FIVE-PART INVENTION

FIVE-PART
INVENTION

a novel

Andrea J. Buchanan

PEGASUS BOOKS
NEW YORK LONDON

FIVE-PART INVENTION

Pegasus Books, Ltd.
148 West 37th Street, 13th Floor
New York, NY 10018

First Pegasus Books cloth edition July 2022

Interior design by Maria Fernandez

Library of Congress Cataloging-in-Publication Data is available.

ISBN: 978-1-63936-203-5

10 9 8 7 6 5 4 3 2 1

Printed in the United States of America
Distributed by Simon & Schuster
www.pegasusbooks.com

To

Margaret Nolan Mullinix

(1931–2021)

invention (n.)

Etymology:

early 15c., *invencioun*, "finding or discovering of something," from Old French *invencion* (13c.) and directly from Latin *inventionem* (nominative *inventio*) "faculty of invention," noun of action from past-participle stem of *invenire* «to come upon, find; find out; invent, discover, devise; ascertain; acquire, get, earn,» from *in-* «in, on» (from PIE root *<u>en</u> «in») + *venire* «to come» (from a suffixed form of PIE root *<u>gwa</u>- «to go, come»).

Definition:
1. a: something invented: such as
    (1) a device, contrivance, or process originated after study
        and experiment
    (2) a product of the imagination
        especially: a false conception
    b: a short keyboard composition featuring two- or three-part
    counterpoint
2. the act or process of inventing
3. productive imagination: INVENTIVENESS
4. DISCOVERY, FINDING

LISE

Letter to Anna, dated 1971

1

This is not a confession.

It is not even an explanation.

I know I was a bad mother to you. That's why I'm here, in the place for bad mothers whose daughters have forgotten about them. Now, don't make that face. I know you haven't forgotten me. But you don't know what it's like here, paralyzed by time, when all there is to do is think of all the ways I have failed you, all the stories you don't know, all the reasons I had, or thought I had. All I have here is time to think, time to replay the events of my life, to undo somehow our estrangement, make things turn out better, change what happened between us.

I suppose it is an unburdening.

That's all I want, to be free of the burden of all this time. Time is slow here, in this place. Minutes take hours, hours unspool with silent inevitability, and days are blank eternities as I think about what I want to say to you.

Back when I played piano, I used to imagine I was free from time, that I was able to float through time as I played. But performing comes with its own burden: the burden of omniscience. Of knowing exactly how a piece is to be played.

And yet, isn't that the trick? To play a piece of music as though the inevitable is actually a surprise? When I performed, I was a fortune-teller, an illusionist, a guide. And yet I know there was some part of me hoping that I, too, might be led someplace unexpected, that there may have been something yet I didn't know.

But now, here in this place, unable to play, I am no longer all-knowing, and without the omniscience of a performer, I can only guess at whether I am doing the right thing in telling you all this. Perhaps this moment, here, right now, is precisely where I am supposed to be, precisely where I was meant to be led: here, leaden, no longer able to float. Perhaps this is what I deserve.

I don't blame you. I know this place is a practicality, not a punishment. Where else would I go?

My wrists ache as I sit here, empty of music, full of time.

So. You discovered the paintings. You learned about your father. And now I need you to know what I know as I know it now, bereft of omniscience but cursed with time to think, so you can understand it all. To understand me, finally.

Note that I did not say *forgive*.

2

In the early days in the hospital, I kept my eyes closed. Especially when he was there. I didn't need to see Mor to sense his presence. I could smell the mix of turpentine and sweat on his coat. I could hear his impatient sighs, the repetitive clearing of his throat, his constant, nervous readjusting in the vinyl hospital chair. He was never able to keep still.

This was 1933, before you were born, before I was married to Samuel, back when I was married to Mor.

It's easier than you might think to not respond, to stay in the dark, dreaming. When your eyes are closed, time passes without you. You hover in suspension. Darkness. Endlessness.

I kept my eyes closed for the doctors, too, at the beginning, but eventually it became easier to give in, open my eyes to shut their mouths. They promised me that if I tried for them, if I opened my eyes, I would be able to play. I had seen a battered upright in the common room. They promised me if I answered their questions and kept my eyes open and stopped trying to slip away, I would be able to play it. They told me I was there because I had tried to slip away. They told me why I was there, but not how. The facts of what had supposedly happened, but not anything that made sense to me at the time. My wrists throbbed inside their bandages, a message from the past.

I couldn't open my eyes when Mor was there. I listened to him fidget and sigh, and I tried to stay very still, still enough to disappear, until I fell asleep and, finally, he was gone.

Once, when he returned, I felt a hand on my hand, and for a tense moment I thought it was him, but it felt at once too gentle and too confident. Then the light above me was adjusted and a cool towel was placed on my forehead, and I realized it was a nurse, changing my dressings.

When I felt the rush of air as the nurse moved away, I opened one eye just the slightest bit, and I saw him, his profile contorted with concern, his posture tense and anxious as he watched the nurse leaving. I had the impulse to comfort him. I remember thinking that if his face were a key signature, it would be C-sharp major, so many worried hatch marks crowding the staff.

But as he turned to me, I was overcome. I immediately shut my eyes. I couldn't look at him. I didn't want him to see my eyes opened. I turned my head away from him, turning my body as much as I could given the restraints on my ankles, my wrists. I lay there, feeling my heart panicking in my throat, my skin cold and clammy, my hands shaking. I tried to breathe, to slow the sharp, spiky inhalations before they became cries, hurt my throat, alerted someone.

The treatments they gave me made me spacious, right from the start, emptying great gaps of time from me, rendering my mind blank as a desert. But every time he was there, I felt a terrible oasis of panic, a looming dread.

I outlasted him by lying there with my eyes closed, waiting for the terror to pass, imagining myself playing through Bach's first Invention, note by note, in my mind, to try to be in this moment, and that one, and the next, and the next, until I remembered my way all the way through. Once he finally left and it was safe to open my eyes, I found his message on the bedside table. A sketch of me, reading a book on a bed, in a room cluttered with books and paintings—was this our bed, our busy room?—and a note: "A few kisses, Lise. I'm sorry. M."

In the hospital they gave me medicine that made my lungs burn as though I'd just finished singing Schubert Lieder. That faded me to an empty blankness. They asked me questions, so many questions. *What day is it? What year is it? What is your name? How old are you? Who is the president? Why did you cut your wrists?*

I was roused from my sleep early in the mornings, before breakfast, and pierced with needles. I kept my eyes closed while they put me on stretchers, strapped me into movable beds, wheeled me into rooms where I was injected with something that flooded me with emptiness before the shaking began. When I did open my eyes, I stared at fluorescent lights on the ceiling, waiting. I came to know what to expect from the treatment.

I saw it, once. Done to someone else. I wasn't supposed to see. But I wanted to know what had been happening to me, what filled the space between the terror rush of adrenaline and waking up in my room, in the dark. I watched through the scratched, clouded window in the door. I saw a woman restrained on a bed. She was so still, no panic, no anticipation. Perhaps it was her first time. I saw the flash of a needle in a nurse's hand. Then it began. The woman struggled against her restraints, moaning, writhing, her eyes rolling back in her head and her body arched with the initial assault. Her body rattled with convulsions, seizures shaking her arms, legs, trunk. It seemed to go on forever, the nurses just standing by, almost impatiently waiting for the flailing to end. Finally, she stopped moving. For a still moment, it seemed as though she barely breathed. Then a nurse placed a stethoscope on her chest, listened for a moment, and glanced toward the window where I stood. I moved away from the door.

Whenever I was restrained on a bed, ready for treatment, I tried to let Chopin études flood my brain. I heard them all at once, my favorites colliding, a snatch of one mashed up against a strain of another. One of them—the "Revolutionary" étude, "Tristesse," maybe "Winter Wind"—would eventually float to the top, and I would allow myself to be filled by it. Every time, afterward, when I was awakened, I felt battered, broken, a heap of shattered bones. It took time, who knows how much time, until I could remember where I was, until my body came back to me and I felt less bruised. The music in my head became hidden, just emptiness inside me. I would drift off to sleep in the blankness, and when I woke, the space inside my head would feel infinite.

He did this to me. Mor did. That's important for you to remember.

The day I finally decided to open my eyes and keep them open for the doctor, after hearing his voice piercing the silent spaces, I was bleary from the treatment. I felt hands on my wrists, my arms, my legs; the sensation of buckles being removed, straps undone; I heard the clank of metal as things were unfastened. I covered my eyes to block out the light, and a voice told me not to close my eyes anymore, that it was safe to look.

He was a collection of facts: square black glasses, reddish mustache and beard. Hands gripping a clipboard, a pencil, a sheaf of paper. Long white coat brilliant in the harsh light. Legs crossed in a low chair. It took a while to register in my brain as he introduced himself.

The other doctors were interchangeable, frowning, rough. They appeared from nowhere to observe each of us in turn, note things on clipboards, dictate observations to the nursing staff in code I didn't understand but felt the intention of. Dr. Zuker was different. He was the one who promised me I could play, who swore that if I kept my eyes open, if I used my voice, if I stayed with him and answered his questions, he would let me practice again.

"When you are strong enough," he kept saying, as if he could possibly know how to determine that.

He pestered me with questions, things I didn't want to answer, and told me things I didn't want to know. There was an absurdity to what he was saying that I could not reconcile with the information he was trying to impart. He told me that I'd cut my wrists. That didn't make sense. And yet there was the proof, my aching hands and arms, bandages still covering the wounds. He told me about the various procedures the doctors wanted to perform, the word transporting me to a concert hall, visions of doctors flourishing their instruments, virtuosos wielding scalpels, a triumphant standing ovation, the surgeons bowing, gesturing grandly to my unconscious form on the operating table.

I didn't remember hurting myself, but I remembered wanting to be dead. To be left alone, with my eyes closed, with the music. I remembered letting the nurses change my dressings, bring me food, change my hospital gown, clean me. I remembered that I didn't care. I was music, pure music, and I would not speak, would not open my eyes, would not be bound by time.

Once, when my eyes were still closed, I'd felt the brightness of an open window to my right, heard noises from the hallway on my left, waited for the nurses to leave, and then I opened just one eye, secretly. The floor was a sea of sick-green tiles, and I was shocked by the presence of even that dull color after so many days of closed-eyed darkness. Shortly after that, I spoke for the first time in the hospital, my voice faltering like a clarinet with a split reed, as I asked for Mor and heard the nurse tell me, "Your husband? He knows where you are, don't worry. He's the one who signed the papers." She surprised me with her hand on my hand, and I imagined for a moment that this was a gesture of compassion until I realized she was shaping my hand around a paper cup, cool and weighted with water. "Now stick out your tongue for the medicine, and drink up."

At some point, after I obeyed them, after I started opening my eyes, I remember being put into a robe stiff from industrial washings, helped into a wheelchair, wheeled down a hallway punctuated by doors with no windows. There were other people in the hallway, sitting in wheelchairs like me, some staring blankly, some sleeping, some talking and gesturing to people I couldn't see. I was pushed through a doorway into a room filled with other people in wheelchairs, old women sitting with blankets in their laps, young women sitting near windows, nurses soothing women who whispered angrily, talking to women who would not answer.

I remember seeing the piano.

It was in the corner of the common room, plants and books on its lid as if it were a side table or a bookcase. It beckoned to me like a beacon, begging me toward it. Together, I knew, we could escape this deadened room with its scuffed black-and-white checkered linoleum, sagging olive-green couches, cafeteria-style tables; together we could transcend time, if I could only play it. It was near a window. I remember the sunlight streaming in, looking warm on the keys. I remember my impulse was to clear the plants and books from the top of it, put them in a more proper place: a table, a bookcase, a cabinet. A piano should not be a desk. Even a spinet deserves to have the fullness of its own sound, a lid unencumbered by objects that could go elsewhere. I remember fingering the C-sharp major scale in my lap. Pressing down against my own leg was not the same as pushing against a real key, but I imagined the hammer striking the strings, the twangy sound of the instrument, as best I could. Most likely the spinet would be tuneless, the action sluggish, the pedals too muddy. It wouldn't matter. I planned to savor every moment of the experience.

I remember Dr. Zuker materializing at my side, telling me, "Do you see, Mrs. Goldenberg? We have a piano here. Perhaps, if you keep your eyes open, and keep talking with me, and if your husband allows, you may play it."

I remember that word.

Allows.

3

The next time I saw Dr. Zuker, he sat before me for several minutes without speaking, simply regarding me, an unresolved chord fading slowly into silence.

"I'm curious about something you said previously," he said finally, leaning back in his chair and paging through his notes. "You said—and I'm quoting here—you said, 'I did everything he asked me to, everything, and he took it away.' You did say that, did you not? Did I hear you correctly?"

I didn't remember saying it, but then I didn't remember so many things. There didn't seem to be any point in disagreeing with him.

"Yes," I said, after a time.

"Can you tell me what you meant by that?"

I looked down at my hands. I still felt music in my fingers, the urge to play, the feeling as though I could play again, the anxiety of wanting to practice but being unable to. The sense of danger around the edges of this feeling.

"Am I correct in assuming that you were referring to your husband?" He waited for me to answer, although it must have been clear to him that I would not. "What was it that he took away? Can you tell me more about that?"

Sometimes I had a flash of it. Mor standing near the door, his coat and hat on, briefcase in hand. Looking like a child in his father's clothes, his shirt too loose, his pants billowing, pooling at his shoes.

Sometimes that was all I saw, just that flash of him standing with his brow furrowed, his angry face on, nervous hands rattling the keys in his pocket.

Other times I could see him standing between me and the piano. His finger up, warning me. A key in his hand. Saying, "No playing. You hear?" In the memory I freeze, and everything else is frozen too, and it seems as though if I could only thaw out quickly enough, I could walk around inside that still space and see it all from outside the moment.

Sometimes I remembered being alone in the apartment. Pulling the stool out from where it nestled against the upright. Feeling around the underside of the fabric seat until I found the unraveling seam. Pulling a key from where he'd hidden it inside the cushion. Unlocking the lid. Standing before the keyboard in silence.

Then he would return, accusing me before he was even through the door, saying, "You have been playing. Look at you, you're flushed. It's disgraceful." In my mind I could see myself telling him I had been listening, pointing toward the radio, putting my hands to my cheeks, trying to feel for the warmth that had given me away.

I remembered him grabbing the key from its hiding place in the stool cushion, heading into his secret room. Locking the door behind him before I was able to see inside. Me sitting down at the piano, playing the Brahms against the locked lid, my fingertips knocking and pressing on the wood, worried that even that might be too loud.

"He locked the piano," I said to Dr. Zuker. "He locked the lid and either hid the key or took it with him, so that even when I was home alone with a moment to myself, I couldn't play."

"And why do you think he did this?"

I shrugged. Blinked back stinging tears.

"Were you having difficulties with your husband?" Dr. Zuker asked. "Is that why you harmed yourself?"

I jerked my gaze back to him, away from my hands in my lap, away from the looming feeling. I remembered what I was supposed to say. Every time we had met, the doctor had reminded me why I was there, had told me again and again what had happened: I had hurt myself, I had been treated for my injuries, I was staying at the hospital while I recovered. I knew the facts. I knew my lines now. I knew I had to say them to him if I ever wanted to leave.

"No, no," I said. "It was just as you've explained it to me before: I was upset. I wasn't thinking clearly."

"Have you had moments like that before, where you made decisions when you were upset and not thinking clearly?"

Dr. Zuker had explained it to me so many times I could almost remember it as though it had really happened to me. A woman stands in her living room, slices her wrists, falls to the floor.

"Have you experienced periods of depression? Of sadness?"

"Well, I'm a musician, after all. I do feel things."

"A musician," he repeated, paging through the papers in his file. "Do you perform? Or did you, before this episode?"

I shook my head. "Not recently."

"Did you teach?"

I shook my head again. "I used to."

"Did you study?"

"Before," I said. "Years ago, before I was married." There was a rising tightness in my chest.

"So when you speak of yourself as a musician, are you referring to that time in your life?"

"I am referring to myself." My voice was shakier than I intended it to be. "It's who I am."

"Your husband mentioned that you enjoyed playing piano," he said. "However, you are not a *professional* musician, correct? You play mostly for yourself, and for your husband, is that right? Why are you crying, Mrs. Goldenberg? Can you tell me what you are feeling right now?"

I remembered Mor's shadow in the doorway, stretching out so much taller than he was, an avatar of his anger. I remembered his face close to mine, his hand gripped around my wrist, the vein on his forehead throbbing as he emphasized his point. I remembered the door slamming. The piano lid locked. A clammy, purple dread. A horrible certainty.

Dr. Zuker forged on. "Were you playing the piano just before you decided to hurt yourself?"

I pushed myself to standing. I'd felt so heavy, so tired, when I was sitting in the wheelchair. But standing up, I felt light. Shaky. New. Still, I moved my legs. I walked toward the dusty spinet in the corner of the common room.

Dr. Zuker stood too. "Mrs. Goldenberg."

His voice was a scolding, and a warning, but I didn't care.

4

My piano had been a gift from Mor after we were married. I had been practicing when I could on the grand piano of the house where I cleaned most days. Then one afternoon, while I was preparing dinner, I heard them on the stairs, Mor and his friends, and then they were all bursting through the door, drunk with the effort of somehow hoisting that upright up so many flights of stairs. He came through first, as Rafael and Samuel helped give the piano one final push over the threshold. It scraped the door, but they were all so giddy and exhausted even Mor laughed.

"Well?" Rafael said finally. "You will say nothing?"

I remember the blood rushing to my face as I wiped my hands on my apron, unable to say a word. I ran over to where they stood, the battered upright just barely through the doorway, already dominating the small apartment. Mor hadn't yet brought the stool up, but I threw open the lid and ran my hands over the keys and began a Bach Invention standing. Only when my eyes welled up so that I could barely tell the black keys from the white did I stop playing and try to speak.

"It is enough to see you so happy," Mor said, putting his hands on my shoulders. I remember being surprised by this rare public gesture of affection.

"Is there wine? We must have wine!" Rafael walked into the kitchen, opening the cupboards, while Samuel hung back in the other room. The brothers were like that in their art, too, as you know, Rafael more daring, Samuel more—well, you know how Samuel was. Already by then they were exhibiting and selling their works more than Mor could stand.

I found the wine Mor had saved from our wedding and brought it out for them. Rafael overtook our one chair, so Mor and Samuel sat on the bed. They stayed and talked and begged me to keep playing until late into the evening, until the neighbors banged on the walls and floor and ceiling for us to stop singing, stop playing music, stop making a racket.

I learned later that Samuel had helped Mor sell his favorite painting to buy the piano. *Man with a Hammer*. It was an oil painting of a worker, hammer in hand, his arms raised as if to bring the tool down on something impenetrable. The worker's exertion was visible, the weight of everything in the definition of his muscles. I had admired the painting for its execution, but to Mor it was a political statement. I was stunned that he would part with it, his proudest work, but all he would say about the sale, trading the painting for the piano, was, "For you, it was necessary," with an awkward kiss on the cheek.

But somehow my music stopped being necessary. Rafael and Samuel stopped loitering late into the night at our apartment, demanding wine or talking about their latest projects. They had become bona fide rising stars, and Mor was nowhere. He was teaching, he was doing factory work, he was going from gallery to gallery on show days, hoping for someone to recognize his genius. He was forbidding me to practice.

He told me I was no longer allowed to play.

5

It hadn't always been like that between me and Mor. How could it? No one chooses to fall in love with the madman; they fall in love with the man and ignore the signs of what he is sure to become. In the early days, he was benign. Here, now, writing this to you, it seems so clear, a progression of chords leading to a predestined conclusion; but in those early days, it was unlike anything I had heard before.

When we met, Mor and I, I was a scholarship student in France. My father had been incensed by my leaving. Hadn't I left enough already? Hadn't I already gone to Saint Petersburg? He couldn't understand that Paris was a stepping-stone. The opportunity to study with Cortot, to have, possibly, a real career in music. He said it was a waste of time, that I should concentrate on finding a husband, that twenty was too late for success as a concert pianist, and almost definitely too late for marriage. *Look at your brothers: their wives were eighteen, nineteen, when they married, and they were considered old at the time. At this rate I'll have to pay someone to take you off my hands. If your mother were alive to see this, she'd die all over again.* When I left, he told me not to bother coming back.

I didn't want to. Paris was a revelation. Not the city, although the city was of course revelatory, but the training. My world was the practice room, the classroom, the music library, my teacher's studio. At the École Normale de Musique de Paris I gained a new perspective on technique, a French approach to complement the solid, strict Russian training I'd grown up with. I learned how to think like a conductor directing an orchestra, rather than a pianist coaxing sound out of a singular instrument. I learned how to blend sounds like watercolors. How to execute technique with subtlety, shade, nuance. When I wasn't in the practice rooms, I was in the library, studying theory and counterpoint and music history, or in my room, poring over scores, or at the school, teaching young students to supplement my scholarship support. At the end of that first year, the hard-to-please Cortot singled me out in the last masterclass of the semester—an international concert career was almost a guarantee, he said, if I continued my level of work. It was more than I ever could have hoped to hear.

So I was giddy when I met Mor, floating on high praise and the thrill of hard work. Normally I would never have taken time off from practicing, never have allowed myself to be persuaded by my flatmates to take a picnic. I remember one of the girls bragging about her American boyfriend, who studied painting at l'Académie de la Grande Chaumière, promising us he would bring some of his American friends, artists we could practice speaking English with. I remember showing up late, having dawdled in the practice room—and once I was there, time stopped completely.

Did you ever believe in something as foolish as love at first sight? The fairy-tale cliché of a heart leaping into the throat of a love-struck princess upon meeting her prince? I hadn't thought I did. And yet as I was introduced to Mor, my ears seemed to block out sound as if I were underwater, my eyesight narrowed into tunnel vision, and my hand, as he reached for it to say hello, felt electrified.

Mor was slight, barely taller than I was, his clothes loose and casual, as though they were castoffs belonging to an older brother. His hair was wavy and slicked down in the style men seemed to favor in those days. He smiled at me and introduced himself, and I couldn't shake the thought that this was somehow momentous, preordained, that we were meant to meet, that in fact we already knew each other from some long-forgotten past. It was profound, this instant connection, and it felt like years before I could formulate words in the presence of his intensity. The entire world, for that fleeting moment, was my hand in his.

And then I found myself saying, "Nice to meet you," and then shaking hands with another art student and then apologizing for being late. My ears went back to normal, my heart stopped racing, the moment passed.

At the end of the day, as the others made their goodbyes, Mor stopped me.

"I'd like to see you again," he said.

"I'd like that," I replied.

And just like that, my life changed.

He wasn't American; he was from Łódź, in Poland, but he had been to America, had even lived in America, had even become an American citizen, in fact, so in a way he was almost quintessentially American. He was in Paris to study, like me, and he planned to return to New York, where he had come to know a great many artists, and begin a new series of paintings of everyday life—street scenes and city landscapes. He'd been studying at the Chaumière but, he said, his real training in France had been self-directed, learning from old and modern masters at the Louvre and other museums. He'd spent days there, months there, attempting to deconstruct the paintings he'd most admired, reverse-engineering their techniques, decoding their secrets.

His paintings were striking—still lifes and portraiture, the requirements for his program of study—but his drawings, to my eye, were the real talent, especially his sketches of Paris street life. I particularly liked how he did not romanticize his subjects. If there was grit, he didn't smooth it away. He aimed for realism, and I appreciated this as a kind of honesty. In my own work, I tried to be as honest, as true as possible to the intentions of the composer, such as I could comprehend them, so I felt I understood his point.

He was passionate even then about politics, had even started a student political organization for artists, who wrote topical articles for its newsletter and took pains to invest their artistic work with a political sensibility. He could argue for hours, and often did, over issues I recognized as urgent to him but about which I knew nothing. I remember how appalled he was to realize my lack of interest in current events, how he seemed to take it personally that I had no opinion on any of it. But I had spent the War in practice rooms, learning repertoire, buried in music, the existence of momentous events taking place only noticeable to me, only relevant, in terse, infrequent dispatches from my father, in the school's name being changed from Saint Petersburg Conservatory to Petrograd Conservatory. "No matter," Mor told me. "You will learn."

He often took me as his subject, sketching me while I read, occasionally posing me more formally, and despite his thirst for realism, he imparted to me a beauty I didn't truly possess. But I liked the way he saw me. I liked the way I looked in his paintings. I liked the way I felt when I was with him. He was prickly sometimes, like all artists, but he was kind to me. And kindness was important. Had anyone been so kind to me before this? Had anyone loved me enough to paint me as a radiant beauty? How he lingered on getting just right the way the light fell on my idealized cheek, the way my romanticized lips curved ever so slightly, full and rounded, as I just barely smiled. He took such care to craft the best version of me.

He was patient with me then, especially in the beginning, when I was shy. He was protective. Sometimes when we were out, even just walking through the neighborhood, he would hold me tightly, defiantly eyeing any man who passed us by and so much as dared to look at me. At an exhibition, he threatened to fight another art student he thought had been spending too much time talking to me. The other man backed down quickly, to my relief, but I couldn't help feeling absurdly flattered. No one had ever fought for me before. No one had ever threatened to fight for me before.

"You belong to me," he told me once as we lay in his bed, whispering so as not to wake his housemate in the next room.

I know now it should have been a warning. It should have made me bolt from his bed, return to the practice room I'd been absent from for so long, return to the studies I'd been neglecting.

But it didn't feel like a warning. It felt like love.

I agreed to marry him. His term at the Chaumière was up, and he was returning to America. I would abandon my studies, give up my scholarship. I had only a year left to go, but New York, he said, was brimming with music; the world would be my instructor, the way the museums in Paris had been his teachers. And we could always come back; I could return to the École Normale and pick up where I left off. The excitement of this new adventure balanced out the guilt I felt telling Monsieur Cortot I would not be returning in the fall, that I would be going to New York, that I was getting married. It was not an easy conversation.

Mor met him once. We were standing outside the entrance to the school when Cortot exited the building. I smiled and nodded to acknowledge him, and for a moment it seemed that he would walk right past us with his grim expression, not even recognizing I was there, and I feared he was angry with me for curtailing my studies. But then he stopped and said, as serious as I had ever seen him look when lecturing about the power of Beethoven's late sonatas or the deceptive frivolity of some Mozart piece, "Never forget that you are an artist."

"Yes, of course," Mor responded. Cortot looked at him sharply, as though he hadn't even realized he was standing there until just then, and said, glancing at me before walking away, "Not you. Her."

I remember writing a brief letter to my father. *You will not have to pay anyone to take me off your hands, as it turns out.* I didn't expect a reply, and I didn't receive one.

"No matter," Mor told me. "I am your family now."

—❧—

His English was better than mine; the city seemed like his city more than mine. He wasn't awed by the skyscrapers or cowed by the pace. Overwhelming, loud, brash, exciting, endlessly new, endlessly reinventing itself; it was the city as usual for him, but startling for me, with no practice room to hide in, no music to distract me. At first I was dazzled by it, seduced even; but soon it became a kind of ache just to be there, a dull pain reminding me that this wasn't really home. Not that Paris had truly been a home, or even Petersburg; my father had made it clear I was no longer welcome. But still, this was different. There was something empty, something frantic, something heavy beneath the excitement, and it struck me as we filled out the necessary marriage forms at City Hall that what I was feeling was dread, because I realized that, although there wasn't anything to return to, we would never be going back.

"We can have a simple ceremony here, a civil ceremony. That will be the most practical thing. And once you've been here a bit longer, we will get your naturalization papers and you can become a citizen, like me," Mor said.

He was right, it was practical. Why should we wait to marry when we had already begun our lives together? And yet it felt so lonely. That was not how I'd pictured my wedding day, in a simple dress before a magistrate, a stranger as witness. My father, as contentious as our relationship had been, should have been there to give me away. I should have been home, getting married by the rabbi in the village, my brothers and their wives and their dozens of children, all loud and celebrating. Or married somewhere in Łódź, surrounded by Mor's family though, curiously, I knew nothing of them, had never met them, had never really heard him speak of them.

What had I done?

Our marriage certificate, issued by the City of New York Department of Health, was stark with facts. Residence, age, birthplace, father's name, mother's maiden name. In the space next to "Occupation," in his column, was a single word: "Artist." There was no occupation listed in my column. Instead, in the space where "Occupation" should have been, across from his declaration of himself as an artist, was "Maiden Name if a Widow." This I left blank. Was I not expected to have an occupation? If the form had required one for me, would I have been as bold as he was? Would I write "Musician"? Would I dare to write "Artist"?

Mor found work, thanks to his small network of friends, who seemed happy to meet me. He taught drafting classes at a local school and spent the rest of his time painting in our apartment, one small room of which we'd turned into a makeshift studio. But this was not enough; living in New York took much more than I had realized, more energy, more emotion, more money. I found work as a cleaning woman, no time for studying music, only occasionally sneaking a touch on the keys of some neglected piano I was now paid to dust.

Living with him in this strange place was different from the time we'd spent with each other in Paris, where everything felt so fated, so foretold. Some nights, as he sketched or painted, his attention focused solely on the canvas before him, I saw him as if he were a stranger. In Paris, we were both expatriates; here, he embraced America with the fervor of a religious convert, requiring us both to speak only English, to be as American as possible, as New York as possible, which was easier for him, since he had lived here already and already felt at home. His bouts of moodiness in Paris had seemed like an endearing idiosyncrasy; here they felt threatening, his anxiety about money, about his work, a spreading stain that tainted even our most benign interactions. Worse, whenever I tried to broach the subject of my returning to my studies, of even considering applying to music school, he became agitated. Couldn't I wait, couldn't I see he was trying to establish himself, couldn't I just support him for now until we were stable enough to afford me some leisure? So I waited.

I worked, I cooked, I took care of him, I did what wives were supposed to do when they had no occupation. And yet, even in that, I was failing. I'd thought maybe a child would bring some meaning to my life, some purpose, to make me feel less displaced, to make him happy, to make us more like a real family. But every month the disappointment arrived.

He did love me, I knew that. He told me that. He cared so much—that was why he protected me, wanted me all to himself, wanted me home with him when he was home, wanted me paying attention to only him. And even though it was difficult in the beginning, there were moments of happiness. His friends—his community of artists, the Collective, Rafael and Samuel in particular—all of them had been welcoming, had provided a feeling of connection that helped me feel more secured in place. And of course he did find me the piano. After months of arguing, months of feeling my fingers aching to practice again, my mind anxious to resolve itself in music, he had taken pity on me. Or perhaps it was his way of apologizing, of telling me he understood, that he appreciated how patient I'd been, without having to articulate any of it. He brought me the piano, with help from Rafael and Samuel—and the sale of his beloved painting—and for a time, that was enough.

6

The treatments increased, became more and more frequent, until I was deemed improved enough, or complacent enough, to have regular visits from Mor. Instead of being confined to bed, I was in a regular chair, not even a wheelchair, a blanket on my lap, a robe covering my hospital dress, as we sat in the common room. I was smoothed out from the treatments. I was able to face him across the table and not feel the urge to close my eyes.

He visited once on a particularly sunny day, and I was caught for a moment on the way the light fell in exuberant stretches across the tables and couches. He sat opposite me, his eyes pleading at me as though he hadn't noticed the sunlight at all. I watched the dust trapped in the sunbeam, floating. It felt like that in the hospital. Warm and comfortable and happy, even though I was trapped, with my head so spacious and empty and floating, like I was suspended in time.

He kept his hat on, his coat on, as though he were ready to leave at any moment, his entire demeanor a wary apology. But I just smiled.

"I'm so glad you've come," I told him.

"Are you?" he asked, shifting in his seat.

"Of course."

He stared at his hands for a moment and when he raised his face, his eyes were bright, and he blinked quickly. "Then I'm glad, as well."

It was easy to smile at him when I was suspended in so much space. Sometimes I felt as though the spaces hid my own thoughts from me too much, erased my memories and my music. But sometimes the spaces protected me. I could float. I could be trapped in a sunbeam.

The common room was always crowded, men visiting wives, mothers visiting daughters, sons and daughters visiting mothers. That day I watched them all hold hands, sit next to each other, walk together, play cards. I felt so disposed toward them. Indulgent. Even their distracting chatter was tolerable. The spaces were a buffer. My heart felt full.

"I brought you something," he said, finally taking off his hat. He reached into his briefcase portfolio, took out a package, and put it on the table between us: the score of Beethoven's *Emperor* Concerto.

"Oh!" I drew in my breath as I pulled the music closer to me. "Thank you so much—and what a rare edition it is! How thoughtful of you. Wherever did you find it?"

He looked concerned, his forehead a wrinkled landscape. "Lise, it's yours," he said. "I brought it from home."

This wasn't true. Couldn't be true. It was utterly unfamiliar to me. And yet, when I looked closely, I could see that the binding was not new, that the cover was yellowing and soft at the edges, that there was writing inside, *my* writing, markings I myself had made on the score. Irrefutably, in the upper right-hand corner of the title page, was my own name, written in neat student script.

I laughed, which was easy to do, for I felt like laughing that day, and agreed of course it was mine, that's right, how forgetful I am sometimes.

I was forgetful. The more treatments I had, the more I was alternately seized by the injection and suspended in a dreamless sleep, the more I forgot. There were spaces that weren't there before. It had become harder to console myself with Études and Inventions, harder to hold the music in my head to distract me from my circumstances. But I was consoled anyway, distracted anyway. The spaces made me more patient with being where I was.

"You asked me to bring it to you, remember? They wouldn't let me before, but now you are so much better . . ."

"Of course," I said again.

"You are feeling better, yes?" he asked. He was so nervous, constantly moving, clasping and unclasping his hands, running his fingers through his hair. I remember thinking that once I was finally home I must trim it. It stuck out in tufts, standing away from his head as though it was trying to escape him. I remember thinking that his nervousness felt familiar.

"Much better," I said.

I paged through the Beethoven score. Notes leaped off the page at me, but I couldn't make sense of them. I could see where I had notated fingering, underlined dynamics, but the musical notes themselves were harder to read. It used to be I could look at a line of music and see it all at once, a paragraph submitted to my brain in its entirety. Now it was too much to take in.

"I have been working," Mor said, drawing my attention away from the score. "I have been doing much work while you've been gone."

I remembered that this was a good thing, that it was good for him to be painting. "That's wonderful. Will you be showing soon?"

He sat back in his seat, frowning. "No. No! This is not for display, to have people gawk at. This work is too important. It is too difficult for the common person to understand." He leaned forward, whispering fiercely, his eyes intense. "I am on the edge of something revolutionary, I can feel it."

This, too, seemed familiar, this intensity. I couldn't think of what to say, so instead I put my hand on the concerto score, still open on the table before us. "Tell me, have I played this before?"

"Lise," he said, flustered.

"I must have, but I don't remember."

"You played this many times. You performed it years ago. You must stop this nonsense."

I closed the score. The spaces made me serene, unmoved, even though I could feel something, some kind of beginning.

"Of course. I'm sorry."

But he was unsettled. He tapped his fingers, fiddled with the hat in his lap, looked around the room worriedly at the other patients and their guests. "Soon you will come home," he said.

"Yes, of course, soon."

"Things will be different, Lise," he said.

"Of course." I couldn't picture in my mind exactly what our apartment looked like. But soon I would be there, soon I would remember.

"Do you remember, Lise, why you are here?" he asked.

I remembered what Dr. Zuker had told me, over and over. That I was there because I had been very sad, and that I had tried to hurt myself. That I had succeeded in hurting myself. That I had cut my wrists with razors. When I tried to think about it, there was a heaviness that filled me, a tightness in my chest. I remembered playing the piano; I could see from the scars on my wrists that something sharp had cut me. But all around me was space, black space, and I couldn't remember for sure what it was that had happened.

"I tried to hurt myself," I told him. "But I'm better now, you see."

His face was grim.

But he looked relieved as he said, "I'm glad."

7

When he took me home, I was startled by the sheer volume of the world outside the hospital. The sunlight made my eyes ache. The streets were so dirty, and the sounds of traffic assaulted me. I'd been in a sanitized space for so long, I'd forgotten what the chaos of regular life was like. The building, too, was a disappointment. I saw too clearly the desperation of our neighborhood, the filth everywhere, the people on the streets who lolled in doorways like the patients I'd spent the last three months with in the ward. Mor kicked the trash out of the way on the stairs as we started up to the apartment. Still, even with the rubbish cleared, I had to go slowly. Stairs were difficult. I was still weak.

He helped me up the steep flights, easing me around the broken parts, the rickety steps in need of fixing, the trash sticking out between the spaces in the wired fence of the empty, unused elevator shaft. We passed children playing on the landings; housewives hanging laundry, yelling; men smoking, playing cards. None of this seemed familiar to me.

"Is this really where we live?" I asked.

He jerked my suitcase impatiently as he gestured for me to go ahead, but he didn't answer my question.

When we finally reached our floor, I remembered the blue-gray of the walls, the ratty, threadbare carpet of the hallway, the series of locks, the sound of his keys as he opened the door.

I stood in the doorway, hesitating before I went in. It was a simple room, two windows on the opposite wall, curtains blocking the light that still managed to poke through aging lace trim, a bed to my right. On the left was a closed door; just beyond that, another door led to a bathroom and kitchen. Against the walls on the right were bookcases, sagging and full of books on art and music. The bed was spare, a simple quilt on the mattress, two pillows. A rug, with an old, faded oriental design, lay across the floor, one corner hiding under a small table and two chairs. I could see his portfolio on the table, photographs in frames on the bookcases and windowsills.

"Lise?" His voice was querulous, full of something. I moved inside and sat on the bed. I was suddenly so tired.

"I'm sorry. Dr. Zuker insisted. He said it was important for your recovery."

"What?" I asked. All I wanted was to lie down in this dark room. I smoothed my hand along the quilt, and it was suddenly familiar: I had a clear memory of sewing it myself, piecing it together as he painted next to me.

"Lise, look." His voice sounded serious and apprehensive as he gestured to the left corner of the room. I looked, but nothing was there. The wall was empty. I wasn't sure what it was he wanted me to see.

"I'm sorry," he said again. "The piano is gone."

ANNA

1954–1967

1

1954

You're going to love her," Tom said, confident with one hand on the wheel as he broke his gaze from the road to wink at Anna. He was expansive today, his charismatic, generous self, the self she preferred. He smiled and barked a laugh. "I just hope she loves *you!*"

Anna smoothed her olive-green smock dress, hands in her lap beginning to sweat. "Well," she said, smiling to hide her nervousness, "now why wouldn't she?" She tightened the headscarf covering her newly set hair as they drove, the wind whipping stray strands into her lipstick. Tom had insisted on the convertible, though he rarely drove it. Usually it just sat in the driveway taunting the neighbors.

It was so typical of Tom to inject the tiniest seed of doubt in the guise of a joke. Plausible deniability for later. *I was just kidding, can't you take a joke, you have no sense of humor, so stupid.* It could escalate, sure. She kept it light. She grabbed his hand. She smiled.

"She's your mother. She has to love me, because she loves you, and you love me."

He yanked his hand away, slapping it to the wheel, gripping tightly now. "Don't be too sure about that," he muttered.

It was uncanny what a shape-shifter he was, uncanny how he could slide so easily from charm to threat. Anna felt the pressure to get him back to the twinkling eye, garrulous story, seductive smile. That was what had snagged her in the first place, the way he had seemed so comfortable in his skin, the way everyone was drawn to him without him having to lift a finger, how easily he commanded everyone around him. He was a natural-born salesman, a gifted mimic, a charismatic liar.

After hours, he was the star of local theater productions, a leading man—not that sissy-shit, he liked to say, but manly roles, parts only a real man could play. At the office, he was the star adman, the dream eligible bachelor chased by all the secretaries, whom he regaled in the lunchroom with corny songs and bawdy anecdotes. He could have had any of them, but he had chosen Anna. She wasn't sure why. She was sturdy, not willowy like most of the girls in the secretary pool. She wasn't frivolous or easily taken in. She wasn't whimsical or daydreamy. She had a determined face, lips meant more for speaking her mind than for kissing, eyes that saw everything. She had no time for his flirtatious ridiculousness. She alone, of all the secretaries, seemed immune to his charms, though privately, of course, she had noted them. Once he made it his mission to make her succumb, she took a strange girlish pleasure in realizing she'd thwarted the whole game merely by not playing along.

What's a smart girl like you doing as my secretary? he'd asked, surely knowing exactly how he was flattering her. *You should be writing copy with me.* Instead, within a month, she was sleeping with him. Not so smart, after all, depending on your definition of the word. Now she was pregnant, as of four months ago, and married, as of two weeks ago, and officially out of a job.

"Don't be too sure about that," he said again, to clarify for Anna that she had indeed been meant to hear him say it, to emphasize the fact that Anna had not yet responded to this bait he had dangled. Did he really intend for her to be nervous about it, to think there was a chance that he didn't really love her? Weren't they newlyweds still? Then again, he hadn't told her anything about his mother until just that morning, when he got a bug in his ear about making this trip. Never, in all their conversations about Anna's estrangement from her mother, did he ever think to mention his own mother. Anna had always been led to believe she had passed. Maybe she had? Maybe this was all some kind of joke?

He looked over at Anna again and laughed. "You look like you're going to be sick, Annie." He gripped her hand again. "Don't be too sure that she loves me, is all. That's all I meant." He turned on the radio. "I'll be damned, you really can't take a joke. No sense of humor."

They drove along a dusty, winding lane that was more of a dirt path than a road. Tom swatted at the occasional mosquito that hovered in the brown cloud kicked up by the car as they rode deeper and deeper into the country. Anna had never thought of Tom as having come from anywhere. He seemed so self-possessed it was as though he had been created, in whole, all by himself, raised up from the sophisticated concrete of the city streets, the smoky theater footlights, the elegant tablecloths of exclusive restaurants. He never talked about a family, ever; she suddenly realized this included their own burgeoning family as well. Yet he drove them, on and on, into the country of his past, finally willing to reveal to her the truth of his provenance.

He said nothing when they passed broken-down gas stations and shuttered-over stores, nothing when they saw clotheslines of drawers and sheets waving over barefoot children playing in the dirt. Perhaps this was the long way toward some kind of civilized country home. She did not dare ask. She had learned to encourage through staying quiet. Sometimes Tom would give her more when he thought she had given up.

Soon they drove up to a squat, faded house, paint baked off by the hot sun. Anna could feel the sweat dripping down the back of her neck, under her breasts, between her thighs. Tom turned off the car and said, "She's going to get the surprise of her life!"

"You didn't tell her?" Anna asked, alarmed, but Tom just chuckled as he sprinted around the car to her door, opened it for her, and held out a hand. He didn't seem bothered at all by the heat or the dirt. He was invigorated, his eyes twinkling again.

"Knock it off, Annie, this is going to be great," he said, closing the door behind her. But he didn't make any move toward the house, just stood there, a hand lightly on Anna's back. Chickens strutted in the yard, and Anna could see off to the right the neat lines of an extensive vegetable garden. Suddenly the front door opened, and a woman as gray as the house stepped out.

"Tom," she said, her arms folded across her chest. She wore a plain housedress, neat and clean, though in a style Anna considered dowdy, and squinted her eyes in their direction but seemed to make a point of not looking at Anna. "To what do we owe the pleasure?"

"Good to see you, too, Ma," he shout-laughed, his voice loud and fake-friendly, the way it got when he bullied his way through an uncomfortable social situation. His mother's face stayed the way it was, and it seemed to Anna that she might not have any other expression besides the dour frown and cruel eyes, the lines and wrinkles of her face firm and unmovable as though she were a molded figurine of an old woman. This was her mother-in-law?

"Ma, come on, Ma, don't be that way," Tom said, his voice a reproachful yet playful plea. He strode to the porch and planted a kiss on the stern and still unmoving cheek of this woman who was, evidently, his mother.

"You come here without so much as a phone call after more than two years and expect me to be happy?"

"Ma—"

"You show up with some new hussy of yours—did you knock this one up too?"

Anna instinctively placed a hand on her belly. Could she be showing that much at almost five months? She had worked hard to stay slim for Tom's sake, and her smock dress was, she had thought, forgiving. Was this woman some kind of witch?

"She's my wife, Ma," Tom said, a hand on her shoulder now, but still his mother's arms were folded, and now she trained her piercing eyes in Anna's direction. Her eyes may have been the only part of her that wasn't gray and washed out. They were blue, the clear ice-blue of her son's, but unlike Tom's they did not sparkle to entice or twinkle to charm. They bore into Anna like the headlights of an oncoming car. The old woman seemed momentarily shocked, for she simply stood and stared while Tom grinned like nothing was wrong.

"Hello," said Anna, still standing in the driveway.

The old woman ignored her and turned to Tom. "You got some things to make right before that can happen."

"Ma, just drop it, will you? This is Anna, my new bride," he said, lingering over the word, draping an arm over his mother's shoulder and squeezing her to his side like they were college chums. "Make her feel welcome!"

She shrugged him off sharply and made for the door, her voice a slap in the face as she hissed, "She is not welcome."

"Wait," Anna commanded, her voice a little more forceful than she had planned. She cleared her throat and tried again. "We don't mean to impose, Tom just wanted the two of us to meet. To celebrate. We eloped recently, and, well, you were right: you're going to be a grandmother." Anna did not mention the fact that she hadn't known that Tom had a mother, that Tom hadn't told her his mother was even alive until that morning.

Tom stared at her with a bemused, indulgent expression, clearly enjoying the show. But Anna's speech did nothing to sway his mother, who grabbed for the screen door and stomped into the house. She paused at the threshold and shot her icy eyes at Anna. "For your information, I already am a grandmother," she said and slammed the door.

"What on earth?" Anna said, walking toward Tom, her eyes pricking with shame.

"Don't worry about it, Annie, don't worry about it. She's a miserable old lady, that's all." He embraced her and she allowed herself to bury her face in his shoulder. "She never did like surprises."

Anna drew back and gently punched his arm. "Then why the heck didn't you warn her? I suppose I'd be mad too!"

He laughed and swung her around in a hug. "But you're cute when you're mad."

Anna laughed, too, and whispered as she looked toward the house, "She certainly isn't—" But she was caught short.

Through the screen door she saw a solemn face. A scraggly, pale girl, thin as the pins Anna had used to fix her scarf to her hair that morning, stood in the doorway. She couldn't have been more than two or three years old, naked except for a sagging cloth diaper, with a plain little face made all the more ghostly by her eerily familiar bright blue eyes. She just stood there, staring at them, her face nearly pressed up against the screen.

"Oh my god," Anna said.

The old woman popped the screen door open, grinning cruelly toward her, and Anna saw she held a baby on her hip, maybe a year old. "Go on," she waved the little girl forward. "Go on, say hello. Go on!"

The girl clung to the old woman's housedress, sucking her thumb and burying her face in the woman's knees. But Tom dove in, scooping her up on his shoulders.

"Hey now, is that any way to greet your dad?"

Anna stepped back against the porch, leaning in case she lost her balance. "'Your dad'?"

The old woman looked Anna straight in the eye and smiled a Tom kind of smile. "I told you, I'm already a grandmother."

"Tom?" Anna panicked.

"Annie, meet my kids," he said.

They drove back in the dark. It was cold, thanks to Tom's stupid convertible, which he refused to convert back into a covered car, but Anna was fuming enough to keep her teeth from chattering. The girl slept on the back seat, wrapped in a blanket, next to the small suitcase Tom's mother had packed; her brother slept on the floor. When Anna looked over her seat she could see the children had fallen asleep holding hands.

"She's four?"

Tom closed his eyes and, in the moonlight, Anna could see his jaw working. "Yes."

"Why is she so small? Why is she still in diapers?"

"How the hell should I know," he snapped. "It's that old woman. Didn't feed her right. Didn't bother to put her on the toilet."

"That old woman," Anna seethed, "that old woman who raised your damn kids for you while you lived the bachelor life?"

The car swerved as he lunged in her direction. "Don't you start with me, Annie. I've had about all I can take from ridiculous women today."

"Who's the mother?"

"None of your business."

"Where's the mother?"

"None of your business."

"God damn it, Tom, if I have to take care of these children, I have to know who they are and where they came from. And they are going to need to know their mother."

He grinned. "Why, you're their mother now, Annie. They won't need anyone else."

Their mother! Here she was, just twenty years old, pregnant, barely married, and already a mother of three?

She looked at the sleeping bodies in the back of the car. Tom's mother had sent them off without even allowing them into her home. After making the cruel introduction, she had thrown a suitcase at them, some cloth diapers and a doll, a few sets of clothes, and told them she wanted nothing more to do with them, nothing. The children should be with their father, she said, and whatever woman was stupid enough to have him. And with that she'd slammed the door and kicked them off her property.

Anna was by no means an orphan, but she knew what it meant to be cut off from the full world of a family. She looked back at the sleeping children. Who else would take care of them?

2

1956

She ran from the kitchen, the smell of eggs nauseating her, and barely made it to the bathroom in time to have all of last night's dinner come up. How could she be pregnant again?

"Pauline! You stop that right now!" she shouted as she returned to the kitchen in time to see the girl reaching up to the range as though she were aiming to bring the whole pan down on her head.

"Baby's hungry," Pauline whispered.

Anna wiped her hands on her apron and turned off the flame. "You don't worry about that, I'll feed him, you just sit down before your father gets . . . well, you know how he gets. Go on." The girl dawdled, her bright blue eyes an accusation. "Scoot," Anna said, swatting her lightly on the bottom.

In the dining room, Pauline made her way to her seat, across from her three-year-old brother, Kevin. Next to him was Billy, his little head barely visible over the table, the baby Anna had been pregnant with when she first took in the children. She'd hoped he and Kevin might be close, seeing as they were only a year or so apart, but Kevin was aloof. Tom thought he was slow, but Anna supposed he was just quiet. Like Pauline. Billy scrambled to sit on his knees so he could see his plate. He was only two, but Baby was younger, so Baby got the highchair at the head of the table. Baby's name was a bone of contention. Anna had spent the latter half of that pregnancy in denial that she was soon to be a mother of four, and when the baby inevitably bore himself into existence, she couldn't bring herself to decide on a name.

"Can't we just call him Baby for now?" she'd asked Tom. "Just until we see who he is?" But no: that was the stupidest idea Tom had ever heard, so he decided for both of them. By the time she left the hospital, she had been informed she would be taking home a baby boy named James. Still, at home, alone with the children, she called him Baby, because James didn't seem right, and nothing else did either. Not Jim, not Jimmy. It wasn't a problem except when Tom overheard her or the kids slipping up and using Baby instead of Jim. Anna sighed. It was probably about time she made her peace with it. She couldn't call him Baby forever. Especially not when there was another actual baby on the way soon to depose him. Another baby. Five children?

She heard Tom make his entrance into the dining room, the thud of his briefcase dropping theatrically by the door echoing in her like the beginnings of a panic attack. Was the table set? Had she remembered to put out the juice? The butter? As she hurried to gather everything, she could hear the jovial rumble of his baritone as he made conversation with the kids. Perhaps today was going to be one of his good days. Her hopes were dashed when she saw him at the table, a glass of last night's whiskey in his hand.

"Okay," she said, her voice unnecessarily bright. "Who wants eggs? Toast? Bacon?"

She served Tom first, giving him the best of everything. The fluffiest, yellowest scoop of scrambled eggs. The medium-burned toast—not too dark, not too light, as he wouldn't tolerate either—with the most butter. The fattiest pieces of bacon.

"Me, me, me!" Pauline waved her hand, and Billy joined in. He was only just beginning to talk—Tom hated that he was so slow—but he mimicked his sister, clapping and saying, "Meee." Kevin sat, silent, moody as a teenager.

"Hush now, Billy, you'll have yours soon," Anna chided. The egg smell was making her nauseated all over again.

"Me, me, me," Pauline chanted. "Me, me, me!"

"I'm coming, hold your horses," Anna said lightly. But she sensed a sudden darkness as she left Tom's side to serve the children.

She picked up Baby's bottle from where it had fallen into the seat of his highchair and popped it back into his mouth, leaving him to deal with propping it up again. Then she served Kevin, piling his plate with scrambled eggs, his favorite, as he grabbed for some toast. She spooned some eggs onto Billy's plate, gave him a piece of toast for one hand and a crispy piece of bacon for the other, and made her way over to Pauline.

Pauline was six now, nearly seven, but she was still small. Spindly, with long legs and arms, she looked sickly, with her pale reddish hair, her cold-white skin, her thick glasses. She was much healthier now than when she had first been thrust into Anna's life. Still, she wasn't a big eater. Food was always a chore, and Anna worried about her thinness, her seeming intention of existing on nothing but air.

She began to fill Pauline's plate with roughly the same amount she had given Kevin when Tom said loudly, "More."

Anna stared at him in confusion. She was beginning to sweat from the nausea.

"I said, *more*." Tom enunciated like she was slow. Pauline looked up at Anna and then back to her father, who was sitting across the table, red-faced and sour. "She's so eager? *Me, me, me!*" he imitated. "Give her more then. Give her all of it!"

"Tom," Anna said.

"You heard me!"

Anna looked down. There was so much food already. Pauline would never eat that much.

"At least let me serve myself," she said, laughing a shaky laugh to make it seem like this was all fine and normal, nothing for the children to worry about. She began to make herself a plate, even as she felt the nausea roil and rise to her throat.

"And don't give yourself more, don't baby her," he snapped. "She asked for it, she's going to get it. Right? That's what greedy girls get, right?"

Anna gave herself a healthy pile of scrambled eggs, the smell of which nearly made her retch, and four slices each of toast and bacon.

"No," he said. "Switch plates with her."

"But—" Pauline began to whine.

"But nothing!" he yelled and reached across the table to switch their plates. "Now eat."

They both just looked at him. Kevin ate his food, seemingly oblivious, while Billy smeared scrambled eggs into his mouth with his hands as Baby sucked on a bottle, but Anna and Pauline were frozen.

"You wanted it so much, eat it!"

He dug into his food dramatically, a mockery of eating, and Anna and Pauline reluctantly began to do the same. Anna could barely choke it down, she felt so green, and Pauline, finally sensing something sinister, began to whimper quietly as she nibbled on a piece of toast.

"Come on," he said, eating his food with gusto. "Your mother worked hard on this breakfast, the least you can do is eat it. Don't be ungrateful!"

"Go on, make your father happy. Have a bite." Anna hoped her smile might divert him and signal to Pauline that everything was going to be okay.

Pauline ate the crust off her toast and then attempted tiny bites of egg.

"We are going to stay here until you clean your plate," he said. "Do you hear me?"

"My plate!" Billy said, but it sounded like *ma pate*.

"That's enough out of you." Tom took Billy's plate and dumped all the food onto Pauline's. Then he grabbed Kevin's plate. "Yours too." The boys started to cry and Pauline sank in her chair. "Now eat!"

Baby began to wail, too, and threw his bottle on the floor. Tom seemed amused by this, for whatever reason, and walked over, kneeling down to retrieve the bottle and chuck Baby on the chin. "Aw, Jimmy, little Jim-Jim, Jimbo!" he said. "Don't be sad, boy!"

While Tom was engaged with Baby, Anna quickly swiped Pauline's plate and scraped half of the food into the frying pan on the table, covering the evidence with a napkin. Pauline looked at her, eyes widening with concern.

"Just pretend to eat," Anna whispered, leaning over Pauline as though she were busy fussing with her napkin. "Pretend to eat it and spit it out in your napkin."

She thought she'd said it quietly enough, thought he had been engaged in favoring Baby, but of course he'd heard it. He heard everything. He was impossible to escape.

"No, you will not *pretend* to eat it," he said. He stood up and came around the table and pried Pauline's mouth open, using his hands to force-feed her the scrambled eggs. She started to spit it out, but he got level with her and looked her right in her eyes. "You will not waste food. You will eat it until it's gone. Now chew!"

It was 7:15 already, far past the time he needed to leave for his commute, nearly time for Pauline to leave to walk to school. How far was he willing to take this?

"Tom," Anna said, as Pauline began gagging on the food he was forcing into her mouth. "She's a child. This isn't right."

Tom stood up abruptly and smacked Anna across the face, his arm hitting Pauline too.

"Don't you ever," he yelled, "contradict me. In front of my children!"

Anna's face smarted and her eyes filled with tears. Baby wailed, shocked by all the yelling, and the boys started crying again. Pauline just sat there, chewing, her eyes fixated on some distant point.

Tom stalked past Anna and grabbed his briefcase. He didn't even say goodbye, just slammed the door after himself as he left. Anna moved to comfort the children, these children, her children. Two of them someone else's children, but they were her children now. They could not be only his.

She placed a hand on Pauline's hair. "Shhh," she said. "It's fine. You go get your things and get ready for school. I'll clean this up."

Pauline obediently slipped down from the chair and ran up the stairs to her room to get her book bag. Anna put Baby in his walker and sat Billy and Kevin in front of the television. She didn't even care what was on, she just needed a moment. She was a robot. She cleared the table, picked up the food on the floor, wiped down the mess, began to tackle the kitchen. She heard the sound of the front door opening and for a moment her adrenaline spiked and she felt sick again.

"Tom?"

There was no answer, so she poked her head out, drying her hands with a kitchen towel. It was just Pauline, heading to school, and Anna felt herself relax.

"You go straight to school, okay?" she said. "And then come right back here at lunchtime?"

Pauline nodded. Framed by the light in the doorway, with her blonde-red hair, the girl looked unearthly, and her silence only enhanced the effect.

"I'm telling you," she said to Deborah. "You see a different side of him at work. The way he is here . . . or at least the way he was this morning . . ."

Anna inhaled her cigarette and sat down on the couch, relishing a scarce moment of relaxation as Baby, Billy, and Kevin napped upstairs.

"It certainly sounds as though he was in rare form," Deborah said.

Anna leaned on her hand as she sat, covering her face, hoping it wasn't still red from Tom's slap earlier. She hoped Deborah wouldn't notice, wouldn't ask. But Deborah seemed oblivious, sitting there in her sweater set, unaware of the privilege she had, the sheer ability to walk out into the world, unencumbered by children or pregnancy, a svelte professional woman. Deborah was no bombshell, but she always looked put-together. It wasn't fair that Anna had to stop working once she experienced the barest hint of motherhood; she, too, would like to have her hair coiffed, her face done; would like to be able to socialize with a friend while on a brief errand and return to the office secretary pool wearing a smart skirt and heels like everyone else. She, too, would like to be free. Deborah was the only one who still spoke to her. What were the rest of the girls afraid of? Most of them wanted what she had, or so they said: a man, a family. So why did she feel like a cautionary tale?

"I'm telling you," Anna repeated and shook her head. For a moment, her eyes stung and she felt the dangerous tide of frustration and exhaustion beginning to swell and show on her face in the form of fat, angry tears. But she wouldn't allow it. Not in front of Deborah. Not sitting here in her housecoat, pregnant and unruly, with Deborah so prim and neat.

"I'm sure he'll come home a changed man," Deborah said. "You know how he is—he has his moods, but then he's Mr. Sunshine."

"True." Anna rested her cigarette on the ashtray and leaned forward. "Now. Since you're already here. Spill. I want the office gossip!"

Deborah laughed and smoothed her skirt. "Well, there's not much to tell. Doris is still Doris."

"Ha," Anna barked. "Still pining after Mr. Harris?"

"As always. And Minna is newly engaged and can't stop devising ways to show off her ring or work mention of her fiancé into conversation."

Anna rolled her eyes. She could just picture it.

"Other than that . . ."

Deborah seemed nervous, somehow.

"Other than that?"

Deborah hesitated, then finally admitted, a smile unable to contain itself. "Well, I do have some news. Though perhaps Tom has already told you? I've been promoted."

"Promoted! Why, that's wonderful! Congratulations! Are you head of the secretarial pool now? How marvelous!"

"To junior copywriter," Deborah said.

Anna almost couldn't make sense of this. "Junior . . . ?"

"Can you believe it? I couldn't believe it at first, either. The first woman junior copywriter!"

This had to be impossible. How could this be? Women were secretaries; men wrote the copy. Tom had always teased her with the prospect of her joining forces with him, but they both knew it was folly. That wasn't how the world worked. The way the world worked was women were secretaries, and when they got pregnant, they got fired.

"Who," Anna began, trying to understand. "What team . . . Who are you working with?"

Deborah smiled at her with a funny expression. "Why, Tom, of course. That's why I thought he might have told you."

"Oh!" Anna understood that she needed to smile back. "Well, that really is marvelous, isn't it?"

"I truly love it," Deborah said. "It's ever so much more exciting than being a secretary. The campaigns, the brainstorming sessions . . . well, you know. I'm sure you've heard Tom talk about it."

"Indeed," Anna murmured.

Just then the front door opened.

"Well look who's home for lunch," Anna said, heaving herself up from the couch. "Pauline, come say hello to Miss Deborah."

The girl put her books down by the front door and walked over. She stood with her hands clasped, eyes down, twisting her arms, fiddling with her dress. She smiled shyly at Deborah and returned her gaze to the floor.

Anna nudged the girl.

"Come on now, say hello," she chided.

"Hi, Miss Deborah." Pauline's voice was muffled, strange-sounding, too quiet somehow. Anna was alarmed. Pauline knew better than to mumble; Tom had made sure of that.

"Pauline!" Anna said. "Let's not be rude, now. I need you to speak clearly! It sounds as though you're talking with a mouthful of food!" She shook her head at Deborah as an apology, but Deborah waved her off.

"Never you mind, Pauline." Deborah leaned down to Pauline's eye level. "I heard you clear as day."

"Thank you, Miss Deborah," Pauline whispered, and a piece of something slimy with spit tumbled out of her mouth.

Deborah straightened up and stepped back.

Anna grabbed Pauline by the shoulders and whirled the girl around to face her. "Open your mouth," she commanded, leaning down to see. "Open it!"

Pauline complied and Anna stood up abruptly.

"We'll just be a moment," she said to Deborah and took Pauline into the kitchen.

Anna held a napkin below Pauline's chin as Pauline cried soundlessly. "It's okay. Spit it out. Go on. It's all right."

Out came the eggs, the toast, the bacon. All the breakfast she had chewed at the table that morning but not swallowed. Once the food was out of her mouth, Pauline began to whimper, saliva stringing from her mouth to the napkin. She must have held it there, tasting it all morning, all through lessons, all through recess, all through the walk home.

Anna threw away the napkin of saturated, half-chewed food and used a clean one to wipe Pauline's mouth. This child. What had she been thinking? How would Anna explain this to Deborah?

"What was that?" she asked Pauline, for she realized the girl was whimpering again, trying to speak.

"I'm sorry," Pauline whispered.

Anna looked at her. Tom's eyes, Tom's mother's eyes, staring back at her, unreachable.

"What am I going to do with you?" Anna sighed and stood up. "Go on upstairs and brush your teeth. I'll have your lunch ready in a jiffy—and this time how about we eat it, and swallow it?"

Pauline nodded, sniffling a bit.

"Don't tell Dad," she whispered, her eyes wide and shining with the beginning of tears.

"Shh, of course not," Anna said, folding the girl into her skirt for a brief hug before swatting her lightly on the backside. "Now run along."

Pauline ran out of the room, ever obedient, and Anna began making a sandwich and warming up the soup she'd started earlier.

"Everything all right?" Deborah asked from the doorway.

"Oh, you know," Anna said, over her shoulder. "It's always something with these kids."

Anna grabbed the sack lunch she had packed for Tom, the lunch Tom had forgotten to take with him this morning when he had stormed out so abruptly, the lunch Tom had sent Deborah here to retrieve. Some junior copywriter. More like a Girl Friday.

She felt a wave of nausea come over her. Though was it nausea, or bitterness? Anna would jump at the chance to be someone's Girl Friday instead of someone's mother. Motherhood had never been something she'd wanted for herself, after the childhood she'd had, and yet there she was, trapped with four kids—soon to be five kids—deep in it. With a pang, she realized she missed her own mother. Or maybe just the idea of a mother. Someone to take care of her, wipe her face, help her spit out what she'd been holding onto. But she knew they would never be able to talk about such things. Anna's embracing of motherhood had seemed like some sort of slight to her mother, some kind of dig at her, or at least that's how she'd made Anna feel. *Why should I bother?* she had asked when Anna suggested she come visit, see her grandchildren. *They aren't my blood.*

Not most of them, anyway. Besides, she was too busy. She had lessons to give, music to learn. Anna had long understood those things came first.

"Here you go," she told Deborah, handing over Tom's lunch. "I suppose you'd better get back before his lunchtime is over."

Deborah nodded and looked back to the stairs Pauline had just run up. "I'm curious, do you ever hear from the mother?"

"My mother?" Anna frowned.

"Pauline and Kevin's mother."

"As far as I know, she's out of the picture. Tom hasn't heard from her in years. I don't even think he knows where she is these days."

"He mentioned to me that she was . . . troubled," Deborah said.

"He mentioned to you!" Anna hoped her irritation came off as surprise.

"Well, I confess I was curious, so I asked a little, once," Deborah said.

"And what did he tell you? Other than that she was 'troubled'?"

"Oh, you know," Deborah hedged. "The kinds of things men always say about their exes. She was crazy, she was a real head-case. He said that after the younger one was born, she just . . . left. Took off. That part does sound crazy to me, not just man-talk. Can you imagine?"

Anna absorbed this, trying to make her face appear calm. She could imagine taking off. She imagined it almost daily. But she could never. She could never abandon them, like their mother had. Like her own mother had, for all intents and purposes. Someone had to protect those kids. But beyond those thoughts was the shock of jealousy. This was more than Tom had ever told her about the kids' mother. She was surprised that Deborah had become such a confidante of his.

"Obviously Kevin is too young for that kind of conversation, but does Pauline know you're not, you know, her real mother?" Deborah asked.

Anna was becoming impatient with Deborah's intrusion, but she tried to keep the edge out of her voice. "Pauline knows what Pauline needs to know. And as far as she knows, I'm her mother."

"Will you tell her, do you think?"

"I'm the only mother she's got."

"But wouldn't you want to know?" Deborah persisted. "If your mother wasn't your real mother?"

"No," Anna said, cutting her off, more forcefully than she had planned to. She could see Deborah pull back, finally put in her place a little. "I'm the only mother she has, and the only mother she'll know. It would only hurt her to know the truth. So she's never going to be told anything different."

She hadn't intended for that last part to come out like a warning, but once it was out there, lingering between them, Deborah seemed chastened, so Anna did not apologize.

"Well," Deborah said, clutching Tom's lunch bag a little more tightly, "I'd better be getting back to the office. I'll tell the girls you said hello. And I'll try to get Tom into a better mood so that he can come home happy."

"You do that." Anna saw Deborah to the door. Deborah's heels clicking the pavement as she walked away, waving goodbye over her shoulder, sounded like ambition, like freedom, as Anna ran back to the bathroom in her house slippers, a prisoner of morning sickness once again.

True to Deborah's prediction, Tom came home as Mr. Sunshine. He burst through the door, singing, carrying a dramatic bouquet of flowers, calling the children over to him.

"There you are, there's my big man," he said to Billy, who rushed over for a hug. "And come on, Kevin, there's room for you too, don't be shy."

He handed the flowers to Anna and scooped up the boys, hoisting them belly-first onto his shoulders like they were barrels of whiskey. They squealed and writhed as he rassled with them and tossed them onto the sofa.

"Now, you be careful," Anna said, holding the flowers out of arms' reach of Baby, who sat on her hip.

"Ooh, boys, did you hear your mom?" Tom said. "We've got to be careful!"

Suddenly he pounced on them, tickling them into shrieking laughter. As they rolled on the sofa, Tom stood up and took off his jacket and tie, tossing them to Anna, walking over to the stereo. "Music! We need music!"

Anna now not only held Baby on her hip, she also had flowers in her other hand and Tom's jacket and tie draped over the crook of her elbow. "What's the occasion?" she asked.

Tom looked at her like she was crazy. "The occasion? Since when do we need an occasion?" He put on his favorite jazz album, the one with the smoky saxophone and off-rhythm piano, and danced toward her. "The occasion is, I'm home," he said, smiling his best kind of smile, the one that tricked her into believing him all the time, the one that kept her from leaving. He leaned in to kiss her as Baby squealed in delight.

"Now, where's my best girl?" he demanded, whirling around theatrically.

Pauline had been lingering just beyond the sofa, watching the fun, but now she walked over to her father and looked up at him as he pretended to search for her and not find her.

"Daddy!" She tugged on his shirt, laughing. It was good to hear her laugh. Her face was transformed by it. She wasn't such a plain girl after all, not when she was smiling like that.

"Oh there you are!" he said and scooped her up into his arms, twirling her around. They danced around the living room while the boys danced with each other on the sofa. Normally Tom would have yelled at them for jumping like that, but they sensed the shift in him and took full advantage, bouncing and throwing pillows at each other.

"Anna, turn it up!" Tom commanded, but his tone was happy, not scolding, so she walked over and fiddled with the knob as best she could with her full hands. She watched them, the boys roughhousing on the couch, Baby bouncing on her hip, excited by the music and the commotion; but most of all Pauline and Tom. He held her and danced her around in time to the music, whirling and bobbing and moving to the rhythm. They danced all over the living room, Pauline smiling so wide Anna couldn't tell if she was laughing. All of the ugliness of that morning was gone, all of it drowned out by the music and the happiness and the easiness and the fun.

Anna watched it all unfold before her and thought *remember this, remember this*, hoping it would be enough, that this happy moment could be some kind of inoculation against sadness, that sometime in the future Pauline and the boys would be able to remember this moment and know that, despite everything, they were loved.

3

1958

The woman at the door was tiny, barely taller than a child, and her eyes darted around like a startled cat's, taking in every possible hint of danger, even though all she was doing was standing on the front porch.

"May I help you?" Anna asked, finally. The screams and whines of the children grew more intense from within the house, and she fought the urge to slam the door behind her, push this woman out of the way, and run, the children's wails fading like sirens in the distance.

The woman smiled blankly, as though she hadn't heard, and Anna sighed. "If you're one of those do-gooders from the church, I already told them . . ."

"Oh! Yes. The church," the woman said. Her eyes finally alighted on Anna's face. She seemed nervous and patted her strawberry blonde hair as she spoke quickly, her gaze skittering away. "I'm from the church."

"Well, as I told the other one from the Ladies' Committee, they're all still contagious, and we have yet to finish up that casserole."

Anna realized as she said it that the woman wasn't holding a Pyrex of beef Stroganoff or plate of baked goods or Jell-O salad. She just held that blank smile, as though she didn't fully comprehend.

"The chicken pox," Anna said, to clarify. "They're all still sick with it." It had been one after the other, emerging from their rooms with fever and spots, and just as one would get past the worst of it, a new one would come to her, feverish and itchy. At this point it seemed as though they'd all been sick for months.

"Oh, of course," the woman said, shaking her head. She wore gloves as though she'd just come from church, but her coat was threadbare, and the dress beneath it quite plain. "Well, I assure you, I am quite inoculated, having had it myself as a youth."

The woman's eyes were bright as she took in the house. They seemed greedy for details, flitting from the front windows to the porch paint to just over Anna's shoulder. Anna instinctively pulled the door closer.

"In any case, as you said, the church sent me to relieve you." The woman sounded relieved to have finally stated the reason for her visit. "If you might like to set a spell, I'd be happy to watch the children while you rest."

At that precise moment, Jimmy's high-pitched wail pierced the doorway, soon joined by the choir of Tommy Jr. and baby Jill.

"Pauline!" Anna yelled over her shoulder. "Mind your brothers and sister!"

To be fair to this strange woman and her strange offer, Anna could use the rest. Her legs were shaky with the effort of standing. She had mostly recovered from her own bout with the illness, after being infected by the kids, but she wasn't fully well, not yet. It might be nice to have the company of someone—to have the help of someone—even if it was one of the relentless do-gooders from the church Tom had joined just to show himself off as the best singer in the choir. She opened the door.

Only once she had welcomed the woman into the house did she realize what a state it was in. Blankies and burp cloths on the floor, half-emptied bottles on every available surface, toys and clothes and this morning's breakfast plates cluttering up the notion that she was an efficient housewife and mother.

But the woman was too focused on her task to be bothered by it. She picked her way through the minefield of childhood detritus and set herself gingerly on the couch. Baby Jill threw a spoon from her highchair as she clawed at her spotted face and screamed to be picked up. Tommy Jr. and Billy fought over a blanket on the floor. Jimmy and Kevin lay listless and pockmarked in front of the TV, the sound blaring.

Anna hoisted Jill from the highchair and wrangled a tiny sock back onto her chubby fist, to keep her from scratching at the pox, then set her in the walker, where the baby continued to cry.

Anna was beginning to apologize for all the chaos when the woman abruptly asked, "Where are the older two?"

"Excuse me?" Anna said.

The woman backtracked. "Oh, I was told by the—well, by the Ladies' Committee, as you put it?—that you had several children, including an older boy and girl. I was just wondering where they might be?"

Something suddenly felt off—there was something off about this whole thing—but she pushed the thought out of her mind, chalking it up to her own exhaustion, plus her irritation at being roped into some scheme of Tom's without so much as a warning. When had he put out the alarm for the good ladies of the church to rush to her aid? Since when did he care?

"Well, Kevin, the oldest boy, is right there, currently being hypnotized by Captain Kangaroo. And Pauline . . ."

She yelled upstairs for the girl and apologized to the nervous woman who sat on the edge of the couch like it might contaminate her.

"Kevin," the woman said, almost under her breath, but the boy didn't hear her.

"I'm sorry, I didn't catch your name," Anna said.

"Oh, my apologies, it's Jean . . ." The woman stopped suddenly, seemingly transfixed by the appearance of Pauline on the stairs.

"There you are," said Anna. "What were you doing upstairs?"

Pauline dawdled on the stairs, hugging the banister. At eight, she was still tiny enough to fit through the rungs.

"Well?" Anna prompted. "We have a guest."

"It was quieter upstairs," Pauline whispered.

"One can't argue with that," Anna said to Jean, but the woman was standing up, walking toward the stairs, toward Pauline, not paying any attention to what Anna was saying.

Jean knelt at the base of the stairs and opened her arms to Pauline.

"Well, hello there, Paulie," Jean said softly, motioning her hands as though she were expecting a hug. Pauline moved back, still clinging to the banister, shrinking to it as if the spindly rungs could hide her. "Aw, don't you remember me?"

Paulie? Remember me? All the hairs on the back of Anna's neck stood up, and she stood up too, moving closer to the woman.

Jean abruptly stood to address Anna. "From church, I mean," she said, looking at Anna apologetically. "I do love to see the little ones at church."

Anna's eyes narrowed. "And when was the last time you saw these particular little ones at church?"

Jean flashed her nervous smile. "Oh, who can say, I'm there so often."

"Well, they aren't," Anna said, scooping up Jill from the walker. Pauline shrank back even farther onto the stairs, absently scratching at the pox scabs on her arms, but her eyes were fixed on Jean, as still and penetrating as Jean's were nervous and darting.

"I appreciate your kind offer, Jean, but on second thought, I don't think it's necessary." Anna began to herd Jean toward the door.

"Oh, it's no trouble at all, I'm happy to stay," Jean said, but Anna held firm, gesturing her to the doorway, blocking her from returning to the stairs, or the living room, or wherever it was she seemed so determined to go. Her nervous energy confirmed Anna's sense that something was wrong, wrong, wrong.

"I insist." Anna opened the door for Jean, baby Jill still sniffling in her arms but finally starting to look tired enough for her morning nap.

"If you're sure." Jean turned to her as she walked through the door and back onto the porch.

"Oh, I'm quite sure," Anna said sharply.

Jean's eyes suddenly grew bright and still, and her brittle, nervous smile relaxed into something far sadder. "It's just that I miss them so much," she whispered.

Anna felt the hot sting of adrenaline rush up her spine and spread throughout her body, but she managed to say before she closed the door in Jean's face, "I'm sure you'll see them at church."

They were all asleep finally, Pauline, Kevin, Billy, Jimmy, Tommy Jr., and baby Jill, who fought sleep most of all these days, and Anna felt the ache of exhaustion right down to her bones, where the viral illness still lurked and made her heavy with flares of pain when she was the most tired. But she couldn't sleep yet. She needed to confront Tom, now that he was finally home.

She found him in front of the television, snoring into his whiskey, and she nudged him with her foot until he was jostled awake and forced to reckon with her, standing there in her robe and curlers, blocking the TV.

"I called the church." Her arms were crossed, and she had that look on her face that he knew meant there would be no chance for him to polish his excuses smooth as the ice in his glass.

"Congratulations," he said. He lifted his drink in her direction like a toast.

"There is no Ladies' Committee."

"What are you talking about?" he said, looking past her to the television.

She walked over to the set and cranked the knob, hard. The picture narrowed itself into a tiny point and went dark.

"There is no Ladies' Committee," she repeated. "Unless that's a clever name you've come up with for your harem."

"Of course there's a Ladies' Committee. I probably just got the name wrong. I don't know what they call these things. Knitting circles, charity groups—you know, it's one of those things they do at the church. To help people like you, taking care of sick kids."

"To help people like me," she said, laughing, before walking back to him and leaning down into his face. "There is no Ladies' Committee, Tom."

"Come on, now," he said, but she slapped the whiskey glass right out of his hand onto the carpet, and he stood up, a head taller than her in her curlers.

"The humiliation!" she cried. "I stood there on that porch and accepted a *casserole* from the woman having an affair with my husband?"

"Listen, that was all her, I didn't know anything about that," he said, finally dropping his pretense. "She's nuts! Totally crazy. She got obsessed with me, and I put her in her place, I told her, look, I'm a married man! But you know, some women are just—they won't take no for an answer."

She rolled her eyes, and he grabbed her wrist, tried to pry open her fist with his hands, tried to hold her hand in his, tried to kiss it. "I swear! I thought it was innocent fun at choir practice, just joking around between friends, but then she just . . . couldn't control herself."

"Uh huh," Anna said, allowing him to hold her hand. She needed him to feel mollified before she could bring up the woman she truly wanted to discuss.

"Well, I mean, honestly, who could?" He smiled at her, that Tom smile, turning it into a joke, pulling her close. "Come here, Annie. Even in this get-up you're my one and only."

But Anna resisted his kiss. "No. Explain it to me. Tell me straight."

Tom sighed and picked his glass up off the floor, poured himself another. "There's nothing to tell, Annie. I swear. This woman had it in her head that she liked me, I rebuffed her—as a married man should—and then she went crazy. Followed me around. Showed up at my work. Found out details about my life. I mentioned at choir practice that you all were sick, and she showed up here with that damn casserole and the malarky about the church committee! Trying to snoop on my private life."

Anna remembered how the casserole lady had peered beyond her shoulder to catch a glimpse of the inside of the house, just like Jean earlier today. How Anna had been so miserable, covered in pox while having to look at the bubbly brunette in full makeup, that she had taken the casserole dish from the woman's perfectly manicured nails, *sure, Ladies' Committee, thanks, no, we don't need anything,* and shut the door abruptly in her face. What had been the woman's endgame there? To know that the wife of her church-choir crush had eaten her handiwork? Was it some kind of power play?

Anna shook those questions from her mind and asked the question she really cared about, giving him ample room to obfuscate, just to see if he would tell her the truth.

"And what about the other one?"

"What other one?" Tom asked, settling back in his chair and knocking back his drink.

"The one from today."

"I truly don't know what you're talking about," he said. And even though he always managed to look convincing as he lied to her face, Anna still felt halfway convinced that he really didn't understand.

"Come on."

"I honestly don't know!"

"The woman!" she said. "Short? Strawberry blonde? Nervous?"

He shook his head, looking mystified.

"She came into the house, Tom. She came into *my* house."

"Anna, I swear." He put down his glass and took both her hands. "You have to believe me. I don't know what you're talking about."

She whipped her hands away from his. "She was here, Tom! She said she was from the church, but she came into the house, she asked about the kids, she asked about Kevin and Pauline. She called her *Paulie*."

But Tom was calm. Amused, even. A half-smile played on his face like he understood something she didn't. "You say she called her Paulie?"

"She acted like she knew her already. Tell me why that is, Tom."

"And what did she look like again?"

"I told you—short, reddish-blonde hair, really nervous, her eyes darting around all the time. She said her name was Jean."

At this, Tom burst out laughing. "Jean!"

"I don't find this funny, Tom."

"Shh, shh," Tom said through his laughter, which sounded like it was more from relief than from anything else. He embraced Anna and held her gently. "I'm not sleeping with Jean."

The way he said the name made Anna think two things: that he wasn't sleeping with Jean, and that he was sleeping with someone else.

"That isn't at all what I'm concerned about." Anna pulled back. "I've given you plenty of opportunity here to explain yourself. And you're still pretending."

He shook his head and rolled his eyes, like he was exasperated with her. "Yes, fine, you figured it out. She's the kids' mother."

Anna hadn't realized until he said it just how hard she'd been hoping that she had been mistaken, that the sense she'd had deep in the pit of her stomach when Jean confessed to missing them had been wrong.

"*I* am the kids' mother."

"You know what I mean."

"I'm the one here every day, taking care of them, feeding them, bathing them, putting calamine lotion on their damn pox that they gave to me, keeping them alive. I took them in when no one wanted them. When *you* didn't want them." Her voice shook, her throat tight with angry tears. "*I'm* their mother."

"Of course you are," he said, embracing her. "Of course you are. I know that."

"What made her think that she could come here? Did you invite her here? Did you tell her to come here? Was this your plan?"

"Jesus, Anna, no," he said. "I'm just as surprised as you are that she found me."

"She can't come back here." Anna wiped angry tears from her face.

"She won't."

"How can you be sure of that? She came here today! What if she wants them back? What if she tries to take them back?"

"She won't," he said, holding her close again. "She didn't want them before, she's not going to want them now. She's crazy, I told you. And probably lonely. Just wanted to make sure they were okay or something, and now she did, and it's done. She won't come back. I'll make sure of it."

Anna pulled away, wanting to demand specifics from him, wanting something more than vague promises. But then she saw a shadow on the stairs.

"Pauline?"

The girl sat on the stairs in her nightgown, hugging her knees to her chest.

"What are you doing out of bed, young lady? It's late!" Tom said.

"I'll put her back to bed." Anna scooped her up from the stairs, Pauline's limbs dangling, too long now to fold into Anna's body like they used to, and wondered how long she'd been there, how much she'd heard, how much she understood.

Baby Jill stirred in the room she shared with Pauline as Anna smoothed the covers over the girl and brushed her bangs off her forehead. "Do you need a story?" she whispered, and Pauline nodded, her face serious, like always.

"The hands one," she said.

"The hands one," Anna agreed and began to tell her the bedtime story she'd heard so many times from her own mother, who had only seemed to feel motherly in the nighttime, barely visible in the darkness as she'd whispered to Anna the fairy tale about a girl whose hands are cut off by her own father, who receives prosthetic hands made of silver from a king who sees her in her handless state and marries her anyway. By the time Anna got to the part where the devil tells the queen mother that the girl is pregnant with a monster and needs to be killed, Pauline was asleep.

4

1964

Well, that certainly took long enough," Lise said after Anna took her off hold.

"Mother. I'm at work."

There was an icy pause before Lise spoke. "Yes, I'm sure you are."

Anna sighed, trying to maintain a professional demeanor as one of the senior associates walked by. Once he was well past, she whispered into the phone, "I'm not sure why that's offensive to you, but I assure you I don't have time for this."

"Offensive! Why would anything you do be offensive to me? I'm sure plenty of mothers never hear from their daughters because they're so busy at work."

Don't start, Anna thought, but started anyway. "We have gone over this. I *am* busy. I have children, I have work, I have school after work—"

"Ah, yes," Lise said. "Still, I'm not sure why anyone would want to pursue a degree in something as useless as art appreciation."

"It's art *history*, Mother."

"At the community college? Surely not." Lise tutted. "I just don't understand why you wouldn't want to study something practical."

"I already went to secretarial school."

"Yes, and look where that's gotten you."

Anna fumed, willing herself to say nothing, to not give Lise the satisfaction of reacting. Peterson walked by and placed a stack of files on her desk, motioning her to get off the phone.

"I'm so sorry," she said, in her best secretarial voice, "but I'm going to have to call you back."

"No, no, this won't take long. I just wanted to let you know that he died."

Anna was still, frozen, as Peterson waved his hands in irritation. "Who," Anna said. "Who, Mother?"

Peterson rolled his eyes and walked away. She shouldn't be taking personal calls at work. She was sure she would be getting a talking-to later.

"Well—your father, of course." Lise cleared her voice, the only indication of emotion Anna could sense.

She felt the tears gathering and tried to speak but found she couldn't.

"You know he was sick," Lise said.

"I know, but—"

"I'm making the arrangements now. You might want to come home for the funeral."

"Of course," Anna snapped. "When was it ever implied that I wouldn't want to attend my own father's funeral?"

"Well, I know you're busy . . ."

Anna's throat was tight and she blinked back tears of rage. "I loved my father. I would never miss something so important."

"And yet I don't remember you coming to see him in his last days," Lise said.

"I'm hanging up now."

"I'm just stating a fact—" Lise began.

"And I am hanging up," Anna said and hung up the phone.

Peterson stood by her desk, looking apologetic rather than angry, as Anna tried to collect herself. She grabbed the stack of files and started going through them. Peterson cleared his throat and said, "Take as much time as you need, Annie. Don't even think twice."

"Thank you," she whispered, the files blurring into shimmering pools as she blinked.

The worst part was he hadn't said anything. In his most recent letter to her, he was his usual self, no mention of the cancer, no mention of any health problems at all. Anna supposed he had been trying to protect her, as he had his entire life, it seemed; but she was flaring with rage as she drove home, thinking about how she had put off responding, thinking she had more time.

If she had known, she would have visited—she would have sent the kids to Tom's against their will, she would have braved the endless disappointment and disapproval from her mother and seen him one last time. It wasn't fair that her mother had had him all to herself. She didn't deserve him. Anna would never understand why he had tolerated her, why he had excused her meanness, her coldness. They had made some pact, evidently, long ago, that she was allowed to be as awful as she wanted to be, for whatever reason. It made no sense. And anytime Anna had gone to him, distraught over something Lise had said or done, he had gathered her in his arms and sighed and said, "You have to understand. Your mother is trying. It's difficult for her. She's been through a lot." Anna could never understand. She could never understand how someone having had a difficult life could excuse them from being kind to a person they were supposed to love. But Samuel had always seemed to make sense of it for himself. Her father was the most patient man alive. *Had been,* she corrected herself. *Had been* the most patient man alive. He was dead now. How could he be dead? How could he be dead and Lise still be living? It wasn't fair. It made no sense.

Anna used the drive to upstate New York to prepare herself, to fortify herself. She remembered one of the last times she had allowed Lise to visit them. Pauline had been nine or ten, and within an hour of Lise's arrival, she had retreated to her room. Anna had left Lise—whose ever just so slightly raised eyebrow indicated her disapproval as she offhandedly inquired as to what kind of parent would allow their child to be so disrespectful to their grandparent, even though she had refused to let Pauline or Kevin call her "Grandma"—and found Pauline curled up with her favorite doll, the one she'd brought with her that awful day when Anna had learned that Tom had children. *What's wrong*, she had asked, and Pauline had looked up at her with those intent blue eyes, spilling over with tears, and said, *Gramma Lise says things with a smile on her face, but it makes my heart hurt.*

Anna had long ago grown past allowing her heart to be hurt, she thought, yet Lise still managed to find ways to wound her. It had always been like that. Anna could never understand it, and could never forgive it, but raising her own children, she had managed to start forgiving herself, or at least letting herself off the hook a little for whatever it was that made things so difficult with Lise. Anna knew from having her own babies that no one comes into this world having wronged it. Whatever evil Lise projected onto her was just that, a projection.

Still, there was a part of Anna that yearned for reconciliation, even as she dreaded the reality that there was no more Samuel to moderate between them. Would it even be possible? Or was Samuel's death also the death of any hope that the chasm between them might be breached?

It had been years since they had seen one another, and Anna was shocked to discover that her mother had become an old woman in the time that had elapsed. Her hair was fully white now, her posture stooped, her limbs frail and skinny as tree branches in winter. She strained to hold the door open for Anna, and Anna walked past her feeling like a giant, at least a head taller, her thick, vibrant body an imposition. She took her time removing her scarf, her hat, her gloves, her coat, while Lise watched, absent-eyed, reserved, until there was no more putting it off, and Anna had to say "Hello, Mother" and perform a perfunctory embrace. It was like holding a birdcage.

As long as there was something to do, it was manageable. So Anna busied herself with the tasks Lise had set out for her, organizing, arranging, calling. She examined Lise obliquely, catching her in mirrors, in quick glances, witnessing her napping in the armchair, her face for once beatific and gentle—kind, even. She had to remind herself this was her mother, experiencing grief. And in a way, that was a good enough explanation. The fragility, the irritability, the snappishness: wasn't that all just the way that grief expressed itself?

"Maybe you should play, Mother," Anna suggested the first night she was there.

"Play?"

Lise seemed so confused, her question so genuine, and it made Anna feel as though there was a part of Lise that Anna could reach that was separate from the part of her that was instantly dismissive of anything Anna might suggest. She recognized that feeling: hope. Evidently it would always be there, this wish that they might be able to understand each other.

"Yes," Anna said. "Perhaps playing something might make you feel better. Was there a piece he loved? A piece that always made you think of him? Some way you might remember him best?"

Lise looked away, waving her hand, pulling her shawl tighter around her for just a moment. But she didn't fight the suggestion. Instead, she went to the piano. There she seemed less fragile, her posture more grounded, solid.

"This was one of his favorites," she said before she began. "The first piece I ever played for him that I played just for him. If you understand."

To Anna, it sounded sad. Mournful. And slightly modern, as though it were a song a person could sing, and not a piano piece from a hundred years ago. She sat and let the sound wash over her, the slightly out of tune piano with its familiar tone bringing her back to her childhood, when she would sneak into the room while Lise was practicing and huddle near the solid back leg of the piano with a blanket, inhaling the smell of the wood and letting herself vibrate with sound, until Lise discovered her and shooed her away.

She had closed her eyes and was allowing the sound to take the place of whatever words her mother couldn't say to her, to accept it as some kind of substitute for affirmation or forgiveness, when Lise abruptly stopped. They sat in silence, the room darkening as daylight ebbed away until her mother was just a shadow.

"What will I do?" Lise whispered. "I don't know how to be in this world without him."

Anna saw her shoulders shake slightly and recognized that her mother was crying.

"I'll get us some tea," Anna said, unable to bear it.

The day after the funeral, before Anna left, Lise asked her if there was any particular painting of Samuel's that she might like to have. Most of Samuel's work was in galleries, or in circulation, or in storage, but there were a few things in the room he'd used as his studio, if Anna would like to look.

The studio smelled like him, cruelly, it was so vivid, and Anna had to stop for a moment and inhale. If she closed her eyes, it seemed like he was only just over there, behind the easel, waiting for her or just gone for a moment to grab something from the hallway. But when she opened her eyes, now full of tears at his memory, he was gone, leaving only the sense of him having just been there.

There was a stack of canvases leaning against the wall, and Anna began to tip them back toward her, trying to make sense of each one. Most were abstract, one or two more figurative, but the last one . . .

"Mother, this is amazing. This is you, isn't it? I've never seen Father paint anything like it before. He never seemed to do portraits. When did he do this?"

Lise frowned and walked over. "That's not your father's."

She took it from Anna's hands and placed it on one of the shelves, face-in, so it was no longer possible to see her face rendered in oils.

"Well, who painted it then?"

"No one," Lise said. "A friend of your dad's from the Collective."

Anna picked it up again, studying it. "Whoever painted it loved you. You can tell."

Lise made a sound that was part exclamation, part negation.

"Look, look at the lines. Look at the attention to detail." Anna held out the painting, forcing her to see it. It was dusty but somehow still vibrant, saturated, and the artist had captured a brittle essence that Anna felt absolutely represented her mother, but also some kind of softness and affection that was alien to her. It was both ethereal and, at the same time, humanizing. The signature at the bottom said "M. Goldenberg."

"Yes, well, don't go using your precious art history degree on my account," Lise said. She pushed past Anna to look through the other paintings. Anna carefully placed the portrait back on the shelf then turned to see what Lise was finding.

"Oh, I always loved that one," Anna said, and Lise held it out for her.

"He never finished it. I'm not sure why he kept it."

Anna took in the half-finished painting. There was a woman, a pear tree, and an angelic figure. The woman in the painting slightly resembled her mother: the same pale skin, the same brown curls, the same facial shape. But he had prettied her, and Anna had never known her mother to own such a frivolous, diaphanous gown. The woman in the painting looked down at the ground so sadly and with such longing, even as her hands reached up toward the angel hovering in the upper corner.

Her hands were graceful, with long, tapered fingers, artfully splayed like a ballerina's hands, painted in a shimmering silver gray that caught the light from the angel's glow. Just below the wrist on each hand was a line, and below that the arms were the same warm flesh color as the rest of the woman's skin, as though the hands were dead but the rest of her was living. At the point where the silver hands met the flesh of her forearms, there were painful indentations.

"I know this," Anna exclaimed. "This is the fairy tale you used to tell me, isn't it? The girl with the silver hands?"

Lise looked closer. "I suppose it is," she said. "He did go through a phase where he was painting fairy tales."

"Can I take it?" Anna clutched it to her chest. "Even though it's not finished?"

"Why ever would you want it?" Lise asked.

Anna couldn't say: *because it reminds me of the nights you sat with me telling me fairy tales and touching my hair in the dark as though you actually loved me.* Or, *because it reminds me of how my father loved stories and symbols, and how we used to love solving puzzles together.*

Instead, she said, "I would also like this one," choosing an abstract piece with colors that pleased her and reminded her of her father.

"As you wish," Lise said and began to walk out of the room.

Anna followed her, but not so close that she was crowding Lise, and as she hung back a little after Lise passed through the doorway, she grabbed the portrait from where Lise had left it on the shelf.

Her mother's eyes stared back at her, but because they had been painted with so much love, it seemed to Anna that the mother in the painting was someone else's mother, and that this mother looked at her as though she loved her.

5

1967

Now, Mrs. Mansfield—"

"Please just call me Anna, I'm no longer anyone's 'missus,'" she said.

"Excuse me," said Principal Neill, clearing his throat. "Of course. Anna. In any case, this is a very serious issue."

Anna rolled her eyes. How many times had she been called in to appear in this office because of Pauline's insistence on wearing miniskirts shorter than the fingertip length mandated by the school?

"I've told you, she leaves my house fully covered. What she does when she gets here is out of my hands."

Pauline sulked in the seat next to her, arms crossed, her long, ironed hair hiding her face. Anna couldn't help but notice that the paisley dress she wore was barely the length of a shirt. Her hair was probably longer.

"Oh, this isn't about that." The principal frowned. "Although she has been cited for that infraction every day this week and risks detention for that alone. No, this is about . . . witchcraft."

"Witchcraft?" Anna laughed as he said it. Was he serious?

"That's the term you use for it, isn't it, Pauline?"

Pauline rolled her eyes as she slunk even further down in her chair pushed up her glasses. "No, that's not the term I use for it."

Anna nudged her. "Don't be disrespectful to Mr. Neill. Sit up and answer his questions."

"Fine." Pauline sighed. She made a show of hoisting herself upright in the chair.

"Well, what do you call this then?" The principal pulled out a wooden board from under his desk. It was decorated with lettered script that, from what Anna could see, looked like it just spelled out the alphabet.

"I call it spiriting," Pauline said.

"Spiriting," Anna repeated.

"Yeah. Talking to spirits."

"Excuse me?" Anna said. The principal caught Anna's eye as if to say, *What did I tell you? Witchcraft.*

Pauline scooted forward in her chair, her dress pushing itself even more into a shirt, and took the board from Mr. Neill's hands.

"Where's the thingy?" she asked him. He looked blank. "The planchette?" He looked at Anna, shrugging. Pauline stood up, she was so exasperated. "The thingy, the thing you use to spell out the words. Come on, man, if you're going to confiscate my stuff, at least take care of it!"

"Pauline!" Anna chided.

"Ah, yes," he said, "I think I have it here." He reached into a desk drawer and pulled out a heart-shaped piece of plastic. Pauline set the board down in the middle of the desk and swiped the planchette out of his hand.

"It's a Ouija board, Mom," she said. "Haven't you seen these before?"

Anna had heard about Ouija boards, of course, but had never actually seen one. She stared at the board, with its antique-looking drawings and lettering. There was a sun, a moon, a YES, a NO, a curved alphabet, some numbers, and the word GOODBYE.

"Look, okay? You do it like this," Pauline said, lightly resting the fingertips of both hands on one side of the plastic planchette. "Go on, you do it too."

Anna looked at the principal and back at Pauline, who was still urging her to touch the thing. She leaned closer and put her hands on the planchette.

"Not heavy like that, Mom," Pauline said. "Lightly. You want the spirit to move *through* you."

"Now, Miss Mansfield," Mr. Neill cautioned, but Pauline spoke over him.

"Right, lightly, like that. So then you just ask a question, like, is a spirit here with us right now?"

Anna felt the planchette move beneath her fingers, dragging her across the board to the place where it said YES.

"See? It's probably Grandpa, since he died recently," Pauline said to Anna, and she addressed the board: "Is this Anna's father?"

This time the planchette didn't move, resting stubbornly on the YES.

Anna felt her heart quicken, even though this was ridiculous, even though she was sitting in a high school principal's office with her delinquent child. If this was real at all, it might make sense for her father to be here, trying to communicate. It was her mother who couldn't, and she was still alive.

"Is this Samuel Sandler?" Pauline asked. Suddenly the planchette jerked to the other side of the board. NO.

"All right, this demonstration is over," said Principal Neill. "Whatever this is, witchcraft or 'spiriting,' it is not allowed in this school."

Pauline made sounds of protest as she sank back into her seat.

"She's been doing this in school?" Anna asked. "Pauline? You've been doing this during class?"

"Not during class—" Pauline said, but Mr. Neill cut her off.

"Not during class, no, but she has been . . . soliciting other students to come to her at lunch and during free periods or study hall."

Anna bristled at the word "soliciting," not liking what he was implying.

"She's basically holding séances in the girls' bathroom," he said, exasperated, "and charging money for it."

"Pauline!"

"What? It's capitalism!" Pauline hugged the board to her chest.

"It's inappropriate," Anna said.

"And there have been complaints," said Mr. Neill. "Several students have come to me worried about the so-called communication that has transpired in these sessions. One girl told me she now believes she's haunted!"

"Jane? She is." Pauline laughed.

Anna wrested the board from Pauline's hands. "Hand over the planche too."

"The *planchette*?"

"Whatever it's called, it needs to be in my hand, now," Anna said. The girl made a show of surrendering the piece of plastic, and Anna handed both items to the principal. "You may dispose of these as you wish."

"But, Mom—" Pauline wailed.

"But nothing," Anna said.

"Thank you," said Mr. Neill. "And now, Pauline, if you will excuse us, I need you to wait outside while your mother and I discuss the matter of your punishment."

Pauline left the room without saying a word, though Anna could tell she was fuming, and went to sit outside the principal's office under the watchful eye of his secretary.

"I'm so sorry about all of this, Mr. Neill," Anna said.

He laced his hands on the desk before him, and the look on his face implied that this was only one of many horrors he had witnessed in his years on the job, just another day in the life of a high school principal. "You know, it's not uncommon. We often see these kinds of behaviors in children from broken homes—the acting out, the desire for attention."

"Excuse me, but my home is not broken," Anna said.

He waved his hand, an apology. "A euphemism, that's all."

"For divorce," she said.

"Yes," he said, but wouldn't say the word.

"It's true, I am divorced. But believe me, my home was far more 'broken' with my ex-husband in it."

"I mean no offense, Mrs.—excuse me, Anna. It's just, Pauline seems to require more attention than perhaps you are able to provide right now. Thus the acting out at school, with her dress code violations and this pre-occupation with the occult. Perhaps you might arrange for her to spend more time with her father?"

Anna laughed before she could stop herself.

"Her father has long since remarried. He hasn't much time for his children," Anna said.

"Well, then perhaps this is the perfect opportunity to schedule a visit, and encourage them to spend more time together. Does Pauline get along with her stepmother?"

"Pauline does not have a relationship with her stepmother," Anna said.

That wasn't exactly true. But the last time Pauline had spent any significant time with Deborah was seven years ago, when she was ten, and she knew her as Anna's best friend, not her dad's new wife. Not her stepmother. Anna flashed back to the day she'd discovered them, Deborah in *her* bed, entangled in *her* sheets, arms around *her* husband. She remembered how Deborah and Tom had both protested, as if what Anna was seeing was some sort of accident or mistake or hallucination. She was done that very day. No more excuses, no more apologies, no more taking him back. *You can have him*, she told Deborah. And that was that.

"In any case, I'm afraid I'm going to have to recommend a two-day suspension," Mr. Neill said.

"Isn't that a little harsh? For just playing some childish game?"

"Come now, we both know it's more serious than that."

Anna smiled. "Mr. Neill, you aren't telling me that you believe in spirits, are you? Or that you believe my child has the ability to summon them?"

"No, of course not, but," Mr. Neill stammered, "but this is a serious matter. And combined with her flagrant and consistent disregard of the school rules around appropriate attire, it seems a suspension is only fitting."

"Well, if that's your decision," Anna said.

"It is."

Anna stood. "Then we need no longer prolong this conversation. Mr. Neill, I thank you for your time, and I apologize for Pauline's behavior. She and I will have a serious talk about it this weekend."

"I appreciate that," he said, shaking her hand.

When she walked out of the principal's office, she didn't wait for Pauline. She just kept going and expected Pauline to catch up to her.

"Mom, wait!" Pauline was scrambling in her platform boots, her tiny dress. But Anna kept walking. She didn't stop until she got to the car.

"Mom, please, come on," Pauline said. "You can't really be mad at me, can you?"

Anna stayed silent as she put the key in the ignition. She was trying her best to keep counsel both because she didn't want to say something she might regret, and because she knew it was a punishment to withhold interaction. It made Pauline frantic and, more importantly, it made her compliant.

"Mom, I swear, I wasn't hurting anyone or scaring anyone," Pauline said. "It's just a tool. I was just . . . translating."

Anna stayed silent as they drove. It was almost time for Kevin and Billy to be let out at the junior high. And Jimmy would be walking Tommy Jr. and Jill home from school soon. She needed to get back to work. Taking off in the middle of the day like this meant overtime later.

"Mom, please," Pauline pleaded, tugging at her sleeve. "Don't be mad!"

"Pauline, I'm driving here," Anna snapped, trying to shake her off.

"But you're not mad?" Pauline held on to her sleeve. "Promise?"

"I promise, if you take your hands off me," Anna said.

Pauline released her and slumped back into her seat. "I'm sorry."

"You should be!" Anna said. "You were very rude to Mr. Neill, and besides that, you shouldn't be 'translating' or 'spiriting' or anything of the sort! Especially not at school. And charging people? How much money did you make?"

Pauline mumbled something.

"How much?"

"Twenty-five dollars," she said, now overly loud to make her point.

"Well, you're paying for groceries this week."

"Mom! That's not fair! That's my money!"

"Ever hear of taxes?"

"That's stealing!"

"You're the one who brought up capitalism."

"Yeah, capitalism! Not fascism!" Pauline said, throwing up her hands.

"I thought you didn't want me to be mad at you," Anna reminded her.

"I don't." Pauline crossed her arms and leaned back in her seat again. They drove in silence for some time before Pauline spoke again.

"You know how we did the thing a little bit in his office though? How you and me had our hands on it and I asked if a spirit was there?"

Anna nodded. "And you said it was Grandpa."

"Well, *it* said it was Grandpa," Pauline corrected. "But that's the thing. It said yes when I asked if there was a spirit there, and it said yes when I asked if it was your dad who was there."

"I'm aware," Anna said, turning into their driveway.

"But then when I used Grandpa's actual name, it said no. And I don't know if you noticed, but it moved really fast. Like it was angry."

Anna remembered how her fingers had almost fallen off it as the planchette skittered to the other side of the board, resting on the NO.

"I assumed that was you," Anna said. "Pulling it toward your side."

"No." Pauline looked very serious, the same serious eyes, behind her glasses, that she'd always had, even as a very little girl. "There was like a bad spirit there, like pretending to be your dad."

"A bad spirit."

"Yeah, like," the girl shivered. "I don't know. I just got a bad feeling."

"I'm sure it was nothing. You know that stuff isn't real, right?"

But Pauline was lost in thought. "Your dad's name was Samuel, right? Samuel Sandler?"

"Yes," Anna said, beginning to become exasperated.

"Well, all I know is, whoever was moving that thing around said he was your dad, but his name wasn't Samuel."

"Pauline . . ."

"Mom! I'm telling you the truth!"

"And I'm telling you, that stuff isn't real." Anna stepped out of the car and slammed the door. "You know what is real though? You're suspended for two days. That goes on your permanent record, you understand?"

But Pauline just looked excited. "Two days! That means a four-day weekend."

"Your permanent record, Pauline!"

"That's your bag, not mine," she said.

"I think your father might care about that, even if you don't," Anna said, and this made Pauline stop, drained the excitement out of her completely.

"You won't tell him. You wouldn't!"

"Don't force my hand then. Behave yourself."

Pauline looked as worried as she did irritated. "Just promise."

"I'll promise if you promise."

Pauline wrapped her arms around herself, shivering in her minidress as though she were besieged by spirits. "I promise I'll stop getting in trouble at school. Just promise you won't tell The Old Man."

"Don't call him that," Anna said. "But fine. I promise."

"Is it okay if Ted comes by later, to help me watch the kids?" Pauline called over her shoulder as she went to the house. Without waiting for an answer, she said thanks and ran inside.

Anna got back in the car to return to work. It was going to be another late night, as she had class afterward as well. She had left instructions on the kitchen table for Pauline to start the oven and heat the meatloaf at dinnertime, but who knew if the girl would actually remember, or follow directions. Ted coming over might be the only way they all got fed tonight. God bless her sweet, patient dupe of a boyfriend, eighteen already and graduating from high school in a few months. He put up with so much. Anna knew Pauline was hoping they could get married once she was old enough; if they did, Anna hoped he would be like Samuel was to Lise, never weary of what he had signed up for. Ted was good for Pauline; he kept her from floating away. He didn't indulge her whims and schemes exactly, but he tolerated her, and that was enough for Pauline to feel free, knowing he would always be there to come back to. Anna prayed for Pauline's sake that he never realized he had any other option. Hopefully he would temper her irrational impulses.

Spiriting! Anna knew what that was really about. Sure, yes, Pauline was dramatic, fanciful, gullible—always had been. But Anna realized that her spiriting wasn't about communing with ghosts or making contact with phantoms. What she was beginning to understand was that Pauline's spiriting was about communicating with one ghost in particular, the phantom that had haunted her her whole life. That high school principal hadn't been too far off in his ridiculous suggestion about Pauline spending more time with her father. He just hadn't realized that was what she was trying to do with that Ouija board.

Tom was elusive. It was a fact. Anna doubted she had ever had access to the real Tom, unless you counted his drunken rages, his irrational arguments. But even those felt like a character he was playing. He always held some part of him in reserve, even in his most volatile moments. Some part of him seemed to remain permanently unknowable, and that was part of the draw to him, what kept Anna there all those years, long after she knew in the pit of her stomach that it was far past time to leave. She could understand Pauline's desperation in that sense. She could understand her quest to connect, to know him, to find him somewhere amidst all that persona and bluster and force him to recognize her, to say *I see you*, to say *I love you*. But he had never said that to the children. Anna couldn't remember the last time he had said that to her.

Pauline had gone to him many times over the years. Anna would lay down the law about something, and in an instant Pauline's bags were packed and she was tearfully shouting that she was running away, that her dad was the only one who ever understood her. And inevitably, within a day, or even hours, she would return in his custody, defeated. He would push her through the doorway and lecture Anna about keeping her kids in line and leave without so much as a goodbye, let alone a hug or even a word of reassurance. Anna was the one to comfort her, to let her cry into her lap as she lay on the couch. Anna was the one to listen to her rage about "The Old Man," about how unfair it was, about how mean he was, about how wrong he was. And Anna was the one to console and soothe and repair and hold her tongue when the cycle inevitably continued the next day or week or month.

The "bad spirit" that Pauline claimed had been pretending to be Anna's father was likely no more than Pauline's complicated feelings about her own father's bad spirit. Samuel had never been bad, never for a moment. He had never raged like Tom, had never been inaccessible to Anna. There was no "bad spirit" in him. It just wasn't possible. So it couldn't be Samuel that Pauline had been sensing. Oh, just listen to herself! Pauline was *sensing* things now! Anna shook off the notion. This was self-indulgent theatrics, not extrasensory perception.

As much as Anna hated to cave to the suggestions of a high school administrator, perhaps it was time for yet another conversation with Tom about having Pauline spend more time with him and Deborah—scheduled time, planned time, when they all expected it to happen, not just whenever Pauline got fed up with following the rules at home and decided to show up on their doorstep.

There was something about that "bad spirit" comment that still lodged in her though. She kept returning to it, worrying like a splinter she was trying to extract. Maybe there really was something Pauline could see that others couldn't. Anna shivered at the thought. But she didn't have time to entertain it for long. She had work to do.

LISE

Letter to Anna, dated 1971

1

Mor stayed with me for a few days once I was home from the hospital, but then he had to leave. He told me in addition to his commissioned work, he had taken a job at a factory. "Honest work," he said, "making steel pots and pans." This is always how he saw it, I believe. That his work was honest. That mine—did I even truly have any?—was merely of a fashion. Whimsical, changeable. Less honorable, somehow, than his.

I hadn't forgotten that, the crest of optimism just before the wave crashed: The way he would take an "honest" job to pay the bills, do it for as long as he could stand it—weeks? a month?—and then quit. He would paint until the money ran out and he was forced to move on to the next job to earn money so he could quit again. I wondered how long this factory work would last. I was not well enough to find my own work, to shoulder the burden of his art.

The first few days, he was kind but nervous around me. He made soup and tea; he read to me from the days-old newspapers he'd swiped from the garbage, just to try to reorient me to the world outside the hospital. He tried to fill the empty space on that side of the room where the piano used to be. I woke up one morning to find him moving the table there. It didn't fit. Its roundness protruded into the room the way the piano never did. I remembered that now, the way the piano's upright case had sat so neatly between the corner window and the doorway to the kitchen, the way the cushioned stool settled in close to the wood panel that encased the instrument's stringed underbelly. The way the keys felt beneath my fingers. My chest tightened every time I realized, yet again, that it was gone; but I wasn't sure what it was, exactly, that I was feeling. The lightness and space I'd gained from my time in the hospital, from the medication, made me feel muffled; a gauze, like the bandages on my wrists, between myself and the rest of the world.

Mostly I slept. Each day I woke up and had to remind myself where I was, had to close my eyes and open them again before it settled in around me that I was home.

I had the bed to myself. Mor slept at the table, his head on his forearms as he slumped in the chair. I knew he could not have been comfortable. And yet I was thankful for the space between us. I didn't think I could bear his uneasy nearness beneath the blanket.

When he was gone, I'd sit at the table in the daytime, remembering. I'd go through the shelves in the kitchen, recognizing some things—a favorite mug, the old spices in the back of the cabinet—with a sudden rush of the familiar; finding other things—a can opener, the silverware, a box full of coupons—new and strange. I felt uncoordinated, out of rhythm, as I paged through cookbooks, my music books, the box of photographs and letters I'd saved. Things from long ago I knew best; other, newer, things I found alien. But when he was home, he tried to explain as much as he could to me, and I tried to remember. I sat at the table in the place where the piano used to be and concentrated very hard on trying to remember what it was like before it was gone.

Once when he put me to bed for the night, he sat next to me, holding my hand. He turned it over in his so that my palm and inner arm faced up. He traced the scars on my wrist with his fingers, as delicate as a paint-brush. I could see his face struggling with emotion.

"I was trying to protect you," he said. "I only did what I did to keep you from leaving."

He grasped my arm then, covering the scars with his square, blunt hands as if he could heal them completely, squeeze them off my skin, but gently, more gentle than I remembered him capable of being.

"Why would I ever leave you?" I asked.

"Shh," he told me, leaning forward to kiss my forehead. "It's fine now. You're here."

Once he'd finally returned to work, he left me with instructions. I was not to leave the apartment or unlock the front door. I was not to use the stove to cook. I was to take my medicine and rest.

"I do not want for you to overexert yourself," he said, sounding like Dr. Zuker.

After he left, I made the bed. I ate the breakfast he'd prepared and cleaned up after myself. I straightened the apartment. I sat at the table.

I did not take my medicine.

I'd decided to stop taking it a few days after coming home. I didn't like the padded way it made me feel, like I was wrapped in cotton balls. The longer I went without taking it, the clearer I felt. Without the medication, that sense of being suspended in limitless space began to wear off, allowing more friction between myself and the world, more feeling in general. Without the medication, I was more impatient at the thought of sitting in that room all day, by myself, with nothing to occupy me.

I tried to think my way through repertoire, the way I had entertained myself during those long, timeless days in the hospital before I opened my eyes, imagining Bach, Brahms, Chopin, Beethoven, Schubert, Mozart.

I lay on the bed and began thinking through the Bach First Prelude, first blocking it out in chords, reducing it to its basic structure, then imagining playing through it as notated. Then I moved on to the fugue, unspooling it in my mind, easily at first, as though I were reading it off a printed page. But as I watched it in my mind's eye, I saw a blankness looming, measures that were completely white, bereft of notes, even the staff missing. When I arrived at that part of the music, I couldn't remember what it sounded like or what should fill those blank spaces. I tried again, and again I came up against the same empty measures. I couldn't remember the music. I skipped on ahead to the rest of the piece, to the ending, which I was able to remember quite clearly, but I was bothered by the missing part that I couldn't seem to recreate.

I got up and retrieved the score from the bookcase and paged through to the C-major fugue, searching for the part that had been a white blot in my memory. Once I read the missing measures, I was relieved: *of course, that's what it was, that's what it sounded like, now I remember.* But my fingers itched. Reading the music and imagining it in my head was a small comfort compared to playing. The blank spot, too, was disturbing. If I had been playing, I might have been able to figure it out, to get it back. Instead I flailed in the utter absence of memory.

I started to put the music back on the shelf, in its place between Bach's "Two- and Three-Part Inventions" and Beethoven's "Klavierstücke." The music books took up the length of the low shelf, volumes from Bach to Villa Lobos, everything I had studied or once planned to study. I was surprised Mor had allowed me this small bit of potential "overexertion," surprised he hadn't confiscated my scores when he'd gotten rid of the piano.

How could he have gotten rid of it? He'd sacrificed so much to get it for me in the first place.

I needed to get out. The one-room apartment was becoming more and more claustrophobic. Perhaps walking around would help my memory, help fill in those white blots of blankness, put a spark in my brain, and give me back my music. He'd said not to leave, but if he weren't here, how would he know? Especially if I went out and returned before he came back?

2

Once I was outside, safely down the stairs and out the front door of our apartment building, I realized I'd forgotten what it took to be in the world. I'd walked out the door without my coat, without my keys. I had no money. I stared up at the sky, at the buildings all around me, the people passing by who didn't notice the significance of a woman on the sidewalk staring up at the sky.

Yet I was outside, in the sun, able to take whatever time I needed, able to walk where I pleased. It was almost decadent to have such leisure, even if it was discombobulating, and I savored it, standing in the sunlight, my eyes closed for just a moment as I took a deep breath.

I took my time. I walked slowly, ambling down 90th Street until it met Columbus and continued downtown, past the stores, the apartment buildings, the restaurants, the brownstones, the pedestrians, the people going about their business unconcerned with me unless I were to get in their way and block their progress. I'd forgotten how pleasant it was to walk, and although I hadn't walked this far in a while, I wasn't tired, at least not yet.

I watched everything. Newspaper boys in the streets, shopkeepers sweeping, old women haggling, people rushing to and from the subway. A violinist played on a street corner, hat on the ground signaling the solicitation of donations, and I stopped to watch him. Men and women walked past him, ignoring his playing—a Bach Chaconne, if I was not mistaken. No one had coins to spare. But he continued, eyes closed, playing as if to an audience of thousands of rapt music lovers, the thin melody floating away from him and merging into the sounds of motorcars and pedestrians and the background noise of the city. No matter what was happening around him, his eyes remained closed, and he swayed with the music. It reminded me of those days when I'd kept my eyes closed to shut out the world and keep the music to myself, the privacy of the world I imagined in the darkness, the music helping me float through time.

Maybe there was a way for me to practice again. I no longer had an instrument, but maybe I could find my way to one, somehow. The violinist paused and began a new piece, more Bach. He opened his eyes for a moment and saw me watching him. He smiled, and I smiled, too, as I nodded a kind of goodbye and made my way toward my new destination: 57th Street, toward Carnegie Hall and the piano stores nearby.

The American Piano Company storefront was a grand two-story expanse of glass, providing a view of grand pianos arranged within like glossy tables in a glorious restaurant. There were people inside, some seated at instruments, playing, some standing nearby, observing. I pushed on the heavy glass door to enter and, once inside, was immediately enveloped by the smell of polished wood and metal strings, the scent of the practice room. The sounds of the practice room too: there was a general cacophony of piano music as several people played pianos at once. A salesman appeared to move toward me but was waylaid by a customer with a question, and I moved quickly toward the back of the hall, where there were upright pianos packed tightly in rows, price tags dangling from their shiny lids, and fewer people.

It had been so long since I'd played. I walked the aisles of beautiful, lacquered pianos, a smorgasbord of keyboards laid out one after the other.

I tucked myself into a glossy upright in the back corner, hoping I would be hidden from roving salesmen. I felt awkward just sitting at the keys, intimidated by their regular, even sheen, so different from the chipped and discolored ivories of my old piano. The finish was so shiny, so deep and clear, it was like a black mirror. I saw myself reflected in it, a dark blur.

I waited until the other people testing out pianos in the showroom were playing at full volume and began the left-hand introduction to Chopin's Nocturne in E Minor, pedal down, a wistful outline of an e-minor chord. But my fingers weren't moving the way I intended. My left hand was slow to respond, and when I tried to play faster, the sound became choppy, loud, overbearing; when my right hand joined in, it was crass and intrusive. My muscles ached and my arms shook with fatigue. I couldn't coordinate them the way I meant to, couldn't evince the tone I expected from myself. There was a fundamental disconnect between what I heard in my head and what my hands were capable of.

I turned my hands over, palms up, the red-tinged ridges on my wrists and inner arms looking like grotesque mountain ranges in the desert of my skin. How frustrating to be back at the beginning, unable to coordinate right against left, unable to play with any sense of subtlety, musicality, intelligence. I thumbed my scars, heard Dr. Zuker's voice in my head, *you hurt yourself when you were feeling very sad, and now you are here, getting better.*

"Excuse me, miss?"

A salesman had materialized next to me.

"I'm sorry," he said. "We're closing now."

"Closing!" I stood up quickly, pushing against the bench. I needed to get home.

"I do apologize. During the week we're only open until four. But on Saturdays we have extended hours—"

"No need to apologize," I said, "I just lost track of the time. Thank you."

I fairly ran as I retraced my steps to get out of the store. I must hurry. Mor was due home soon. It might already be too late.

3

The walk back home took longer than the walk there. The streets were busier, filled with people who pushed past me, bumped against me, rushed by me as they crossed against the traffic. The cars were packed more tightly together, too, taxis honking irate horns as if that might help. This was an ill-considered plan, I realized slightly too late, to walk so far when I was still not fully recovered. How far had I walked that day? Three miles? Four? I'd walked that far before, sure, back when I was a woman who could sit and play for hours without ever tiring. But now?

The flurry of activity on the streets no longer seemed exciting, but instead manic, frantic. I began to feel a sinister undercurrent as people moved around me and cars raced past, as if they knew something I didn't. I walked faster and tried to calm myself by focusing on the street in front of me, counting my steps. I walked in four-four time, then twelve-eight time, then six-four time. I tried to step in triplets, in sixteenth notes, in time with a mazurka, the nocturne I couldn't play that day, anything to distract myself from the panic. The sky was beginning to darken as I finally reached the apartment building.

I was relieved to find the main entrance to the building unlocked. The lock had been broken for so long now. I remembered, back when I was well, being irritated that it was never fixed, but now I was glad to find it still in its state of neglect. I had no keys; if it had been locked, I'd be stuck outside with the men who sat on the stoops asking passersby for money, sleeping in boxes on the corners near the steam vents.

My legs ached from walking, and I still had seven flights of stairs ahead of me. What had I been thinking? I hadn't been thinking. And yet I remember feeling glad I'd tried. As tired as I was, I felt exhilarated to have accomplished something on my own after so many months of sitting, waiting, resting, sleeping.

When I finally rounded the corner of the stairwell on our floor, I was filled with dread to hear the murmur of male voices and see the door to the apartment ajar.

I walked into the apartment and found Mor there with Rafael and Samuel.

"Lise, my god," he said, leaping up from his chair and stalking over to me. He grabbed me by the elbow, squeezing too hard. "My god, where were you?" His voice broke slightly, and I realized he hadn't meant to hurt me.

Before I could explain, I felt myself becoming light-headed. My feet and hands disappeared, and the room swirled to the right as he and Samuel helped me to the bed. I sat for a moment, my head on my knees, while they scrambled around me. Someone gave me a cool towel for my forehead; someone else brought a glass of water. I lay down and the tunnel vision began to expand, my arms and legs coming back to me.

"What were you thinking, leaving the apartment?" Mor demanded, pacing. Rafael sat at the table, smoking, though Mor usually forbade it. Rafael alone seemed more amused by the situation than concerned.

Samuel sat at the end of the bed, holding my glass. He stood up to close the door. "She's home now, let's give her a chance to rest before the Inquisition," he said. Mor glared at him then ran his hands through his hair, making it stick out from his head even more than usual.

"Of course, of course." He sighed, kneeling next to the bed. "Lise, I was so worried. To come home and find the door unlocked and you . . . nowhere. What was I to think?"

I sat up slowly, leaning against the wall.

"I'm sorry," I said. "I didn't mean to worry you."

"Where were you?" Exasperation cut through his attempt at concern. So he was angry after all.

"I took a walk," I said. "I went to the piano hall. I wanted to practice."

He stood up and paced again, unable to pretend he was anything but mad. "I can't believe what I'm hearing. Are you crazy? Of course you're crazy, you're barely a month out of the hospital. I knew I should have left you there, you're still unwell!"

"Mor," Samuel said, a hand on his shoulder. But he thrust it away.

"Do you have any idea how dangerous that is, what you did? What if you had become confused, what if you couldn't remember where you were going? You have no money, you didn't take your keys—what if someone had attacked you, what if you got lost, what if you collapsed? Did you not think of any of this?"

"Mor," Rafael said from the table. "You heard her. The woman wanted to practice. Who are you to stop the work of true art?"

"She is not an artist." He spat the words out. "She is a damaged woman who tried to kill herself. The only true art in this house is in that room," he yelled, gesturing to the room that he used as his studio. "Do not lecture me about art!"

I was crying, my body shaking with the force of it, my face wet with tears, my arms wrapped around myself, my knees drawn up to my chest.

"I have no music here," I said. "You have your room, your work, but what do I have? Nothing! I can't even remember the things I don't have."

"You have plenty of music," he shouted. "Look at all your scores."

"But no means of playing them. You took away the record player, the records, the radio. You took away my piano."

"I did it for your own good, Lise, so you can get better. Music excites you too much, playing piano would make you overexerted. This is for the best," he said. Samuel stood near the door, watching; Rafael drew on his cigarette.

"Now I am left with the problem of what to do with her," he said. "Do I send her back?"

"To the hospital?" I asked, panicking, rising from the bed. "Mor, you wouldn't."

But he ignored me. "What can I do? I must go to work, and clearly she's in no state to be left by herself. How can I be sure she won't try to leave again? Maybe next time she won't be so lucky as to make it back."

"Mor, I swear, I didn't mean to worry you, I'm better, I swear it, please don't make me go back," I begged.

"I'll stay with her," said Samuel. We all turned to look at him, and for a moment I could barely breathe. "I have time now. I can stay with her this week if that will help." His eyes flickered to mine for a moment and he turned to Mor.

Rafael cleared his throat. "I would volunteer, of course, but I'm working on such a large-scale piece at the moment, readying it for a show. Good of you to jump in, Samuel. You're not doing anything."

Mor sat hunched over the table, his hands in his hair again. He glanced at me as I sat down on the bed. I couldn't tell if he was still angry, exasperated, or ready to give up.

"Thank you, Samuel," he said finally, standing up to shake his hand. "That would help me very much."

"Of course," he said. "I'm glad to do it."

Mor came over and sat next to me on the bed. "Do you hear, Lise?" he asked, his eyebrows knitting together in a straight line above his deep-set eyes. "Samuel will be here to watch you. There will be no more escaping, you understand?"

I nodded my head.

"Say it," he commanded. So I did.

—m—

Now that my fate had been decided, I cooked the men dinner and then I cleaned the dishes while they talked in the next room. Rafael's voice floated over the others, expansive and loud, laughing over a joke he told at someone else's expense, with Mor arguing about art and taste and whether or not subjectivity matters, Samuel a murmur of agreement here, a note of dissent there. I stood at the sink for a long time, even after the dishes had been washed and dried.

"Lise," Samuel said, surprising me. I turned around to face him, wiping my cheeks with the backs of my hands.

"Oh, yes, I'm sorry, can I get you something?" I looked down at the floor, at my apron as I dried my hands on it. I couldn't look at him. I was humiliated by what he'd witnessed tonight.

"No, thank you," he said, smiling at me strangely, as though there was a joke I wasn't getting. "I just wanted to make sure you were all right. We're leaving now."

I realized that he had his coat on, that his hat was in his hands. He had such long fingers. Artist fingers. Good piano fingers, I thought, looking down at my own hands, with their short fingers, knuckles hiding under smooth skin, not muscled like they were before, when I could play.

"I'm fine, thank you," I said.

"I'll see you tomorrow then." He smiled again in that strange way, standing too close to me, as though he were waiting for something.

"Lise! My love!" Rafael pushed past his brother to squeeze my shoulders with both hands as he leaned down to my eye level. "You had us worried today."

"I know that now. I apologize."

He smiled, tilted his head with a shrug. "I'm thrilled to know you were on a mission to make music. So much better than just wandering the streets, as Mor feared—though that, too, might be thrilling, I'm sure, after convalescing for so long."

I nodded, smiling too, though I sensed a strange scolding behind his words.

"But now, listen to your husband and stay home. We don't want to worry him any more than he already is. Let him go to his job, so he can quit and get back to his real work! I can't be the only one suffering for art!" He laughed at himself, turning away from me as Mor gestured to both of them out into the hallway.

"Goodbye," I said, but none of them heard me, and I listened to the sounds of men talking in the hallway as I sat on the edge of the bed, staring at the table where the piano used to be. When Mor came back in, he stood in the doorway, waiting for me to look at him, but I wouldn't meet his eyes.

"I'm going to be working now," he said finally, his hand on the door to his studio. "I have some ideas I'd like to sketch before they are gone." He fished the key out of his pocket and unlocked the door, careful not to open it too wide, careful to block my view of what he kept in there.

"I think I'll try to sleep," I said.

He must have nodded as he slipped into his room, taking care to lock the door behind him. All I heard was the sound of the lock tumbling into place.

I'd been asleep awhile when I heard the door open, saw a sliver of light slice across the room before I heard the click of the light switch, the key in the lock of his door again. I closed my eyes and he moved to the kitchen, where I heard him wash out a glass, move some dishes on the counter; when I opened my eyes again, he was standing next to the bed.

"I need you."

He was a dark presence silhouetted by the light coming off the streetlamp just outside the window.

"I'm so tired," I began, but then he was on me, rough hands smoothing the hair away from my face, lips on my lips.

"I need you," he repeated, and I closed my eyes.

He moved the quilt away and climbed on top of me, reaching up under my nightdress. I felt my body respond, even though I didn't want it to.

"It's been so long," he said. "We have not been living as husband and wife for so long now."

He sat up to take off his clothes and then came back to me. He pressed my knees open, spread my legs.

"Dammit, Lise," he said, his voice an angry whisper. "I am trying to love you, and you make it so difficult."

I rubbed my eyes and, for a moment, I thought it might be over, that he was so frustrated he'd given up, but he was only waiting. I moved my hands away from my face, and he was there. I could see his eyes staring into mine in the dark, and I turned my head. He kissed my neck, his chin rough and scratching, and then I felt him pushing into me, his hands finding the place first.

In my mind, I began the Bach Invention in C Minor. I was halfway through it before he was done.

"Don't leave me again, Lise," he said, his breath hot on my ear.

After I heard him snoring, I moved his arm from where it lay across my chest and made my way to the bathroom. I cleaned myself and washed my hands, wiped my face with a cold washcloth. I returned to the bed and lay on the edge, looking at the window, the table, all the shapes in the darkness of the room. It was a long time before I slept.

4

In the morning I awoke to the sounds of him slamming plates together, throwing silverware in the sink.

"Get up," he said as he carried his plate to the table and sat down. "Lise! Up!"

I rolled over to the wall to avoid the light streaming through the window.

"Lise! Samuel will be here soon. He cannot see you looking like . . . this," he said, gesturing. His upper lip curled with distaste.

There was a knock at the door.

"Ach." He stood, nearly spilling his coffee. "Make yourself presentable!"

I got out of bed and grabbed my robe, heading to the bathroom. I heard Mor opening the front door, talking, as I sat on the side of the bathtub. I was not making myself presentable, I was motionless. My insides felt moved around, my stomach unsettled. Eventually I stood and put on my robe, brushed my teeth. I allowed myself a look in the round mirror next to the sink. My hair was frizzy and I tried to smooth it back with my hands, gather it into a hair band, but curls escaped, framing my face. Annoyed, I took the band out. Why not let my hair be disheveled, crazy. Wasn't that what he thought I was?

"Lise, I'm going now," he said, opening the door and startling me. I put the mirror down and turned to him. "Please just stay in bed today.

Samuel is here if you need anything. I trust you won't be making any more excursions."

I couldn't read his eyes, couldn't tell if he looked at me with irritation, concern, or malevolence. Now I think perhaps I misread him, that perhaps I had always misread him. Perhaps he always meant to be tender.

He leaned closer and came to me, kissing my forehead. I could smell the soap and shaving cream on his skin. He stepped back, one hand tugging a strand of my hair, and said, "Fix this."

Then he left, shutting the bathroom door. I heard him saying goodbye to Samuel, and the lock of the front door as he left.

I leaned my shoulders and head against the bathroom door and closed my eyes.

"Lise?"

Samuel's voice was perilously near, so I smoothed my hair again, trying to wrestle it back into the hair band and make myself presentable, before I opened the door.

Instead Samuel opened the door and came to me, gathering me into his arms, embracing me so tightly that for a moment I couldn't breathe, kissing my hair, my forehead, my mouth.

"Oh, god," he said. "I've been so worried, Lise. I've missed you so much. I wanted to see you, I wanted to visit you in the hospital, I wanted to come here as soon as I heard you were home . . ."

I fought my way out of his embrace, pushing him back, struggling to pull my robe tighter around me as I moved away from him.

"Lise?" He looked at me with utter confusion as I backed away from him; then as he reached his arms out to me, he realized.

I shook my head.

"Tell me you remember," he said, coming closer. "Mor said you'd had some memory loss, he said there might be gaps. But surely . . ."

I stumbled backward until I was sitting on the edge of the bathtub. "No, no, no, no, I would remember this, I would remember."

This was the way time worked now. In my days of being open-eyed at the hospital, in my early days at home. People visited me from the past and told me things that changed the future. They had reports to give me, information to impart. *You hurt yourself; the doctors had to perform; you were out for days; this score is yours, you asked me to bring it to you.* And my role was to accept the information. To assimilate it. To allow myself to dissipate, to float, to become a cloud enveloping all of it. To accept it as reality.

This was no different.

Another fact I hadn't known. Another piece to the puzzle.

"When?" I said. "How long?"

We sat at the table, uneasy, strangers now that I had failed to remember our ever being familiar. I searched his face for clues, something that might transport me even a little into my own past. But he merely looked like Samuel: angular, lean, thoughtful as he considered what to say.

"It was new." He reached across the table for my hand, gently placed his fingers on mine. This I did remember: I knew somehow, without remembering exactly why, that he had always been gentle with me, kind, a calm place when Mor was stormy.

It bothered me, these gaps in time, the things I had forgotten. Like the gaps in the music when I tried to play it in my mind. My life should be knowable, easy to track, everything clear. Otherwise, how was I to make sense of things? The gaps left me uncertain, blankness where there should have been facts, confusion where there should have been understanding. A wall where there should have been a piano.

After a time, Samuel sat at the table and took out his sketchbook. I was surprised to see him begin to draw, to see that he didn't hide his process from me. He sat there drawing, erasing, shading, starting a sketch and abandoning it in dissatisfaction, returning to it later after refining some unfathomable detail in another sketch—all right in front of me. He didn't even shield me from his mistakes. He allowed me to watch him as he worked, even when what he was working on didn't turn out as he had hoped, even as he was trying something new, he told me, a new style for him, something less grounded in realism. He tolerated my questions, even encouraged them, and smiled as he answered, still sketching as he talked, never snapping at me to be quiet or to leave him alone. It was fascinating to me: his process, and also his willingness to be so transparent in it.

"You look as though you've never seen an artist at work before." He chuckled, raising an eyebrow briefly as he looked up from his sketchbook and the figure taking shape upon his page.

I sat on the bed with my dress covering me, my legs pulled up to my chest, my arms a pillow for my chin on my knees, thinking of Mor's locked door, the invisible work that went on behind it.

"Honestly, it's been some time," I said.

"What does that mean?"

"Mor decided some time ago that his work is private."

Samuel looked confused. "He's no longer going to show?"

"No, no. I mean, his actual working process. He's forbidden me to go into his studio. I haven't seen any of his work in months."

"You can't be serious." Samuel laid his work gently on the table.

I shrugged, gesturing to the room just off the kitchen. "See for yourself."

Samuel walked over and tried the doorknob. Locked, just as I'd said.

"How strange," he said, returning to his work at the table.

For a few minutes the only sounds were Samuel's charcoal pencil scratching on the page, the rustle and chirp of birds outside the open window, the occasional sound of car horns and buses. Then he blew some stray eraser peelings off his work and set it down.

"Forgive me if I am speaking out of turn," Samuel said, "but I think it is wrong. I think it's wrong that he has locked you out and shut himself in. It's wrong that he forbade you to play or even practice piano. It's wrong that he has taken away your piano. I know you don't remember what's happened between us, but I do. I remember how you cried, I remember how you told me of the cruel things he said to you, how he hurt you. I remember what you told me about what he'd done to prevent you from playing. I remember the day I found you . . ."

At this, his voice broke.

Samuel had found me?

He came over to the bed and sat next to me. He took my hands and smoothed his thumbs along the undersides of my wrists, where the scars were, held me in his arms, tentatively, let me lean against him. "I think you should be able to make music."

You mustn't blame me.

I had been so starved for kindness.

I should be ashamed to tell you any of this, of what we did, of what he made me feel. But perhaps it is the only way you will be able to understand why I did it. Perhaps it is the only way you will know what I needed. And perhaps it doesn't matter now, here, at the end of the story, where nothing comes next for me anyway.

His hand moved to caress my hair, and I felt my body remember, awakening, a thousand tiny shivers along the path his hand drew. He traced the side of my face with his fingers, tentatively outlining my ear, my jaw, my neck, and I finally reached up to him, my fingertips in his hair.

It was as though I saw him for the first time. His hair so dark brown it was almost black, flecked even then by slivers of gray. His sharp jaw, his deep eyes, greenish brown and heavy lidded. The way his face broke into a smile, his strong, even teeth surprising me, making his handsome face even more handsome. His arms, his arms around me.

He pulled me closer to him and we kissed. All thoughts of Mor were gone as he touched me and I filled with a sensation I had never felt before, terrifying in its directness, its intensity. For a moment it was the entire world. A fumble of clothes onto the floor, and I was looking into his eyes and finally my skin was alive with sensation, every nerve firing, every point of contact a new heightened dimension. I allowed myself to be transported into the feeling, willed myself to stay with it, to not float above it, a spectator to it all, but to stay inside it, inside the gravity of it. There was no music in my head. Only Samuel. And me: I was there, that time, for the first time. And when it peaked, when I was released from that sweet tension and flooded with the indescribable, exhilarating relief of it, I couldn't speak. It was a wordless kind of grief, a wordless kind of joy.

For a time, I lay like that, floating, resting in the fact of his body curved around me, my head nestled below his chin, my back against his chest, my knees bent alongside his bent knees, my breath rising with his breath. With his arms around me, I was safe. With my eyes closed, there was no emptiness, no longing, no missing piano, no yearning. Just us, on the other side of what we had done.

5

After being with Samuel, I remembered. It all came flooding back to me, and I remembered what it was that had set Mor off, what had precipitated my hospitalization. It was the dinner party and salon held by Mrs. Whiting, his patron.

When we'd arrived that night, I had been struck by the sheer extravagance of the Whitings' place, an entire two floors, twelve stories above Fifth Avenue, far too grand to be an apartment. They had a library, a full dining room, an elevator, servants' quarters. There was opulence everywhere, art I'd only seen in books. The floors shone, and I thought about the effort it would take to clean them.

Mrs. Whiting greeted us, taking my coat from my shoulders as gently as a mother drawing a blanket over a baby. As soon as the coat was off, I wished it were back on. I'd worn my best dress to the dinner party, at Mor's insistence, but I could see that it was utterly out of place. Mrs. Whiting was trim and elegant, her hair shining and artfully arranged, her face made up with vibrant lipstick, dark mascara. What must she have thought of my thinning coat, the fading dress, my plain face?

But she merely smiled as she turned, her skirt twirling in a perfect arc, and led the way to where the rest of the guests had gathered.

The drawing room was a series of tall windows framed with lush velvet drapes, white with a pale daffodil-yellow pattern, the kind of yellowed sunlight shade that I could only contemplate in the context of the difficulty of stain removal. The furniture was heavy, men's chairs and sofas, but everywhere there were touches of yellow: daffodils in a vase decorated with yellow and copper designs, a luxurious-looking yellow-and-white throw over the masculine sofa. Mrs. Whiting herself was a study in yellow: her gauzy white dress studded with yellow throughout, daisies in the lace, her slender waist wrapped in a shiny yellow ribbon. "Ah, yes, my yellow phase," I heard her say to a guest. "I daresay William is thankful I've moved on from mauve!" Then Mrs. Whiting led me by the hand to a tall, bearded man, one hand in his vest pocket.

"I believe you know my husband, William."

"My dear! A pleasure. Mordecai!" He shook Mor's hand heartily. "How is it you never paint your beautiful wife? Were I a painter I'd never use anything else for a subject!"

"Surely you mean to say you'd be painting your *own* beautiful wife," Mrs. Whiting laughed.

"Of course, my dear," he said, drawing her to him and kissing her hand.

My cheeks flushed as I watched their easy exchange, a husband and wife half-embracing in mixed company. Neither of them could have been more than a decade older than Mor and I were at the time, and yet they seemed more comfortably adult than I could ever imagine feeling. I looked over to Mor. He seemed flummoxed by both Mr. Whiting's characterization of me as beautiful and the accusation that he had neglected to capture it on canvas.

"I do paint Lise, occasionally," Mor said.

"That's my boy," Mr. Whiting said. "A nice change from the political stuff, eh? A woman's body is always more pleasing to look at than an urban landscape."

I felt Mor bristle beside me. "I believe you are aware of my opinion that the purpose of art is not simply to please."

Mr. Whiting waved his hand while he puffed on his pipe. "Of course, by all means, make a statement, promote a cause. But, by God, give me a naked woman sometime!"

I could sense Mor tensing, ready to fight, but Mrs. Whiting laughed and said, "Good heavens, William! Can we save the risqué talk for later, when the women have retired to their sewing?"

"Oh, I didn't bring my sewing," I stammered. Had I really been expected to? I couldn't picture working on Mor's old socks, his shirts and fraying suit jacket, in this opulent place.

"What, dear? Oh, no, no, just a figure of speech!" Mrs. Whiting clapped her hands together. "Come on, all. Let's move this conversation to the dinner table. Rafael? Samuel? Peter? Alfred? My goodness, you seem to be having your own salon over there!"

The men looked up, mid-argument, it seemed to me, but Rafael quickly regained his usual ease among company and arranged his face in a magnanimous smile. "My dear Mrs. Whiting, we're only plotting out exactly how to flatter you into singing for us later."

"Please, call me Alice. And your flattery will have to reach staggering levels before I will agree to sing a single note!"

Mr. Whiting walked ahead of Mor into the dining room, and Rafael put his hand on the small of Mrs. Whiting's back as he guided her through the massive arched wooden doorway. He leaned close to whisper something in her ear, and she laughed girlishly and leaned against him. He looked over his shoulder at me, raising an eyebrow in greeting. *Please, call me Alice.* Oh, Rafael.

Suddenly Samuel was a tall presence beside me. We stood for a moment watching Rafael and Mrs. Whiting leave, and then he said, "Shall we?"

The food was exquisite. It was food unlike any I'd ever eaten before, much less cooked myself. I'd never seen such fine silverware, or so much of it at one table. The plates, of course, were china, and decorated with dainty gold flourishes. The runner along the length of the table was a vibrant yellow, the candles yellow, the centerpiece a floral conglomeration of yellows and oranges, a burst of sunset. Mor urged me with his eyes to follow the lead of everyone else there, who seemed so comfortable with everything—the courses, the forks, the servants bringing things on platters whenever Mrs. Whiting tinkled the small bell near her wineglass.

"Please," Mrs. Whiting said again. "You're sure I can't get you some wine?"

"Thank you, no," Mor replied. His voice was firm, and I heard the impatience behind it. "Lise and I do not imbibe."

"Then I'll take your share, gladly," said Rafael, making a grand gesture with his wineglass. "Really, Mor, you must be the only artist I know without a vice."

I saw his jaw clench and unclench. Why couldn't he be jocular like Rafael? Why couldn't he be gracious like Mrs. Please Call Me Alice? I remember silently pleading with him: Couldn't he relax, just for a few hours?

"Well, we all know *your* vices, Rafael." Mrs. Whiting laughed.

Her husband sipped his brandy and said, "What is it, brandy? Cigars?"

Everyone laughed good-naturedly except for Mor and Samuel.

"Women," Samuel said, too loudly.

Rafael put a hand on Samuel's shoulder, slapped him on the back. His eyes flicked to Mrs. Whiting for a moment. "Ah, yes. Women. Were it ever thus. This is why you shouldn't paint the beautiful women, William. It's impossible not to fall in love with your muse."

Mrs. Whiting smiled, leaning toward her husband, who was seated at the other end of the table. "I'm ever so thankful you're not a painter, William."

"Yes, well." He gestured to Rafael in a kind of toast and drained his glass. "Now tell me, what are you working on these days? How is your group of renegades—what is it, the Imperative?"

"The Collective, dear," Mrs. Whiting corrected him, rolling her eyes indulgently.

Everything I knew of the Collective—Alfred and Peter, Rafael and Samuel, and Mor—was entirely funneled through Mor, with his stories of their lackadaisical work ethic, their weak artistic points of view, their ever-evolving positions as his rivals. The Collective had been intended as a core group of like-minded artists, working together to advance their political beliefs about the place of art in the modern world, and to advance each other in their careers as artists. The five of them, taking on the world together. And it was like that when Mor first began, buoyed by the new-ness of the endeavor. But success arriving individually to one or the other and not all of the group at once had a splintering effect, at least that was what he believed. As a group they had made only small progress, moving forward in staggered steps, which only seemed to increase the anxiety of those who were slightly behind. I doubted Mor would feel the same about the importance of group integrity were it he who was breaking out. I knew it had been difficult between him and Rafael, with Rafael's recent successes. Between him and Peter too. And Alfred. And Samuel. Between him and everyone, I supposed.

Mor talked about his latest work, another political commentary, another piece on urban development and the way man changes the natural landscape into something solid and concrete instead of organic and fluid. I knew he felt proud of his work, felt it to be superior to the others'. His nightly rants about the slights and insults he had accumulated in the course of working with them were almost like a lullaby to me at that point. Just on the way to the dinner party, he had told me that of all of the Collective, it was his work that most represented the true face of man. Rafael's work—preposterous fluff, pandering to the masses. Samuel's? What was his art now, anyway, but a pale imitation of his brother's? Peter Franklin he dismissed as a mere child, with his delicate features, his nose like a baby's, lips like a woman's. "He is more vain than my wife," he liked to complain to people, though vanity was never my particular crime. But Mor resented him for it, saying Peter was popular the way a shallow picture star is popular: for his looks, not his craft. *Watercolors!* he would say contemptuously—as empty as his mind. And yet I could not help but note that Peter had had several solo exhibitions, while Mor had none.

As for Alfred DeMarco, I suspected the only reason Mor went easy on him was because he was threatened by him. He said that he considered Alfred a "courageous painter," which to my understanding meant he considered Alfred a bad painter. But he was always quick to qualify his praise, calling Alfred's work too abstract for his taste. Alfred painted on huge canvases—something Mor noted, with some satisfaction, that Rafael had recently begun to copy—immense, outsized creations, overvibrant with color and intentionally random form. Mor never understood the appeal of such things. *Why paint on such a large scale?* he would ask me. To impress people? To frighten people? To make one's work seem more full, more intense, more important than it really was? Standing before one of Alfred's finished pieces, taking up the entire wall of his studio, Mor told me, left him with a feeling of aching emptiness. Something that big should fill a person, not eviscerate.

But Alfred, too, had been showing successfully. The only explanation Mor could fathom was that people must not be ready for art that forces responsibility on its audience. How else might one account for the success of painters like Alfred, or Peter and his painfully lighthearted diversions. His own art, Mor was sure, was too complicated for anyone to fully appreciate. He would be like all the greats, revered only when he was dead.

"I'm eager to see it," I heard Mr. Whiting say as I returned to the conversation. "But—and forgive me, for this is quite off the topic—may I ask you something, Mordecai?"

"Of course," he said.

"Have you ever considered changing your name?"

"My name?"

"Mordecai Goldenberg—really, don't you agree? It's a mouthful."

"It is not a mouthful. It is my name."

"Of course," said Rafael, leaning into his wineglass as he enjoyed a sardonic smile. "But you must admit, it's difficult. What about something more palatable, easier to the American ear? What about . . . Morty? Mort? Morty Gold?"

Mrs. Whiting clapped her hands together and cried, "That's perfect!"

Mor sputtered, incredulous. "Morty Gold? You cannot be serious."

"Why not? I changed my name," Rafael pointed out. He gestured to Samuel. "We both did. Yehuda and Shmuel were not the names of famous artists. But Rafael—now that has a nice ring to it." He clinked his glass with Samuel's. "And Samuel, too, of course."

"My word," said Mrs. Whiting. "Rafael, I haven't seen your latest work of course, but that may be the single most brilliant thing you've ever done, changing your names like that."

Mor was red-faced, and I knew the effort it was taking him to not stand up and walk out.

"I could not dishonor my heritage that way," he said through clenched teeth.

"It would be a dishonor to become a famous painter?" Rafael asked.

"You're saying a Jew with a Jewish name cannot be a famous painter?" he said, his voice rising.

"Now, now," interrupted Mrs. Whiting. "Let's not get political."

"Madame, art is political. Everything is political," Mor hissed.

"Please, call me Alice!" She waved away his righteous anger with a delicate hand.

Rafael pressed on. "What I'm saying is that when you have a difficult or intimidating name, people won't say it. And if they won't say it, how will they talk about you? And if they don't talk about you, how will you be a success?"

"Your shame is not my shame. I keep my name and keep it proudly. I will not change it."

"It's not shame—" Rafael began.

"Gentlemen, gentlemen," said Mr. Whiting. "It was an innocent question, and now I have my answer. Mordecai, I admire your principles."

"Women, of course, are expected to change their names without incident," said a woman at the end of the table. She was small, older, almost regal-looking, dressed in a fashion that had been popular years ago but was no longer, swathed in a marvelous matching caftan and turban. She waved her hand in dismissal, making music with her many bracelets.

"Yes, that's quite true, Helaine," said Mrs. Whiting. "Aren't we all expected to peacefully surrender our names upon marriage?"

The women at the table nodded. I felt Mor again growing impatient beside me. Women's marital name changes were not equivalent to the problems of men.

"But of course, you have quite the story about a woman changing her name, don't you," Mrs. Whiting said. "Please, won't you share it with us? I don't think anyone here has heard it."

The woman shook her head. "I don't think anyone here is interested in an old woman's story."

But at this the table erupted in a murmur of interest and reassurance. "Madame Helaine Augustine! Please, don't make me beg," said Mrs. Whiting. "Really, it's quite the tale!"

Madame Augustine held up her hands in surrender as the other dinner guests cheered politely in anticipation. She took a sip of wine before she began.

"Years ago, there was a young pianist, very promising, very ambitious," she said. "Bent on having a career as a concert artist at a time when a woman contemplating such a thing may as well have been considering flying to the moon under her own power. She was a scholarship student—a full scholarship student, the first full scholarship student, in fact, and the first American scholarship student—at a well-regarded music school in Paris, the Conservatoire.

"She worked very hard, practiced hours and hours of course, learned all the repertoire she could, worked harder than everyone else, all so she could combat the double prejudice of being both American and a woman. Eventually she performed in Paris and also made her London debut, all to respectable notices. She was certain that upon her return to America, she would be able to realize her dream of having a concert career.

"But she was in love with a certain French diplomat, and when he proposed, she accepted, though it meant staying in Paris a while longer.

"It was a heady time for her, performing to some acclaim, getting married. But soon after the wedding, her French diplomat began to become irritated by all the attention she was getting. For one thing, she had refused to change her performance name—although she went by his surname in polite society, her concert programs still read Minnie Aderholt, and that he simply could not abide. He also resented the time it took for her to practice, and indeed couldn't stand the 'racket,' as he called it, when she played at home. She was forced to use the practice rooms at the Conservatoire to rehearse.

"But eventually even that was not enough to mitigate his jealousy, and he forbade her to practice—and to perform. He wanted a wife, not a 'career woman.' And so she acquiesced. For a time. But she was miserable. After spending almost all of her twenty years on this earth playing the piano, to suddenly stop? It became clear to her that this was an untenable situation. And so, one night, while her fine French diplomat slept, she left. And by the time he realized she was gone the next day, she was already on a ship bound for New York."

Madame Augustine paused, clasping her hands, considering, as the dinner guests murmured in response to this development.

"She was lucky: she had money saved from her concertizing, money her husband hadn't known about, and so wouldn't miss. And at that time in New York, finding a job was very easy, so she felt confident that if her plan to be an immediate concert sensation fell through, she would be able to support herself somehow. But in the meantime, she reinvented herself. She used her savings to rent a piano to practice on, and then decided to rent out a concert hall and orchestra. Unheard of for a woman to do! She was laughed at by the concert manager! But she was undeterred. She performed an ambitious program—two concertos, a selection of Chopin and some French music, some of her favorites—to which she invited all the top music critics. And it went marvelously. Very nice reviews.

"On the basis of this, and some other fortuitous connections, she gained some minor fame, at least among music fans and critics, and gained some patrons along the way. And soon her dreams of concertizing across the country materialized—the concert manager who had laughed at her became *her* concert manager, arranging for her to perform all over, with small orchestras, prestigious orchestras, in solo concerts, with chamber musicians. Soon all the important music aficionados knew her name.

"Ah yes, her name. The point of the story Mrs. Whiting wanted me to share with you all, in light of our previous conversation. That was the stroke of genius for her concert career: she changed her name. She wouldn't change it for her husband. But she did change it for herself. Because no one was quite prepared to take her seriously when she was Minnie Aderholt, American player of the piano. But when she was a rising young star, direct from training in Paris and European acclaim and a national concert tour—when she was Madame Helaine Augustine . . . well, that made audiences sit up and take notice."

She smiled at the dinner guests as Mrs. Whiting broke out into applause. "And the rest is history! How positively brilliant of you to reinvent yourself like that."

"Yes, well, reinventing," Madame Augustine said. "It's what's required of us women. Especially those of us who cannot abide when something gets in the way of our passion."

I was dazzled by this woman—a pianist, like me; who had trained in Paris, like me; but one whose path had diverged so sharply from mine.

Already by then Mor was locking the keyboard, hiding the key or taking it with him when he left so that I couldn't practice even when he was no longer around to hear me. He hadn't yet hit upon his most ingenious solution. But at that point, I was still obedient, still obeying his commands, still playing only when I was allowed. I hadn't yet forced him to become cruel.

Did he remember telling me that? That I had brought it all upon myself?

I did. Finally, I was able to remember it all.

Mrs. Whiting shooed the guests into the drawing room and placed a hand on my arm as I began to walk past her. "My dear, I wonder if you might be able to accompany me in a few arias tonight—and I'd love for you to favor us with a piece or two of your own, if you feel up to a solo performance! I hear you're quite the virtuoso!"

"I do not think it would be appropriate for Lise to perform," Mor said, his contempt barely concealed.

"Oh, I couldn't," I murmured. But she waved us both off with a flutter of her yellow cloth napkin.

"Oh, won't you say yes? Mor, think of it as a personal favor to your favorite patron. Won't you?"

Mor sulked in his chair, glowering, before grudgingly saying, "One piece."

6

The buzz among the guests and the artists that night was talk of the government's new Public Works of Art Project, announced just days before.

"'In approving the PWAP,'" Rafael read aloud from the newspaper clipping he had brought with him, "'it is recognized that the artist, like the laborer, capitalist, and the office worker, eats, drinks, has a family, and pays rent, thus contradicting the old superstition, that the painter and sculptor live in attics and exist on inspiration'—though of course, that is no superstition! After tonight's event, all of us artists will return to the attics we crawled out of." He paused as the guests laughed and continued: "'The approximately 2,500 artists, now unemployed, are to be given employment in their own field under conditions calculated not to deflate their inspiration.'"

"And how," asked Mr. Whiting, "is this different from a handout?"

"Because it's not free," Rafael said. "Artists have to apply—and I assume not everyone gets chosen—and then they are assigned work."

"And what is the application process?"

Rafael scanned the article. "It says the 'chief requirements an applicant must have are ability, sincerity, and enthusiasm for "the American Scene."'"

"Not exactly rigorous," Mr. Whiting scoffed.

"Oh, don't be absurd," said Mrs. Whiting. "Why, it sounds like it's tailor-made for you boys. I do hope you'll consider applying. How fantastic to have a dependable kind of artistic opportunity, in addition to all the other exciting work you're doing."

From across the room, I could see that, despite Mor's natural cynicism, he was interested in the idea. I hoped he would put forth the effort to apply. "The American Scene"—that was practically all he painted.

Rafael folded the clipping and put it back inside his jacket pocket. "We'll see." He sighed. "It sounds to me as though they're looking for artists to paint a fairy tale about America, to distract us all."

"It's no fairy tale," Mor said, standing up. "The American Scene, as they call it, is quite real. And from what you quoted, there is no instruction to sugarcoat it, or to make some kind of propaganda. We may paint what we see, the real America we see, in progress, all around us. If your version of America is a fairy tale, by all means, paint that."

Rafael laughed. "I leave the fairy tales to Samuel these days. Haven't you seen? He calls them 'character studies,' but—"

"Fairy tales can be quite dark," Samuel said. "Just because they are stories doesn't mean they aren't true."

"I prefer to paint realistically," Mor interrupted. "Capture the contemporary landscape, and its interaction with man and machine."

"Oh, yes, we've all seen your marvelous construction scenes," Rafael said dryly.

"Do you not believe those scenes to be worthy of art?" Mor demanded. "Do they not deserve to be painted?"

"Ah, but you're asking the wrong question," Rafael replied. "The question is, do you deserve to paint them?"

There was a murmur from the guests as Mor's agitation became visible. He strode toward Rafael, and though Rafael was more than half a foot taller than he, it seemed as though Mor became bigger the closer he got.

"'Do I deserve,' you ask?" Mor said. "Do *I* deserve? How dare you question my right to create art. I am an artist. I must make art. Of course I deserve to make art!"

All of us stood very still, and I felt Samuel beside me, discreetly taking my hand. It felt as though we were all holding our breath, waiting for the fight, unsure of what might happen next.

But then Madame Augustine stepped forward, toward where Mor and Rafael stood, and laughed softly, breaking the tension. She leaned on her wooden cane as though it were a fashionable accessory rather than an aid in her walking.

"My dear," she said, addressing Mor. "Do you understand how presumptuous that is? Every single music student I have, every single one of them, thinks they have the right to make music. Not all of them do. And not all of them will. Right now I have dozens of students, all of them quite talented. Of these, perhaps one—*one*—will make a career of performing. A handful will go on to become conservatory teachers, or music teachers at professional schools. The rest?" She shrugged. "They may teach in their homes, or accompany the church choir, or quit entirely once they marry. The point is, the odds are small. And all of them believe themselves to be artists, and all of them work very hard to fulfill that belief.

"But no one 'deserves' to make art. None of us do. So while I'm happy to hear that you feel so passionate, that you 'must' make art, that you feel you 'deserve' to make art, I must advise you that your personal conviction does not make it less impossible."

Mor started to respond, but Samuel saved us all from a scene of surely unbearable awkwardness by saying, "It is heartening indeed, then, that the government is making such an effort to support those of us who feel so compelled, despite art's impossibility."

And with that, Mrs. Whiting clapped her hands and invited the guests to adjourn to the music room for the next part of the evening.

It did not take much flattery at all for Mrs. Whiting to perform, and I accompanied her as best I could. She performed the first piece, an Italian art song, reasonably well, but went spectacularly flat on the higher notes of her second selection, a more famous aria that was, unfortunately, familiar to all in attendance. Luckily, as she was the hostess, and patron to many in the audience, both selections were met with polite applause, and no one was rude enough to offer a more critical response.

Then it was my turn. I sat at the Whitings' 1894 Model D Steinway grand, with its bass strings nearly the length of my entire living room, and began to play "Une Barque sur l'ocean" from Ravel's *Miroirs*. Mor was in the back of the room, talking with a man who had been interested in his diatribe about art and who deserves to make it.

The instrument was marvelous. I barely had to touch the keys to coax a sound, and when I used more force it was sonorous and broad, not harsh or abrupt like my small upright. The action was so responsive my *pianissimo* was like a breath across the keys. It was a pleasure to play such a fine instrument. My fingers flew as I performed passages meant to call to mind a boat rocking gently on the waters, being tossed by waves, being swirled by the current. When I reached the end of the piece, there was a hush in the room, and I held my hands above the keys, not wishing to break the spell. Finally I dropped my head, lifted my foot off the pedal, and placed my hands in my lap.

"Brava! Brava!" exclaimed Mrs. Whiting as the guests applauded. "My dear, I knew you were rumored to be a talent, but I had no idea you were such an *artiste*!"

I shook my head, declining her praise, and then I was surrounded by partygoers anxious to share their impressions. Somewhere on the other side of the room was Mor, his growing irritation festering like humidity.

I shook hands and accepted compliments, and then suddenly Madame Augustine stood before me.

"You made some beautiful moments," she said. "Where did you study?"

"L'École Normale de Musique. With Cortot."

"And how many years ago was that?"

I counted silently. "Fourteen."

"And what was the degree? Artist's diploma? Master of music?"

"I—I didn't complete my degree."

"Ah." Madame Augustine regarded me with a kind of wordless understanding as the room buzzed around us. "Keep playing. And if you ever want to resume your studies, please let me know."

She handed me a thick rectangular card. It read: *Madame Helaine Augustine. Chair, Piano Department, The Institute of Musical Arts at The Juilliard School, 120 Claremont Avenue, New York, N.Y. Monument 2-9336.* On the back, in handwritten script: *1170 Fifth Avenue, New York.*

"We may not all deserve to make art," she whispered, "but it is required of some of us nonetheless." She squeezed my hand and walked away, to allow me the chance to greet the other guests, who seemed eager to shake my hand, to touch the fingers that had just made such music.

I sat back down to the piano and played encore after encore, until I'd exhausted my repertoire. It was only when Mrs. Whiting announced that she was so taken with me that she would like to sponsor a solo concert that I remembered: she was Mor's patron, not mine; I should not be drawing any focus away from him. But it was too late. I could see him seething in the corner. I could tell how incensed he was.

"I thank you for your interest in my wife, Mrs. Whiting," he said as he stalked to my side and grabbed my arm too tightly. "But we cannot accept your offer."

"Nonsense!" Mrs. Whiting said, laughing, but she was caught short by his anger.

"Yes. It is absolute nonsense." His voice was loud enough to carry over the general conversation. "It is nonsense that you should take any sort of interest in her amateur displays. I will not have her perform, not under your aegis, not under anyone else's. Her job is to support me, as my wife, not indulge herself in pathetic attempts at art."

"My dear," Madame Augustine said as the silence settled around us. "I believe that is not entirely up to you to decide."

"And that is where you are wrong, Madame."

He steered me roughly from the piano and Mrs. Whiting, past Madame Augustine, past Samuel and Rafael, through the guests with their shocked faces, until we reached the front door.

"Silence!" he said, although I hadn't said anything. "We are going home."

After that night, my world became very narrow. I was no longer allowed to work, even though we needed what little salary I had. I was no longer allowed to go out, though since I had no work, I had no place to go.

After that night, I was no longer allowed to practice. He no longer locked the keyboard and hid the key; he no longer threatened to burn the piano for kindling; he no longer castigated me for finding the key in its hiding place or taking it out of his pocket, or for breaking the lock on the wooden fall covering the keyboard when the key couldn't be found. After that night, he was forced to resort to other measures.

You brought this on yourself, he told me. *Otherwise I would never be so cruel.*

After that night, he got the razors.

PAULINE

1979

1

The phone rings and rings. Pauline almost doesn't want to hear the chirpy answering machine message again, but she also doesn't want to hang up on the off chance that Nomi might answer, instead of forcing Pauline to leave another message. Before Steve brought home that ridiculous machine, Nomi *always* answered the phone promptly. Having a machine around to do it for her is just lazy. A person can just sit on their couch, ignoring phone calls from their best friend.

Why *is* Nomi ignoring her? It's been days. Well—it's been *two* days. But still. It's not normal. Though can she really say that? The way things have been going, it kind of *is* normal. Maybe part of what's making her feel crazy is that her suspicion that Nomi *has* been avoiding her is actually right. Hasn't she been pulling back? Saying no to working dinners and lunches? Suggesting they work on their stuff separately? Doing their own—separate—creative visualizations?

"Hi, you've reached Naomi," Pauline mouths along with the message, imagining she has Nomi's breathy relaxed-lady-in-a-Calgon-commercial voice instead of her own, which she thinks of as impatient and thin. She remembers those sing-alongs with her family, The Old Man urging her to sing more and more quietly until she was barely singing at all, and everyone laughing at how much better it sounded.

" . . . and Steve," the message continues, in a man's deep voice. At this Pauline rolls her eyes. We get it, Nomi, you two are the perfect couple, you do everything together. She acts out Nomi's giggle and continues to lip-sync the rest of the message: "Yes, and Steve. We're not home at the moment but leave us a message and we'll get right back to you!"

Pauline can hear the exclamation point in Nomi's voice, and this enrages her. How easy it is for Nomi to be happy. How easy for her to be likable! It isn't fair. Is that why she's been avoiding Pauline? Is Pauline giving off a stench of desperation that Nomi can't bear to be associated with? Pauline rolls her eyes as she tries to control her surge of anger so that she can better match Nomi's recorded carefree tone when she leaves her fifth message of the day.

"Hey, Nomi, it's me—again! Pauline. In case you didn't remember. Ha. Just leaving you another message because I haven't heard from you, and I'm wondering if you're actually getting these, or just ignoring me?" Pauline hears herself laugh and immediately cringes as she knows it sounds manic and cackling, not cool and casual the way she'd planned, not like Nomi's girlish giggle. "I don't know if this thing is broken, or just full, or if you went away and didn't tell me or something—although, you wouldn't go on a girls' trip without your best friend, would you?—or, gosh, I don't know, anything's possible, maybe you're mad at me?"

The machine cuts her off, and Pauline slams the phone onto the receiver on the wall, hard enough to make a buzzing, ringing sound that is only slightly satisfying.

She paces the kitchen. Great, now she'll have to make another call since she got cut off. It's going to make her look really crazy, calling again like that, but what can she do? She hears Hope in the other room, still playing with her blocks. She peeks around the corner. Hope's reddish-blonde wisps are barely corralled into tiny ponytails, and her brow furrows in concentration as she places a green triangle on a stack of red rectangles. She looks up and sees Pauline, and she smiles. "Look, Mommy, I made a house!"

"You did," Pauline says, but she's back to pacing, her mind racing. What could possibly be going on to make Nomi go silent like this? Pauline feels the edges of a certainty she doesn't want to admit—the sense that Nomi *knows,* that she has picked up on what Pauline has tried to be so careful to hide, that she senses what's been going on with Steve—and pushes it away. Instead, she plays back their most recent conversation in her head—didn't it feel like Nomi was pulling back? Saying all that nonsense about working independently, about how important it is to grow? Oh, okay, fine, she doesn't want to work with Pauline anymore, is that it? She should just come out and say it then. That's fine with Pauline; she can find someone else to go into business with. Someone who isn't going to flake when things get tough, someone who won't be a fair-weather friend, someone who won't be so jealous, someone who won't shut out her *best friend* for really no good reason.

Pauline scoops up Hope, who squeals in protest and grabs after her blocks. "We're going for a ride in the car, Hope-Hope."

"No," Hope says.

"Yes," Pauline says.

"I need Bunny," Hope whimpers.

Pauline sighs and leans down to grab Hope's gray beanbag bunny. Hope takes Bunny and rubs its ears where the fur is the most slick.

On the drive over, the radio plays, and Pauline sings along, windows down, not caring who hears her. The nerve, to be told to sing more quietly. If The Old Man could hear her now! She's on-key, she even has some vibrato. At a red light, the man in the car next to them smiles as she sings along with Olivia Newton John.

"What are you looking at?" Pauline yells and floors the accelerator.

"Fast, Mommy," Hope says.

Pauline glances in the rearview mirror, seeing Hope holding Bunny, seeing the man in the car now behind them. "Yes, fast," she says, feeling a speck of satisfaction.

When they pull up to Nomi's house, Pauline turns to Hope and says, "I'll just be a minute, okay? You stay here with Bunny and I'll be right back." Whatever Hope might have said in response is lost in the slam of the car door.

Pauline marches up to the front door. *Sorry, Pauline, I can't make it. Actually I have plans that night. How about we work on our ideas separately and then we can meet in a few weeks to talk about things*—has Nomi been planning this all along? To dump her as a friend? To sabotage their business together? Pauline realizes it now: Nomi has been planning this for weeks. Nomi must have figured it out; she must have made up her mind and decided somehow, and now this is the result. Shutting Pauline out. Banishing her.

"Hello?" Pauline knocks on the door. "Hello?" She leans her ear to the crack, but she can't hear anything. Nomi's probably in the back. Pauline could just go in and take a look.

The door is locked, but Pauline knows where Nomi's spare key is. She retrieves it from beneath the fake rock in the front garden and lets herself in. "Hello?"

There doesn't seem to be anyone home, but it doesn't look like Nomi is necessarily gone. There are plates out on the counter, a cardigan draped across the back of a chair, a magazine open on the couch. And then she hears it: the sound of women's laughter.

She stalks to the sliding glass door that opens onto the back patio and the pool, but her face when she makes it outside is all smiles.

"Well, there you are!" she says. "I've been trying to call you all day!"

Nomi looks at her with a kind of surprise, and maybe dread, and definitely guilt. She *should* feel guilty! Look at her, hosting some kind of pool party with the other moms. Look at all of them, Honey and Sarah and Maria and Katherine, lounging on low chairs, drinks in hand, sunglasses disguising their eyes.

"Pauline," Nomi says, and her voice is shaky, "nice to see you."

"Is it?" Pauline asks and laughs to let them all know she knows it was a big joke and a simple misunderstanding. "I've been calling you all day! Now I know why you didn't hear the phone—you've been sunning by the pool! Ladies of leisure! Where are the kids? Was there a play group planned that I didn't know about? Besides this one, of course."

Nomi laughs uncomfortably and walks over to her. "No, no, of course not. The kids are at Honey's house, with the au pair. No plan or anything, it just kind of happened. Can I get you something to drink? Did you need to speak with me about something urgent?"

"Oh no, nothing terribly urgent, just the state of our *friendship*." Again, she says this with a smile and a laugh to let them all know everything is fine.

"Let's go inside—" Nomi begins, but Pauline cuts her off.

"You know what? I believe I will have that drink! What are you ladies having?"

Honey raises her glass and says, "Strawberry margaritas."

Pauline fumes. How could Nomi *do* this? That was *their* drink. How many afternoons had they spent by the pool dreaming up ideas together over strawberry margaritas?

But she just laughs. "Of course! I should have known! It's Nomi's specialty."

"*Naomi*," Nomi says.

"Excuse me?" Pauline is trying to keep it light, but the annoyance chokes her voice, making it reedy, high-pitched.

"I've told you, for a while now. It's *Na*-omi. Nomi is a family nickname. I prefer you use Naomi."

Pauline looks at the women, frowning at them comically and throwing her arms up as if to say, can you even believe this? "Oh, so, I'm not your family now?"

"Pauline," Nomi says and reaches out to put a hand on Pauline's arm, but Pauline yanks it away, inadvertently hitting the table where all the women's jewelry is sitting. The rings and bangles make a jarring rattle, jarring also because it means they truly have had a pool party without her, leaving their jewelry on the table to prevent it from falling off in the water or getting wet while they stood in the pool and sipped their margaritas and laughed and gossiped about her.

"*Steve* calls you Nomi," Pauline counters.

"Steve is my husband," Nomi says.

Pauline can't stop herself. Before she even realizes she plans to, she grabs Nomi's wedding ring from where it sits on the table, next to the bracelet Pauline gave her for her birthday last year—at least Nomi still cares about that—and throws it into the pool.

"Not anymore!"

The women gasp as they stand up, finally, saying things like "what the hell" and "Pauline" and "oh my god." Her laugh isn't convincing enough, or they're too dumb to get the joke, so she laughs more loudly.

"My god," she says, shaking her head like they're idiots, "it's a joke! Haven't you ever heard of a joke?"

"Pauline," Nomi says, and this time it's not kind or reassuring. It sounds like a scold. It sounds mean.

"Fine!" Pauline says, rolling her eyes and sighing. "Jeez, I was kidding, I'll get your dumb ring."

"It's not a dumb ring, it's my wedding ring," Nomi says, "and don't bother." She walks over to get the pool net to fish it out, but Pauline has thrown the ring into the deep end. She knows it's going to be too hard to scoop it with that thing.

"I insist!" Pauline says and runs to the edge of the pool. The water when she hits it rushes over her like a cold realization, and her clothes become heavy and wrap around her as she tries to find the bottom of the pool. Her sunglasses float off the top of her head, her sandals separate from her feet as she kicks, and her rings slide off as she wrestles her way to the bottom. She feels around for Nomi's ring and manages to grab something, but when she pops up, head above water, she sees it's her own wedding ring she's found.

"Oops," she says to her shocked audience, all of them standing with their mouths open dumbly in their unflattering cover-ups and kaftans. Why the hell wasn't she invited? Do they all not like her? Did one of them poison Nomi against her, is that it? She leaves her ring on the side of the pool, takes a deep breath, and plunges back under water. Where the hell is Nomi's ring? Finally, she spies it. She grabs it and holds it up over her head as she surfaces.

"See? Found it!"

She throws it toward Nomi a little harder than she means to as she hoists herself up on the side of the pool. Only after she's sitting down, feet still in the water, does she remember her own things are still in there.

"Be right back," she says, but the women are attending to Nomi and her ring, and they don't seem to notice or care. Why would they? It's clear they all hate her. She dives in once again. She finds her other ring, her sunglasses, her Dr. Scholl's—it's like a scavenger hunt, the ring at the bottom, the sunglasses floating midway down, the sandals bobbing to the surface—and places them poolside. She tries to hoist herself up again, out of the water, but she can't.

"Just go to the shallow end," Honey says, sounding irritated. "Use the steps."

"It's fine," Pauline says, and she pulls herself up, elbowing the pavement, scraping her skin, struggling, but trying not to seem like it's a struggle. Her blouse catches on something sharp in the cement and tears a little as she crawls out of the pool. "There. I'm fine. Not that any of you care."

She mutters this, but it's clear that Nomi, at least, has heard, because Nomi comes over to her, standing close, closer than she's been in a long time. At first Pauline thinks she's going to apologize, but instead she can't even believe what Nomi is actually saying.

"No, I don't need you to call Ted, and I don't need you to call a doctor," Pauline says, loudly, to show the other women how confident she is, how little she cares, how above it all she can be, how ridiculous Nomi's suggestions are. "I needed you to return my calls and be my friend. But I guess now I know who my real friends are. Turns out, it's none of you!" She laughs, as if what she's saying is truly hilarious. "Joke's on me, right?"

"Can I at least get you a towel?" Nomi asks, and Pauline pushes right past her.

"I don't need anything from you," she says as she walks through Nomi's house, dripping on the linoleum floor, the shag carpet, the leather couch. She can hear the women saying things literally behind her back as she walks away, but she doesn't care. She is too mad to care. She is also too righteous to care, because she was right, she was right! She knew Nomi had been pulling away, she knew Nomi had been mad at her. They could say whatever they wanted to about her, but at least she wasn't wrong.

She pulls open the door of the car and inside it's like an oven. Even with her wet clothes, it's too hot to sit down.

"Mommy?" Hope says, her voice weak and tired like it is when she wakes up from a nap, and then Pauline remembers: *Hope.*

Hope, still strapped into her car seat, is nearly as drenched as Pauline, wisps of hair now plastered to her head, her face, her cheeks, bright red and her neck and chest flush with rash. Pauline suddenly feels sick.

"Bunny fell down," Hope whimpers. Her face is streaked with tears. She must have been crying. She must have been sweating. She must have been baking, trapped in here while Pauline jumped in the pool.

"Shh, shh," Pauline says, reaching to get Bunny. "Here's Bunny, he didn't fall, he's right here, I've got him, there you go, there's your Bunny."

Hope holds Bunny limply and a look of confusion comes over her face.

"Mommy, you take a bath with your clothes on?"

Pauline laughs with the sheer relief of Hope being okay. What was she thinking, leaving her in the hot car like this? What if Pauline had been longer in the pool? What if she had been too late?

"I guess I did, Hope-Hope," she says, laughing, partly to try to get Hope to laugh too, to stop her from looking so concerned, to get her to liven up instead of being so limp and tired. "You have a very silly mommy!"

She's still laughing. It's one of those laughs now where she can't stop laughing, but Hope isn't biting. The laughter is not contagious. Maybe Hope is too worn out to laugh. "Isn't that right, Hope? Don't you have a very silly mommy?"

Hope is already starting to close her eyes again, rubbing Bunny as she drifts off from the heat, but Pauline is wide awake, crying, laughing, sweaty in her damp clothes and the hot car. She turns on the engine and cranks the AC and pulls away as she sees Nomi shadowing the doorway, the kitchen phone cord stretching out beside her, probably calling the police on her. Some best friend.

2

It had actually started out because their kids were best friends. Hope and Ben had bonded from day one of preschool, and thank god for that, because that had been Pauline's way in to the hip mom crowd. She had been intimidated by them, in their broad floppy hats and giant sunglasses, their fringed maxi dresses, their effortless pantsuits, their casual bell-bottoms, looking like languid models instead of moms, so offhandedly wearing outfits that Pauline would spend hours calculating the importance of, analyzing in her gold-flecked bathroom mirror, talking herself into and then out of. But then Hope and Ben ran up, hand in hand, and Ben asked if they could keep playing, so Nomi and Pauline were aligned like star-crossed lovers, destined to be friends because their children were. Pauline studied her elegance as they sat at the playground, and at home she tried putting into practice what she'd observed. The way Nomi held her hand just so in front of her face as she leaned in to gossip about the other moms, gracefully shielding the children and any onlookers from the information she shared. The way she tossed her hair when she laughed. The way she stood with her feet in sixth position, like the ballet dancer she'd once been, while chatting about the minutiae of parental life. Pauline tried working it into her usual repertoire of postures, gestures, stances, but every time she posed too obviously and Ted would frown and say, "What's happening, are you practicing for another role?"

And she'd have to say yes, yes, she was thinking of auditioning for a part in this year's community theater production, and he would say, "Hmmm," and go back to his book.

But soon they became more than just mom-friends, friends because their children were friends; very quickly they were inseparable, hanging out when the kids were in school and there was no reason, really, for them to be spending time together. Pauline always got a little thrill when Nomi would wave her over at drop-off and say, "How about a little constitutional?" because that meant they would stroll around the neighborhood together, and Nomi would confide in her about this and that, and everyone would see them and know that they were best friends, and then they'd end up at Nomi's house having strawberry margaritas, even though it was 10:00 A.M.

Nomi seemed to know everything about everybody, but she wasn't mean—people confided in her precisely because she was so nice. And even when she shared the juicier tidbits with Pauline, she never did it in a mean way. She always framed it compassionately, like wasn't it so unfortunate that Shelley's husband was having an affair, how brave she was to continue to show up at the planning committee with a smile on her face; or wasn't it a shame that Penny hadn't been able to lose the baby weight after her last pregnancy, what a struggle it was for her, poor thing. Each thing she told Pauline was like a quarter Pauline put in the bank, and all of it added up to how much they were best friends.

Pauline confided in her too, but mostly she just listened and watched, and tried to mirror what Nomi did so that she, too, could be popular and effortless and liked by everyone. She tried not to make it obvious, but of course Nomi noticed, because she noticed everything. They were in Nomi's master bath suite once, and there, along the pink Formica, was arrayed an entire rainbow of lipstick shades like it was a department store cosmetic counter, and Pauline was startled to look up and see Nomi watching her in the mirror, ashamed to realize Nomi had witnessed her hungry gaze as she'd tried to imagine the names of the colors, tried to commit the arrangement to memory so she could replicate it at home. Pauline felt naked, as though Nomi had seen right to the core of her desperation and wanting, but instead Nomi merely winked and said, "This one's my favorite," and tossed it to Pauline, urging her to try it. *Mystic Melon.*

Pauline drew it on her lips self-consciously, and it was rich and smooth and shockingly bright, not like the lipsticks she normally bought, which left little crumbles along her mouth and dried too fast and cracked, or sat too thick and felt like glue, and whose colors looked more garish than they did fashionable. She tried not to think about the fact that technically her lips were now touching Nomi's lips, by way of this shared lipstick. But then, after declaring the color "absolutely devastating" on Pauline, Nomi squinted, crossing her arms, sizing up Pauline, and pulled her into the closet. Pauline felt suddenly electrified, standing that close to Nomi, breathing in her perfume.

"There's a set in here I think would just look *divine* on you, with that lip color," Nomi said, riffling through the racks and heaping hangers full of clothes onto Pauline's arms until she found the item she wanted. It was a pants set: houndstooth-checked black, orange, and white pants that flared at the bottom, a black top with a dramatic orange-and-white stripe marking the V-neck, and a matching sweater, black with orange and white vertical stripes outlining the garment, orange and white horizontal stripes on the cuffs of the sleeves.

"Take it," Nomi said. "I can barely squeeze into it anymore."

"Oh, I couldn't," Pauline said.

"Oh, but you could." Nomi took the clothes from Pauline and returned them to their spot, handing her the pants set. Pauline fingered the ridged pattern of the pants, the ribbed edges of the sweater, and looked up to catch Nomi watching her again. "See? You could take it. The lipstick too."

So Pauline did.

She felt excited and nervous the next morning when she put it all on, nervous like she was dressing for a date. She felt almost beautiful. At the right angle, didn't she look a little like Nomi? If her hair were different, if it were that dark honey-brown, and styled with those bouncy loose curls, wouldn't she look like Nomi in this? Couldn't someone be forgiven if they mistook her for Nomi from a distance? She checked her teeth for lipstick three times and changed her mind about her shoes twice. Ultimately she settled on black pumps and completed the outfit with an orange scarf she found that just about matched the orange in the set, if you didn't look too closely. She felt energized. Confident. Nomi-like. Ted barely noticed, of course, though he did manage to say she looked nice as he walked out the door, which was something. But all her ebullience vanished when she showed up at school to see Nomi frowning at her over her sunglasses, in a cluster of other moms.

"You weren't supposed to actually *wear* it," Nomi said behind a delicate hand, just so against her face, so the other moms wouldn't hear. But Pauline heard, and she was mortified. She searched the other mothers for a reaction, any sign that they recognized the outfit as Nomi's, that they, too, were aghast that Pauline would wear it out in public. No one's face betrayed anything. But that of course meant nothing.

It turned out Nomi wouldn't be able to do their normal walk that day. Pauline claimed to be relieved as she, too, was busy, and had so many things to do, and then returned home and changed into her own clothes and lay down on the couch. Later, she hung Nomi's outfit in the closet, away from her everyday clothes, next to the dresses she kept in plastic for special occasions. She felt humiliated by her attempt to be like Nomi—surely everyone had seen it, had witnessed her pathetic attempt to embody that kind of cool, had laughed among themselves at her sad earnestness—but Nomi never mentioned it, never brought it up, never reminded her. They resumed their usual routine, and it was almost like it had never happened. Pauline was relieved, but on guard. She had trespassed, and she understood that at any time Nomi could withdraw in retaliation. That was the way friendship worked.

One day, when it was time to pick up the children from school, Nomi wasn't there. Hope and Ben played on the playground together, thrilled to have more time to run around, and Pauline waited, her stomach tightening with anxiousness as each minute passed. It felt a little like hunger. She sat on the playground bench and tried to appear calm and casual to anyone who might be watching, trying to affect Nomi's graceful hand pose as she leaned forward into her one crossed arm and tried not to feel conspicuous about being alone.

Then suddenly a man materialized next to her: lanky, bearded, though what man wasn't these days; gradient sunglasses; dressed more for business than the playground, with his short-sleeved dress shirt and wide tie, his brown polyester pants. He put his briefcase on the bench, too near Pauline for her taste, and she moved to the side and looked up at him with what she hoped was her most Nomi-type gaze. "May I help you?"

"Ben!" he called, waving an arm over his head, before acknowledging Pauline. "I'm here to pick up my son."

Ah, so this was Steve! Pauline had heard tell of him: how he worked long hours as some sort of computer engineer, how he remembered their anniversary with a dozen roses, how he did things around the house, like wash dishes, that Ted would never, at least not without a thousand arguments and reminders from Pauline.

She stood, smoothing her dress. "Oh hi, I'm Pauline." She smiled familiarly, but he seemed more perplexed than anything else.

"Okay," he said. "Are you one of the teachers here?"

Pauline could feel her face slipping from its Nomi-type coolness, a plasticky slide between amusement and offense and confusion. "I'm Pauline," she said.

He continued to stare at her blankly.

"Nomi's best friend?"

For a moment it seemed his stare would go on forever, but finally he appeared to have a moment of realization, and he smiled and said, "Oh, right, Polly," and she said, "Pauline," and he said, "Right, Pauline."

He sat back down on the bench. "So, is this just what happens? You wave to your kid that it's time to go and they just ignore you and keep playing?"

"Usually," Pauline said. "Where's Nomi?"

"Oh," he said. "She's a little under the weather, so she asked me to pick up Ben. I had a half day today, so it was on my way home."

Under the weather? She had seemed fine that morning. Also, why hadn't Nomi called *her*? Pauline would have picked up both kids and brought them home. No need to involve Steve.

"That's odd," she said. "I just saw her a few hours ago and she was fine. Plus, she needn't have bothered you—I could have dropped Ben at home just as easily."

He looked at her strangely. "It's not a bother. He is my son, after all."

Pauline reddened. "Oh, of course! I just meant, I would have been happy to, if I'd known she was sick."

Why *hadn't* she known Nomi was sick?

They both watched as Hope and Ben chased each other around the merry-go-round and up and down the slide, shrieking and screaming as they went.

Steve relaxed into the bench and stretched his arms out along the back. Pauline felt adrenalized by the sudden proximity of his arm as it rested near her shoulder blades, and for a moment she wondered if Nomi had meant to do this, had meant for them to meet.

But then just as abruptly, he withdrew his arms and stood up, clapping his hands together. "C'mon, Ben, time to go."

He picked up his briefcase and started walking toward the children, who seemed determined to ignore his entreaties.

"I can watch them if you'd like—I can drop Ben off later," Pauline said.

Then Ben barreled into his dad's arms, and Steve swept him up into a big hug, and Pauline felt jealous of Ben for a moment, she realized with a jolt, and Steve said, "Thanks, Polly, but I'll wrestle this little bear home myself."

"I'm not a bear!" Ben shrieked, and Hope joined in, defending him. "He's not a bear!" Steve put down his briefcase again and crouched low. "But what if *I* am?" And the children screamed ear-piercingly and ran off to hide behind the slide while Steve stalked the playground, pretending to be a bear.

Pauline could hardly believe it; she almost held her breath watching, and for some reason her eyes were stabbed with tears, seeing Hope laugh as she tried to elude the bear's grasp, seeing Ben hang upside down as the bear grabbed him and tickled his tummy. Had Ted ever done anything like this?

"Okay, okay," Steve said, while Hope and Ben clutched his calves, sitting on his feet. "I surrender! You have caught the bear!" He began walking with them on his feet, and with every lumbering step the high-pitched laughter caught her heart more and more.

"You okay?" he said, when they'd made it back to the bench, and she realized her face was wet with tears.

"Oh, yes, I was laughing so hard I was crying, isn't that right, Hope? Wasn't that so funny?"

"Funny!" Hope said.

Later, almost accusingly, Pauline said to Nomi over the phone, "You never told me Steve was so great with kids!"

But Nomi just sighed and said, "Isn't he though? He wants another one, but I just don't know if I'm ready."

Pauline felt herself become very still and said, "Nomi."

"What?" Nomi seemed almost irritated.

"Is that what was wrong today?"

"What do you mean?" Now Nomi was definitely irritated.

"Is that why you were feeling sick," Pauline clarified. "Could you be . . . ?"

"Oh god," Nomi said. "I don't think so? Oh, I hope not. I don't want to go through that again."

Pauline felt her brain clicking into some higher gear, making calculations, forming plans. She could see it all unfolding before her, how perfect it would be. "Oh, but just think: What if we went through it *together*? I could get pregnant too! We could go maternity clothes shopping together, we could do those Lamaze classes together—we could be pregnancy buddies!"

"Pauline," Nomi said sharply. "Just because we're friends doesn't mean we have to do everything together."

"I know, I just—"

"Even if I *was* pregnant right now, I'd have a head start on you. What would you do, start trying to get pregnant tonight to catch up? I swear, Pauline, sometimes you're just too much."

Too much. Everyone always said that about her. The Old Man had said it every time she'd had a feeling or expressed an emotion: "Too much, Pauline, you're too much." And Anna—Anna had said it too. She'd say, "Pauline, tone it down," but that really meant the same thing. Pauline was too much. Said too much. Wanted too much. Needed too much.

"Oh, I'm just trying to make you feel better," Pauline said. "But seriously, next time, just call me. I can take the kids home. Save Steve the trip."

She flashed back to the sight of Steve with the kids laughing, clinging to him as he pretend-struggled to walk.

"Hey, what do you think about getting together, the four of us? We could do a bridge night or something? You and Steve could bring Ben here—the kids could play and the adults could play. What do you think?"

"Could be fun," Nomi said. "Listen, I'm exhausted. I'm going to go to bed early."

"Maybe you *are* pregnant," Pauline said.

"Maybe," Nomi said, but she didn't seem convinced.

Still, that night Pauline made a point of wearing the negligee Ted had bought for her one Valentine's Day, and when she suggested they do the thing he liked but she didn't, he was too caught off guard to say no. Afterward, she lay on her back with her knees bent for a long while, thinking about the electricity that had raced across her back when Steve's arm was near.

Maybe they would be pregnancy buddies after all.

3

Nomi was restless, and that made Pauline feel both energized and hypervigilant, because it meant she was never quite sure how to anticipate Nomi's moods. Sometimes Nomi seemed perfectly content with her life, which to Pauline seemed picture-perfect, with her adoring Steve and charming young son. Pauline often found herself comparing lives as she sat with Ted eating TV dinners, listening to him talk back to the news or tell her about whatever boring thing was going on at the bank while Hope played at their feet. Surely the dinners at Nomi's house were more interesting—surely Nomi was as talented a cook as she was a friend, serving Steve steak and baked potatoes and greens, listening raptly as he told her and Ben about his exciting work with computers. Computers! They were the future! But then Nomi would complain to her, would say that Steve wouldn't leave her alone some nights when all she wanted to do was sleep, that she felt ridiculous being a housewife, that it was impossible to be both a housewife and a feminist at the same time, that she wished she'd had the chance to go to college like her brothers—she had been smart enough; she just hadn't been male.

"Do you know, I've been keeping a secret from you?" Nomi said once, leaning forward as they sipped their margaritas near her pool.

Pauline felt nervous, but she played it off. "You're a Nielsen family?"

Nomi playfully swatted at Pauline.

"You're going to be the next Bond girl?"

"Come now," Nomi said.

"You're pregnant?"

Nomi didn't answer her right away. Instead she narrowed her eyes and looked off toward the pool, and for a moment Pauline's stomach lurched. None of her entreaties with Ted had resulted in anything so far, and she felt her hopes of being pregnant alongside Nomi start to fade.

"I've been taking courses at night," she said. "At the community college."

"No!" Pauline was truly surprised. She had been running down a list of potential Nomi secrets in her mind, but community college coursework was not one of them.

"Yes!" Now Nomi beamed. She seemed excited to share her secret. "In business!"

"Business!" Pauline said. "You, a businesswoman?"

"You can't see it? Me, in a sharp suit and heels?" Nomi got up to model her imaginary businesswoman outfit, but quickly sat down again after doing a turn. "Actually, business and education. You see, I have an idea: I want to start a school."

"A school!"

"Yes!" Nomi got up again and paced by the pool. "I want to create a space where children can express themselves, not become little automatons who have to sit in their seats and raise their hands. Don't you want that for Hope? For Ben? Look at how they love to play—once they start real school, that kind of play will disappear. It'll quash their natural love of learning."

Pauline hadn't thought about that. She had just been looking forward to the long hours that would stretch before her once Hope was in full-day kindergarten.

"So that's what I want to do: I want to start my own school. I want to design my own curriculum, hire my own teachers, run it like a business—oh, Pauline, isn't it exciting?"

It seemed to be, at least for Nomi. But all Pauline felt was Nomi slipping away, disappearing into her project.

"Could I help you?" Pauline asked. Nomi sat down.

"Help me how?"

"Well, I could help you with marketing—getting the word out. I could help you find a place to build a school, or find a building to turn into one. I could interview teachers. I could literally do anything you wanted me to do, honestly!"

Nomi grabbed her hands across the table. "Can you imagine? The two of us, working together to do this important thing!"

Pauline could imagine, and she squeezed Nomi's hands. "Absolutely!"

From then on, their morning walks and afternoon time while the children played were consumed by talk of Nomi's project—"*our* project," Nomi would say whenever Pauline would call it that—and at night in bed, Pauline would think of more things they could plan together when they spoke the next day. They might not be pregnant with children together, but they were pregnant with ideas together, and that was even better in a way, because ideas were more bonding and less needy.

Ted seemed pleased that Pauline had a project to keep her occupied, and he merely sighed when he would come home to find the house in disarray and nothing thawed for dinner. It was good for Pauline to be busy.

4

Bridge night was probably where things started to go wrong, if Pauline had to pick a point in time when everything began to unravel. Of course, she couldn't really put a finger on it, but she had the sense that that was where it might have started.

They fell into a routine of taking turns each week, one night at Nomi and Steve's, one night at Pauline and Ted's. Whoever's house it wasn't would bring the wine; whoever's house it was would handle the food. And the kids would play and watch TV and crash on the couch until it was time for one of them to be scooped up and put in their own bed and the other to be scooped up and driven home.

It had been decided early on that teaming up as spouses would present an unfair advantage, so they split up the couples. Nomi and Ted played as a team, and Pauline and Steve played as a team. At first, Pauline watched jealously as Nomi and Ted bantered, for they seemed to get along so well and were so simpatico. When they brushed by each other in the kitchen or on their way to get a drink, they seemed too familiar for Pauline's liking, even though if someone asked her in a court of law exactly what had crossed a line, Pauline would be forced to admit that nothing had. But it sharpened her own focus on Steve, and she tried her best to be extra clever, extra witty, to look her best on bridge night, to pounce on the jokes that emerged between them during the course of a night and make them "their" jokes, their private code.

After that, Pauline liked teaming up against Nomi and Ted. She liked studying Steve's face behind the cards, his brow furrowed, his glasses slightly crooked. His beard was handsome, she had decided, and she was irritated by Ted's refusal to grow one. He had those lambchops and that mustache—why not just take it a step further? But no, it wasn't *professional* at the bank. Steve was taller, too, more broad-shouldered. Pauline watched as he got up to tend bar or check in on the children playing in the other room, noting how his muscles moved beneath the shiny polyester of his shirt. When they teamed up, it felt like they truly were a team. They had pet names, private jokes; they could mind-meld and win against Ted and Nomi, which felt like a bigger victory than just a game-night victory. It felt *significant*.

Was it her imagination, or did his hand linger on her lower back as she pressed by him in the kitchen? Did he look her in the eye a little too long, a little too meaningfully, when they sat across the table from one another? When he took her coat, did he mean to draw his fingers along the back of her neck the way he did, making her skin a sudden relief map of desire?

And then there was that one night at Pauline's house when they had seemed so truly in sync. They had flirted all night and had beaten Nomi and Ted so badly, and were so triumphant, toasting one another while the two losers sulked, when a sleepy Ben wandered out from the family room and clung to Pauline's side and said, "Mommy, can we go now?"

Nomi stood up and said, "Hey, Benny, I'm over here. Sure, we can go. The grownups are all done playing."

But Ben, still half asleep, grabbed Pauline even more tightly and said, "No, I'm talking to *my* mommy!"

Pauline said, "Shh, shh, Ben, I'm Pauline, I'm Hope's mommy—*your* mommy is right over here," but Nomi walked over too quickly and grabbed Ben, picking him up too hard, and he cried, saying, "I want my mommy!"

Nomi whisked him over to the coat closet while Pauline and Steve and Ted stood awkwardly.

"He's just asleep," Pauline said. "He's confused."

"Of course," Steve said.

"Steve." Nomi's voice was a dagger thrown from the other room.

"That's my cue," he said, shaking Ted's hand.

"Good game," Ted said.

"It certainly was for us," said Steve, and he embraced Pauline—his hand thrillingly low on her back—saying, "Good job, partner," his voice low and sexy in the curve of her neck, and Nomi said "Steve!" again in a way that sounded angry as Ben whimpered about wanting to go home.

After they had left and Ted had deposited Hope in her bed and Pauline had cleared the table, Ted found her in the kitchen, running dishes under water in the sink as she stared out the window, replaying the night's events in her mind. He cleared his throat.

"Is this another Carl situation?"

Pauline nearly dropped the dish she was holding. "Excuse me?"

"You heard me," Ted said. "Do I need to be worried?"

She let the water run as she soaped up another dish, scrubbing too hard, making a show of it. Finally it seemed she had waited him out, because he turned and walked away.

"Take your medicine, Pauline," he said.

After that, it seemed like everyone was more distant. Ted buried in books like always. Nomi still mixing margaritas and going on walks and talking about plans, but muted, like she was only pretending to be interested. And Steve. For a couple of weeks, it turned out that he was too busy at work for bridge night. "It's a shame," Nomi said when she called to cancel. "But what can you do?"

—⁂—

At the preschool carnival weeks later, she was so busy looking for Nomi that she literally bumped into Steve. Nomi had been elusive ever since that bridge night, and as much as that fueled Pauline's panic, it also fueled her imagination. Was there trouble in Perfect Marriage Land? It hadn't been her imagination that there had been tension between her and Steve, and she knew Nomi was no slouch: she saw everything and, more than that, she noticed everything. She had probably seen the way that Steve held Pauline just a little too long as they said goodbye. How he had looked at Pauline over his cards, across the table, so directly it had made her face flush. And yet as enjoyable as those memories were for Pauline—and she replayed them, over and over, wondering what Steve thought and felt, wondering what Nomi thought and felt—they also irritated her, because she couldn't revel in them completely, because she was sure that they were the reason why Nomi had become so distant. Pauline became irritable, without their friendship to define her daily routine, and soon Hope was reacting, too, acting out, throwing tantrums, being defiant. And of course she was. Pauline had always felt as though Hope was an emotional tuning fork, picking up on the vibrations around her and feeling them resonate in her own body. Of course she had sensed the anxiety and sadness and happiness and desperation and fantasy and overall checked-out-ed-ness that was Pauline's current state.

Steve seemed happy to see her, unless he was putting on a show for the kids, and she felt herself smiling idiotically, out of proportion for a school carnival hello. Hope and Ben, too, seemed super-energized, shrieking and hugging each other and jumping up and down, as though they didn't see each other in class every day, and pleading with Pauline and Steve to let them get in line to do the limbo together.

"Where's Nomi?" she shouted over the music.

Steve had to lean in close to her so she could hear, and she could smell his aftershave. "She wasn't feeling well."

"Oh! Sorry to hear that." Once again, Nomi hadn't said anything to her about feeling ill. Pauline felt a familiar irritation rise.

Then suddenly Steve was placing a balloon hat on her head. The intimacy of his hands on her hair shocked her, but then he put a balloon hat on his own head and smiled and said, "When in Rome." Pauline looked around and saw that all the children, and most of the parents, were wearing balloon hats.

"It looks good on you!" she said and instantly wished she hadn't, as he made a face as though to say he couldn't hear her, and she realized she would have to repeat it. He came closer to her and put a hand on her back, on her shoulder blade, ever so gently, and leaned his ear toward her so she could say it again.

"I said, you wear it well," she told him, shivering at the feeling of his hand touching her, and abruptly he dropped it and stood up so that they were farther apart again.

"Just wait 'til we get to the face painting!"

She watched him being led, by both hands, by the children toward the face painting booth and, for a moment, let herself slip into the fantasy she had been trying to resist ever since the last bridge night: that she wasn't just the other woman but the other mother, that this could be her life, her and Steve and their sweet children. What a family they could make.

Ted's comment still rankled. She couldn't get it out of her head. She was mad at him for saying it, and ashamed of herself, and also indignant, all at the same time. This wasn't a *Carl* situation. Carl had been a totally different thing. Carl had been . . . well, he had taken advantage of her. She had been lonely and Ted was away on business, and Carl had just pounced. She had been the victim there. Though perhaps that wasn't fair to Carl—sweet Carl, who had only ever called her *missus*, never her actual name. He was so young, and she was so flattered that this stunningly handsome, strong man, so unaware of his power, so unaware of the power he could have over women like Pauline, had paid any attention to her that she didn't notice when they crossed a line, or at least she didn't care. His body was like a Greek statue, and she told him that as he stood naked in her bedroom, the sweat beading on his chest, his legs. *You like, missus*, he said, and she said yes, oh, yes.

When Ted came back from his trip, he wondered why the front lawn was so unkempt, the flower beds a mess, the trees untrimmed. *Oh, I had to fire Carl*, she said, hoping he would just leave it at that, but no, he just kept pushing until it all came out, and she finally confessed how lonely she had been, and how unhappy she was, and how good it felt to be physical with someone who worshipped her, who appreciated her, who knew what to do to make her feel good, until he finally said, *Dammit, Pauline*, and left the room.

This was different. This wasn't a misguided fling with the gardener. Steve was a father, a husband—a good father, a good husband. What she was beginning to feel for him wasn't purely some kind of physical urge, it was . . . familial. She wanted to be a family with him.

Ted had made her see a shrink after the Carl situation. He said it was either that, or he would file for divorce. So she went. Pauline told her about Carl, about Ted, about everything that had happened. The shrink had a habit of correcting Pauline every time she referred to Carl as her friend. She insisted on pointing out that Carl was not Pauline's friend; that Carl was technically her employee; that Carl was barely nineteen to Pauline's twenty-five, which might not seem like that big an age gap but actually was; that Carl had limited English; that Carl wasn't even his real name—it was Carlos. She kept telling Pauline that she needed to ask herself some hard questions, questions about why she might want to stray from the person she had been with since she was seventeen years old, but she wouldn't tell Pauline what those questions were, and she wouldn't give Pauline any answers. After the first session, Pauline swore she wouldn't go back, but she spent a day cleaning the house, doing serious, penitent cleaning, like the kind of cleaning a person might do to save their soul, the whole time replaying every single interaction, conversation, look, glance, thought she'd ever had concerning Carl, and she decided fine, she'd do it, she'd ask some hard questions.

She saw the shrink for about a year. By then, they had long since moved past Carl, and what that situation had to do with her marriage, and onto what that situation had to do with her parents' marriage (or lack thereof), and what everything had to do with her father. She didn't tell the shrink much about The Old Man, but everything she did tell her made the shrink's eyes get wide before she managed to calmly say things like, "And how did that make you feel?" She did tell her about Anna not being her real mom. About not knowing her real mom. About having a memory of maybe once having met her real mom, but not being sure whether or not it was a dream. About the way The Old Man had finally told her about her real mom. About the shame of knowing her real mom didn't want her.

"How wonderful, then," the shrink had said, "to have grown up with a mother who *did* want you."

Pauline had shaken her head, had become exasperated, trying to tell the shrink she just didn't get it, Anna was the mother she *had*, not the mother she *wanted*, but instead she'd found herself crying. The shrink asked her if Anna had ever told her any stories about her birth mother, and Pauline said no, Anna had kept that all to herself, the only story she'd ever told her was a fairy tale, which—come to think of it—was kind of gruesome, and the shrink indicated that she'd like to hear it, because of course a shrink would be interested in a story like that.

It was about a girl who'd had her hands chopped off by her father, Pauline told her. He'd made a deal with the devil, and then the terms came due, and he had to chop her hands off with an axe. So he did, but the girl cried tears that were so pure they cauterized the wound and the devil said he couldn't take her. The deal was off, and the girl's father cast her out, because she was a mutant with no hands. The girl set off into the forest, having no idea where to go, and ended up in a field of pear trees. Some angels saw her awkwardly trying to pick some of the pears and took pity on her and gave her some. Around this same time, a king happened to ride by and see this handless girl trying to eat the pears. He, too, took pity on her and brought her to his castle. He thought she was beautiful, so he married her and gave her as a wedding gift a pair of hands made out of silver.

Then she was pregnant, but the king had to go away on important business, and while he was gone, the baby was born. She sent a message to him announcing the birth, but the devil got a hold of it and changed it to say that she had given birth to a monster. The king read the message and wrote back to say that he would love their child, monster or not, but the devil changed the message to read that the king wanted the child to be killed. So the girl with the silver hands left the castle with her child and went back into the forest.

Some angels saw them and led them to a house where they could stay. The king looked for them for years and refused to stop until he found them. In the meantime, somehow, over seven years, her hands grew back. Then one day the king knocked on the door and told them he was looking for his wife. And the girl said, I am your wife, but he said, no, you can't be, because my wife had silver hands. The girl went and got the silver hands, which she had saved in a box, and showed them to him, and they went back to the castle and remarried and lived happily ever after.

Pauline started crying as soon as she finished the story and said, "You know what's dumb? I'm not crying about the girl having her hands chopped off, I'm not even crying about all the suffering she had to endure. I'm crying because of those stupid idiot angels. Like, that's great that they were able to help her to get a pear or find a house. But where were they when her father *chopped off her hands?* Why didn't they stop it? Why didn't they stop the devil?"

The shrink sat silent for a time and asked, "What about the girl's mother?"

Pauline was confused by the question.

The shrink said: "In the story, you said the girl's father did this deal with the devil, the girl's father cast her out. What about the girl's mother?"

"She wasn't in the story," Pauline said.

The shrink nodded. "Maybe you need to put her back in."

By the time the carnival was nearly over, they all had their faces painted. Hope had a flower on one side and a heart on the other. Ben had opted for a four-leaf clover on one side and a lightning bolt on the other. Steve looked quite handsome with hearts on both his cheeks. And Pauline had a flower on one cheek, with glittery stars around it, a design element courtesy of Hope. They bought tickets to throw darts at balloons, to try to land a ring around a small bowl with a goldfish in it, to aim beanbags at a target and dunk the elementary school principal. There were no rides at the carnival, but it had the feel of a county fair, and Pauline wished she could feel the rush of the evening air on her face hundreds of feet up on a Ferris wheel, clutching Steve in fear and exhilaration as they circled the sky.

"What do you think, should we call it a night?" Steve asked. They were walking with the kids, holding hands, taking turns swinging each kid between them.

"Nooooo," the kids whined, and Pauline said, "Do we have to?" and Steve laughed.

He pulled her toward him a little, under the playground streetlamp, and leaned so close it made her stop breathing for a moment, and said, "Here."

He took his thumb and smoothed the upper part of her cheek, just under her eye.

"You had a little glitter smear."

"Oh, well," she said, feeling her face flush, her body ripple with adrenaline, "we can't have that, can we?"

But then he hoisted Ben up on his shoulders, tickling him in a cascade of laughter, and said, "Okay, see you around, friends!"

"Bye, friend!" Hope shouted.

"Bye, friend!" Ben managed over his laughter.

"Bye, friend," Pauline said lightly, but she was angry as she watched Steve walk off, swinging Ben down easily as they headed to their car. What was that? What was he doing being so close with her all night, only to be so abrupt and take off?

He must not be able to reckon with his feelings, she decided, as she got Hope settled in the back seat. There's something happening here that's undeniable. But he's a good man, so he's conflicted. She sighed as she realized that's what she loved about him, that he was a good man, a family man. Then she started as she recognized what she'd just thought. *She loved him.*

5

Maybe it actually was the carnival night, not bridge night, that was the start of everything going downhill. Because it's true that after that is when it seemed official that Nomi was pulling away. Morning constitutionals were rare. Whenever Pauline would ask about getting together to brainstorm or work on their project, Nomi would come up with excuses, or seem noncommittal, or redirect Pauline into some other conversation Pauline would be so happy to take part in she wouldn't notice until afterward that they hadn't actually made any plans.

It made her feel paranoid. It made her feel insane. Like, actually insane. She started stalking Nomi, checking up on her, driving by her house to see if her car was there, if she was home. Once she even called Steve at work, just to try to have a conversation about it, to see if he, too, had noticed anything off with Nomi, or if he was concerned. He hadn't been able to talk—no, Nomi seemed fine to him, totally normal, nothing out of the ordinary—but listen, it was a busy day at work, so he had to go. She'd gotten the feeling that he, too, was trying to give her the brush-off, but she told herself that was just crazy talk. Steve, of all people, understood her, and understood her concern. He was just busy. They'd talk later.

She had taken to talking to him all the time, in her mind. Imagining, fantasizing. Sometimes she would put on the outfit Nomi had given her and pretend to be Nomi, getting ready to go out on a date with Steve. Sometimes she would obsess over what was going on with Nomi and their friendship, replaying all their conversations and berating herself for saying this or not saying that, or for just not being worthy of Nomi in the first place, how stupid was she to not have seen that before; and when she had tired of the rehashing and had run out of the likely and terrible possibilities of how it would end, she would switch over to obsessing about Steve, flashing back to their bridge nights, the night of the carnival, the endless imagined conversations she'd had with him as she lay in bed trying to fall asleep. Sometimes she worried that she was lost. That she was disappearing. Sometimes she felt like she was grieving, practicing for the inevitable end of her friendship with Nomi, the inevitable loss of Steve when they were finally able to confront the impracticality, the impossibility, the inappropriateness of what they felt for one another.

Other times, she was filled with an indignation close to rage, if she were ever allowed to feel something as powerful as that. How *dare* Nomi? How *dare* she be the one to decide if Pauline was worthy or not, if Pauline deserved the favor of her company, if Pauline should be shunned by the other moms—because make no mistake about it, she was not imagining things, there was a coldness at the morning drop-offs that was palpable. It wasn't fair. She needed a group. She saw the older mothers of elementary schoolers, middle schoolers, the hardened high schooler moms with their burgeoning jowls and brittle hair, their in-group cackling through gossip like old ladies—she saw the way the loners were excluded, shut out of the planning committees, the bake sales, the PTA. Was this her future? Without a pack to protect her, she was just hurtling toward irrelevancy, invisibility. Disappearance.

Well, Nomi didn't get to decide that for her. Pauline would be the one to decide. She would try to repair their friendship, if it was even truly broken. She would get on Nomi's bright side again. And if she didn't? Or couldn't? She'd find another way. She always did.

Still, it felt like a constant wound that needed tending, and Nomi's absence from her day-to-day life was noticeable to other people, not just her. Ted had even asked about it.

"Not that I mind, necessarily," he said one night, over a meal of soup and sandwiches Pauline had taken too long to prepare and had come out worse than should be possible for such a simple dinner, "but what happened to bridge night?"

"Oh," Pauline said, trying to keep her voice bright. "Nomi and Steve are just having a busy couple of weeks. Work stuff, you know. Computers."

"Hmm," Ted said. "And what's the status of your project with Nomi?"

"Moving along, moving along," she said, cutting off crusts for Hope. "We're making progress."

"Glad to hear it," Ted said. "Always good to have something to keep the mind engaged."

Keep the mind engaged? What did *that* mean? Pauline fumed but tried to keep the irritation off her face. Everything Ted did seemed to bother her these days. His boring conversation. His stupid comments. How did some people go through the world like that, never snagging on anything rough? He just sailed right through, everything easy and calm.

Later that night, she called Nomi, trying to make it like old times. She called from the kitchen line, far away from the bedroom where Ted was holed up with his book, to make sure he couldn't hear her, and she launched into a litany of his annoying behaviors. Normally this would draw Nomi in, she would laugh at Pauline's exaggerations and dramatic storytelling, and then she would share something annoying that Steve had done, and they'd go back and forth trading dumb husband stories and cementing their bond as best friends. But that night Nomi seemed bored, even yawning audibly, excusing herself afterward with an insincere-sounding apology that pretended to marvel at how she could be so tired. And she didn't join in. She didn't even laugh. Instead, she actually defended Ted.

"Oh, he's not so bad, Pauline," she said, even though Pauline had just told her how condescending he had been to her, urging her to keep her mind *engaged*. "Honestly, I think he's a pretty great guy."

"Except when you two lose at bridge," Pauline said, hoping to lure her with an opportunity for some easy Ted-bashing. But Nomi avoided it.

"Maybe you two just need to go to couples counseling," she said.

Pauline was shocked, absolutely incredulous. The temerity, the sheer audacity! To suggest couples counseling!

"I wasn't aware my marriage was in trouble," Pauline said, trying to be as frosty as possible. Channeling her grandmother, the queen of frost. Anna could be blunt, but Grandma Lise had been a one-woman ice storm. Nomi, however, appeared to be thoroughly insulated.

"It's not like that," she said, yawning again. "You just go and talk things out. You get on the same page."

"Uh huh."

"It can be very helpful during those times when you're just out of sync as a couple."

"And how would you know," Pauline said, adding silently, *Mrs. I Have a Perfect Marriage.*

"Steve and I went a few times. I can give you the number, if you like."

So she and Steve had been "out of sync"! Pauline wondered how recent this was, just how out of sync they had been. She wondered: Was it because of her? Because of her flirting with Steve at bridge, because of his obvious feelings for her? She felt a thrill, her stomach floating like she was about to plummet from a great height, the way she always felt whenever she thought of Steve. She was convinced she could tell when he was thinking of her too: randomly, throughout the day, she would get an all-over body shiver and feel it in the pit of her stomach, this sense that she was in his thoughts, that she had infiltrated.

"No thanks," Pauline said. "No offense, I just don't think Ted would ever go for that kind of thing. You know he hates shrinks."

"You could still take the number," Nomi said. "You could use it for yourself."

There was something going on here, Pauline was sure of it. Nomi *must* be jealous of her and Steve. Otherwise why would she so deliberately try to hurt Pauline with these suggestions, all of which added up to: *You are crazy. You need help.* Nomi was supposed to be her best friend. How could she say such a thing?

Pauline summoned her best version of her grandmother's icy disdain and said, "I'm sure I won't need it. Thank you though. I'll speak to you soon," and hung up the phone.

She waited in the silence, willing Nomi to call her back. But the phone just sat, an infuriatingly silent brick-orange oracle, refusing to speak.

It was the first time Pauline had ever hung up on Nomi. But it felt like an ending.

6

Her first stop is five houses away. Honey's house isn't as fancy as Nomi's—no pool—but she tries in her own way, which is to say too hard. Tibetan prayer flags. Plants and Buddha statues. Macrame everywhere. Pauline is fairly sure proximity is the only real explanation for Nomi and Honey's friendship, because, really. Who could stand to be actual friends with someone who brings every conversation back to themselves and how they visited their astrologer to do past-life hypno-birth regression therapy and realized they'd been a nun in the eighth century and that their mission now was to let the kundalini power flow through their chakras, perform five thousand prostrations to the goddess Tara each week, and embody the feminine divine so as to become a bodhisattva to manifest the rainbow body for the enlightenment of all beings?

Still, she seethes with envy at how close Nomi and Honey are, at how close they've become in the past few weeks. It should have been Pauline serving strawberry margaritas today, offering them up to a confused Honey, not the other way around. It should have been Pauline watching Honey flail as the uninvited guest today, not the other way around. *She* was Nomi's best friend. Not Honey.

Pauline pulls up, a teeny bit onto the front lawn, but really, who cares, and pulls Hope out of the car with the engine still running. Hope is groggy from the heat and sleep, still, and recoils at Pauline's wetness as Pauline hoists her onto her hip.

"You're gonna see your friends!" Pauline says with fake excitement. "Isn't that fun, Hope? You'll get to play with Ben, and Lydia, and Ashley, and . . ." She can't be bothered to remember the names of Katherine's twins. But Hope is squirming in her grasp, twisting and protesting to the point where Pauline worries she might drop her as she rings the doorbell.

The au pair opens the door, the sounds of rambunctious pre-schoolers shrieking into earshot, and just stands there. Honey should be worried—the girl is stunning. Stick-straight blonde hair down to her butt, a truly impractical minidress, Nordic features. Pauline wonders how much Dan is allowed to interact with her.

"Hi, Olga, you remember me." Pauline breezes past her into the house. "Just dropping off Hope for a bit!"

"But—" the girl begins. "Miss Honey didn't say—"

"Oh, of course she did," Pauline says, smiling as she pushes sweaty strands of hair from Hope's face. "The kids are all playing here while the ladies gather at Nomi's house, yes? For the pool party?"

She keeps the smile on her face as she stands there, literally dripping, water pooling on Honey's linoleum, while Olga tries to make sense of things.

"Right. So I'll see you in a few hours!" Pauline bends down to kiss Hope on top of the head. "You have fun, now, Hope-Hope!"

"I wanna go home," Hope says, beginning to cry, but Pauline is at the door, calling over her shoulder, "Don't let her have too much juice, Olga."

Once the door is closed, Pauline can barely hear the girl's cries.

Her second stop is a bit of a drive, but she cuts down on the commute by taking the back roads, running stop signs when the coast is clear. She doesn't have time to waste. Nomi could have already called him.

She pulls into the parking lot and screeches to a stop, nowhere near an actual parking spot, and gets out. She's no longer dripping wet, but she's not exactly dry. She can see herself in the glass door, briefly, as she yanks it open: blouse clinging to her breasts, bell-bottom jeans still heavy with water, her hair plastered to her face, her eye makeup running like exaggerated tears. She doesn't care.

"Excuse me—" a man says, but she pushes past him to the elevators and punches the up button.

"You're going to need to sign in," he says.

"No thanks," she says, her voice as bright and happy as Nomi's on her answering machine. "I'm here for a meeting. They're expecting me!"

The doors open and she runs in, pushing the door close button as quickly as possible, before someone is able to stop her, or pull her out. She is in too deep, for the second time today, but she's in control. Can't they see that?

When the doors open on the fifth floor, Pauline is relieved to find there is no receptionist, no waiting area, no second set of security people to navigate. Instead, she is confronted by a maze of desks and filing cabinets, with no clear direction of where to go. She strikes out on a path that appears to take her toward the heart of things, past men on telephones surrounded by stacks of papers that ruffle in the breeze she creates as she strides through the room. She looks to see if any of the men look familiar, and they do, because they all have beards and long hair and glasses and short-sleeved shirts and ties—but none of them are Steve.

"Steve?" she says, loudly, over the din of men talking. "Excuse me, does anyone know if Steve is here?"

"Steve Carter?" says a man in the distance, standing up, and Pauline says "Yes!" and rushes over, but before she can get there, a man steps in front of her, and she almost pushes him out of the way before she realizes who it is.

"Pauline?" he says. "What on earth is going on?"

"Oh my god, Steve!"

Now that she's found him, the sheer relief of it makes way for the rest of the feelings she's been holding at bay, and she finds herself shaking, falling into his arms, holding him, leaning against his chest, his warmth and solidity contrasting with her still-wet clothes, her emotional permeability.

"What is it? Is Nomi okay? Is it Ben—? Pauline, you have to tell me, are they okay? Has there been an accident?" Steve grabs her arms and holds her away from him, shaking her. His face no longer seems understanding and kind; he seems angry with her, terrified, confused. "Did Ben fall into the pool? Is he okay?"

"What?" Pauline is exasperated, and a crowd of concerned office people has formed around them. Someone asks if they need to call 911, and someone else says that might be a good idea, just in case, even though no one knows what's happening.

"No, no," she says, shaking her head. "I mean, yes, he's fine, no one fell into the pool—I mean, *I* was in the pool, but I'm fine—and Nomi's fine too. This isn't about them, Steve! This is about *us*."

Steve gets a look on his face Pauline can't decipher, close to the kind of look he gets on bridge night when he tries to be inscrutable to Nomi and Ted, and people begin to step back and disperse as he tightens his grip on Pauline's arm and leads her back toward the elevators.

"It's fine, everyone," he says, "just a misunderstanding," but there's a murmur as they walk past people, and Pauline suddenly feels very cold, very much aware of her wet clothes, which drag with the weight of the water they still hold as she's pulled along by Steve. She feels like she's sinking more now than she did when she was in the pool.

"*What*," Steve spits through his teeth when they are as far as possible from the ears of his coworkers, "the *fuck*, Pauline?"

She's never heard him speak this way. Certainly not to her. It throws her off a bit.

"I just—"

"Keep your voice down," he shout-whispers, and she shrinks at his tone, shrugging her shoulder to get her arm out of his grip. They are standing closer than they have ever stood, outside of those lingering goodbye hugs. Closer even than the night at the carnival, when he smoothed the glitter from her face.

"You know we were going to have to have this conversation sooner or later," she says.

In some ways, they have already gone through all these stages. The shy newness and intensity of getting to know each other, the deepening crush and flirtation, the waning and doubt and pullback of plausible deniability, the reconnection. It's a dance, that's all it is.

Pauline reaches up and puts her arms around him, pulls him closer to her, and kisses him, running her hands through his hair, feeling his shoulders and arms, before Steve pushes her away. No, not pushes—*shoves*.

"Jesus Christ!" he says, wiping his mouth. Pauline is stunned to recognize a look of disgust on his face. Is that what he feels for her? Disgust? He backs away like she's some big desperate pathetic disease he doesn't want to be contaminated by. But then he notices her tears.

"Pauline," he says.

Pauline isn't fooled. His voice sounds like the kind of voice Pauline uses on Hope when she's trying to de-escalate a tantrum. When she's humoring Hope to avoid a scene.

"Pauline. I'm sorry, Pauline."

"Stop saying my name over and over," she cries. "I'm not a child."

"Of course you're not, of course not," he says. She can see him signaling someone with his eyes, but then he looks back to her and leans down so their eyes are on the same level, and his eyes are focused only on her and his voice is filled with patience.

"I think we've had a misunderstanding, you and I. That's all."

"No. No, Steve! We haven't had a misunderstanding—we've had an *understanding*. That's what I'm trying to tell you. I understand you, we understand each other. It's okay for us to acknowledge it."

"I want to be really clear with you," he says. He looks into her eyes very seriously, and she feels that surge of adrenaline, that stomach flip, so powerfully that it takes her a moment to comprehend what he's saying. "We. Do *not*. Have an understanding. I am happily married. To a woman who is your best friend, I might add."

"I'm conflicted about that, too, of course I am—"

"There is nothing to be conflicted about," he says, his voice loud enough to register with the office busybodies pretending to do work near them, so he lowers it again as he continues. "Pauline. There is nothing between us. I apologize if my friendliness toward you was misinterpreted, but I assure you. That is all it was. There is no *us*. I do not have feelings for you. I don't know what happened today to cause all this . . ." He gestures to her damp clothes, her chlorinated hair, her pool-watered makeup stuck permanently mid-streak down her face. "But I don't want any part of it."

"If there's no *us*, if you *really* have no feelings for me, then why have you and Nomi been avoiding me? She told me the two of you were going through a rough time. Why else would you be avoiding me, other than the fact that you're scared of what you feel for me, freaked out about how connected we are and the kind of life we could have together? Why else would *she* be avoiding me, other than the fact that she knows about us? That's why I look like this, that's why I'm standing here sopping wet—she planned a whole day behind my back, invited everyone else but me, and I went over there and called her on her bullshit, I crashed her pool party."

Steve closes his eyes for a moment and Pauline briefly cheers—this is it, she's broken through his resistance—but when he opens them, they're as cold as the pool water.

"Nomi has been 'avoiding' you—and we have been having a 'rough time,' as you put it—because she has been avoiding *everyone*. She had another miscarriage, Pauline. She's been a little busy dealing with that."

Pauline refuses to believe it. How? How could she not know this? How is it possible for Pauline to not be the first person Nomi told she was pregnant, let alone that she had miscarried?

"I—I didn't know she was pregnant," Pauline says. "She's my best friend. Why didn't she tell me she was pregnant?"

"That's a good question to ask yourself, isn't it?"

Behind Steve, the elevator doors open and Pauline hears walkie-talkie radio chatter before she registers that it's the police.

"What seems to be the problem?" one of them says, and Steve says, "It's fine, we're taking care of it," but the other one says, "There's been a report of trespassing," and looks Pauline up and down before asking Steve, "Is this woman harassing you? Do you need to press charges?" and Pauline starts crying and saying, "No, no, no, I'm sorry, I'm sorry, please, it's fine, I'll go, I'll just go, it's a misunderstanding, right, Steve?"

They agree not to take her in but insist on escorting her downstairs, and Pauline is humiliated to think that this will be Steve's lasting impression of her, wet and pathetic and manhandled by cops. She looks to him one last time as the elevator doors close, but he's already turned his back on her. He's walking away.

The cops aren't so bad after all. They give her a ticket for parking illegally, but they seem to take pity on her—a scorned woman, confronting her husband at work. She'd been through so much that day, finding out the truth that her husband had been cheating on her with her best friend, being pushed into the pool by that best friend after confronting her with what she knew.

"Maybe we should go back upstairs and arrest *him*," one of the cops says after she tells them her sad story, but Pauline does her best to laugh it off flirtatiously.

"Oh, no, Steve and I will work it out," she says. "We always do. As for my former best friend . . ."

"Next time, make sure she's the one standing closest to the pool. That way you can shove her in first," the other cop says.

"Oh, there won't *be* a next time," Pauline says, and they all laugh.

They wait for her to leave, and once she pulls out of the parking lot, it seems like they're following her, so Pauline drives aimlessly, turning down streets that are the opposite direction from her house, circling back, going the other way. Eventually she loses them, or they give up, and she finally allows herself to relax as she starts to drive home. Hopefully she can get out of these clothes and get dinner in the oven before Ted arrives.

But then she remembers: *Hope.*

She taps the brakes too hard, and the car slams to a sudden stop. The car behind her comes perilously close to crashing into the back of the station wagon, and Pauline raises a hand to say sorry before she turns the car around and finds her way to Honey's house. What time is it? It is only just barely starting to get dark. How long did that whole misguided ordeal take? It couldn't have been that long. Well, at least Hope is in good hands—surely the sexy au pair will have given her dinner if it comes down to it. Honey would never keep a good-looking girl like that around if she wasn't actually competent at taking care of kids.

She pulls up on Honey's lawn, right on the grass, but before she can even get out of the car, there's the whole army on the front porch: Honey, Sarah, Maria, Katherine—and Nomi, standing with her arms crossed. Pauline opens the car door and begins to stand, saying, "I'm just here to pick up Hope," but Nomi walks toward her, with an expression on her face that Pauline has only ever seen her deploy on tetchy school administrators.

"*Ted* has taken her home," she says. "You know. Ted. Your husband?"

"Well, of course—"

"*Your* husband," Nomi says. "Not Steve. Who is *my* husband. In case you need some clarification on that point."

"Nomi—"

"For the thousandth time, it's *Na*-omi," she says, practically yelling.

"Come on, Nomi—"

"Go home, Pauline. Just go. I don't have the energy for this right now."

"I'm sorry, Nomi," she says. "I'm sorry about the baby. I'm sorry about everything. I just want to be your friend again. Like it used to be."

"Hm." Nomi looks angry, but it seems to Pauline like her lip might be quivering, like she might be filled with sadness or regret, like she might forgive her.

But instead Nomi says, "I don't think so," and walks away.

When she finally gets home, it's dark, and she can see from the mess in the kitchen that Ted has made dinner and fed Hope, and she hopes that he is buried in a book somewhere unwilling to talk to her, because she doesn't think she can face him right now, she can't have this conversation. Her clothes are dry now, wrinkled in weird places because of how she sat, and her hair feels crunchy and wrong, and it's starting to sink in just what she's done, just how badly she's screwed everything up. Ted was wrong: this isn't a Carl situation. This is worse.

She hears the shower running and breathes away some of her anxiety. She can avoid him for a few minutes, shed these clothes, fix her hair and face, shed the proof of what happened, even though it sounds like Ted already knows. Steve must have called Nomi. Nomi must have told Ted. What must they all think of her?

She stuffs the clothes in the laundry basket and pulls on some old pajamas—not the good ones, not the fancy ones Ted bought for her; she doesn't deserve those. She deserves something worn-out. Old. Full of holes.

Bottles of medication roll to the front of her nightstand drawer as she pulls it open looking for a hair band. They're practically full. Another indictment. Would they even help at this point? She pushes them aside until she finds the hair band she wants and ties back her hair, stiff with chlorine.

She steals into Hope's room, avoiding the squeaky part of the floor in case she's asleep, and stands by the side of the bed. Hope is sleepy but not sleeping yet, holding her bunny close to her face, and Pauline gently touches her hair, her fingertips just barely brushing through its fineness.

"Mommy," Hope says, and Pauline says, "Shh, I'm here."

Pauline kneels down so that she's on eye level with Hope and whispers, "Did you have a good day? Did you have fun with your friends?"

Hope nods her head. Her eyes look serious. "I missed you."

"Oh, sweetie, I'm right here, you don't have to miss me."

Hope sighs and rubs the slick part of Bunny and says, "Mommy, one time you were the baby and I was the mommy, and I was a really good mommy to you."

This, of all the things that happened today, is the thing that finally breaks Pauline. She starts laughing, without meaning to or understanding why, and then her laughter turns a corner, suddenly falls in on itself and becomes an endless well of grief, and now she is crying, sobbing, and she can't stop.

"I'll be better," she says. "I'll be a better mommy to you. I'll be better, Hope. I promise."

LISE

Letter to Anna, dated 1971

1

Suddenly the blank spaces were filled for me, flooded with memory. It was all coming back to me: not just my own actions, but the actions that had spurred me to act in the first place.

After the night of that salon, he'd gotten the razors.

"I'm putting these here," he'd told me the next morning, pointing to the keyboard with one of his used razors, the edges orange, rusted. "You won't know which key hides them; I'll change them every day if I have to. There could be five, there could be ten, there could be one. There could be nothing. You don't know. But if you risk it, if you try to play—slice!—your finger is gone. There is the end of your playing. Forever."

"Isn't that what you want?" I'd asked.

"Of course not. Someday you'll play. Just not now. Not in my house."

After that, every day, while he was gone looking for work or visiting the galleries, trying to interest someone in his paintings, I lifted the lid and searched methodically, staring into the sliver of darkness between the keys, looking for the gleam.

Every time it was a risk. Every day I pulled the stool out, felt around the underside of the fabric seat until I found the unraveling seam that fell away a little where it joined the wood, and pulled the key from inside the cushion. Every day I unlocked the lid and stood there in the silence, willing the notes to sound, afraid to cross the razor-thin line he put between me and the music. He kept me in the house for weeks, isolated. My punishment for performing at the salon, for outperforming him. Every day I defied him.

One day, after locking his studio door and preparing to leave for the afternoon, he told me to be presentable later; Rafael and Samuel would be stopping by for dinner. My heart quickened. I hadn't seen anyone other than Mor since the night of the salon. I did my best to remain nonchalant. I accepted his kiss on my cheek as he said goodbye. I waited for the sounds of his footsteps to decrescendo down the stairs. And then I went, as I always did, to the piano.

I started at the lowest note, the low A, pressing down with one finger slowly, careful to keep my other fingers out of the way. Key by key I searched, until between the twenty-third and twenty-fourth key I saw it, toward the back: a metal flash against the black wood. I held down the key with my left hand and slid the razor up the side of the G-sharp with my right hand, pulling it out completely. When I held it like that, thumb and forefinger pinching a small gray rectangle, it seemed innocuous. I placed it on top of the piano and pulled out a scrap of paper from my pocket, wrote down "G#, key 24" so I would remember where to put it back later.

It took me nearly a half-hour to find the blades. I went over the keyboard twice, from bottom to top and top to bottom. There were only four blades, and I noted each one: G#, key 24; D#, key 43; B, key 63; F, key 72. Mor must have a similar scrap of paper somewhere, some crumpled thing keeping track of where he put the blades, so he could retrieve them later. I was strangely comforted by the thought of both of us writing down the names of the notes, secreting the notations in our pockets, composing in furtive antiphony. I played each of the notes one at a time, letting each sound fall away into silence before going on to the next. Was it random, the placement of the razors? Was it a message? Could he know, for instance, that today's four blades were placed next to notes that spelled the opening chord of *Tristan und Isolde*?

I smoothed my hands over the keys, the ivories pockmarked and nicked in all the familiar places. Even knowing I had searched each crevice, I was afraid to play. What if I had missed something? Eventually I decided to try an old favorite. Brahms, the Op. 118 Intermezzo, a love song, bittersweet and unrequited. When I first learned it as a girl, it seemed full of mystery, a message from some distant world. Now I understood it. Now it was merely heartbreaking.

When I was done, I was greedy for more. I wanted to feel my fingers moving, making music, I wanted to keep sculpting sound out of the twanging upright and the cramped acoustics of our apartment. I wanted to feel the power of the music coursing through me, the omniscience of deciding dynamics, voicing, timing.

I played the Schubert Impromptu I'd been hearing in my head all morning, then began a Chopin Ballade. For a moment I lost myself in the dreaminess of the slow, quiet beginning, but soon I became irritated by the unevenness of the keys, the way the instrument made it impossible for me to truly control the sound the way I intended to. I lingered for a moment on a resolved chord, voicing the melody a little more clearly before moving on to the next part.

I had studied the four Ballades with Cortot, and according to him, this one, the second Ballade, was said to tell the story of a town swept away by a devastating flood. The pastoral beginning was supposed to capture the proverbial calm before the storm. It was my favorite part; I always loved to play the lullaby-like melody of the first part as though nothing, ever, was to exist after it—then dive into the dramatic, fast-moving flood music as if to obliterate everything that came before it. This time, though, as I got to the flood, as I began to crash through the low octaves and fast-moving passages, I was startled by a flash of something, a sudden movement, and a tinny sound.

I stopped, my heart racing.

The apartment was suddenly claustrophobic with silence. I leaned over the left side of the keyboard, peering into the narrow spaces between the keys, looking for what I dared not believe might still be there. I played the first four bass notes of the flood section with my left hand, a low A octave, then an E octave, then a B octave, then a C. And there it was: a rusty blade, millimeters from my thumb.

My heart pounded in my ears. How could I have missed this?

I tried to ease the blade out with my fingernail, pressing the C key down and trying to slide the blade up the side of the B key. I couldn't quite catch it; it kept slipping back. Finally I pressed the C and B keys together with my thumb and second finger, expecting the blade between them to pop up for easier extraction—but as I played the minor-second interval, I realized that even with both keys depressed, the blade could not be seen. It was too short. The key bed was too deep. The blood pounded louder in my ears as the truth made itself fully known to me.

The blade was too short.

The key bed was too deep.

I attempted a *glissando*, dragging the side of my thumb across the keys for the length of the keyboard, from bottom to top. When I passed the deadly spot, the B and C where the blade lay, nothing happened. My thumb glided right over the keys, unimpeded, unscathed, uncut.

The blade was not tall enough to slice me.

I stopped again, and the silence was oppressive. There should have been music to accompany this discovery, thundering octaves, diminished-seventh chords; there should have been a wailing coloratura. Instead there was nothing as I realized I had spent nearly two months working to avoid something that never could have happened in the first place.

I could have left in every last blade and never been cut.

My hands rested on my thighs. My fingers on my lap interrupted the dull brown checkered pattern of my skirt, and I studied the way the pattern disappeared and reappeared between them. The silence became punctuated with noise of the traffic outside, the sounds of neighbors, who were no doubt thankful my practicing was over.

What a fool I had been. What a fool.

All that wasted time, finding the blades, extracting the blades, replacing the blades; all those papers I'd saved, the maps of key bed minefields, a tally of nothing.

I had trapped myself. I had not put the blades between the keys, but I was the one who believed in their power, who let myself be enslaved to the terror of violent possibility.

Mor could never have done this without my consent.

I tried again and this time successfully extracted the final blade from the keys, the one between the B and C, the one that had told me the truth.

"I will show you the consequences," I said aloud, standing up. I was crying, the blade, the keyboard a blur before me. "I will show you what you want to see, I will show you what happens when I defy you. This is what you have wanted all along."

The razor blade was dull. I scraped it along the length of my left arm, the pale underside with its blue veins like delicate branches beneath my skin. The blade didn't cut. I pushed harder, with the kind of slicing motion I might use to cut vegetables. Still the blade did nothing, and that made me laugh. What a fool I had been.

On the lid of the piano was the paper where I had written down that day's locations of the blades, the blades themselves a gray pile on top of that. I grabbed the handful of blades from the top of the piano and fumbled to make them all face the same way, sharp side down. Then I took a deep breath and jabbed them into the slender white space of my wrist, the place where Mor first kissed me years and years ago when I was too young to know what it meant to choose the life I lived.

Together, the blades were sharp enough to matter. I heard the Ballade in my head, sweeping me away, and the flood this time was not water but pain. My blood was a bright red upon the keys.

2

I found myself awakened by the abrupt clatter of teacup on counter, the faucet squeaking into action as it blasted water against the sink and then just as sharply was turned off, the cracking whip of the newspaper being opened, angry mutterings as Mor slammed through his breakfast routine.

"Fix yourself," he grunted from behind his paper. "You have overslept. I leave in ten minutes."

I felt lethargic, heavy with grief and medicine. Then I remembered: in talking with Samuel the day before, in reminiscing about the night of the salon, it had all returned to me. The memories of what Mor had done to me, and what I had done to myself.

Samuel had held me as my breathing became jagged with panic, as I told him about the flood of music, the flash of something sharp, the world falling away. I could see myself slashing at my own arms, could feel the feeling of being suspended in time before I fell, the sensation of the floor on my face, everything sideways, my eyes closing, the music in my head overtaking me. He had scrambled to find my medication, the kind that could calm me, and brought it to me with water, his hand trembling. After that there was only sleep, where I dreamed, blessedly, not of razors and floods, but of Samuel, my head on his chest, his arms around me. We were in the sun and almost-summer air, and I hadn't felt that feeling, that happiness, in so long I almost didn't know how to place it.

Mor slammed his paper onto the table, onto the breakfast plate, teacup clattering as it spun away from the storm.

I stood up, drawing my robe around me. "I'm sorry to have slept so late. I must have been very tired yesterday."

"Of course you were tired. You were not resting, as you should have been. Instead you were talking all day with Samuel, making yourself crazy. Making yourself sick!"

I sank back onto the bed, shrinking away from his anger.

"I'm not angry with you," he said, but his face was red with it, his eyebrows furrowed down to the point of nearly obscuring his flashing eyes, his hair seemingly vibrating with rage. "It was Samuel's idea, I know. Talking about the past. To help you recover," he said, mockingly.

I shook my head. "We were just making conversation."

"Bah!" he shouted, his hand pushing away the air around him. "Do not bother defending him, Lise, he and I have already discussed it—while you slept so soundly, exhausted by your ill-advised chat and the medicine he was forced to sedate you with after making you so agitated. Why are you still sitting there? Go! Fix yourself! Rafael will be here at any moment."

I shook my head in confusion. "Rafael—"

"I can't take you to work with me. I certainly can't leave you here by yourself. And Samuel has proved himself to be as weak in his life as he is in his art. Rafael has given me his word that he will not exhaust you, so I expect you to be rested and awake when I return. Then we will have dinner together. Later, I may need you."

"Of course," I said, my face flushing as I walked into the bathroom. I overheard Rafael's arrival just as I closed the door, the overly loud, overly friendly overtones of Rafael's greeting, the low rumble of Mor's response.

When I emerged from the bathroom, I found Rafael at the table, newspaper spread, cigarette ash tapping the sill beneath the slightly opened window.

You were only small when you met him, so you don't remember, but you've seen the pictures: in his youth, his features were similar enough to Samuel's to be uncanny, so it appeared to me as though it were Samuel's imperfect ghost sitting before me at the table.

"Ah, the lovely bird, returned to her cage," he said, smiling. "You don't mind, do you?" He raised his cigarette hand slightly. Mor would mind, of course, were he here. But Rafael's question was a formality. He barely waited for a response, his attention returning to the morning's paper as he paged through.

"Please," he said, looking up from the paper briefly, "do not feel obliged to entertain. I'm quite content."

He had an easy smile on his face, as though he truly were content to sit there, at our table, with nothing to do other than leaf through the paper and babysit me. But his irritation was clear.

I made myself a cup of tea and brought it to the bedside table. I didn't want to sit here all day with Rafael as my reluctant jailer. I was still trying to make sense of all I'd begun to remember. But neither did I truly want to think about what I could no longer avoid thinking about. I needed a distraction. I grabbed some piano scores from the bookcase and sat down on the bed.

I tried to read through the Brahms First Rhapsody, playing it in my mind, trying to slow myself down and imagine playing it in real time. Near the music box–like middle section of the First Rhapsody was a notation from my teacher. In his old-fashioned script, he had written *pedal* and then, nearby, in all capital letters, *INTENTION*.

Is intention the same as choice, I wondered. Is it possible to make a choice without intending to?

I made myself restart that section in my head, trying to think my way through it as if I could physically play it, but I continued to be distracted by the thinking beneath my thinking. I felt divided, the music on top, everything else churning underneath.

I tried to focus, talking myself through each measure, reading the fingerings and notations in the score. The first triplet, don't rush. Shape the left hand three-note phrases. Make the first opening phrase a long decrescendo, but subtle. Suggested, not literal, because the passage is marked *forte*. Just the idea of it. But clear enough so that it doesn't sound like an accident, it needs to sound like a choice.

It was unsettling to realize how many things I had chosen without being clear about my intentions. Unsettling to realize I had been choosing at all, when all this time I'd felt as though I had no choice in anything.

Build the phrase, rising left hand, falling right hand. A crescendo now, not too loud, there's still more *forte* to come. "*Forte*" doesn't mean "loud," it means "strong."

At every point along the way, I realized, I had had a choice. When I left the practice room to meet with my friends picnicking with the students from the Chaumière—that was a choice. When Mor asked me to leave school and go back with him to America, and I did—that was a choice. When Mor asked me to put my music aside to help support his work, and I did—that was a choice. When Mor forbade me to go into his studio, and I respected his wishes—that was a choice. When Mor forbade me to play the piano, and I didn't play—that was a choice. When Mor forbade me to play the piano, and I did play—that was also a choice. I had been choosing, all along, whether I realized it or not.

After the *forte*, fade away. This part should sound like a mystery. Pedal, but not too much pedal. Right hand blending into the background, left hand taking the melody. Keep it staccato, but just the merest intention of staccato, amidst the pedal, amidst the long phrases. And then the richness of the closing thought, expansive but still quiet. The first lyrical section, a new theme, a quiet, almost inverse version of the main melody. Still speaking, still shaping, even though it's *pianissimo*. A sad lullaby.

Maybe it had simply been easier to think of choices as things bestowed upon me, rather than actions I could take.

Dr. Zuker had told me, over and over, that I'd been in the hospital because I had been very sad, and that I had tried to hurt myself.

But my injury didn't happen because I was sad, or weak, or crazy.

It happened because I chose to make it happen.

I'd blamed Mor, but all of it was a choice I'd made.

It was beginning to dawn on me: I could choose something different.

"Quite a day yesterday, or so I hear," Rafael said, startling me out of my thoughts.

I attempted an approximation of his smile. There were layers to it, a kind of calculation beneath the easiness. The smile of someone used to others finding him charming. As you know, I have never been a person whom others would find charming, and the smile wilted on my face, a failed experiment.

"Samuel has been quite a welcome distraction."

"Really," he said, looking amused, holding my gaze just slightly too long. My cheeks burned. He knew.

He looked at his watch. Extinguished his cigarette on the brick windowsill. Lit another one. Folded the paper. Folded his arms as he leaned back in the chair. Crossed his leg. Jiggled his foot impatiently. Sighed.

"I apologize for all this," I said. "I'm sure you have better things to do."

"I do have work waiting for me at the studio," he admitted. "Did Mor tell you? I've been invited to show at the Whitney. It's a group show, of course, but still. It is significant. It's caused the requisite amount of tension at the Collective, of course."

No wonder Mor had been in such a dark mood. This news must be killing him. Rafael showing at the Whitney, but not him?

Rafael stood up abruptly, finally unable to contain his restlessness. "Look, my dear Lise. I believe your husband, though admirable in his concern for your safety and well-being, is, shall we say, overreacting. You seem quite capable of spending the day here by yourself, sipping tea and looking through your music or what have you, without collapsing into a nervous heap or escaping on another ill-advised excursion. What do you say we strike a deal here?"

"What do you mean?"

"I mean," he said, the charming smile working overtime, "I leave here and go work on what I need to work on for the show. And you stay here, like a good girl. And sometime before Mor is due home, I'll return, and we'll swear upon our lives to your dear husband that both of us have been here the entire day, doing nothing but sitting here and marking time. Is this acceptable to you?"

I hesitated only because I was so thrilled with the thought of reprieve, and from the relief of what he was proposing. "It is absolutely acceptable."

"Very well, then, this is our plan," he said, gathering his jacket and hat. "A good day to you, and I shall see you at . . . let's say four-thirty, just to be safe."

"Four-thirty," I repeated.

"Be good," he said as he let himself out, an eyebrow raised, his smile this time the kind of mischievous grin that I was sure he depended on seeming tempting to most women.

"I will," I said, but the door had already closed. I listened to his footsteps down the stairs, the jaunty tune he whistled fading as he descended. I waited at the window, craning to see him exit the building and head south.

Then I raced to get properly dressed, find my shoes, make up my face, and gather myself. For I, too, had a plan.

I found my good dress in the closet, hanging where I'd left it all those months ago, and I reached into its pockets to see if my memory held any truth.

There it was, in the right pocket. I fingered the thick paper, feeling the embossed print.

Madame Augustine's card.

3

This time, as I walked, I was not tired. I was not foggy, or confused, or aimless. I had a purpose. I was of a piece with all the purposeful New Yorkers walking so determinedly down the street, with all the people who knew exactly where they were going and were single-minded about getting there. I was one of them, and I felt borne along by our ferocious collective focus. In the sunlight, the noises of the city all around me, I caught a glimpse of my reflection in a shop window. A woman in motion.

It was a long walk, but I couldn't stop. Even if Mor had rounded the corner and seen me walking, I wouldn't have stopped. The thought of him sobered me for a moment, but not enough to slow my pace. I consulted the address on the card. *Madame Helaine Augustine. Chair, Piano Department, The Institute of Musical Arts at The Juilliard School, 120 Claremont Avenue, New York, N.Y. Monument 2-9336.*

When I arrived at the school, I paused to catch my breath, taking in the arched windows along the ground floor of the building, the grand entrance marked by cement filigree at the apex of its archway, the set of steep stairs guarded by wrought-iron railings.

Everyone there seemed young, so much younger than I was, their clothes brighter and more modern, their ease in the place palpable. Once inside, I saw the marble foyer, floors as polished as mirrors, and an impossibly wide staircase leading to a landing dominated by a stained-glass window of Orpheus playing a lyre. From there the stairs split into two, one left, one right, gliding upward into what I could only imagine might be ever more elaborate chambers. Even the ceilings were intimidating—intricate geometrical moldings, a massive chandelier.

A group of students clustered before me, moving slowly with their instruments and music bags as they headed toward the grand staircase. I could hear them talking about a concerto someone was working on, a chamber music recital another had next week. How I'd missed the details of this world, being steeped in it. I moved closer and followed them as they ascended the stairs.

"Excuse me," I said to the one I thought might be a pianist, due to her carefully kept fingernails. "Can you tell me where I might find Madame Augustine's studio?"

"Third floor," she said. "All the way in the back."

I thanked her and continued up the stairs until I'd reached the third-floor landing. My heart raced, my breath shallow from the stairs. I was giddy with the rush of trespassing, the thrill of breaking out of the apartment again, of infiltrating this place at once so familiar and so foreign. I stopped at the landing and closed my eyes, forcing myself to breathe, to be calm. I walked down the hallway, a series of practice rooms on either side emitting muffled sounds of Mozart, Beethoven, Poulenc, Chopin, Brahms, Debussy. These small chambers, each with a single small thick-paned window near the top of the door, each with a single person inside, lost in their own world, reminded me of the rooms at the hospital.

At the end of the hallway was a set of wooden doors, one of which appeared to be slightly open, and I walked toward them, the muted cacophony of students in practice rooms fading as I moved farther away. There didn't appear to be any sound coming from behind the doors, but I hesitated anyway, listening at the crack, waiting to hear the rustle of pages turning, conversation, scales, arpeggios, anything.

I knocked. After a few moments with no response, I cautiously placed my hand on the oversized brass doorknob and pulled.

The room smelled musty, the smell of old rugs and wooden walls and rarely opened books in rarely dusted bookshelves. It was lit by dim wall sconces, its series of windows flanked by heavy curtains, parted just enough to allow slashes of sunlight here and there, dust particles floating in the brightness. I could barely make out a desk in one corner, with music piled on it; a portrait on the wall of a younger-looking Madame Augustine; some chairs stacked on the other side of the room. And there, in the middle of the room, two Steinway grand pianos, side by side.

The last time I was in a studio as grand as this, it was to tell Monsieur Cortot that I was leaving to follow Mor to America. I remembered his look of disappointment, how quickly it had turned to impassivity and resignation, the cultivated face of a teacher used to the squandering of potential.

I walked toward the piano and breathed in that idiosyncratic grand piano smell, wood and felt and metal and ivory and the scent of high-carbon steel strings stretched taut along the length of the instrument. My upright piano had smelled only like the polish I used to shine the outside of it, and its metal frame and strings had been shut up inside its case, the soundboard, hammers, and all the other inner workings tucked away, invisible.

I sat down on the concert bench, adjusting its height by turning the knobs on either side. This was a force of habit. If the bench was too low, my elbows would sink below the key bed, my wrists forced to bend unnaturally; too high, it would feel as though I were tumbling down the stairs or falling from a precipitous height just attempting to play a note, my forearms angled almost straight down, no bend or dip in the wrist at all. When the bench was just right, I would have the advantage of gravity that height gives, the ease of fingers falling toward the keys, but also the comfort of leveling with the keyboard, approaching only just slightly from above, with no strain whatsoever on the wrists, if I were to play.

My wrists—I ran my fingers lightly over the scars, then clenched my hands into loose fists, rotating them in small circles, first this way, then that, to loosen the joints and muscles. I squeezed my forearms, massaging them.

But no, I couldn't play—not while I was waiting for her. I allowed my fingers to just barely, silently brush the keys, feeling their smoothness.

And then, from behind me, a sound. I drew my hands back from the keys and stood up quickly.

"Please, don't let me stop you."

Madame Augustine arose from the desk in the dim light of the corner of the room.

"I beg your pardon, I'm so sorry," I began. "I didn't realize you were here."

"Not at all," she said, walking toward me. She leaned on her cane, her fingers gnarled and arthritic, and gestured at the piano, a bemused smile on her face. "You were about to play?"

For a moment I was tempted to run from the room and back down the staircase, past the stained-glass window with its graceful Orpheus strumming his lyre, past the crystal chandeliers and the shining marble floors and back out into the grimy streets, back to the apartment.

"Actually, I'm here to see you." I fumbled in my skirt for the business card and held it out to her. "Do you remember, from Mrs. Whiting's salon?"

The old woman regarded me. "I do remember. Your playing. And your untimely exit."

"Yes," I said. I couldn't meet her gaze, ashamed by the memory, ashamed by the understanding we shared about it. When I finally looked up, I saw her flick a hand toward the piano as she took a seat on the other piano bench.

"Sit," she said.

I settled back down on the bench, facing her instead of the keys.

"I have been having difficulties," I said, rubbing my wrists. She sat, still as the portrait of herself on the wall, waiting.

Finally, I said, "I have been thinking about intention."

At this, she stirred.

I didn't know how to explain, not the scene Mor had caused at the salon, not the scars on my wrist, not the memory I had finally regained, not the razors, not my actions. I paused, tears threatening to collect in my eyes.

"Intention," she prompted, waiting for me to go on. We sat in silence, my body tense with words and music I couldn't allow myself to express.

"It's hard for me to talk about," I managed.

"So don't tell me. Show me," she said. She gestured to the piano. "Play."

I shook my head. "Oh, I couldn't—I have been injured, I . . ."

She reached across and put her hand on my hand. Her knuckles were ridged like mountains, and blue veins snaked across the back of her hand. I could feel her muscularity, her power. My hand looked like a baby's hand next to hers, formless and undefined.

"Show me," she said.

It was tempting to think about playing such a beautiful instrument. Maybe I could try something quiet, something languid, something easy, for the most part; something short, something I'd played for forever.

Beethoven. The *Pathétique,* second movement. *Adagio cantabile.*

I looked at the keys, placed my hands on them, took a deep breath. I readied my third finger, left hand, preparing the A-flat just over an octave below middle C; fifth and third fingers, right hand, preparing middle C and A-flat, respectively; right foot preparing the sustain pedal; my mind preparing a balance between left and right hands, between melody and inner voices, between *piano* and *mezzo piano.*

I played the first chord and faltered; it was too loud, and yet, at the same time, the melody note was not loud enough. I stopped and tried again.

"Center yourself," Madame Augustine said. "Take your time. Make sure you are ready."

I tried to prepare. Closed my eyes, breathed in through my nose. Imagined the first notes, the tone, the weight of the melody.

My opening bar was timid. It took me a full measure at least to feel the depth of the keys, to adjust to the instrument's idiosyncratic range and know how hard to press before what should be *piano* became an inadvertent *mezzo forte*. I tried my best to respond quickly, to voice the melody, inner voices, and bass line so that they were all in perspective, each layer where it should be. Backing off the pedal. Trying to articulate the phrasing. Attempting to make the piano sound like a string quartet, then a chamber orchestra.

It was difficult. My muscles did not respond the way they should. Even extending my fingers, stretching my hands to their full range, felt like trying to unclench something frozen. I heard only too well the difference between how my playing should sound—easy, expansive, full—and how it actually sounded—plodding, obvious, unbalanced.

And yet—I was playing.

I was playing.

My wrists strained and my forearms ached and my fingers felt stiff, like cement fingers, and my ears were even out of the practice of listening, but I was playing.

Making music. Making choices. Remaking myself as I went along.

The realization of it caught me, caught my breath, and I tried to absorb the shock of it, the joy of it, the relief of it, as I continued.

Crescendo building, I lifted the pedal to clear the sound and just as quickly depressed it again to open the strings, creating a fuller sound, an orchestra of vibrations, as I approached a series of *sforzando* octaves. Just as I brought my right hand off the keys, taking a moment's hesitation before attacking the *sforzando* E-natural octave, the apex of this rising, insistent right-hand melody, I was stopped. Madame Augustine stood behind me, her hand weighting my shoulder, defusing its tension.

"When you say you are thinking about intention," she said, "I think what you mean is that you're asking yourself big questions. But let's ask the small questions first. What about this *sforzando*, this octave right here? How does it follow from what came before?"

I started to try to answer her, but she shook her head. "This isn't an answer I need you to give me in words. It must be a decision you make—internally, silently—and express through your playing."

She gestured for me to play.

"Just the *sforzando*?" I asked.

"Just the *sforzando*."

Out of context it was difficult to muster the momentum that would normally come naturally amidst a growing wave of sound as the crescendo built within the phrase. I tried to imagine it in my mind, imagine that I was playing everything that came before the chord she wanted me to play, and I hovered my hands above the keys until it was time. And then the chord—abrupt, stark in the small room.

"Crass," she said. "You must have both intention *and* technique. Technique without intention is boring; intention without technique is unclear and uncommunicative. It breeds misunderstanding. It's not enough to just drop your hand on the keys and bang a chord. Feel it from your diaphragm, feel it in your shoulders, feel it in your back, feel it in your body. Let it come from a place of grounding, not pouncing from above."

I tried again, tried to summon a sense of groundedness, of music emerging through me, not dropping from me like water flung from hands that are being shaken dry. My wrists ached. I played the chord again. It sounded timid.

"Again," she commanded.

I tried again, tried to imagine the sound of the chord originating from my foot on the pedal, all the way up through my body, the span of my back, the tendons of my outstretched arms as I embraced the keyboard, high chord in the right hand, booming octaves in the left.

"Come on. Don't do it because I tell you to—do it because *Beethoven* tells you to! Again," she commanded.

And this time I felt it, felt the expansiveness, the connection between my intention and my execution, felt the chord resonating in my body, the sound enveloping me warmly, strongly, not harsh or cutting in the least.

"Do you see?" she asked, sitting back on the other piano bench. "Now your intention is clear to me. Perhaps now it is clear to you."

How wonderful it was to be able to think about music this way again. Even with my damaged hands, my out-of-shape technique, it was thrilling to hear these differences, to feel these differences, to manifest it in my playing. How I had craved this. Not just access, but guidance.

"What do I do next?" I asked.

"Next? You ask yourself these small questions for every note in the piece. Every measure, every section. What choice am I making? How does this relate to what came before it, and how does it set up what comes after?" She chuckled. "Easy enough."

But I found myself crumbling, the joy I'd felt a moment ago eroding. I could ask myself these questions all day, every day, and it would matter not at all without a way to put them into practice. And more than that, the full weight of what I had done to myself, how I had turned Mor's cruelty even more pointedly against myself, the choice I had made, settled on me as my wrists throbbed. I held my hands up to her, exposing my wrists, my scars angry, pink, puckered lines.

"I have been complicit," I whispered.

She took my wrists in her hands, inspecting, her wrinkled fingers tracing the artless, jagged ridges.

She dropped my hands and returned to sit at the other piano, collecting her thoughts for a moment before she spoke.

"I will tell you what I tell all my students: that the best performance—the best art—is, at its heart, a lie. What we do, when we play, is an illusion. We are illusionists. The sound decays as soon as the hammer hits the string, and yet we must make it continue, imagine that it flows continuously, no decay, from one note to the next. It is a lie. It is also a lie that when we perform it is the first time we have ever played the piece, and yet to the audience it must seem fresh and revelatory, a discovery we all make together.

"To tell a lie and be believed, one must herself believe the lie so fiercely as to defend to the death its truth. One must make the lie become its own truth. Its own world. The performer and the audience both must enter it. A folie à deux, each reinforcing the other, until the world of the lie is the world of the truth and we all can relax in its beauty.

"But that is the truth of it: that it takes both the performer *and* the audience. A lie doesn't work if the person being lied to doesn't believe it. In that sense, we are all complicit."

She stood up, using her cane to walk slowly to the door of the studio. "Whatever the circumstances of your injury—and it is not for me to know the details—your playing still has a certain sensibility. I encourage you to focus on that."

I stood up from the bench and followed her.

"Thank you for your time today," I said.

She nodded and opened the door for me, and before she closed it, she gave my hand a squeeze and said, her voice thick, "Do not blame yourself."

The door closed behind her as she retreated to the studio, and it was as if a spell had been broken. Suddenly I was aware of the sounds of practice rooms down the hallway, the chaotic mesh of genre and instruments mixed with the sounds of students heading to class. For a moment I was tempted to open the door again, to see if Madame Augustine really existed and was still there, sitting behind the desk, waiting for her next student.

But for that moment, my intention was to return home. Before Rafael arrived, so we could sit, awaiting Mor's arrival, each with our own secrets, pretending that we had been sitting there all along.

4

It was just slightly past four-thirty when I arrived at the apartment, and as I turned the key in the lock I heard the sounds of someone walking toward the door. Anxiety coursed through me like a sound wave traveling the length of my body, vibrating in the pit of my stomach, and I briefly considered turning back. I couldn't face another confrontation with Mor, couldn't face another encounter with his anger and disappointment.

But it was Rafael who greeted me, my key stuck in the lock as the door pulled away from me.

"Well," he said, stepping aside and gesturing with an exaggerated flourish. "By all means, do come in."

He was irritated, I could tell. I walked past him quickly, and when I turned around he was standing, arms crossed, an eyebrow raised. I willed myself to hold his gaze, and finally he shook his head and smiled a tight version of his charming smile.

"I have to hand it to you," he said. "You are determined."

"You say that as though it is not a compliment."

At this he laughed and returned to the cigarette he had left on the table. He sat down heavily. "I just hadn't expected you to go anywhere or do anything. Oh, come now, you know what I mean. In your state."

I continued to stand, continued to force myself to maintain eye contact. "My state?"

He exhaled, smoke encircling him, and waved the cigarette at the windowsill, ash falling, a tiny heap.

"What was it like in there?" he asked, his eyes narrowing as he considered me. "In the hospital. The freedom to be mad! I daresay I envy you. The drama, the darkness—the solitude, I imagine. Now that's an experience an artist can use."

I wanted to correct him, to disabuse him of this notion that my time in the hospital was an amusing diversion, mere material to be used later for some more exalted, artistic purpose, but I sensed that he was goading me, that that was exactly what he hoped my response would be.

"Perhaps one day you will be lucky enough to experience it for yourself."

He laughed again, this time a genuine, full laugh, and crushed his cigarette before tossing the stub out the window. We appeared to have arrived at a truce.

"Perhaps. Perhaps, indeed. In the meantime, let's get our stories straight before Mor arrives. Rather than working in the studio, refining my pieces for the show and hearing some, shall we say, interesting news about its most recently invited participants, I, of course, sat here all day, reading and watching over you. And you . . . ?"

"I slept and looked over my music," I said. It wasn't entirely a lie. It seemed entirely plausible that the entire afternoon had occurred in a dream—leaving the house, going to the school, no longer feeling lost, being found. *You have a certain sensibility. Intention. Complicity.*

Rafael was speaking, I realized. "I assume the real story is that you went, yet again, to find a place to practice."

"I went to Juilliard. To meet with Madame Augustine," I said, thinking about how it was to narrow down my intention to one note at a time, to focus on each thing as it arrived, not anticipating, not remembering, all while still preparing and reminding.

"This is a secret we shall keep," he said, waving a hand to indicate this new depth of generosity. "But I must advise you against too many more secrets. Secrets rarely stay secret for long. And, that aside, they can be quite difficult to keep track of when one has so many."

"You speak from experience then," I said. I felt my cheeks burning as I struggled to maintain an impassive expression, and I hoped he would be surprised enough by my response to drop this line of conversation altogether. I did not want to speak with him any further of secrets. You might be surprised to know that, back then, I had no mastery over secrets, deception, duplicity. That it took a kind of bravery for me to speak this way.

But he smiled as though he had hardly noticed our exchange. "My dear Lise, you have no idea."

When Mor arrived, I was sure he must be able to sense my nervousness, but he accepted my innocent accounting of the day absentmindedly and without interrogation. Rafael attempted to engage him, too, in a way that seemed to me to be a bit frantic, but again Mor didn't seem suspicious in the least. In fact, he seemed barely present, his mind preoccupied as we talked to him too quickly, tried too hard to seem casual about the way we had spent our time while he was gone. I watched him closely, but all I saw was the look he got when what was going on in his head was far more interesting to him than what was happening before his eyes.

It was only when he inquired about dinner that he became a full participant in reality, because I had not prepared anything. Caught short, I fumbled for an explanation, and finally I saw his eyes flare with attention, his brow furrowing.

"I forgot," I said. "I apologize."

"Ah, can you believe it?" Rafael said, slapping him on the back far too jovially for his liking. "It's my fault, Mor. I was such a strict jailer—I forbade your poor wife to do anything more than rest and look at musical scores all day."

I was grateful for this lie, for our commitment to complicity, but I could see Mor was skeptical.

"So you have nothing for me?" he asked. "Nothing prepared?"

I hid in the kitchen, rummaging through the icebox, the cabinets.

"I have soup I can warm up," I said. "Eggs. Bread?"

Suddenly he was awake, no longer sleepwalking through the conversation. He slammed a hand on the table, the repercussions of which I could feel all the way in the kitchen. "This is unacceptable. You are doing nothing here, there is nothing to distract you—you have nothing but time! How is it that you could 'forget'? And what am I supposed to do now?"

Rafael stood, a hand on Mor's shoulder. "Now, now. All is not lost. I'm due to meet Samuel down at the Brevoort for a quick bite. Why don't you join us?"

Mor shook off Rafael's hand, shook his head. "I am not as profligate as you. I can make do with whatever it is we have here."

"Mor . . ." Rafael rolled his eyes. "You are perhaps the only person I know who can turn the prospect of an enjoyable evening into a moral indictment. This is my treat—no, I insist—and I have already decided that it is happening. So put your coat back on and let's go."

I could see Mor deciding, could see how tempted he was to drop his outrage. How exhausting it must have been for him to be so outraged all the time.

"Ach," he said, shrugging into his coat. "Fine, fine. You are a terrible influence, my friend."

"Nonsense. You're hungry, I have dinner reservations, it just makes sense. Besides, this will be fun. When was the last time you and Lise had a night on the town?"

"Lise?" Mor repeated, his brow darkening, ready to take up outrage again.

"Of course," Rafael said. "We can't leave her here all by herself. And I'm sure she's just as starving as you are."

Mor looked at me, considering.

"I couldn't possibly," I said.

"So it's decided," Rafael announced, shrouding my coat around my shoulders like a cape and guiding me toward the door. Mor stood behind us, disgruntled again, and I couldn't tell whether it was his usual irritation, anger at me, or frustration at being outmaneuvered by Rafael. Finally he shrugged and put on his hat and headed to the door.

"Thank you," I said as I wrestled with my coat sleeves, hoping my voice would be too muffled for Mor to hear.

"Not at all," said Rafael, close to my ear.

And then he was loud, grinning at Mor as he said, "It'll be good for Lise to get some air, after being cooped up inside all day."

5

I hung back, walking behind Mor on the way to the subway line as he talked with Rafael, a mixture of gossip and politics. "Don't be ridiculous," he'd said when I'd hesitated at the door, wondering aloud if I should change my clothes, at least make up my face. "We are eating dinner, not performing a play." But I knew the kind of people who would be there: artists, writers, musicians, thinkers. The kind of people he and I were once, together, in Paris, young and vibrant with creativity and forever in the midst of practice and innovation and discovery. "Just be quiet," he'd snapped. "Or I might change my mind about allowing you to come."

Though it was barely six o'clock, the lobby of the Hotel Brevoort was packed. Men huddled in groups, smoke rising from cigarettes forgotten in the rush of conversation. Women's laughter blended with the clashing of ice in innumerable cocktail glasses. There was something familiar about the excitement there, the bubbling tremolo of connections being made, collaborations being born. It reminded me of the way I felt in music school, eager for the work of creativity, eager for the rest of my life to begin. But now it felt subversive, as though I were intruding on a once familiar world. Trespassing into a home where I'd once lived.

I followed Mor and Rafael to the basement, where the hotel transformed itself into a Parisian café. The room was smoky but brilliant, mirrors flanking the walls. A jazz combo played: saxophone and upright bass, accompanied by a slightly out of tune piano. A tuxedoed old man took our coats and bade us entry with a low bow. Mor took my arm forcefully and tried to catch up to Rafael as he snaked his way through the marble-topped tables. Then we were there, at the large booth I was made to understand was Mor's "regular" table, although I hadn't realized he was a regular anywhere, or at anything. Peter and Alfred stood to greet us. And Samuel.

"You can blame your brother for our presence," Mor said to him, after shaking hands with Peter and Alfred.

"If by 'blame' you mean 'commend,' then yes," said Rafael.

"Well then, I commend you, my brother," said Samuel.

"Although, if I'd known it was going to be a dinner party, I wouldn't have been as easily convinced to intrude," Mor said, looking pointedly at Peter and Alfred before he turned back to Samuel.

"Nonsense. You are always welcome. Of course." Samuel hesitated. "Both of you."

Mor elbowed his way in next to Rafael, who had already slid next to Peter and Alfred. I sat next to Mor in the only spot left, on the outside edge of the semi-circular booth, across from Samuel.

"You're looking well, Lise," Peter said.

I didn't know how much Peter and Alfred knew about my time away. But even a small-talk-making remark like that seemed to hint at the uncomfortable, unspoken fact of my absence, at the fact that I had not been well, or looking well, before.

This is just conversation, this is a give-and-take, this is not something that requires a real answer, I reminded myself. *This is a politeness.* In fact I did not truly look well. I saw myself reflected in the speckled mirror surrounding the booth. I saw how the golden flecks and veins couldn't hide my splotchy cheeks, still red from the walk over, my out-of-fashion hairstyle.

Alfred raised a glass in my direction and nodded hello. I watched as the men caught up with each other, curly-haired Alfred laughing as he raised a finger to make a point; Peter smiling, his baby face making him seem even younger than he was; Rafael leaning in with a droll expression; Mor a forcefield of nervous energy beside me, asserting himself in the conversation with what could sound like conviviality but I could tell was anxious vigilance. And Samuel. I smiled as I realized he was watching me watch everyone else, and I dropped my eyes for a moment, not wanting to draw Mor's attention to our silent communication.

"Here," Samuel said, reaching across the table toward us. "Let's get you some champagne."

"Champagne!" Mor sat up straight in disapproval. "You know we don't—"

"One sip isn't going to kill either of you," Rafael said, rolling his eyes.

Rafael took the bottle from Samuel and made an exaggerated show of pouring the smallest amounts possible of champagne into the glasses in front of us. "There! I am positive you can survive that much celebration."

I looked to Mor, who seemed torn between indignation and acquiescence. He sighed and flicked his eyebrows toward me, and I could tell that meant yes, that I had his permission to participate. I felt myself smiling again, on the verge of laughing again, as they all watched me take a sip. The bubbles bounced on my tongue, bitter and glittery, and I felt a warmth expand inside me as I swallowed.

A waiter manifested beside the table, reciting a list of dinner possibilities that seemed like musical instructions. Persian melon, clams a l'Ancienne, snails a la Parisienne, Royal Squab en cocotte Bonne Femme, Halibut Hoteliere, Pommes de Terre Soufflees. Rafael took the liberty of ordering for the table, and the waiter bowed and whisked himself away.

"Is dinner here always this fancy?" I asked, emboldened by a second sip. Mor's glass remained untouched.

"Only on special occasions," said Alfred.

"And this is quite a special occasion." Peter raised his glass.

"Peter," Samuel said, like a warning.

"Is it?" Mor asked.

"You haven't told him?" Alfred turned to Rafael. Rafael took a long drink. I could feel Mor growing tense beside me. I looked to Samuel, but his expression was pained and apologetic.

Rafael drained his champagne and set the glass down. "Well, you see. It happens that I am not the only distinguished artist to be included in the upcoming show at the Whitney. Samuel, Peter, and Alfred have also been invited to show some work—what is it, two watercolors and a gouache? Three watercolors? In any case. I put in a good word for all of us, I swear it. Mor—perhaps it's not too late, perhaps you will be invited as well. At some point."

There was a moment of silence before Mor erupted.

"So, all of you have been invited. The entire Collective, save me. You couldn't have told me this *before* asking me here? Or did you invite me here precisely to humiliate me? Was that the point of your so-called generosity tonight? To savor my failure, in public?" Mor's voice carried over the clink of silverware, the muffled laughter of other patrons' conversations.

"I only just found out myself," Rafael said, hands up in a show of innocence. "Truly, up until this afternoon, I thought it was going to be only me representing the Collective at this show. But evidently there's always room for more." He paused to look at the rest of the table, raising his eyebrows. "Well, at least three more."

"How *dare* you," Mor said, standing up as best he could within the confines of his seat in the booth.

I stood too, to mollify him, and I moved out of the way so he could move out of the booth and stand properly. How this must have hurt him. Rafael must have known this, yet he sat there, lighting a cigarette, unperturbed.

"Mor," I said quietly, moving to place a hand on his arm.

"Do not placate me," he shouted, turning to me and waving my hand off his arm so abruptly, so forcefully, that his hand connected with the side of my face.

I recoiled, but not quickly enough, and for a moment it seemed all I could hear was my own heartbeat pulsing in my stinging ear. Time hung as I felt myself breathe, blinked my eyes slowly, put a hand to my cheek, saw Mor's face, a mix of astonishment, anger, guilt, satisfaction.

Then time sped up again. The sounds of the restaurant came back to me, the jazz combo in the background, the conversation, the clash of plates and silverware as busy waiters delivered food and cleared away remains. Everyone at the table was standing now. Samuel's hands were on my shoulders as he sat me down gently in the booth. Someone offered me ice, from the champagne bucket, wrapped in a cloth napkin.

"Lise," Mor began.

"No," I heard Samuel say. Everything seemed so far away.

"I only meant to help," I said.

"Help?" Mor's voice was choked, constricted, as though it might be gripped with tears, but his words were more angry than sad. "How are you helping me? How are you ever helping me? How can I work like this? If I hadn't had to drop everything while you were sick, if I hadn't had to take on yet another job to afford your stay in the mental hospital, I could have produced more, I could have had the time to create work for this show, I could have created my own show! And you," he turned to Rafael. "Has there ever been an opportunity you haven't slept your way into? Stand there and preen all you want, pretend your talent alone is what accounts for your success, pretend you weren't planning on my humiliation, relishing my humiliation—I know the truth! Come, Lise. We're going."

I sat, the napkin of ice numbing my cheek, a numbness that seemed to spread throughout my body. Mor's voice had stilled the activity around us, and I felt the eyes of everyone in the restaurant watching me, felt the tension of a collectively held breath as everyone waited. The weight of everything hung on me, making me too sluggish to move.

"No," Samuel said. "You're going. Lise is staying here, with us."

"She will do no such thing," Mor said, his voice filling the room. He lunged for my hand, to yank me out of my stasis and pull me away from the scene. But Samuel stood before me, blocking his way.

"Just until you've had a chance to calm down," Samuel said.

"Calm down!" Mor was becoming more belligerent by the second.

"Sir," a waiter said in a low voice, "I'm afraid we'll need to ask you to leave the premises if you can't quietly resolve this situation to your satisfaction."

"You cannot silence me," Mor shouted. "And this will never be resolved to my satisfaction!"

"Very well then," the waiter said, and men in suits seemed to materialize around him, ready to provide escort. For a moment everyone was still, a tableau reflected in the mirrors on the walls surrounding us, refracted into reflections of reflections of all of them standing, waiting, paused mid-scene.

"That will not be necessary," Mor said, grabbing his hat from the stand next to the table. He didn't even look back at me as he stalked away, his reflections walking with him.

Gradually the restaurant resumed itself. The combo picked up again and the murmurs of diners regenerated into normal sounds of dinner conversation. Waiters returned to their routes, gliding past bearing coffees, silver platters, trays of desserts. Rafael and Peter and Alfred sat uncomfortably across from me while Samuel stood by my side, a hand on my shoulder, watchful of the doorway in case of Mor's return.

I was grateful for the napkin, wet with melted ice now, to hide my face. I didn't want to cry in front of everyone. I didn't want the other patrons to see me so uncomposed. I wished I could make it so they weren't able to see me at all, so they were able to unsee everything that had just happened.

Samuel gently moved me over so that he could sit beside me.

"Shall I get you more ice?" he asked.

I shook my head. Laughter erupted from a table across the room. The combo finished their piece to a smattering of applause.

"I apologize," I said into the napkin, unable to look at the men across from me. "He's under a lot of stress right now. This isn't like him."

Rafael almost laughed. "Sadly, it is. It is exactly like him."

"I know he values your friendship, Rafael, I know when he's calmed down he'll regret his words." My voice was shaky, as though even it doubted the truth of what I was saying.

"Madame, Messieurs." Beside the table, someone cleared his throat, and I was shocked to see a trio of waiters bearing plates of food, placing colorful, steaming dishes before us, proffering steak knives and soup spoons. That's right, I reminded myself: this was supposed to be a dinner.

"Ah, *merci*!" said Rafael to the departing waiters, and he smiled at the rest of us apologetically before starting on his soup. "No reason to let a good meal go to waste. This *is* a celebration, after all."

Peter and Alfred looked to me and Samuel hesitantly. The food did smell delicious. And I was surprised to find myself quite hungry. Rafael was already helping himself to some of the pommes de terres from Mor's plate. Or the plate that would have been Mor's were he still there.

"Of course," I said.

6

I was surprised to find that I had an appetite, that I was able to eat at all. And yet I did. The food was excellent, and I savored the richness, the textures and flavors, the satisfaction of one single, perfect bite, and then another, and then another after that. After a time, the company was excellent too. Somewhere into the second course, we all somehow agreed to forget about the tumultuous pre-dinner drama, and all of us, myself included, genuinely laughed over Rafael's stories of Mrs. Whiting's more notorious salon events, Peter's spot-on imitation of Rafael, Alfred's recounting of a blistering review in the *World-Telegram* referring to a rival's attempt at modernism as "the death of art," and other art-world gossip about people I didn't know but felt as though I could. I had more champagne—an entire glass of champagne, two glasses of champagne—and by dessert I felt so comfortable, so relaxed, I was almost able to bear the guilt I felt for being there, enjoying it so much, in Mor's absence. If he hadn't thought me a traitor before, he certainly would now, sitting alongside his enemies, sharing food with them, allowing myself to relax in their presence. Occasionally I caught a glimpse of myself in the gold-flecked mirror, the redness on one side of my face proof of what he was capable of.

After the dessert—an assortment of small cakes, rich with candied fruit—and coffee, bittersweet warmth—Peter and Alfred excused themselves, citing the lateness of the hour and the earliness of their work the next morning, and just like that, the night was over. Everything transformed. The room around me seemed not joyous but claustrophobic, all those mirrors reflecting in on me, and now it seemed all the people were ominously clustered at tables and in booths, frantic with laughter. Our table was no longer festive, no longer a feast, but instead crowded with stained napkins, crumbed forks, plates skidmarked with chocolate, cups puddled with coffee dregs. The messy aftermath of celebration.

I moved out of the booth, watching the men shake hands with each other, as the reality of the evening intruded. What was I doing here, eleven o'clock at night, alone, without Mor? How would I get home? Should I go home? If I did, once I got there, what would he say to me? What would he do to me? The anxiety I'd kept at bay during dinner returned with a queasy shock, and I was only dimly aware of saying goodbye to Peter and Alfred, of nodding in agreement to Rafael's question of whether he should get my coat.

"I'll go with you," Samuel said, but neither of us moved to leave. "If you're sure you want to go home."

I shook my head. Where would I go, if not home? "I'm sure he's calmed down by now."

But his hand was on my arm, tethering me. "And if he hasn't?"

I didn't have an answer.

Samuel guided me through the maze of tables, toward the door leading back to the hotel, and soon we were on the stairs, the world of the restaurant fading behind us. We found Rafael in the lobby, already cozied between two women, laughing with a crowd of people for whom it seemed the night was only beginning. Samuel retrieved our coats from Rafael, who raised a glass of whiskey in goodbye, and then we were outside, watching a silent movie of the activity in the hotel lobby through the plate-glass windows.

"Shall we find a taxi, or would you rather the subway?" Samuel asked.

"Actually, I wouldn't mind a walk," I said.

I was tired, and the walk to the apartment would be long. But walking would take longer than a subway or taxi ride. It would forestall the inevitable. It would help calm the tangle in the pit of my stomach so that I could be ready, when I arrived home, for whatever awaited me.

We walked in silence, the sounds of the evening falling around us. The city at night was only slightly quieter than it was during the day, nearly as busy with people, traffic, activity. I still felt a little of the buoyancy of the champagne in the way my legs seemed as though they were not quite connected to my body, the way things had metabolized from ease and laughter into a kind of fuzzy anxiety. I tried to focus on my breathing as we walked, to bring myself to a calm place.

Finally, I spoke. "In the midst of everything, I forgot to congratulate you about being invited to show. That's wonderful."

"Oh, it's nothing," he said. "Just a few watercolors."

What Mor would give to be chosen for a show like that. Although, truly, would that even be enough? Would he even be satisfied? Or only upset that he wasn't asked for more, that it wasn't a solo show? What would he be happy with at this point?

"Of course, I'm grateful to be included in the exhibition at all. Perhaps there's still a chance Mor will be invited as well."

"Perhaps," I said. And we lapsed into silence again.

The closer we got to our building, the more anxious I became, despite my calm pacing, my deep breathing. Mor had never hit me before. And although I knew it was accidental, that it happened in the midst of his rage at Rafael and his disappointment about the news of the show, I also knew that he had not apologized. He didn't rush to my side to make sure I was okay. He didn't acknowledge the gravity of what he had done; in fact, if I remembered correctly, he blamed me for his having done it. I felt a sickening certainty that he and I had crossed into territory from which we could never return.

Then we found ourselves at the front door of our building, and Samuel said, "I'll walk you upstairs."

"Can you?" I asked, my voice shaky.

"Of course," he said. "But, Lise. If he's still as angry as he was before, you don't have to stay."

"I have nowhere else to go."

"Yes, you do. You can stay with me." His face was serious and shadowed in the streetlight. "For as long as it's necessary. For as long as you want."

He took my hand. I understood the gravity of his suggestion—it was a bold offer, and not without implications for him, inviting a married woman to his home without a chaperone—and I appreciated his concern, but I couldn't stop myself from trying to rationalize what had happened. This was just a spat, I wanted to say, stop taking it so seriously, it was just an argument like any other argument we've had in front of you. But I couldn't stop thinking: *Except it happened in public. Except he struck me. Except he didn't apologize.*

"I'm sure it's not necessary," I said, freeing my hand, turning, taking in a deep breath before opening the door, beginning the climb up the stairs. *He just needs some time to calm down. He'll be contrite. He'll say he's sorry. It will be okay, eventually, like always.*

When we reached our floor, I felt Samuel's arm suddenly bracing me, forcing me to stop. I was puzzled to find the door to our apartment wide open, the lights on, framing a scene of disarray. I couldn't make sense of it, and a panicky nausea overtook me as I tried to understand the facts of what I saw before me: the door hinging open, the chair tipped over, a blanket on the floor, books, a cup, a saucer.

"Let me go in first," Samuel said, and I watched him enter cautiously. My thoughts raced, my heart raced, as I imagined what he might find. Had we been burglarized? Had Mor been attacked? Was he in there right now, on the floor, hurt—or, God forbid, worse? I couldn't stop myself from rushing in behind Samuel, dreading the scene I might be confronted with. But there was nothing. Just the bed unmade, music books strewn across the floor, newspaper falling off the table, closet door ajar. I checked the door to the studio: locked.

"Is anything missing?" Samuel asked. I scanned the room. What could a burglar possibly desire? We had nothing, really, no more than the basics for a practical life, nothing worth taking. I looked inside the closet. Saw the empty hangers. The place where Mor's suitcase would be.

"His suitcase is missing, his clothes," I said.

I crouched on the floor, peering under the bed, reaching my arm out, sweeping the area beneath the bed until I found the lockbox. Unlocked. Open. Empty.

"He's left."

"What do you mean, left?" Samuel asked.

I held the lockbox on my lap, gray, dented, empty. I'd never had the key, of course; that was Mor's concern.

"He took the money," I said.

Samuel stopped. "How much money?"

"All of it," I said. "Everything. He doesn't trust the banks."

Samuel sat beside me on the bed, took the box from me, closed it.

"If his studio is still locked," Samuel said. "He must mean to come back. His work is still in there."

I was too shocked to cry. If I breathed too quickly, I could sense the roiling waves underneath, the purple, creeping darkness of panic. But I needed to stay numb. Otherwise it would be too much.

"Has he done anything like this before?" Samuel asked.

"No," I said. We both waited, because we both knew that there was an endless possibility of definition in the words *like this.* But no. Of all the things he'd done, he had never left.

"He'll come back," I said, looking at my hands in my lap, watching my thumb move across the scar on my wrist.

"Do you really want him to?" Samuel asked.

This was a question I couldn't answer. This was a question that, until now, I couldn't even fathom having the right to ask myself. This was a question that somehow pierced through the numbness enveloping me, that triggered the grief and fear and sadness that seemed to be endlessly lying in wait.

Samuel held me until I couldn't cry anymore and laid me down, and placed the blanket over me, and picked up all the fallen things, the books, the newspaper, the cup and saucer, the chair, the lockbox, and came back to me, lying beside me, his body cradling mine, his arm around me, holding me close.

HOPE

1994

1

I s it fucked up that Hope is eighteen and has never met her grandfather? That the first time she'll meet him in person will be at the
train station, when he picks her up with his new family and her ten-
year-old uncle?

A ten-year-old uncle—that's definitely fucked up.

She'd asked her grandmother if she minded.

"Mind? You're a grown person," Anna had said when Hope called.
There was the flick of a cigarette lighter in the background and then a
long exhale. "You can make your own choices. You might as well see for
yourself what he's all about."

What he's all about. All Hope knows is that he's the black sheep of
the family. She has only ever heard him referred to, ominously, as "The
Old Man."

Hope wanted to explain to her that it wasn't a choice. That the conservatory dorms were closed for spring break, and she had nowhere to be.
That she couldn't afford to go to Florida like seemingly every other college
student she knew. That she couldn't stay at Matthew's place, now that
things were over between them. That she couldn't go home and be around
Pauline with her relentless, aggressive positivity that allowed no room for
Hope's "mystery disease," this weird pain and debilitating fatigue that no

doctor had yet been able to diagnose, but which Pauline was sure could be cured with a daily routine and disciplined diet. That she felt stupid having to pretend to her friends that she had something cooler lined up, so they wouldn't have to know the truth: that her so-called ex-boyfriend (because had he ever truly been her boyfriend? Matthew had always refused to use that word, had always gently corrected her, saying, *don't say boyfriend, say soulmate*) was repulsed by her very nature, so she'd be spending her spring break with the grandfather she'd never met, the floozy he'd taken up with, and the uncle who was eight years younger than she was. It was fucked up. Hope was fucked up. Her fucked-up family proved it. But she couldn't talk about these things. She was a grown person. She was supposed to make her own choices.

Pauline was the one who'd arranged everything, of course. Which was perverse because, from what Hope had managed to piece together, The Old Man was the determining factor in her insanity: a domestic terror, a loud drunk, an abandoning, withholding, faraway father. Pauline's frantic aspirations had always made Hope suspect she was playing for a wider audience.

Hope had tried to call Pauline when she'd gotten The Old Man's wife's letter in the mail, but of course Pauline wasn't home. Pauline was a "life coach" now, lending her expertise to women in their forties who also didn't know what to do with their lives. Pauline had been a high school teacher, a small-business owner, a laundress, a hospital clown. She once ran a dog-grooming studio out of their house, in the back room, and for a summer sold her hand-crocheted whatevers at the local craft place. For a while, she did customer service for a local department store, and she even did seasonal work as a wrapping-paper lady at the mall. One awful Christmas she'd worked at the mall as Mrs. Claus.

"Who *better* than me to be a life coach?" she'd always say. "At least I've done something with my life! At least I'm living it! No regrets!"

No regrets for her, true.

When Hope called to find out what the deal was, her dad answered the phone, and she was surprised.

"Where's Pauline?"

There was a stern kind of pause before he said, "Your *mom* is out. I think she's coaching someone's life."

"You shouldn't make fun of it," Hope mock-scolded. "She's really making a difference! She's really helping people!" These were the standard things Pauline would say when one of them questioned her "life coaching" skills. "What are you doing home?"

"Sick—a cold," he said quickly, preempting any attempt to pry. He'd had a heart attack two years ago. At the time, Hope didn't know what was worse, the possibility of him dying, or the thought of being left to deal with Pauline, alone.

"Do you know, did she ask The Old Man to get in touch with me?"

"No. Not that I know of. Why?"

"I got a letter from his wife, saying it was high time we met, and that they'd like to buy me a train ticket to come see them for spring break."

"Do you want to do that?"

"No," she said. "But it's not like I can afford to go anywhere else."

There was, as usual, the uncomfortable silence. Nobody was ever supposed to talk about money, about being able to afford anything, or not being able to afford anything, especially when someone had decided to go to music school instead of going to college like a regular person who wanted to have a job someday. Hope was on her own. She had made her bed. Now she'd have to lie in it, student loans and all.

"So I guess it's settled then, right?" she said. "I have to go see The Old Man, whether I want to or not?"

"Perfect timing! Your life coach is here," he interrupted.

"Dad!"

"I think it's your mom you need to talk to about this," he said, surrendering the phone to Pauline.

"Hey, you, what's up? Is there something going on?" Pauline sounded breathless and energized, excited to talk. It was impossible to tell, even after all these years, whether she was for real or faking.

"The Old Man."

Pauline was silent for as long as Hope had ever witnessed her attempting to be silent—an impressive three seconds—before recognition finally dawned. "Oh! Yes, oh, that's great! He got in touch, did he? Of course he did, I knew he wouldn't pass up a chance to meet his only granddaughter."

Hope was aware of The Old Man's long-standing familial estrangement, but she couldn't help wondering: Hadn't there been chances to meet her before? Like, say, when she was born?

"So this was your idea?"

"Of course!" Pauline sounded so pleased with herself. What planet was she even on?

"I can't believe you arranged this without even talking to me! You couldn't have at least warned me about it? They want me to come for spring break!"

"That's perfect! Isn't it perfect? Oh, and you'll get to meet Richard—I always like to call him 'Little Richard,' since he's, what, twenty years younger than me—"

"Thirty," Hope said, but Pauline didn't hear.

"—and of course you'll see—what's the wife's name?"

"You mean Gran's *ex-best friend's* name? It's Deborah."

"Oh, water under the bridge," she said, laughing. Hope could picture her moussed too-auburn hair moving just the slightest bit out of place as she tossed her head back, rolling her eyes. "Anyway, what's the problem? I think this is a wonderful opportunity."

Hope wanted to point out that Pauline had gone over her head with this, that having a ten-year-old uncle was deeply, deeply weird, but Pauline cut her off. "I'm sorry, hon, I have to meet another client in about five minutes, so I have to run. Here's Dad."

The phone clattered to the countertop, and Hope heard the muffled sounds of Pauline's heels clicking away into the living room. Then nothing.

"Hello?" Hope said into the silence.

"I'm here." Her dad sighed, sounding none too happy about it.

"Well, what do I do?"

"About what?"

"The Old Man!"

"I don't know, go, if you want to. It sounds like your mother would really like it if you did."

"But what about you?" Hope pressed.

"Me?" He paused for so long that Hope wondered if the line was dead, but then he said, "There are very few people in this world that I actively dislike. The Old Man is one of them."

"Great. That helps."

"Glad to be of service," he said, hanging up.

Why bother having parents if they can't give you any guidance, especially if one of them is a certified life coach?

Hope read The Old Man's wife's letter again and weighed her options. It was a train to DC and a view into the part of her family no one had ever openly discussed, or living on the street for two weeks.

She chose the train.

2

The worst part about her parents not being super supportive about her going to music school was that they were probably right. It probably was a total waste of time, a way to hide from the world of real responsibility. What was she doing, locking herself away in a practice room for six hours a day, if not hiding? Was she really going to emerge from this experience with some kind of international performing career? A record deal? No. She would graduate, like so many other piano majors, and become a teacher, walking student after student through Big-Note versions of "Moonlight Sonata" or "Clair de Lune" or whatever. She could do that now, right now, without going further into student loan debt or daily humiliation in her performance classes.

The last piano lit class before everything fell apart with Matthew, before the Incident, had almost made her quit right then and there.

"Never in my life have I been so disappointed to see you," Professor Stephens said as she walked in, and she thought, *you and me both*. His comments to her were always so plausibly deniable—just a joke, Hope, lighten up!—ever since she'd run into him and Matthew the end of freshman year. They'd never talked about it, the moment she'd witnessed, Stephens coaching Matthew in the practice room, but she'd sensed an odd aggression toward her ever since.

That day, he was behind the desk—Soo-Jin's desk, Hope's teacher's desk—with his perfectly shined shoes propped up on the edge. Slacks store-creased smooth. Shirt sleeves rolled up, but perfectly, an origami theater of rolled-up sleeves. Jacket neatly hung on the back of the chair—Soo-Jin's chair. That smug, entitled look on his face. Smoke wafting from the cigarette dangling between his long fingers. Had he ever once, during class, thought to open a window? Hope could swear that when she had her private lessons with Soo-Jin in this room, the fog still lingered, the nicotine drawn into the porous wood of the pianos, steeping into the bookcases. Stephens only wished this were his studio, his desk and chair, his pianos, his thick, huge, faded rugs dampening the sound, soaking up the smoke. His department. But it was Soo-Jin's. No matter how much he wished it weren't.

Stephens's eyes were obscured by a glare in his glasses; she couldn't tell what he was thinking. But she saw Matthew looking at her sharply, shaking his head, a warning, even though he had a smile on his face, and everyone else was laughing. There was a joke. This was a joke. Hope was the joke?

"I was just predicting to the class that you would be Jennifer arriving with my coffee," Stephens said, sulking, from behind the desk, finally letting her in on it. "So you can understand my bitter disappointment in seeing you entering the room, coffee-less. Ah! But here she is."

Jennifer gave an apologetic smile as she pushed past Hope, practically running to the desk.

"So sorry I'm late," she said, her voice breathy from the sprint. "Huge line today."

Stephens waved her away as he took a sip. "Well, it's here now, as are you, so all is forgiven, I suppose."

Jennifer and Hope settled into seats next to Matthew, and Matthew wrinkled his nose at Jennifer, a perfect imitation of the way Jennifer wrinkled her nose when she talked. He was a chameleon.

"Teacher's pet!" he whispered.

She wrinkled her nose back and smiled. "Jealous?"

Matthew smiled too, but he looked at Hope quickly and she noted a familiar coldness creeping into his eyes, as though he had detected some hidden meaning in the comment for which Hope was somehow responsible.

Suddenly his smile became playful again, and he leaned toward Jennifer. "Super jealous. Why can't *I* be my teacher's slave? I love going out of my way to fetch coffee and cigarettes!"

"Oh, stop, I'm not his slave," she said, rolling her eyes.

"*Sex* slave," Matthew whispered, and Jennifer started to respond, all faux-offended, but then Stephens emerged from behind the desk and moved to his second-favorite lecture position, which was leaning on the front of the desk like he didn't care, and began to talk.

"Goldberg Variations," he announced wearily over the sounds of music bags being opened and scores shuffling. He stubbed out his cigarette and took a deep swig of coffee. "Before this class, had anyone played or performed or otherwise encountered the Variations in their feeble music education? Anyone?"

He surveyed the class with his usual look of disdain. Hope was tired. Although tired wasn't a strong enough word to describe how she was feeling. Not fatigued, even. Not exhausted. Not wiped out. Not weary. There hadn't been a word invented yet for it, for this feeling in her bones, this extra gravity, this pain. She'd started calling it "mystery disease" as a joke, but it had become less and less funny the longer it had gone on without any sort of diagnosis. Or relief.

Hope took the opportunity to close her eyes. The room was so still for a moment, as no one answered him. Full of tension, yet without anxiety; the students expected the tension by this point, so it no longer unnerved them. It was just a muscle tightened, a jaw clenched. A state of being. A state. A fact. That's what Hope's tiredness was. A fact. A thing that just *was*.

Stephen sighed and drained the rest of his coffee. "Incredible. No, not incredible. Pathetic. Not a single one of you?"

Matthew nudged Hope and slid a paper onto the score she had on her lap. A sketch of Stephens, holding coffee in one hand and a cigarette in the other, with a giant dick in his mouth. His own.

"Stop it," Hope whispered and shoved the paper back to him. Matthew folded it into his crossed arms, doing his best to look innocent, thoughtful even, as Stephens caught his eye and began to stalk the room.

There were thirty students, and each one had been assigned a variation to learn and perform for the class. The aria, the main theme upon which the variations was based, was to be performed at the beginning of each class by someone different, picked at random.

Stephens scanned the room, looking at all of them meaningfully over his glasses. He worked so hard at seeming menacing.

"Today is variations one, two, and three, so that means Lara, Young-Nam, and Keiko. And let's see, for the aria . . . Hope Parker. For the crime of not being Jennifer with my coffee."

Hope laughed at first, along with everyone else, but then she realized he was serious. She was in trouble: How could she possibly play right now? Her arms were shooting tendrils of pain. Her wrists ached, and her fingers existed only as the sensation of heavy rocks at the ends of her hands, pulling her downward into a swirling eddy of discomfort and fatigue.

"Can I—I mean, would it be possible—I'm not feeling well—I just came from a doctor's appointment," Hope started. But Stephens was already seated behind the desk, feet up, cigarette glowing.

"We don't need your life story here. Just play."

The room narrowed itself to the score she held in her hands. The score she hadn't practiced. As much as she resented his bullying attitude, his narcissistic assumptions about his own musical supremacy, Stephens was right: Hope was pathetic. She hadn't practiced the aria, or her assigned variation—the hardest one, of course, as though he'd chosen it specifically to illuminate her weaknesses—at all.

She walked to the first of the two pianos that sat side by side, the one closest to the rest of the students, her favorite piano. Soo-Jin's piano, the one she always sat at during Hope's lesson.

"Sometime this century, please."

Her hands moved like someone else's hands. Hope looked at the score, watched her hands to make sure they were moving, shifted to make the fingering work. She knew she was using too much pedal, but she needed it to smooth out the rough edges, to make the aria sound sweet and not plodding, as though she'd just gotten off a bus from a doctor's appointment. She needed to fill the prescription she'd gotten. It might help her, the doctor had said; it might make her drowsy, sleep the pain away. These variations were supposedly composed to help someone sleep, to make someone drowsy. To help with insomnia. Hope hadn't yet found a piece of music to help with this pain and fatigue.

She tried to play the piece as she'd heard it played, but everything she did was too loud, too over-pedaled. It should have been the easiest thing in the world. It was the simplest melody, so spare; playing it should have been effortless. But it was a struggle and what's more, Hope was sure it sounded like a struggle to everyone listening. She finally reached the end and lifted her hands from the keyboard, her foot from the pedal, to half-hearted applause from her fellow piano majors, the sound of pity for Hope mixed with relief that it hadn't been any of them that had played so badly just then.

"Do *not* applaud that," Stephen barked. "That was a train wreck. An absolute disaster. I can't even critique that. That performance was an *insult* to this incredibly important work."

Hope stared at the keys, at her hands in her lap, her head down, avoiding his gaze as he walked toward the piano. But he really wasn't going to critique her. Instead he motioned for her to get up.

"Matthew," he said. It was a command. Hope looked up to see Matthew standing. "Come show us how it's supposed to sound."

Matthew walked toward her with a smug smile and a shrug. It wasn't his fault that she had failed, publicly, and that he had been chosen to illustrate, by comparison, the full extent of her failure. Though, of course he had been chosen. Who else would Stephens choose?

Hope stood up from the bench. Matthew had no music with him.

"Do you need the score?" she asked.

He shook his head. Of course he had it memorized.

Hope grabbed her music and headed back to her seat through a blur of angry tears.

Matthew played it at the perfect tempo. He used no pedal. Suddenly, as Hope heard him play it, the phrases all made sense to her. He executed the tricky ornamentation with such ease it sounded preordained, as though that was the way Bach had always meant for it to be, no room, no need, even, for any other interpretation. The melody was sweet but sad in his hands, and delicate, but perfectly held, perfectly balanced, a sleeping baby carried in firm but tender, careful, strong arms.

"Bravo, my friend, bra-*vo*," Stephens said, clapping Matthew on the shoulder, his hand lingering, Hope noticed, sliding down Matthew's back just slightly, before tapping him to send him back to his seat.

"Sorry," Matthew whispered as he sat back down next to her, but she knew he wasn't sorry. "Shoulda practiced, Hop."

Afterward, they walked toward the elevator to the practice rooms, Jennifer trailing them.

"Wow. That was brutal," Matthew said.

"For me, not for you," Hope reminded him.

"Oh, I know. Believe me, I know. We all had to sit there and listen to you butcher it, remember?"

Was this his idea of a joke? Was this a game right now? In front of Jennifer?

"You okay?" Jennifer asked. "You said you went to the doctor?"

"Yeah," Hope said. "I'm just tired."

"Aw, I bet." Jennifer wrinkled her nose, and Hope could see Matthew doing his Jennifer nose-wrinkling imitation just out of her sight.

"Yeah, yeah—we're all 'tired,' Hop." Matthew rolled his eyes. "Come on. You don't have *tired* cancer. You're not *dying*. Just, I don't know, at least make an effort."

An effort.

Jennifer's eyes widened, and she looked at Hope and then at Matthew.

"Okay, well, I've seriously got to practice, so I'll catch up with you guys later," she said, sounding bright but practically speed-walking toward the elevator to escape the conversation.

"Yes, you do!" Matthew called after her. "You need to work on that coffee-fetching technique. Do some sprints, maybe."

"Good idea," she said, laughing.

"Also maybe work on that Beethoven," Matthew said under his breath to Hope, when Jennifer turned to face the elevator. "Have you heard it recently? Total mess."

"I haven't heard it," Hope said, trying to keep her voice steady. "I guess I'll have to make an *effort*."

"Oh, come on! I was joking," he said, pushing her lightly. Still hard enough to jostle her off balance. "You know I'm kidding. Hop. Hope. *Hopeful*. Look at me! Seriously. It was just a joke."

"I thought you said you weren't going to do that anymore."

"What, make jokes? I never said that."

Hope was too tired to do this. Her vision was cloudy at the edges, tunneling. She needed to get back to her dorm and sleep. She couldn't think, couldn't focus. She walked past the elevator and kept going.

"So you're just leaving?" he called after her. "That's it? You're not even going to practice? Because I hurt your feelings? Come on!"

"I'm tired," Hope said. "I have to sleep."

She didn't want to turn around to see the look on his face. She didn't have to. She knew it would be his cruel look, his disgusted look. The look he had when he hated her. The look he sometimes had when he said he loved her.

"I'll call you later," he said.

It sounded like a threat.

3

When she arrives at Union Station, she scans the crowd for The Old Man. Would she even recognize him if he were here? She's only seen him in pictures. She can't shake the slight feeling of shame about this, as if it's somehow her fault for not knowing him.

As she looks around, shifting her duffel bag to her other shoulder, she sees a plumpish older woman standing apart from the crowd of commuters and other travelers making their way through the station. The woman fiddles with the buttons on her salmon-colored sweater and looks around with a frown of concentration. Her graying pageboy hairstyle and old-fashioned glasses remind Hope of an elementary school librarian. She shifts her weight and turns to her left, and Hope can see she is standing with a little boy who looks to be about nine or ten. He's skinny and his smallness is only emphasized by his baggy striped T-shirt. He has dark hair in one of those unfortunate bowl cuts, and he grips the straps of the woman's purse, swinging himself back and forth. Could this be The Old Man's wife and Hope's little uncle?

The woman's eyes lock on hers, and Hope sees her smile as she starts toward her, the boy straggling behind. "Hope?"

Hope walks over and reaches out her hand. She thinks of the many times Pauline characterized The Old Man's wife as some young floozy. If this grandmotherly woman is a floozy, Hope is Vladimir Horowitz.

"I'm Deborah," she says, clasping Hope's hand. "And this is Richard."

"So nice to meet you," she says to both of them.

"Nice to meet you too," says Richard, with a prominent lisp. Poor Little Richard, Hope thinks. That can't go over well at school.

"Shall we?" Deborah asks, as she starts leading them out of the station to the car.

"Where's . . ?" Hope catches herself just before she says "The Old Man," but she doesn't know what else she's supposed to call him.

"Your grandfather couldn't make it," Deborah says. Her voice is as calmly matter-of-fact as her writing style, and Hope has to check Deborah's facial expression to make sure she's as fine with that as she sounds. She's relieved to see a smile. "He'll probably be home by the time we get there. I know he's anxious to see you."

"Hey, my dad is her grandfather? That's *so* funny!" Richard laughs. He has that gangly, boneless walk of little kids, arms swinging, legs splaying. Deborah reins him in and guides him out of people's way.

"We've been over this, Richard, you know that," she says. She sounds irritated, but she smiles at Hope, her eyes friendly through the shield of her glasses.

"Doesn't that mean you're my niece?" He clearly isn't getting the message, and Deborah grips his arm a little more tightly. But Hope smiles at him and says, "Well, technically, I guess. Why don't you just call me Hope?"

It's easier than she imagined to pretend as though all of this is normal, but still, she's fighting the urge to compulsively crack her knuckles, fighting to stay above the weight of the seemingly endless fatigue. Her ankle throbs, even though it's wrapped in an Ace bandage. Her bones hurt. All of them.

"Okay," he says, swinging his arms around. "Hey, Hope, when we get back to the house, do you wanna hear me play the clarinet?"

Do I have a choice? she thinks, but she says, "Sure."

On the way to The Old Man's house, Hope sits in the front seat and answers Deborah's polite questions about music school. Deborah doesn't ask much about her family, just a general "how's your mother doing?" and a comment about her dad's health. In the back seat, Richard sings to himself, every once in a while asking them if they want to hear another song he learned in choir.

"He's very imaginative," Deborah says. "You'll have to excuse his enthusiasm. We don't get many visitors."

Hope feels vaguely ashamed, as though her personal lack of visitation is responsible for The Old Man's alienation from everyone else in the family. She feels a guilty compulsion to be the most exceptional visitor ever, to make up for the lack of sociable guests over the years.

"Well, I'm glad I'm here now," she says.

Deborah smiles, and they spend the rest of the ride to The Old Man's house listening to Richard sing "The Crawdad Song."

The Old Man's house is way nicer than Hope had imagined. After hearing him spoken of obliquely for so many years, she had envisioned him living like a troll under someone's bridge, but in fact the house is the usual kind of spacious, modern dwelling inhabited by normal people in the suburbs. She guesses the decor is Deborah's touch: everything is modest and understated and expensive without bragging about it, all in a basic oatmeal, burgundy, green palette. Though for all she knows, that could be her grandfather's taste. What does she know about him, anyway, that hasn't been told to her by people with an axe to grind? Deborah takes her upstairs to the guest room, where she'll be staying for the next week, and Richard clamors to share his turtle collection. There are framed photos everywhere, but none of Pauline.

"Why don't you get settled, and I'll start making us dinner," Deborah says. "I'm making pork chops, if that's okay."

"Sure," Hope says, even though she hates pork chops. She is determined to be easy.

Richard pulls her sleeve and whines. "You said you'd come see my turtles!"

Deborah yanks him to her side, and they have an intense whispered conversation.

"Ow," he says, "Okay! O-*kay!*"

"Hope, Richard can wait a few minutes while you unpack. You just get your things settled and go in to see him when you're ready."

Richard looks pouty and mad, and Hope feels for him. What hell it is to be a little kid. Still, she finds him incredibly annoying, and she's only been around him for an hour, tops. "I'll come see your turtles, I promise," she says. "Give me fifteen minutes."

"Yay!" he shouts, jumping and flailing his arms.

"Go, go." Deborah shoos him into his room before she heads downstairs to make supper.

Hope closes the door to the guest room and sits on the bed, massaging her achy hands. It's a pretty room. A generously soft bed with quilts and a down comforter, a muted paisley pattern on the wall, heavy oak furniture with curlicued legs, a non-offensive carpet of faded sapphire. It feels homey, like the rest of the house. This surprises her even though it shouldn't. But the stories she's heard have colored her expectations.

The photos decorating the guest room appear to be mostly of Deborah and her family. On the bookcase there's a svelter, younger-looking Deborah, with the same hairstyle she has now, standing with two women who look like her, all wearing the kind of dresses women wore in the '70s: short skirts, boldly patterned in chartreuse and yellow and hot pink. On the bureau are a few black-and-white photos of Deborah as a little girl. Hope can tell it's her; she has the same serious expression in that picture that she has as an adult. Her little-girl dress has an old-fashioned collar and puffy sleeves, and her hands are folded in her lap. She looks like the kind of child who would remember to say "please" and "thank you," who would say "may" instead of "can." Hope can't imagine Deborah doing something spontaneous or disrespectful.

And yet she knows, from what she's heard, that Deborah has done exactly that. According to Pauline, Deborah has done one of the most spontaneous and disrespectful things a grown woman can do: she stole her best friend's husband. More to the point, she stole Pauline's mother's husband. Pauline's dad. Hope's grandfather. Hope can't square the idea of risky, backstabbing Deborah with the straightforward person she's met today, or with the innocuous representations in these photos. She doesn't look like a home-wrecker. She's not a blonde beauty queen. Even in the picture of her in a tight sweater, her hair coiffed and tall, she doesn't exactly have that come-hither look. Hope wonders what it was that drew her to her grandfather, and what drew him to her.

There is one picture of the two of them together, smiling at each other in fancy clothes. Hope is struck by her grandfather's profile: it's her mother's face on a stranger's body. She holds the photo up to the mirror on the dresser, scanning her face and his for telling resemblances. How much of Hope is him? Even though she's never met him, he's part of her, technically. This thought creeps her out. It reminds her of the direct link between him and Pauline, and between Pauline and her. She prefers to liken herself to Athena, sprung whole from her father's head, never dependent on a mother who wasn't there to begin with.

4

If Hope was honest with herself, Matthew's games had started from the beginning. She had been next door to him, in one of the side-by-side third-floor practice rooms with grand pianos, reserved for piano majors only. It was her second week of school, and she was already failing. Was anyone else crying in a practice room instead of actually practicing? Hope was sure she was the only one.

First of all, the teacher she had been supposed to study with hadn't wanted her. Or at least hadn't bothered to show up for her lessons. There had been some sort of mix-up, the administration had said, nothing personal, even though it felt incredibly personal, an indictment of her ability and talent, and eventually she had been assigned to someone else's studio. Her new teacher was an imposing mystery, a virtuoso with limited English who communicated through the force of her intimidating eye contact and occasional death grip, fingers strong from years of practice poking into students' tendons to correct errant technique. She had sentenced Hope to going back to the basics—not even playing repertoire, just doing finger exercises, scales, arpeggios. In their lessons, she frowned as Hope played and stopped her only to say inscrutable things like "play like squirrel" and "strike from belly button." Hope had no idea what a squirrel's belly button had to do with anything, and she had even less idea what the point was of being a piano major if a person was only allowed to play basic beginner warm-up exercises. And evidently play even those badly.

From the practice room next door, she heard thundering chords and an incredible filigree of fast-moving fingerwork as the person next to her played some kind of actual piano piece, as though to personally humiliate her. Finally, she wiped her angry tears away and began slamming down the beginning notes of the first finger exercise. Although surely a squirrel wouldn't slam anything, so she was already doing it wrong. Just as she was beginning to feel tears of frustration again threatening to fall, she heard, from the practice room next door, the sound of someone playing the same exercise.

She listened for a moment, then played the opening again. Again she heard the person next door join in. She stopped as she listened to the player next door keep going, playing it faster and faster, throwing in some variations and chords—making fun of her.

She stood up from the bench, fuming, and yanked open the door of her practice room. She banged on the door of the room next to hers until the playing stopped—she didn't even know what she planned to say to whomever was in there, taunting her—and stood there, disarmed by Matthew's smiling face as he opened the door.

"Pischna, right?" he said, opening the door. "SJ's having you go through the Pischna 'Technical Studies' book?"

"Who?" Hope was angry, but thrown by his friendly attitude, the way he was acting like he hadn't just mocked her through the practice room wall. He was at least a head taller than she was, dark hair, dark eyes, brilliant smile.

"Soo-Jin. Mrs. Park? That's who you're studying with, right?"

"Oh. Yes. I was actually supposed to be with Professor Stephens, but I don't know, something happened."

"Oh god, consider yourself lucky. Stephens is the worst. He thinks he's Liszt incarnate. I'm honestly surprised he doesn't wear a cape when he performs. But SJ picked you, so you're safe. She's great. You should be flattered."

"I don't know about that," Hope said. "She was kind of forced to take me."

"Bullshit," he said, with that smile again. "They could have foisted you on Harriet, or, god forbid, Irving. If SJ took you on, that means she thinks you're talented. She only takes the best."

"Right. That's why she's making me practice this stuff instead of actual repertoire. Because I'm so talented."

"How do you think I knew what you were doing in there?"

Hope frowned. "She made you do that too?"

"Yup. Don't let it get to you. This is totally 'wax on, wax off,' 'snatch the pebble from my hand, grasshopper' stuff. It's all good, trust me. If she didn't think you had talent, she wouldn't bother."

Hope sighed, sniffing away her tears, still unconvinced.

"Did she do that whole 'belly button *here*' thing?" he asked, tapping on the back of his hand.

"Yes!" she laughed. "What does that even mean?"

"Belly button *here*!" he said, a perfect imitation of her accent. "Strike from *there*!"

"Yes, exactly!"

"It took me like a year to figure out what she was saying. And like a whole other year to actually know what any of it meant. In the meantime, I just nodded and tried to do whatever in the hopes that I was actually doing something remotely close to whatever it was she wanted me to do."

"So it's not just me," Hope said.

He laughed. "It's definitely not just you. Anyway, you're fine. You're better than fine—I've heard you in the practice rooms playing stuff besides Pischna. You're very good."

"Oh, no," Hope said.

"Hey now," he said, looking stern. "I know my competition when I hear it. Now get back in there and practice, or I'll tell SJ on you."

"Okay, okay."

"And I promise I won't make fun of you from next door."

"Okay."

"And I'm Matthew, by the way," he said, sticking his hand out. It was easily twice the size of Hope's. Long fingers, strong. The perfect piano hand.

"I'm Hope."

"Hope," he repeated, shaking his head, looking faux-thoughtful. "Is that short for something? Hopeful?"

"What?"

Matthew's eyes grew wide with pretend shock. "Oh, no, don't tell me your parents named you Hopeless! How could they do that? So mean!"

"No! Of course not! It's just Hope."

"Are you sure it's not long for something? Hop, maybe? That's got to be it. I'm going to call you Hop. That's your new name. Get used to it!"

Hope laughed as she began heading back into her practice room. "And you? Should I call you Matt?"

Suddenly Matthew looked dead serious as he stood in the practice room doorway, his hair grazing the frame. "No. Why would you ever do something as stupid as that?" Hope scrambled to apologize, to process his sudden shift in tone, but just as suddenly his face relaxed back into a smile. "Ah, I'm just messing with you, Hop! See you at closing time?"

It was his first game, Hope realized now. But back then, Hope had smiled as she shut the door behind her. Smiled as she sat back down on the bench, smiled as she heard Matthew begin playing again next door, smiled as she attempted the first Pischna exercise again. Smiled as she played it, striking from there, quick like squirrel, belly button here.

Matthew walked her home from practicing that night, escorting her all the way to her dorm. Everyone seemed to know him; he seemed to be endlessly saying hi to everyone who walked by them, making jokes to people in passing, making everyone laugh. He was like a celebrity.

There were clues, even then, but Hope didn't notice.

"I see Matthew has wasted no time," her dorm resident adviser, an opera major, said when he dropped Hope off at the door.

"What do you mean?" Hope asked.

She had an eyebrow raised, a sour look on her face. "He's a popular guy."

And the next week, at her first real lesson, when Mrs. Park—or SJ, as Hope was increasingly thinking of her, thanks to Matthew—asked if Hope had met any of her students, Hope told her that she had talked with Matthew, and her teacher looked momentarily disapproving.

"He is not serious."

"Yes, he's very funny," Hope said. "And very talented."

She made a dismissive sound. "Talent is nothing if you are not serious."

Hope nodded, looked at her hands.

"Maybe find other students. Younger students, like you. Freshmen, sophomores. Jennifer perhaps."

"Okay," Hope said.

It had felt like a warning, like she was warning Hope away from him. But he was so funny, and so charming, and he'd already made Hope feel so much better about being there. So what if he wasn't serious? Who wanted to be serious all the time?

Their friendship was quick and intense. They were inseparable, practicing next door to each other so they were still together even when they were apart. Sometimes, when Hope was working on something hands separately, drilling the right-hand part, for example, of a Mozart sonata, she would hear him through the wall, playing the left-hand part to accompany her. Or when she played a dramatic ending—in the midst of the silence that hung in the air after the chords died away, she'd hear the faint sound of him appending his version of the old cartoon "shave and a haircut, two bits" melody to her ending. When they took practice breaks, they took them together, and when they were done practicing, they walked home together, sometimes ending up talking for hours about everything from music to philosophy to their pasts to their futures on the front doorstep of her dorm. He took her home with him over Christmas break, had her stay with his family, joked about how they should just get married, because they were soulmates after all, weren't they? And besides, wouldn't it be fun? Wouldn't SJ be scandalized if they came back from winter break married?

Hope noticed how other people longed to be in his company and felt absurdly proud when he brushed them off to be in hers. She felt chosen by him, elevated by her association with him, the most popular, the most brilliant, the most talented pianist in the school. She was in love.

Even when she was startled by an ex-girlfriend of his, who sought Hope out to warn her away from him; even when she was confronted by another former friend of his, betrayed, who told Hope he was dangerous—even then she didn't believe. They were just bitter. They were jealous. They hadn't loved him enough. He'd told her as much. So when the games began in earnest, it was a test, that was all—how much could she take, could she love him enough not to leave. And it was a test Hope vowed to pass. She wouldn't be like everyone else. She would prove him wrong. She would stay.

5

Hope hears Richard singing to his turtles in his room and decides to sneak downstairs and avoid what she assumes will be a painful and lengthy lecture on the salient facts of the species. When she walks into the kitchen, Deborah is there, assembling dinner, all the burners fired and loaded with bubbling pots and pans.

"Can I get you something to drink?" she asks, wiping her hands on a blue-and-white striped apron she has over her outfit.

"No, that's okay, I'm fine," Hope says. "Can I help you do something?"

"Oh, no, I've got it under control," she tells her, smiling, the gracious hostess. "But I could use the company, if you want to have a seat."

Hope pulls out a stool from the marble island in the middle of the kitchen and sits down. "Sure. This is fun to watch, anyway."

"Watching someone cook dinner is fun?" Deborah asks, looking over her glasses at Hope as she goes to check on what's in the oven.

"Yeah," Hope says. "My mother isn't a big fan of that whole tradition. Cooking dinner."

"Really. That's odd."

"Well, yeah, that's Pauline: odd." Deborah shoots her a look, and she remembers that, as bizarre as it sounds, Deborah *is* Pauline's stepmother—in theory, at least, if not in practice. Plus, as his wife, Deborah's on The Old Man's side, and even though everything Hope has heard has implied that he's not a guy with a lot of allegiance to his own children, she imagines it's probably bad form to bad-mouth one of them in front of Deborah, his representative here on earth. "Well, you have to admit a mom who doesn't cook dinner is a little odd. Right?"

Deborah lifts the lid of one of the pots and stirs what's inside. "Not really. When I was working full-time I rarely cooked. And we do order a lot of takeout around here. It sounds like your mother is a very dynamic, busy person. Not cooking dinner might be one of those trade-offs women have to make when they're busy trying to have it all."

What is she talking about? Pauline busy and dynamic? Pauline making a trade-off? Pauline having it all? Pauline truly has everybody fooled.

She continues, "I bet you learned a lot about cooking for yourself growing up then."

"Me? No," Hope says. "I don't know the first thing about it. I eat cereal and instant mashed potatoes, sometimes toast. That's the extent of my cooking."

Deborah smiles at her absentmindedly and reaches into a cupboard for plates. "Actually, I could use your help, if you don't mind."

"Sure." Hope takes the plates and Deborah gathers up the silverware, and they head to the dining room to set the table.

"Thanks," she says. "Your grandfather should be here soon."

"Deborah?"

"Yes?"

"Can I ask you a question?"

"Sure," she says. Deborah's hands are fists full of forks as she stands near the table. Hope can see her take a deep breath and steel herself against—what? What kind of question is she expecting? There's so much Hope is dying to know, so much she's dying to ask, the anxiety is making her nuts. She's surprised to realize that perhaps she's not the only one feeling that way.

"How old are you?"

Deborah visibly relaxes, leaning over the table and laughing. "Oh, Hope—"

"You don't have to tell me," Hope says, embarrassed.

"No, no," she says, waving the forks back and forth. "That's an easy one to answer. I'm fifty-four."

Fifty-four—that's just eleven years older than Pauline. That would have made her forty-four when she had Richard, practically Pauline's age right now. Can Hope imagine Pauline getting knocked up now, her and her dad announcing they'll soon have a baby brother or sister for her? The thought is disturbing.

Deborah holds up a hand, as if reacting to Hope's thoughts. "Richard was a long time in coming. It was a difficult period in my life. I'm very happy to have him. And that's all I'm going to say on the subject."

She doesn't sound upset, the way Pauline gets when Hope asks her about something messy that has the potential to make her look bad. There doesn't seem to be any subtext to Deborah's message. When she said that was all she was going to say, she really meant that that was all she was going to say. No deeper meaning, no subtle implication that Hope might be a horribly rude houseguest to pry into her life the way she did. Hope doesn't quite know how to interpret a conversation that does not require interpretation.

"I'm sorry, Deborah, I didn't mean to make you feel uncomfortable."

She straightens one last steak knife and smiles, as genuine a smile as Hope can recognize. "Oh, no, not at all. I realize you must have a lot of questions. I'm sure your grandfather will be happy to try and answer more of them when he gets here. Now, where are those candles?" She walks back into the kitchen, ostensibly searching for them.

Deborah is such a mystery. She seems so normal, in a way, cooking dinner, being diplomatic, saying things that she means. And yet it's clear that she can't be normal. Otherwise she wouldn't be with The Old Man. Otherwise she wouldn't have betrayed her best friend. Otherwise she wouldn't be older than Pauline with a kid younger than Hope.

The front door slams, and the cold air from outside gives Hope goose bumps on her arm. It's The Old Man. He's home.

Standing in the dining room, it feels like she's in one of those awful dreams where something terrible is happening and she has to run away, but her legs are paralyzed, or she's in a swimming pool and has to run underwater and her shoes are made of cement bricks, or she's stuck in slow motion while everyone else moves in hyper speed. Hope can hear The Old Man making the kinds of sounds people make when they get home from work—taking off his coat, dropping his briefcase on the floor, clanking his keys and change onto the table just inside the door—yet she can't move from where she is to go see him, to make herself known.

"Deborah?" He rummages in the coat closet in the entryway then moves into Hope's line of sight, standing next to the staircase and peering up. "Richard?"

She wants to say something, but she's frozen, so she just stands there looking at him. He is taller than she'd imagined, and older-looking. She forgets how much older he is than Deborah—ten years? Fifteen?— but he looks old. Silver-gray hair in an old-man pompadour, deep lines on his face. He has a jutting, strong jaw, set slightly off-center as though someone has just told him something of which he disapproves, and his shoulders are naturally thrown back, like he's attempting to make himself look even taller. But more than anything else his overall appearance seems grandfatherly, which Hope supposes is appropriate. Not that she'd expected him to come complete with ominous music and signs of evil intent, but she'd assumed he might look more the part of The Old Man than he really does. He has a bemused look on his face that reminds her of Pauline's self-satisfied grin when she's got something up her sleeve.

Then he turns and stares right at Hope, expressionless. For a moment, neither of them says anything; then she sees him just barely grin as she finally frees herself from her cement-shoe-dream catatonia and walks around the table to greet him.

"Hi. I'm Hope."

He regards her with an expression she has come to know via Pauline that roughly translates into "you are a complete moron."

"Well, of course you are! You couldn't be Deborah or Richard, now, could you? And there's very little chance you're a thief, breaking and entering into my home, since if you were, you wouldn't have been standing there idly while I had you in my sights." His face is plastic, his animated expressions providing a competing narrative to his remarks. Hope wills her face to betray nothing.

"Oh, come here!" he says, opening his arms and gesturing. He motions like this a few times before she understands that he means to give her a hug.

He presses her onto his shoulder like she's a baby in need of burping and slaps her on the back a few times. He has that Dad kind of smell: the smell of dress shirts and fancy suits and discreet businessman sweat.

"So, we finally meet," he says, ending the hug and framing her by the shoulders with his hands to scrutinize her face. "You're the spitting image of your mother at your age."

"How would you know?" Hope blurts out before she can stop herself. To her surprise, he doesn't appear to be offended. He raises an eyebrow and appraises her, that bemused expression back on his face.

"She's got spunk, this one," he says to no one in particular, wagging a finger at her. "Yep, definitely Pauline's girl."

Deborah comes in from the kitchen, candles in hand. "Tom! I didn't even hear you come in!"

Tom? Until Deborah said it, Hope hadn't realized she'd never known The Old Man's first name. Or that it was an acronym.

"Well, as you can see, I'm here," he says, looking at Hope knowingly, though she doesn't actually know what else he could mean by it. Deborah doesn't seem to notice the innuendo, or if she does, she pretends not to. She gives him a kiss on the cheek and says, "Yes, you are. Now go wash up, dinner's almost on the table."

"I'll just go up and see my boy, then we'll be down to eat." He stops, one hand on the stair rail, and looks at Hope. "How do you like your ten-year-old uncle?"

He's doing it again, that knowing look, as if to imply that they both know they're really talking about something else.

"Uh, I like him?"

He throws back his head and laughs like she's just made the funniest joke ever.

"Oh, you like him, all right. What did I tell you, Deborah? Just like Pauline."

He keeps chuckling as he goes up the stairs to see Richard, and Hope looks at Deborah to gauge her reaction. She's not giving anything away, but she gives Hope a hang-in-there kind of smile and says, "Come on, Hope, help me put the food on the table."

Dinner is stressful—and not in the "Pauline forgot to cook and now everyone's eating leftovers standing up in the kitchen" kind of way, or even the "Pauline makes the breathless announcement over takeout that this time she really means it, she's found her true calling" kind of way. Or even the "meeting a person's grandfather and step-grandmother and ten-year-old uncle for the first time" kind of way. No, it's stressful because of the grilling. And not in a cooking kind of way.

"Which would you choose: death by hanging, or dismemberment?" The Old Man asks, making a show of carving up the meat on his plate.

Before Hope can answer, he amends his question through a mouthful of pork.

"Excuse me. Would you choose to be hanged, drawn, and quartered, *or* would you choose to be dismembered? While conscious."

"Oh, Tom!" Deborah frowns while Richard dances in his seat, unfazed. "This is not appropriate dinnertime conversation!"

"I just want to get a feel for our guest here. You can tell a lot about a person by the kind of gruesome death they might choose." At this, he winks her way. "Hope, you don't mind being called our guest, do you? Of course, you're my granddaughter, but I don't know any more about you than I do the girl who answers the phone in my office. Here, have some salt. You know, your mother likes salt."

The way he says it implies some kind of unseemly understanding, but Hope is baffled, truly baffled, as she accepts the salt he has passed her way.

"You also know she sent you as her emissary," he says, wiping his mouth and taking a swig from his third glass of wine.

"I'm sorry?"

"Yes. She sent you in her place."

Hope looks at Deborah, at Richard moving the applesauce busily around his plate. "I don't think—"

"Ask yourself this," he commands, leaning in. "Why did she never let you see me for all these years? What has she been hiding from you, what has she been protecting you from? Do I seem like a horrible, evil person to you?"

"No, I—"

"Do I seem *scary*?"

"No—"

He sits back in his chair and throws up his hands, as if that proves everything. "Well, she's evidently too scared to come here and stand up to me herself. So I guess you'll have to do."

Deborah and Richard are both looking down at their plates while The Old Man holds Hope's gaze. It's as if he knows that Pauline is the last person she'd want to represent, the last person she'd want to stand up for. Suddenly his face breaks into a smile and he resumes sawing his pork chops.

"So, what'll it be? Death by dismemberment, or being hanged, drawn, and quartered?"

Hope isn't sure whether to risk it but, in the end, she decides *why not* and shrugs.

"I kind of feel like this conversation has been intended to draw and quarter me, so why not go all the way and throw in hanging too?"

Deborah seems especially stiff, across the table from Hope, as if she is holding her breath. Richard, too, is still, finally free of his endless fidgeting. The Old Man pauses, his knife and fork over his plate, and looks at Hope, his face inscrutable.

"That's my answer," she says to the silence. "Hanged, drawn, quartered."

He begins to nod slightly, considering, his mouth screwed up in faux contemplation, and finally nods emphatically, looking around the table, encouraging everyone, and finally Deborah begins to breathe again and Richard goes back to wiggling. They can tell it's going to be okay. Hope breathes, too, as The Old Man lets out a bark of a laugh.

He points his knife at her, gesturing as he says to Deborah, "What did I tell you? Just like Pauline!"

6

Sometimes Matthew's games were benign. "Guess what I'm thinking." Except he'd draw it out for an hour, and she'd keep guessing, until she'd get irritated and start to give up, but then she'd see his satisfied smile, satisfied because that was what he'd wanted, to wear her down, to make her leave; so she'd jump back into the game, guessing more, over and over, until he'd finally pretend she'd guessed correctly and say, "Your turn," and when she'd say, "Okay, guess what I'm thinking," he'd say it was a dumb game and he didn't want to play anymore.

Sometimes he'd just repeat what she said, endlessly, like they were kids on a playground, or siblings fighting in the back of the car. Except when she tried to trick him into saying something nice, by saying something nice that he would have to repeat, he wouldn't do it. "Hope is an awesome person," she would say, and he would just look at her, his face blank, and say, "Hope is not an awesome person." But then if she said, "Come on, Matthew, cut it out," he'd say, "Come on, Matthew, cut it out."

But sometimes the games were cruel. Sometimes it would start out like a joke, like him saying, "You're so cute, I want to bite you," then actually biting her, playfully at first, then painfully, sinking his teeth into the back of her arm or her calf. Sometimes it would start out like nothing, like a regular conversation, like, "Tell me about the scariest thing that ever happened to you as a little kid," and Hope would get tricked into it, would tell him the truth, would confess about the time Pauline set her hair on fire, the curled end of Hope's braid whooshing into flames before Pauline clamped a fist around it. Pauline telling her it was a lesson, that kids should never play with matches, even though Hope hadn't been, and that Hope shouldn't be so vain about her hair, even though she wasn't. "Why would anyone ever do that?" he asked, and Hope felt the shame of it, the guilt of having a mother who had done that to her, the guilt of deserving it. Then later, after he'd confessed his own childhood trauma, his shame at being the fat kid that everyone made fun of, the kid no one wanted to be friends with, the kind of stories Hope couldn't reconcile with his current charisma and charm and popularity, the kind of stories that made Hope feel let in on a secret; after all that, he took his lighter and tried to set her hair on fire.

But then after the games there would always be the apologies. He was sorry, he was so sorry; he didn't mean it; Hope was the only one who understood him, who understood that he kept trying to push her away because he loved her so much and hated himself. Someone who didn't love him would have left already, but Hope wasn't someone who would leave. She wasn't like the others, the ex-girlfriend who had tried to warn her, the ex-friends who'd left him behind. She had grown up with Pauline; she knew how to wait out an episode to get to the part where the person she loved was themself again. Hope was proving herself, Hope was showing him how much he was worthy of love by staying, by surviving, by waiting out the games until this part of the night, when he would hold her close and cry into her hair and promise he would be better to her. And Hope heard the part about hating himself and being sorry, but what pounded in her ears with the rush of her own heartbeat was *I love you so much, I love you so much.*

7

Hope's recital is in a few months, and she's behind schedule. She's practicing on Deborah and The Old Man's barely tuned upright, but all she can think about is how she is failing.

Even before the appearance of Mystery Disease, Hope had felt out of place. Just waiting to be unmasked. And now, with this sophomore recital, it's the ultimate test. All semester, she's struggled with the demands of the repertoire she's learning, the side effects of the medication she's taking. The endless fatigue affects her memory, making it difficult to hold the music in her mind. The pain limits her practice sessions, forcing her to practice in smaller increments, which means she accomplishes less and takes longer to make progress, due to all the stopping and starting.

She learned not to make a big deal of it in front of Matthew. He would get so upset with her, as though she had been personally trying to annoy him by being in pain. When it had first started, at the end of freshman year, he was concerned, but the longer it went on and the worse it got, the more impatient he became. Luckily, thanks to growing up with Pauline, Hope is a virtuoso at hiding her feelings.

She's tried not to bring any of it into her lessons, either—Soo-Jin is not interested in her students' personal lives, they do not have a place in the teaching studio—but it's almost impossible not to, when Hope has so many memory slips, when it's too much for her to make a decent *forte* or have any intensity behind her music.

In the middle of a lesson once, when she was playing through Chopin's third ballade, Soo-Jin stopped her, impatient with her lackluster performance, telling her, "You are absent. You are not here." Hope confessed that she was having trouble, that she was sick and that she didn't know what was wrong and that it wasn't getting better, and that she was scared. This was more than Soo-Jin needed to know, possibly more than Hope herself wanted to know. "It's just not fair," Hope said, before she could stop herself, because that was all she could think of. Soo-Jin shook her head and said, "There is no fair." Soo-Jin waited for Hope to stop crying, to wipe the tears from her face. For a moment, Hope thought she might be about to offer some words of comfort, or maybe wisdom. But all Soo-Jin said was, "Play."

In a way it's a relief that Soo-Jin doesn't care about how she's feeling, only about how she plays, because it offers Hope the chance to forget about it and focus on piano. That doesn't make it easier though. Soo-Jin keeps asking her to listen, to voice things properly, but Hope isn't sure what she means. She never knows if she's doing what Soo-Jin is asking her to do, if she's doing it right. Only when Soo-Jin says *yes* does she know if she's been successful.

"You must listen with three ears," Soo-Jin tells her. "One to hear what you want to play. Two to hear what you are really playing. Three to hear if someone else can hear either of those two things." Soo-Jin tells her a story about her own Carnegie Hall debut, and about how that night, suddenly, in the middle of a Mozart sonata, she understood how to listen, how to find where the music was hidden. "You can't plan for that," she says. "It happens or it doesn't. But you must try."

Hope tries to listen with three ears, to hear something that drowns out the pain and fatigue, but it doesn't always work.

Right now, she's battling Deborah's piano, with its short key bed, twangy tone, and dull action. It's hard to hear anything subtle as she practices the Brahms First Rhapsody. When she listens to recordings of it on her Walkman as she lies in bed at night, the music sounds like a message from another world, something sinister, triumphant, sad. Something inexplicable, something she can only understand as she hears it. Trying to explain it in words makes it dissipate, a chord fading away. Trying to play it breaks the spell.

Matthew played this piece last year. Perfectly, of course. Whatever his deal was, there was no denying his talent. She knows it's not possible, but a part of her wishes she could go back and start over, find some way to understand how all this could have happened with Matthew and prevent it. Before things got bad, before she got sick, she could say anything and he would look at her like she was the most amazing person in the world, and it seemed they really were soulmates, just like he said. Even now there's a part of her that wants to believe that if she could just go back and fix things from the start, it could all make sense. She could stop his games. She could be pain-free. She could be what he wanted. He could love her. She could play music and have it make sense.

"I don't mean to interrupt," Deborah says, suddenly next to the piano, a stack of fresh towels in her hands. "Just wanted to make sure I gave you these."

She peers at the score Hope has open on the music rack. "Ah, Brahms. I remember learning that piece. Back when I played."

Deborah had played this?

"Not like you, of course, I never went to conservatory, but I did play fairly seriously for a number of years."

Hope understands that Deborah is just making conversation, but she feels a surprising edge of defensiveness, a need to separate herself from Deborah. Hope is training to be a concert pianist. She doesn't intend to be the kind of musician who ends up with only memories of having once made music, married to a weird dinnertime interrogator in the suburbs, an upright piano doubling as a photo and knickknack stand in some dusty parlor, talking about how she played something once, proof of talent she used to have, talent that wasn't enough.

"I'm sure I didn't play it as well as you," Deborah says, as though she can sense Hope's resistance.

"Well, I can't play it at all yet, really," Hope says. "I'm just learning it."

"You know, your gran's mother, your great-grandmother, was quite a talented pianist. Or so your gran told me."

This is the first time Hope has heard anything about another family member being a musician.

"Really?"

"I think your gran was estranged from her for some reason, but I remember her being proud of that, how talented her mother was."

"I guess it must be in the genes," Hope says.

Deborah makes a polite, noncommittal sound as she hugs the bundle of towels.

"You know, last night," she begins. "That's just his idea of lively conversation. Your grandfather is an incredibly smart man. He likes a little verbal sparring to keep him sharp."

"It wasn't much of a conversation," Hope says. "I felt like I was on trial."

"He can be very . . . intense."

"You could say that."

Deborah smiles that placid everything-really-is-okay smile and changes the subject.

"I hope the piano is decent enough for you to practice on while you're here. I'm sure it's not exactly up to your standards."

"Oh, believe me, I've played on way worse." She realizes this may have sounded ungrateful and tries to amend it. "I mean, thank you."

"Well, I'll just put these on your bed for you." Before Deborah leaves the room, she hesitates then says, "He's going to ask about the flat tax."

He does, and Hope's attempts at an answer at that night's cross-examination result in her being pronounced as idiotic as someone believing in a flat earth. The Old Man proclaims her a living example of the kind of "ignorati" produced by this country's horrid public school system. She fares no better at his other debate topics—Catholicism versus Protestantism, Hegel versus Kant, Edison versus Tesla, Mozart versus Salieri—before he finally gives up and goes for the question Hope supposes he'd been waiting to ask her all along.

"How do you expect to support yourself?"

Hope plays dumb. "Excuse me?"

"This music school thing," he says, stabbing at his green beans. "This *piano* thing. Do you actually believe you'll be able to make a living?"

"Right now I'm just training," she says, and he guffaws.

"Oh, you're *training*! Excuse me! And what is it, exactly, that you are training for? Is there some sort of developing military coup requiring the skills of a highly trained pianist?"

She struggles to find the words to defend herself. "I'm *learning* about music and history and piano technique and repertoire, and how to perform what a composer wrote so that it's something everyone can hear and understand."

He chews his vegetables, staring blankly at her to make sure she understands how dumb this is. "I don't *hear or understand* anything in there about a *job*."

"It's not like that, it's—"

But he turns his attention away from her. "What about you, Richard? Don't get any ideas that your clarinet is going to pay the bills."

"I love my clarinet!" Richard says.

"I'm sure you do, but it's not exactly a viable career option," The Old Man says, as Deborah lets out a quiet, "Now, Tom."

"I'm going to be a herpetologist," Richard announces. "That's a scientist who studies reptiles and amphibians, including turtles."

"I know what a herpetologist is," The Old Man snaps.

"Do you know what a cheloniologist is?" Richard is practically vibrating with excitement over the opportunity to enlighten us all.

For some reason, The Old Man is fuming, his face terrifyingly still, reddening as some unimaginable irritation grows. Then he slams his palm on the table, rattling the plates and silverware, and Hope jumps.

"Out!" he bellows.

Richard looks to Deborah, whimpering.

"Get him out of my sight!" The Old Man yells.

"But—" Richard blubbers.

"OUT!"

Deborah talks in a whisper, easing Richard out of his seat and moving him out of the room with soothing words.

"It's just a herpetologist—who specializes—in studying turtles and tortoises!" he lisps between sobs as they go up the stairs, Deborah saying, "Shh, shh, I know."

The Old Man picks up his silverware and resumes eating. After a few bites more, he lets out an aggravated sigh and fixes her with his icy eyes.

"You're excused!"

Hope feels paralyzed. Why had Pauline wanted her to come here, knowing how awful he was? Was it to punish her? Or to explain, somehow, in some convoluted way, what had made Pauline the way she was?

"You," he says, his eyes bright with something dangerous. "Are. Excused."

He looks away from Hope with disgust, his attention seemingly focused entirely on the food still on his plate. "Go!"

Finally she manages to push her chair back from the table, tears of anger burning her eyes. She throws her napkin on her plate and runs up the stairs, leaving The Old Man to finish his dinner.

—⚏—

She expects to find Deborah still consoling Richard upstairs, but instead Richard is in his room, alone. His breathing is still ragged from crying as he sits near his turtle habitat fiddling with some small dolls, army men. Hope knocks gently on the open door to get his attention.

"Hey. Whatcha got there?"

"Come see."

"Ooh, what's that?"

He's putting some of his army men inside an airplane. Another airplane lies on the floor, encircled with rubber bands, and small fallen soldiers lie around it with strings tied to them, like the remnants of teeny parachutes.

"Sometimes I like to crash test my guys," he says.

"Crash test? Like, you put them in there and throw the plane and see which ones fall out?"

"No, no," he says. "I try to make sure they're *safe*."

He grabs the other plane, to show her. "I tried strapping them in with rubber bands, but that didn't work. They all fell out when the plane crashed. So I tried using string. But that didn't work either. Now I'm taping them in. I tried this once before and it almost worked."

He reaches inside the small toy plane carefully, applying liberal amounts of scotch tape to each tiny soldier.

"Do you want me to help?"

He shakes his head, his bangs flopping over his face as he concentrates on his tape seat belts.

"There, I got it," he says. Then he picks up the airplane and throws it into the wall, hard. It falls to the floor and several of the army men spill out, tape hanging off them like clear plastic entrails. Richard investigates the crash site and shakes his head, more sad than frustrated. "It doesn't matter what I do. I just can't save them."

Summoned by the sound of a plane full of doomed army men hitting a wall, Deborah hurries into the room.

"Richard, what on earth? Did you make a dent in the wall? What is your father going to say about that?"

"Sorry, that was me," Hope says, looking at Richard and willing him to stay quiet. "My mistake. I didn't realize my own strength. Just threw it a little too hard, I guess. Sorry."

Richard looks like he might burst into tears again at the mention of his father's disapproval. Deborah looks like she doesn't believe Hope.

"Please be more careful," Deborah says, after a pause, taking in the two of them, and Hope accepts the admonishment as the price she must pay for Deborah agreeing to this version of reality. "Richard, let's get you to bed."

Richard protests with a moan. He is full; the emotional events of dinner are still too near for him to stop himself from full-on sobbing, his tears escalating into hyperventilation almost immediately.

"You can show Hope more of your things tomorrow," Deborah says, cajoling him into bed, trying to get his shirt off him and a pajama top on him as he goes boneless.

"Yeah, totally," Hope says. "We can hang out all day tomorrow. We can do more army guys crash testing, you can show me your turtles. Whatever you want to do."

"Whatever I want?" Richard says, a smile breaking on his blotchy face as it bursts through the pajama top.

"Absolutely!"

"Yesssss!" he says, fist pumping with both fists and dramatically falling back onto his pillow as Deborah tucks his blankets around him. "I know *just* what I want to do! It's going to be a surprise! It's going to be the *best day*!"

"Can't wait," Hope says. Poor kid. He needs a best day.

After Deborah has read Richard several bedtime stories that Hope overhears through the wall, there's a knock at her door. Hope sits up as Deborah comes in and sits stiffly on the edge of the bed.

"I'm sorry about your grandfather," she says. "He does have his moods."

Hope immediately feels the impulse to brush this off, to minimize her grandfather's cruelty, to make Deborah feel better, to be a better houseguest. She makes a sympathetic sound, meant to convey a dismissal, an "it's all right," but she finds herself unable to actually vocalize anything.

"We just all have to be a little more careful," Deborah says. "Tread a little more lightly. When he's like this."

Suddenly, any urge to be accommodating vanishes as Hope shakes her head in astonishment. *Message received: this is how we survive in this house.* This is the lesson she's learned her whole life—be careful, tread lightly, don't fuck it up—but she's never actually heard it said out loud before, and watching Deborah rationalize in real time is unsettling, because even beyond the rationalization, she recognizes what Deborah is doing: she's sharing her strategy for surviving the games.

Until this moment, Hope hadn't connected the dots between The Old Man and Matthew, but now she sees it, and she feels repulsed by it. The Old Man is cruel and ugly—he was charismatic once, she's been told, but now he just seems mean—and it would be easy to see him as someone totally different from Matthew, to wave away his actions as those of a sad old man. But Hope can feel it now, she can see it, and she can't deny the similarities. She also can't deny that as horrified as she is by Deborah's willingness to just go along with it all, Hope has done the same thing. If Matthew is The Old Man, does that make her Deborah?

"When is he *not* like this?" Hope says, her voice almost a whisper. Deborah looks shocked, her eyes big behind her glasses. "I mean, I know some of the stories."

Deborah nods and looks down. "You mean about your Gran."

It feels like breaking every family rule to talk about this, to even hint about knowing this, but Hope is dying to know the truth. "Weren't you best friends?"

Deborah holds up a hand in defense. "We were *friends*. And yes, I regret the way things transpired. And I do miss her friendship. I'm not sure what to tell you, Hope. I suppose I thought I could change him."

Like it had been Gran's fault that he hadn't been able to change. Not *his* fault that he was a jerk, but Gran's fault for not controlling him, for not understanding him, for not curbing his behavior. Hope wants to say, *how's that going for you*, but the hypocrisy of it stops her. Isn't that just what she told herself the whole time with Matthew—that she still tells herself sometimes, when, for whatever shameful reason, she misses him—that if she just loved him enough, things would be different?

"I'm sure you've had relationships with challenging people before. Your mother, I think you mentioned earlier, for instance. Sometimes the best you can do is let them love you the only way they know how. Your grandfather is, shall we say, limited in some ways. But I understand his limits."

Hearing Deborah spell it all out like this makes Hope feel sick. She doesn't want to identify with Deborah, yet this must be exactly what Hope's pathetic internal monologue sounded like, if she said it out loud, trying to justify things to herself. She doesn't want to think of herself this way, as someone like Deborah, who has to believe nonsense to keep herself from acknowledging how broken she is. She shakes her head to brush away the thought. No, she tells herself, she and Matthew were nothing like Deborah and The Old Man. Or Gran and The Old Man. Or Pauline and The Old Man. It was totally different. Wasn't it?

They're silent for a while, and Deborah laughs a little and shakes her head as she confesses. "You know, it used to be worse—as genius as he is now, he was even more brilliant and incisive when he was younger. Those dinner table debates would go on all night. Literally, all night. Until whoever it was he was arguing with properly conceded his point."

Hope blinks. It had been *worse*?

"But he's getting older," Deborah says, patting Hope on the knee as she stands up. "Sometimes you can actually win."

8

It was just a few weeks after Christmas break, the bleakest part of January, when the Incident happened. When, she thought at the time, she fucked up and ruined everything. Sometimes, in her most shameful, self-hating moments, she still regrets having said anything and beats herself up for opening her big mouth, but she tries to keep reminding herself it was for the best, she needs to move on. And besides, there's no taking it back now.

It was like a scene out of one of those embarrassing Lifetime movies. In a rare Matthew-free moment, Hope was hanging out at Jennifer's place, laughing and talking and eating dinner, and suddenly Jennifer saw it. She asked Hope, carefully, "How did you get that bruise?" And Hope looked down and actually said, actually lied to her face, actually, literally told her, "Oh, that? I just bumped into the door the other night, hit my leg." As soon as she said it, she realized how scripted it felt, how cliché. *I'm just so clumsy. I'm always bumping into things.*

"Hope," Jennifer said, her tone worried, serious, as she moved closer for a better look. "It looks like teeth marks."

"What? Come on." Hope laughed, looking away and moving her leg so Jennifer couldn't see the bruise. It was already starting to yellow around the edges, though most of it was purple, ugly, an angry welt on the back of her calf. There was a scab where the bite had broken her skin. "I told you, I just—I bumped my leg. That's it." Hope forced herself to meet Jennifer's gaze, so she could see Hope was telling the truth. She focused all her energy on keeping her face in a smile. But she couldn't keep it up. Jennifer saw her eyes water. She saw her break.

"What the hell did he do to you?"

Hope knew she was talking about Matthew.

Finally, Hope broke her silence. And once she started, she couldn't stop. She told her about the games, about the difference between public Matthew and private Matthew, about the things nobody else knew that Hope had carried as proof of how much she mattered to him, but which were tearing her up inside. Hope didn't tell her everything, but she told her enough. Jennifer held her, and she cried from the sheer relief of not having to pretend everything was okay anymore, and she cried because she was so ashamed, and she cried because Jennifer's tenderness made her realize how long it had been since someone had been tender to her.

All day the next day, Matthew avoided her. He didn't call, didn't return her calls. They'd had plans to have dinner and study together after evening practice, but now she wasn't sure what was happening. By the time Hope finally saw him signing out a practice room for the night, she was adrenalized with worry. Did he know? He must know. He had sensed somehow that she'd betrayed him. He must have, she realized, as he walked past her like she wasn't there.

Hope ran after him, trying to catch up with his deliberately long stride. She was close enough to smell his leather jacket, the scent of his cologne, to see the battered Henle edition Beethoven sticking out of his music bag. People walked by them, fellow students used to seeing them together, and offered pleasantries as if everything were normal. She smiled like everything was fine. Like she always did.

Finally Hope caught up to him at the elevator, and they stepped in, the two of them, alone. He pulled the door shut and hit 3, then 6. He still wouldn't look at her.

"Matthew—" she started.

"I'm going to three, you're going to six," he snapped.

"Please," she said. "Just talk to me."

He faced her, finally, and pulled the emergency stop on the elevator. The elevator was so old it didn't even have an alarm. You could just pull the stop out and stop the elevator. No one would know. It came to a creaking halt somewhere between the second and third floors. Through the small narrow window in the elevator door, Hope could see people's feet walking by just above Matthew's head.

"Talk to you? You mean, like you talked to Jennifer?" He came closer and, in the claustrophobic elevator, the scent of his cologne was overwhelming. "What the fuck were you thinking? Why the fuck would you do that? You have a problem with me, you come to me. Me! Nobody else."

"I'm sorry," Hope said. What an idiot she had been to say anything. She was starting to have trouble breathing. He was so close to her and the elevator was so small.

He noticed her panic, his finger hovering above the emergency stop.

"You want to get out?" he asked, blocking her from the door, from the panel of buttons. Hope nodded, trying not to hyperventilate.

"Say it!" he barked.

"I want to get out," Hope blurted.

"Fine." He pushed the button and the elevator jerked upward. It stopped at the third floor, and he slammed the gate back, pointing at Hope as he started to leave the elevator.

"But not here. I don't want to hear you butchering Brahms next door to me. Go up to six and practice there where no one can hear you."

"Can't we just talk about this?"

He let the gate go and locked it back into position. "You promise me you won't ever talk to her again and then we'll see."

"Okay," Hope said as he began to leave. She said it so quietly she wasn't even sure he'd heard her. She felt even more pathetic promising to give up her friendship with Jennifer than she had confessing what he'd done to her. But in the moment, the thought of being cast out by Matthew was worse than anything. Who even was she, if she wasn't with him?

She went to the sixth floor, because the elevator took her there, and numbly walked to the only practice room with a grand piano. The tiny stalls lining the floor, windowless closets barely big enough for an upright Yamaha, were fully stocked, opera singers shrieking, string players sawing tunelessly through double-stop études, cellists and flautists and trumpeters all adding to the cacophony. But Hope's ears rang with a high-pitched sound that nearly blocked out everything else as she staggered toward the room at the end of the hall in a daze.

Her own hand, turning the handle of the door, appeared to her as a teary blur, and she felt her arms throbbing, her head pounding, her heart racing, her breath catching. Then the handle gave way in her hand, and the door opened seemingly by itself.

"Hey! This is a surprise!" Jennifer said. "Did you want to play through for me? I'm almost done with practice."

Hope couldn't tell by looking at her if she knew what Hope knew, if she had any idea of the damage she'd caused.

"Hope, are you okay?"

"What did you do?" Hope asked.

Jennifer folded her arms. "Is this about Matthew?"

"I know you talked to him." Hope's voice wavered as she forced herself to be steady.

"Hope. This is an abusive relationship. What he's doing to you is not okay."

"No one asked you to do anything," Hope said.

"I know that."

"And now everything is terrible. And I can't talk to you anymore."

"Listen, let's just take a minute, okay? Let's figure this out. We don't have to talk here," she said, putting her hand on Hope's arm. "We can go to the café or something, or we can go to my place—"

"You don't get it." Hope cut her off, shaking her hand away. Hope felt sick to her stomach. She couldn't even look at her. "I shouldn't have talked to you. I can't talk to you."

"What, you mean, you can't talk to me *ever*?" Jennifer said, laughing a little at the ridiculousness of the idea.

"Yeah. Matthew—"

"Matthew what? Matthew *forbade* it? Matthew *commanded* you to not speak to me?" She stared at Hope, incredulous.

"He says it's over if I don't stop being friends with you." Even as Hope said it, it sounded so feeble, so third-grade.

"And that's not enough of a reason that it should be over? Jesus Christ, Hope, he bit your fucking leg!"

Hope felt so ashamed, so weak, so incapable of explaining how terrifying it would be to be permanently out of his favor. She stared at the floor, tears falling, unable to look Jennifer in the eye.

"Fine," Jennifer said, gathering her things. "If this is what you want, fine. There are things you don't know about him," Jennifer said. "You aren't the first person he's done this to."

"I know all about him," Hope said.

Jennifer stopped picking up her things from where they lay around the room and looked at her, her eyes as intense as when she played Prokofiev. "Really? You know about him and Professor Stephens?"

Hope felt sick to her stomach, cold and clammy with the certainty that she was about to retch.

"You can have the room. I'm done." Jennifer put on her coat and swung her music bag over her shoulder.

Hope closed her eyes, unable to speak, and heard the door slam.

Later, the hammering on the door shocked her out of the Beethoven third movement she'd been practicing for hours.

"So are you coming or what?" Matthew barked through the door.

"You still want me to come over? I thought we weren't talking."

"Would we be having this conversation right now if I didn't? Just come. Be there in twenty minutes." Hope heard his footsteps and the creak of the elevator door before she could even formulate a response. Evidently their dinner plans were still on.

It was dumb, she knew it, but she felt herself almost weeping she was so grateful. Yes, Matthew had played games with her before—but he had never been *angry* with her. Not like that. Even as Jennifer's words metabolized within her—*this is an abusive relationship, you know about him and Professor Stephens?*—Hope felt the relief of knowing she was not being abandoned by him.

She gathered her things and stopped at the dorm to cram some clothes into her music bag before she made her way to his apartment. It was cold, the wind biting through her thin coat as the snow fell like lint, her boots slipping on iced-over puddles she hadn't realized were there until they were already threatening to displace her.

"What took you so long?" he asked when he opened the door. He was cooking; Hope could smell pasta and tomato sauce from a can.

"I had to go slowly, it's really icy out there."

He returned to the stove and stirred the sauce. Brahms played on his expensive stereo. It was like nothing had ever happened.

"What is this," she asked, "a piano trio?"

"The C-minor piano quartet," he replied, without looking away from his cooking.

"It's beautiful."

He took the pot off the burner and looked at her like she was completely missing the point. "It's about suicide. He wrote it to stop himself from committing suicide. He was in love, but he was rejected. He wanted to kill himself, but instead he wrote this."

Matthew moved to the couch with his food, eating spaghetti right out of the pot. Hope still hadn't put her bag down. Was she really staying? Was he really speaking to her? Was everything really okay?

"Hop." He paused in his eating. "Sit down, you're making me nervous."

She sat. She dropped her bag. Evidently, she would be staying.

"It's fine, okay? I talked to Jennifer," he told her. "At practice tonight. I talked to her. She's not going to bother you anymore."

"She wasn't bothering me, she was . . ." Hope paused. *My friend,* she realized. Her only friend.

"She was butting in," Matthew said, poking the air with a forkful of pasta. "But whatever. I told her not to interfere. And that you're not going to be her girlfriend, so she can stop trying."

Girlfriend?

"It wasn't like that—"

"Look, I'm trying to tell you I'm not mad anymore, okay?"

He scraped the fork against the bottom of the pot. Could she be hearing this right? Was this some kind of Matthew version of an apology?

"You're not?"

"I thought you were talking shit about me, but she said all you guys talked about was your disgusting bruise. You should put some Neosporin on that."

Hope stared at him as he continued eating from the pot. "Oh, I'm sorry." He looked up, all mock polite. "Did you want some?"

Hope still felt too numb to even recognize whether she was hungry. She felt nothing. She couldn't afford to feel, at this point. Feeling things took away attention from trying to figure out where he was going, what he was thinking, what he would do next. His abrupt shift into "I'm not mad"-ness was a trick. It had to be. She knew he didn't let go of things so easily.

"More for me," he said, shrugging, shoveling another bite in his mouth. He wiped the back of his hand across his face and put the pot down on the table. "Anyway, I thought you'd told her about last year. About how you thought you saw something you didn't. And I didn't want you spreading any rumors."

This was the first time he had ever acknowledged that anything had happened, that there had been something she had seen at all, let alone something she saw that could have been misinterpreted, that could have been fodder for rumors. But she had seen it; she was sure of it. In the foyer outside Soo-Jin's studio, through the barely opened door, she had seen them standing so close to one another, Professor Stephens's hand on Matthew's lower back, her view of Stephens's face obscured by the back of Matthew's head, Stephens leaning forward, pulling Matthew closer. Then she had bent down to rustle scores in her music bag, to make it obvious that someone was there, and Matthew had walked out acting like nothing was wrong as Professor Stephens raced past them, barely saying goodbye. They'd never talked about it, never spoken of that night directly. Not even when the games got bad. Not even when she got sick.

"Hello?" he said, exasperated by her evidently blank face.

"Okay."

"So, we're clear?"

"Clear . . . ?"

He stood up and took the pot over to the sink. "That I'm not gay for Professor Stephens."

Then, as she absorbed the shock of that, he switched back to his favorite topic: how he thought she was faking her illness for attention. Didn't the doctors think she was faking, too, he wondered, seeing as how they couldn't figure out what was really wrong with her? He told her he thought she was acting out this psychosomatic drama because she was scared she wasn't good enough at piano, and if she was sick, she'd get out of having to do the recital and thus escape the possibility of fucking up and proving to everyone how untalented she was. He told her he thought she was doing this because her mom didn't love her. He told her he thought she was doing this for attention, and that everyone was tired of it, tired of seeing her drag herself around looking exhausted and mopey, tired of having to treat her gently. He told her he knew people who were sick for real, his cousin who was sick with HIV, who could be actually dying of AIDS right now. People like that had the right to be terrified, to display their pain—it was real. Not like her, playacting for attention. This was a tough-love speech, he told her, but she didn't feel like there was any love in it at all.

Later, after she cleaned the dishes, they opened the couch, transforming it into a bed. The apartment was so cramped the couch-bed couldn't unfold all the way, and the mattress slanted down into the back of the couch. They lay there listening to Brahms with their feet elevated like hospital patients.

"Who was he in love with?" Hope asked.

"Clara Schumann. She was married, though, and even after her husband went completely insane and was committed to an asylum, she was still faithful to him. So, no go, Brahms."

Hope wanted him to keep talking, to talk about love, about drama that wasn't related to them.

"The first movement is all about Brahms and his pain, the whole love-makes-you-want-to-die thing," he said. "But that third movement—it's about love. It's the most beautiful unrequited love song ever written."

She lay next to him, not touching, but close enough to sense his arms and legs next to her, and listened to the bittersweet opening melody.

"It is beautiful," she said, but he shushed her. She stopped talking and closed her eyes. The music was yearning, sad, and hopeful all at the same time. It seemed to encompass everything she felt in the moment, and she wondered if Matthew could tell. When it was over, he turned to her. Their faces practically touching, their bodies drawn together.

"Hop," he began, then stopped, staring into her eyes as if to forgive her. He enfolded Hope in his arms and they lay there for a while, their heads sloping down into the back of the couch. Hope wanted to say something, but she didn't want to break the spell. Eventually he brought her face up to his, brought his lips close to her lips. Hope began to close her eyes, to yield to the moment, but he suddenly pulled away.

He whispered in her ear, "Unrequited."

She woke up to the smell of breakfast. She was uncomfortable, her neck already aching from the deformed sofa-bed.

"Hey, Hop, come on, rise and shine," he said from the corner of the room that served as the kitchen. "Seriously, we're late."

"What time is it?" she asked, stretching underneath the covers.

"Time to get your ass out of bed. Here," he said, placing a mug on the coffee table. "All yours."

He was already showered and dressed. Hope was a mess, groggy, still in her clothes from the night before, day-old makeup smeared under her eyes. The coffee smelled good.

Matthew grabbed his coat from the closet.

"Are you coming or what?" he said.

"I'm trying—I'm just waking up, and I'm tired."

"You're always tired." Matthew rolled his eyes and said something Hope couldn't hear.

"What?"

"We . . . have . . . to . . . go!" He said this extra loudly while using pretend sign language, as though Hope were deaf or slow or both. He slung his music bag over his shoulder as she put on her shoes, ran her hands through her hair. By the time she stood up, Matthew was already walking out the door, heading down the hallway.

"Come on!" he yelled.

"Where's my stuff?" Hope was trying to move quickly, but she was still hazy from sleep.

"Now, Hop! I can't wait for you!"

"Fine," she said, grabbing the last of her things and running after him, pulling the door shut behind her.

"Why didn't you wake me up earlier if you're in such a hurry?" she asked once she caught up to him in the foyer.

"What am I, your fucking mother?" He yanked the door open and pushed her through. Outside was gray, wintry, the drab look of leafless trees and melted brown city snow. It was freezing, and she stopped short for a moment to catch her breath, the icy air shocking her lungs.

"Hop, GO!" He pushed her again, hard this time. Before she realized what was happening, she was falling, slipping on the icy steps in front of his building, falling onto her ankle, onto the gray ice-slick sidewalk. She felt a sharp burn in her right foot.

"Oh my god," Matthew said. He was laughing. "That was fucking hilarious. You should have seen yourself!"

She didn't move. She couldn't move.

"Oh, fuck, come on, Hop, I'm late!"

He stood there, not moving, just watching her as she struggled to gather her things spilled all over the melting slush, watching her as she struggled to stand. She tried to put weight on her foot, but she couldn't. He saw her wince.

"What, are you hurt?"

She didn't say anything.

"So this is my fault?"

She didn't say anything. He hoisted his bag back over his shoulder and started walking.

"Whatever," he said over his shoulder. "I'm late."

"Matthew!" she yelled after him. "How am I supposed to get home? I can't walk!"

He turned around, walking backward to face her for a moment. "Call a fucking cab."

She sat down on the icy steps, the cold seeping through her coat onto her pants, her legs, as he turned and walked away.

9

The next day, while The Old Man is at work and Deborah is out doing whatever Deborah does, Richard reveals his *Best Day* plan: they are going to ride the Metro. All day.

It's his favorite thing to do, just ride the Metro aimlessly, taking a line to its inevitable conclusion then riding back to the start again. He says Deborah bought him a pass, and that he just likes it. He likes watching the people, likes wondering about where everybody is going, likes listening to the musicians performing in the stations, likes going to places and not knowing quite where he'll end up.

"I like going by myself because I can go wherever I want! I'm the boss of me! But today will be even better, because I get to show *you!*"

"Isn't it dangerous?" Hope asks. "I mean, aren't you worried riding the train all by yourself?"

"Nobody notices me," he says. "I'm just a kid."

Since today is *Best Day*, their Metro excursion is not one of Richard's usual meandering missions. Instead, they take the Metro to Pentagon City so he can show her the mall. It's one of his favorite places, he tells her. Better even than the Smithsonian, he says.

"Better than turtles?" she asks and is treated to an earnest rundown of his personal hierarchy of which turtles are best and why.

Once there, Richard swings her hand as he leads her to the music store he likes, with its listening stations, where he can hear the kind of music he's not allowed to play at home. Then they go to a Borders bookstore, where the people working there seem to recognize Richard, bolstering his claim of being a mall regular. Richard pores through a pile of books about turtles while Hope browses; then they eat in the bookstore café. Richard orders a latte, and Hope lets him. As he continues his attempts to educate her about turtlekind, his face lighting up as he tells her the difference between cryptodires (who can retract their heads fully into their shells) and pleurodires (who can only kind of pull their heads back to the side, which is why they're sometimes called "side-necked" turtles), Hope recognizes she has been unkind to dismiss him as just an annoying kid. Richard is a soulmate of sorts, another sensitive misfit. Another kid trapped in a fucked-up family.

"Hey," Hope says as he finishes his latte, a foamy mustache on his upper lip. She hopes she's not putting a bad idea in his head, but she has to ask. "Don't you ever get tempted? Riding the Metro and stuff."

"Tempted by what?"

"I mean, tempted to just . . . not go home?"

Richard looks confused, and then kind of worried, or maybe shocked.

"I just mean, you're so free, riding the Metro all day, and it goes so many places. If I were you I'd be tempted to just keep riding."

He looks at her with his eyebrows scrunching together as he thinks, frowning, and he looks a lot like Pauline, like The Old Man. "Why would I do that?"

Hope immediately winces. She had thought that maybe he was already at the stage where he realized how fucked up his family was. Hadn't she already started to figure that out when she was eleven? Twelve? But it appeared to be news to him that not only was there a way out, but that he should want to leave in the first place.

"Oh, you know . . . I read some storybook once, about kids riding the rails, living on trains by themselves, without grownups. It seemed fun, and I always wanted to do that. And here you are, kind of doing that."

"Yeah!" he says, visibly relieved. "It's my favorite thing! That's why we're doing it on *Best Day*!"

They take the long way home, Richard humming and bouncing in his seat while Hope looks at the Metro map, thinking about the way she, too, keeps traveling over the same worn path, giving herself the illusion of freedom while never truly running away from home.

At dinner, Hope braces herself for another round of The Old Man's bizarre personal quiz show, but tonight his questions seem more benign. How was everyone's day? How was everyone feeling? Had anyone read the news? Was there anything interesting that had happened? Perhaps Deborah had spoken to him after last night's scene, urging him to cool it. Or perhaps this Good Grandpa Making Chitchat thing is calculated on his part, a role he plays in alternation with the role of Evil Shouting Grandpa to keep everyone wary and hypervigilant and eternally unsure of when the next lightning round of questions will strike. His attempts at normal dinner conversation are almost more unnerving than his death penalty questions.

"The Metro, eh? What do you plan to do tomorrow?" The Old Man asks. Richard bounces in his seat, excited, but Hope can feel the tension underneath everything, like a tightly coiled piano string waiting to be struck by a hammer, waiting to sound.

"I'm gonna take Hope on the Metro again! This time we'll ride to the aquarium! Or the airport! Or we'll just ride around all day to different places!"

For some reason, his son's simple exuberance seems to trigger The Old Man's irritation. Hope feels her stomach drop, and the emotional tone of the room shifts as he mimics Richard and his lisp in a smarmy singsong.

"'Ride around all day to different platheth!' When are you going to grow up and lose that girly lisp? Now, tell me again: Where are you taking Hope? And no lisping!"

"I'm going to—" Richard considers his word choice carefully, avoiding anything with an *s*. "Take her on the Metro."

The Old Man throws his silverware down in disgust.

"That's the stupidest idea I've ever heard. That's just *stupid*."

In a flash Hope is at home, and Pauline is telling her the same thing. "Stupid" is Pauline's highest insult, the word she uses to describe anything she considers pathetic or hopeless, or anything she doesn't understand. According to Pauline, there is nothing worse than being stupid. Especially if you're smart. Hope has always made a conscious effort to never use that word, because she hates Pauline, and she hates that Pauline dismisses everything she's afraid of as being stupid. Now she understands where that has come from. Hearing The Old Man say it is a shock that jars everything into place.

"I enjoyed exploring the Metro with Richard," Hope says. "It was great."

"Really," says The Old Man, amused, leaning back in his chair, that Pauline grin on his face again.

"Really."

"You really thought it was great," he says, daring her.

"Yeah. It was fun."

He regards Hope and Richard for a moment then laughs a sharp, bitter laugh. "Then you're both stupid."

Richard starts to cry.

"Oh, look at you—your girly lisp, your stupid plans, and now you're crying? How are you ever going to be a man, Richard? How are you ever going to be tough? Come here, give your old Dad a punch. Come on, take me! Just stand up and hit me like a man. You can do it, Richard!"

Hope is frozen again, held in place by her sheer inability to accept that this is truly happening, that The Old Man is truly goading his ten-year-old son into hitting him, that he is truly playing the part of some old-timey bully, that nobody is stopping him.

But no: it is happening. There he is, face red, fueled by who knows how many glasses of wine, mocking his own child, demanding that he be "a man," whatever that is. And there is Richard, standing up from his chair and walking to the end of the table where The Old Man is sitting.

Richard is sniffling and hyperventilating, his head down, and The Old Man reaches out and grabs his chin, pushing it up so the boy's tear-streaked face is visible to him.

"Come on, hit me! Hit me!"

Richard just stands there, sniveling.

"I'm not asking you, I'm *telling* you," The Old Man shouts.

The Old Man grabs Richard by the arms, and Richard reflexively flails, pushing against his father.

"That's right, that's what I'm talking about. Come on, Richard, just do it! You know you want to hit me, so just hit me!"

Richard yanks his arms away from The Old Man and hits him, just barely, fists closed, on the chest. He is sobbing.

"What's that?" The Old Man laughs. "That's nothing!"

Deborah finally intervenes, rushing over to the end of the table and enfolding Richard in her arms, his jerky sobs muffled by her soft body. "Tom, he's just a boy."

"Of course he's a boy," he says, his lip curling with disgust. "He's a mama's boy, that's what he is."

Deborah ushers Richard out of the dining room and into the kitchen. His crying picks up volume and intensity as they leave, and Hope can hear Deborah trying to soothe him, though how this awfulness can be soothed away, she has no idea. The Old Man cuts up his steak and forks it into his mouth like there's nothing wrong. He says nothing for a while as Richard sobs in the distance. Finally he says, "This is good. A little tough, but Deborah's done worse."

Hope is still frozen in place, unsure what to do, what she is allowed to do. She hasn't made a sound, but The Old Man shoots her a look as if she's said something impertinent to him. She's expecting an abrupt dismissal, like last night, but again he knocks her off guard.

"Looks like it's just us chickens," The Old Man says, chuckling a little as he gestures to indicate the two of them. "Eat up, Hope! Go on, finish your dinner."

"I'm not hungry," she says, and she's not lying. She feels sick to her stomach after what just happened.

"Come on now, Hope, I won't bite," he says, leering, waggling his eyebrows as he takes an intentionally large and dramatic bite of his steak.

"Won't you though?" she says. His face transforms itself into an angry frown. He looks like Pauline when she gets mad. Hope feels herself flush with adrenaline at her own boldness. "I get it now. I get why Pauline ran away from home. Why she ran away from you. I can't believe you would be so cruel to your own children."

Pauline had told her the story many times. How she had tried to run away many times over the years. How the last time she'd run, as a teenager younger than Hope is now, she'd met up with Hope's dad, dropped her suitcase on his doorstep, told him she'd left home for good. How they went to the justice of the peace and got married. How it was her rite of passage, suddenly going from being a child to being a grownup.

She expects rage, but instead, he laughs. Genuinely laughs. Sits back in his chair, his hands on his belly. He even uses his napkin to dab at his eyes. Then suddenly he is still, his expression now one of mock surprise.

"Oh, you don't *know*," he says. "Of course you don't know! You've only heard Pauline's version all these years. Ah. Of course, Pauline *did* run away from home, a bunch of times. But she didn't run away from *me*. She ran away from *Anna*."

"That's not true." And yet as Hope says it, she realizes that it *could* be true. Didn't Pauline's stories always favor herself, make herself the hero and everyone else the bad guy? Didn't she always dramatize things, make them complicated with details that showed her in a better light? Growing up with Pauline was a constant lesson in learning that Pauline's version of the truth was never actually the full truth. Hope has the uneasy feeling that, as much as The Old Man is a game player, he might actually be right.

"Are you going to sit there and tell me the facts of my own life? No. You weren't there. I was," he says. "And I'm telling you, Pauline ran away from *Anna*."

"But she said—"

"'*But she said*,'" he mimics. "Whatever she said, the facts are this. The last time she tried to run away from home, I was long gone. I was living across town. We were divorced, Anna and I. Had been for years. And then Pauline shows up one night, really playing the sympathy card, waterworks, the whole thing. 'I hate my mom, she hates me'—blah, blah, blah. Oh, she always was so dramatic! So loud, going on and on, she even woke up Deborah. But that's what happened. She came *to* me. She didn't run away *from* me."

Hope sat, arms crossed, determined not to buy it, determined to over-rule the sense in the pit of her stomach that he might be telling her the truth.

"That's not what Pauline told me, and it's not what Gran told me."

"Oh, it's not what your *Gran* told you," he says, doing that thing again where it sounds like he's making a double entendre.

"Why would she run away from Gran to you? Gran was the one who took care of her. Gran was the one who had to pick up the pieces after you left."

Again, she is expecting rage, but instead he sits smiling like he's watching an amusing show, like he has a satisfying secret.

"She ran away to *me* that night," he says slowly, as though Hope is extremely stupid, "because she wanted to find her *real* mother."

His smile twitches with delight as he watches her absorb what he's said.

"That's right. *Gran* isn't your real gran. Anna isn't Pauline's real mom." He takes a sip of wine and leans forward, lacing his fingers, steepling them beneath his chin. "She didn't tell you that part of the story? No?"

Hope shakes her head.

"She came to me that night and demanded that I put her in touch with her real mother. I told her it was a mistake, but there was no stopping her. She wanted to talk to Jean, she wanted to know everything about her, she wanted to know who she was and why she gave her away and where she was and what she did and on and on and on and on. God knows why. That woman was a nightmare. Anyway, I gave her the last phone number I had for her, and then, as far as I know, she went to see your dad."

Hope tries to process everything he's saying. Her grandmother is not her grandmother. Pauline's mom is not her mom. There is another woman out there, somewhere, who is Hope's grandmother, who is Pauline's mom. Why has no one told her before now? Why does The Old Man get to be the one to do it, smiling his self-satisfied smile, so happy to break the news?

"Gran," Hope says, her voice breaking, "*is* my real Gran."

"Well, but biologically speaking, no," he says. "Zero relation to you."

Hope stands up, tears piling up in her eyes. "May I please be excused?"

"Oh, are you running away now too?"

Hope is halfway up the stairs, but he says it loudly enough for her to hear: "Like mother, like daughter."

Upstairs in the guest room, Hope calls home, praying Pauline isn't around to answer the phone. The ringing on the line serves as a countdown to potential Pauline, and Hope scrambles to come up with some kind of plan if she answers, some way to convince her to willingly hand the phone over to Hope's father without prying or demanding to know what's up. But to her relief, her dad picks up.

"Why didn't you tell me?" Hope says, her voice tight with tears.

Her dad just waits. He doesn't insult her by saying "Tell you what?" He just waits on the other end of the line.

"Hello??"

"I'm here," he says.

"Well?" she demands. "Gran isn't Pauline's real mom?"

Her dad sighs. "I'm assuming it was The Old Man? I can't imagine Deborah dropping that particular bomb."

She is so angry she wants to scream, she wants to throw a plane full of taped-in army men right in The Old Man's face, in her dad's face, in Pauline's face, wants to tear down the walls of this room, throw away all their fake happy family photos, burn everything.

"How could you not tell me?" she cries.

"Your mother—"

"Oh, it's Pauline's fault now," she says.

"It's not your mother's fault, but it was her choice, and I respected it."

"Her choice not to tell me that my family is a lie?"

"Listen . . ." He sighs. "Do you want me to get her? She's downstairs, I can go get her, you two can talk this through."

"No! I don't want to talk to her right now, I just want to know the truth. The Old Man said Pauline ran away from Gran, and that she came to him, and that he put her in touch with her real mom, and then she went to you and you guys got married or whatever."

Her dad is silent for a while.

"Well? Is that true?"

"That's not what happened," he says. "Look, you've got to understand. She idolized The Old Man. She still does, I don't know why. She ran away from Gran a dozen times, trying to get him to let her live with him. That night, she came to me in hysterics, sobbing, because she'd showed up on his doorstep saying that Gran had had enough of her, that Gran didn't love her. Now, that wasn't really true—I mean, they fought, but Gran absolutely loved her. *Still* loves her. But anyway, they'd argued, and so

Pauline had gone to him and said that she needed to live with him because Gran didn't want her anymore. He told her that that didn't surprise him, because her *real* mother hadn't wanted her either. And that's how she found out Gran wasn't her biological mother."

Hope tries to imagine herself in Pauline's place, just slightly older than Hope is now, discovering in the cruelest way possible that the only mother she's known is actually not the woman who gave birth to her.

"He told her her real mom was in the loony bin, crazy. He told her she'd abandoned her, probably because Pauline was too needy, always wanting something."

Hope pictures Pauline standing on The Old Man's doorstep—it's raining, for some reason, and Pauline has no umbrella so she's drenched, shivering in the white velvet miniskirt from the wedding pictures Hope has seen, her long, iron-straightened blonde-red hair beginning to clump into curls in the rain—watching his face as he tells her these cruel secrets, the joy he takes in hurting her, in ridiculing her need.

"He turned her away. Sent her home. But she couldn't go home, couldn't face Gran. She was too mad, and too sad, and felt too guilty for being angry with Gran for keeping this secret while also taking care of her all this time when she didn't even have to. Or so Pauline thought at the time. Anyway, she came to my parents' house right afterward, and they said we couldn't live together unless we were married. So I proposed."

"Romantic," Hope says.

"Yeah, well."

Hope wants to ask more. Now that there's a crack of the truth letting some air in, she wants the whole window open. She wants to know every-thing. How did Gran agree to be Pauline's mother? How did she keep on being her mother even after The Old Man left? Why did Pauline care so much about The Old Man's affection? Why didn't Pauline ever tell her about any of this? But suddenly she hears a sound on the line.

"Hello? Hello? Is someone there?"

"What?" her dad says.

Is it Pauline listening in? Is it The Old Man? There's another click as whoever it was hangs up. Hope says goodbye to her dad and hangs up with an unsettled feeling. No place is safe here.

Hope brings the phone back up to her ear, the dial tone's mechanical note soothing in its blatant simplicity, no variation, no vibrato, just a single blaring tone. Her fingers rest on the holes as she fights the urge to dial Matthew's number. What would be the use in calling him? What could he say to her now that would make any difference at all? Finally, she replaces the phone in its cradle, slowly, gently, the way she imagines whoever was listening to her call did, easing themself away in the hopes of forgetting whatever they had overheard.

10

After the Incident—the push down the stairs, a moment of violence she had finally allowed herself to fully acknowledge—Hope was totally frozen out by Matthew, this time for real. He couldn't even look at her. The only time he even talked to her after she showed up at school in an ankle brace was to threaten her, to tell her that if she told anyone her twisted ankle was his fault, she'd pay for it. The thing was, she realized with a shock—she almost didn't care. She was so unmoored by what had happened between them, and by how afterward she had become consumed by how sick she was, by how the doctors couldn't come up with any diagnosis other than her pain being her fault somehow; so thrown off by the anticlimax of slogging through appointment after appointment, test after test, only to have herself be identified as the culprit; so exhausted by the pain. It made her numb. And the numbness made it almost as though he couldn't hurt her anymore. Nothing he could say would be as hurtful as the pain coming from her own body. Nothing he could say would be as devastating as realizing that everyone seemed to agree she was in a prison of her own making. But if that were really true—if her illness was something conjured up from her own imagination—why couldn't she imagine her way out? Why couldn't she just imagine it gone?

Before, being shut out by Matthew was unthinkable. It would mean she would disappear. But as she pushed her way through the reality of it, she was surprised to discover that she didn't mind the exile. It wasn't as awful as she had imagined it might be. She reached out to Jennifer, made tentative attempts at repairing their friendship. She went to her doctor appointments. She floated in a haze of medication and exhaustion. She moved through the world as though she were underwater, heavy limbs displacing invisible, heavy currents as she made her way to the practice rooms. She practiced half asleep. She dreamed that she was practicing. She dreamed that she was awake.

Then there he was, two days before spring break, pounding on her practice room door again. After shunning her for weeks, now he demanded to come in, and when he looked at her, he seemed like a stranger. She saw him more clearly, suddenly. He was just a normal person, standing there in his jeans and rumpled T-shirt, his dumb cologne. He didn't look like a person who had any power over her.

"I don't want to fight anymore," he said.

"Okay."

"I have to tell you something, but you can't sit there all mopey and pretend-sick, you have to just stop fucking around and be normal."

"Okay."

"I'm serious, just drop the act," he said.

Hope just sat on the bench. No reaction. This made him mad.

"This is what I'm talking about, Hope, this is why it's so impossible. You pushed yourself into my life, you just *had* to be my best friend—you asked for this! And now you're acting like it's some kind of punishment."

"What are you talking about?"

"I kept telling you and telling you—didn't you get it? I kept pushing you away, but I couldn't get rid of you. Do you even know how desperate you are? You really are hopeless. That should have been my pet name for you. Not Hop."

Hope sat blankly, staring at the piano keys, not him, letting the game continue, trying to wait it out.

"And then this 'illness,' like, it's so obvious that it's about attention! Your mom doesn't love you, I don't love you, no one loves you! Poor Hope!"

"I thought you said you didn't want to fight," she said quietly.

"Listen," he said, coming over to her, suddenly contrite, kneeling in front of her at the piano bench, tears on his cheeks. Suddenly he was kind again, holding her hands gently, looking at her with a sadness that seemed like it was genuine, like it was not a game. "The problem is, I *do* love you, Hope. I love you so much. I love you *too* much. And all of this, all of the games, everything was just me trying to protect you, okay? That's what all of that was about, I was trying to save you. I pushed you away because I'm a terrible person, I'm a fake and a liar and you deserve better than someone like me."

"What are you talking about?"

"I'm . . ." he said, breaking down. "Me and Professor Stephens . . ."

"You and Professor Stephens what?" she asked, and he stopped mid-sob to stare at her with something like despair or disappointment in his eyes, she couldn't tell.

"Jesus, Hope, what do you think?"

She didn't know what she thought. She thought about all those nights they'd lain in bed next to each other, touching but not touching. She thought about him introducing her to his family, spending the holidays together, him telling his mom *meet your new daughter-in-law*. She thought about him telling her he loved her, that he loved her more than he'd ever loved anyone, that she knew him better than anyone ever had, that she was closer than he'd ever allowed anyone to get. She thought about him and Professor Stephens, about him telling her over and over she hadn't seen what she thought she saw. She thought about him saying *soulmates*. She thought about him saying *unrequited*.

"You were supposed to make it okay," he said, sobbing. "This was my last chance, and I thought if I loved you enough, if you loved *me* enough,

it wouldn't be real, but it didn't work. And then instead this happened."
He stood up and gestured to Hope, as if he were gesturing to her illness,
her pain itself. "And I had to watch it happen, I had to watch you be sick.
And it broke my heart and scared me to fucking death because either
you're legitimately sick, or you're pretending to be sick, and if you're really
sick, then maybe you're sick because of me. Because of who I am. Which
means maybe I'm sick too."

It all clicked into place for her, finally.

"I don't have HIV," she said. "That was one of the first tests they did.
It was negative. So whatever I'm sick with, it's not that."

He looked sick with relief, until she stood up and started to get her
things together, preparing to leave.

"Where are you going? We're not done."

Hope tightened her ankle brace as she leaned down to shove her music
back into her bag. "I think we are."

He grabbed her arm, twisting it a little, holding it too tightly. But she
stood her ground.

There was a time when she couldn't have even thought the words, and
now she heard herself saying them. "I need you to let me go."

He stared at her, as if seeing her for the first time, and released his grip
on her arm.

That was the last time they would speak before her trip.

11

Hope dreads having to face The Old Man the next day, but as she wakes up to the sounds of Deborah busy readying the house for guests, she remembers: it's Easter. Perhaps the neighborhood kids and their parents coming over for Richard's egg hunt will provide a buffer against him. Or The Old Man will be tame today, due to having to be on his best behavior in front of witnesses. Either way, it's Hope's last day here. Soon she will be out of this madhouse and back to her regular life. Which is, of course, also a madhouse.

Is it fucked up that The Old Man is insanely obsessed with Easter? Hyping it up for Richard, talking about the egg hunt like it's a matter of life and death? Pauline, for all her craziness, had never been religious, and mostly Hope grew up not really celebrating anything, but she remembers Pauline telling her once that Gran was actually Jewish. Until now, Hope thought that technically made *her* Jewish, since she understood it was something passed down from mother to daughter to daughter. But The Old Man overruled that notion (as surely as he'd overruled Gran's traditions when they got married) when he told her the truth about Gran not being related to her by blood, and now here she is, not knowing anything anymore, not knowing what to believe, having to participate in a holiday she doesn't care about on behalf of someone who doesn't care whose traditions he ignores.

Deborah has her help with the macaroni salad, dumping whole jars of mayonnaise over giant bowls of pasta, then sends her to set up the paper plates and plastic cups and utensils on a porch table festooned with pastel-colored streamers. The Old Man is outside, surveying the backyard, a glass of whiskey in his hand, even though it can't be later than 10:00 A.M.

"Is it time yet? Can I start?" Richard yells as he runs onto the porch.

"Whoa there," The Old Man says. "We have to wait for all our guests! Wouldn't be right to start the hunt without them!"

Richard deflates good-naturedly, his arms drooping at his sides. "Aw, no fair!"

"That is precisely the definition of fair," The Old Man says, but he's smiling, so Hope feels less worried for Richard.

Then Richard grabs The Old Man's free hand and smiles up at him, blinking his eyes rapidly, looking as innocent as possible. "Can you give me a hint, at least? About where to start?"

The Old Man laughs at this appeal, swatting him away. "Of course not!"

Richard deflates again, this time for real.

"I can give you one piece of advice though," The Old Man says, taking a sip of his whiskey.

"What's that?"

The Old Man smiles, and it's a cold smile, a mean smile. "Look hard."

The neighbors begin to arrive, everyone in their church best. Little girls in frilly dresses with ribbons in their hair, boys with their hair combed and shirts with buttons. The grownups are all old and beige like Deborah and The Old Man. Some of them are the dressed-up kids' grandparents. They are all pleasant to Hope, tell her it is lovely to meet her, inquire about where she's visiting from and how she's enjoying her stay. Everyone mixes around, sipping drinks and eating Deborah's lunch spread, until finally it is time, and the egg hunt begins.

"And they're off!" The Old Man says. He's on his second drink by now.

Richard is so excited he trips over his own gangly feet as soon as he tries to run, much to the amusement of The Old Man. But he picks himself up and starts chasing after the other kids to look for the eggs. Then he runs back and grabs Hope by the hand.

"Come on! You have to! This is my *favorite* holiday," he says, breathless from scampering between potential egg hiding spots. "I've waited for this all year!"

"You might want to pace yourself, Richard," The Old Man calls. "It could take awhile to find all of the eggs." He's standing on the porch, looking incredibly pleased with himself. Hope isn't sure if it's the alcohol, his natural narcissism, or if he has some plan they don't know about.

Richard becomes increasingly panicky as the egg search drags on and he's finding nothing. In fact, none of the kids seem to have found any of the eggs.

He pulls Hope as they run to places he's looked before, desperate for her help. He's starting to cry. "I can't find the eggs, Hope! Where are they? They have to be here!"

"Oh, you can't find them, Richard?" The Old Man calls out from the porch. "Did you look *everywhere*?" He asks this like it's a trick question, and he laughs like a crazy man. Hope feels the hairs on her arms stand on end. Everything about this feels wrong. Richard falls against her, sobbing.

"I can't find them anywhere," he says, tears and snot running down his face.

"Sure you can, Richard," says Deborah. "Here, let me help."

"No." The Old Man stops her. "Let him do it himself! He's such a baby, with you always babying him, and this is a baby's game. He's looking for eggs, for Christ's sake. How hard can it be?" His mouth quivers with laughter when he says this, though, like there's a joke they're not in on. The other kids retreat to the porch with their parents, confused, and the parents, sensing something is up, begin to herd them into the house.

Hope stands there with Deborah, both of them helpless as Richard begins making his rounds of the yard again, alone, looking behind flower beds, kicking over rocks, checking between bulging tree roots. Hope can hear him sniffling all the way over where she's standing, and she wishes she could go grab him and take him away, run away from home with him. Why doesn't Deborah do that?

"I—I—I—" Richard is crying full force now, stuttering and hyper-ventilating, his hair sweaty on his face.

"Spit it out!" The Old Man commands.

"I j-just can't f-find the eggs anywhere, and I looked everywhere they could possibly be, and they're not there! I can't find them!" he sobs.

The Old Man looks triumphant.

"Of course you can't find them!" The Old Man is practically jumping with excitement. His face is red, his smile leering. "Of *course* you can't find them, Richard. Do you know why? Do you know *why?* It's because *I buried them!* That's right, I *buried* them!"

He laughs and claps his hands, and his laughter doubles him over, it's so strong and loud. His eyes are watering, and his face is red when he stands up. "I buried them!"

Richard runs to Deborah and drags her back into the house.

"Tom!" is all she can say. Her face is a cloud of betrayal, disapproval, fear.

Hope watches The Old Man laughing, thoroughly enjoying himself, while the other parents look on in shock.

"Oh, come on, you sticks-in-the-mud! It was just a fun prank!" He walks out onto the lawn, unsteady and half falling over. "What a bunch of spoilsports. I'll dig them up. Richard, where'd you go? Come help your old man dig up these Easter eggs!"

But Richard is inside, and the other children are crying and clinging to their parents in confusion, and Hope hears the grownups begin to make excuses to Deborah, who stands helplessly in the doorway, trying her best to be a good hostess as The Old Man drunkenly wanders the yard.

Hope can't help it: her first thought is that she has to tell Matthew what just happened. He would love it, the awfulness of it, the shock of it, and she can imagine herself telling him the story, boasting her way out of the shame of it, as she goes upstairs to her room to pack. She grabs the phone and sits on the bed. Her train is in a few hours. She feels so guilty leaving Richard behind, but what can she do? Richard, Deborah, and even Pauline—they're all trapped by The Old Man, but Hope has a way out at least. She'll leave a note for Richard, she tells herself. She'll promise to come back for another *Best Day*, just the two of them, or have him come visit her for a *Best Day* wherever she is. They'll ride the train together as far as it'll take them.

She dials the phone and the line rings and rings in her ears, and for a moment she allows herself to imagine that it might be Matthew answering, that he might be happy to hear from her, just like in the old days, that everything they knew about each other could be forgotten—that he might say *thank god you called, Hop. I missed you.*

But instead, she hears the comforting voice of her grandmother on the other end of the line.

"Gran?" Hope manages to choke out before the tears close up her throat. She didn't expect to cry, but somehow all the emotion of everything—her fucked-up family, her fucked-up relationship, her crazy grandfather—tumbles out of her.

"Well, hello, my dear! This is a nice surprise! I thought you were at your grandfather's. Are you surviving your visit?"

"I just . . ." Hope sniffs back tears, unable to hide the fact that she's crying. "I just don't understand."

"Don't understand what, dear?"

"Why Pauline sent me here," she says. "It's really bad, Gran. I mean. I know you know. But."

Anna sighs on the other end of the line. "I do indeed know."

Hope's hitched breathing is the only sound for a few moments before Anna finally speaks.

"You know and I know that your mother is her own spectacular person. And you know and I know that you two have had your challenges. I, too, had a, shall we say, *complicated* mother—as you might know from the stories your own mother may have told you. But she did give me some very good advice once. She said: 'You can't change other people. *You* are the only person you can change.' I used to think that meant changing myself to accommodate someone else's behavior, or changing myself to allow the other person not to change. But that's not what it means. Sometimes it means you need to limit contact with someone. Sometimes it means setting boundaries with someone else. Saying no. Or just moving on. And that's okay. Now, it took me a long time to really understand that, and to put it into practice in my life. But it's very true. And I believe it applies here."

"To Pauline?"

"To your mother, sure. And to your grandfather, of course. And to anyone else who might be in your life who makes you feel like it's a full-time job trying to make them love you."

Hope holds the phone to her chest for a moment as she tries not to cry out loud.

"Can I call you when I get back home?" she says, finally.

"Yes, you do that, and you can tell me all about your visit. And about anything else you'd like to tell me. We're due for a lengthy phone call."

"You may regret making that offer after I talk your ear off," Hope says, trying to laugh.

"Well, you let me be the judge of that. Talk to you soon, dear. I love you."

"I love you too," Hope says. She hangs up the phone and packs her bag, and even though it's full of heavy things, she feels lighter than she has in months.

LISE

Letter to Anna, dated 1971

1

A week passed, and I crescendoed and decrescendoed between anxiety over Mor's absence and elation over how his absence freed me. But more than anything, his absence was an *ostinato*, a low nibbling worry that ran beneath everything I did. Even when I was concentrating on other things, even when I was not actively trying to detect it, it was there, the subtle, constant hum of wondering where he had gone, and why, and when he would return.

Samuel had stayed with me that first night, I had allowed him to stay, because it felt wrong for me to leave the apartment and go to his place, which was the only other option I had; but I was chafing with worry, with the feeling that all of this was wrong. I had lain awake, tense with the waiting, my ears alert for Mor's footsteps in the hallway.

Samuel stirred in his sleep and his arm drifted, heavy across my stomach. For a moment, I allowed myself to think: It would be so easy. I could abandon this place, and all the memories in it. I could go with Samuel. Trade the uncertainty, the instability, the guilt, the shame, for the safety of him.

You might wonder why I felt such allegiance to Mor, to our obviously broken marriage. You might ask why I didn't say yes to Samuel right then, why I didn't leave with him that very night, why I didn't walk away and let us begin our life together. These are fair questions. You were already destined to find me, and I was already destined to be your mother; but so much could have been different. So much could have changed if I had walked away then instead of later. I wouldn't have had to lie to you for all these years. I wouldn't have felt so guilty.

But I was not omniscient, I couldn't know then what I know now. And more than that, there was something crystallizing in me that was only beginning to take shape, that had to do with what Madame Augustine had said at my brief piano lesson, before everything fell apart. She had spoken of playing with intention, and I was beginning to recognize that that was what I needed to do. I needed to stop just allowing things to happen and having those things become my choices by default. I needed to make choices in the first place, with intention.

How exactly to do that in life and not music, I wasn't sure. But I was able to know this, finally: I did not want to be some helpless woman, taking shelter with whatever man could protect me. I needed to make choices with intention. If I was choosing Samuel, I needed it to be a choice.

"And what will you do," Samuel had asked that first night, his finger-nails lightly tracing up and down my arm as we'd lain in bed talking, after I told him I couldn't go with him to live at his place.

"I'll find a job," I'd told him. "I'll find a job and pay for the rent and electricity and food, and . . ."

"And wait for Mor," he'd said, his fingers the slightest bit heavier, slower, blunter.

I'd sat up, drawing my knees to my chest. I did not want to wait for Mor. I did not want to continue to make myself a prisoner to his choices. But I was trying to be careful about my own choices. I was trying to be right, in the midst of all I had done wrong.

"No," I said. "Not waiting. Preparing. When he returns, I want to be ready. I want to be able to speak to him clearly and to explain to him the decisions I've made. And to know for myself that I've made those decisions because I meant to. Perhaps this doesn't make sense."

But Samuel had sat up, too, had put his arm around me and kissed my hair, had stayed with me in the quiet.

"This doesn't mean I can't see you," he'd said, after a time. And I'd kissed him, deeply, and leaned back beneath the weight of his body, turning away from the door, forgetting about waiting for footsteps, everything forgotten but the two of us, together, a furious kind of mourning.

But when it came time for him to leave, finally, when he could no longer stay with me, keeping vigil for the sounds of Mor's footfall on the stairs, it seemed it didn't make sense to him after all.

"I don't understand why you won't come stay with me, rather than be here, alone. Are you performing some kind of penance? Are you punishing yourself over his leaving? Over us?"

"It's nothing like that," I told him.

"You are as obstinate as he is when he has a mind for something. Do you know that?"

I wanted to be obstinate. Needed to be obstinate. An obstinate woman wouldn't be shut up in the hospital on her husband's say-so. An obstinate woman wouldn't stop making music so as not to be an inconvenience to someone else. An obstinate woman wouldn't be slapped, be abandoned, wouldn't have let her husband leave. An obstinate woman would make her own choices.

We stood near the door, preparing to say goodbye, and I felt hyperalert to each murmur of voices, each rustle of sound that approached. I tensed as I heard heavy footsteps growing louder, then stopping, and watched the doorknob for signs of movement, for the door giving way to Mor with his suitcase, his pained expression. But then the footsteps continued, and I heard the sound of keys against a faraway door, and I knew it was just a neighbor, not Mor, not Mor returning, not yet. The sounds waxed and waned, nearby tenants walking past and continuing down the stairs, away from where we waited.

Samuel pulled me into an embrace. "There are a thousand ways to imagine undoing what's already done. Don't torment yourself. None of this was your fault."

I would have liked to believe that. But I would also have liked to believe that if I retraced my steps thoroughly enough, I could erase them, erase what happened, undo everything, make everything better. And yet, as I laid my head against Samuel's chest, felt his heartbeat, the warmth of his arms around me, I couldn't help but ask myself, wasn't this better? Wasn't this so much better?

Then he kissed me and was gone, and I stood, resting my back against the door, listening to his footsteps diminuendo away until they were *pianissimo*, triple *pianissimo*, inaudible, and I was left in the apartment, the morning sun brightening the windows, Mor's absence filling everything.

I had no luck at my old job—cleaning houses was not as lucrative as it was a few years ago, my former boss Mrs. O'Brien told me, when more people could afford a cleaning service—but I was directed to a Mr. Kirsch, supervisor of a button factory in Queens, who was rumored to be hiring. This rumor proved to be unfounded, as I discovered when I was turned away, along with dozens of other women. But I persisted and, as much to shut me up as anything else, Kirsch suggested I speak to a Mr. Farber, who oversaw a sewing factory near Brooklyn that was in need of piece workers.

The work was brutal, and paid by the piece, six cents each, so I had to work quickly and take care not to overstress the machinery, which seemed to break if I so much as looked at it directly. The longer I had to wait for a supervisor to repair it, the less money I made. So I was careful. There was no time for talk, for socializing. We were given an hour for lunch, supposedly, but no one took it, not when there was money to be made by continuing to work. Some women kept their food with them at the tables, and ate when they could, but space was at a premium, and seniority mattered. I, like the other new girls, stored my lunch under the bench where I sat. The rats pilfered some of it, but there was usually enough left over for me to manage. I took the subway each morning at 6:00 A.M., worked my 7:00 A.M.–6:00 P.M. shift, and took the subway back, exhausted, numb, my fingers sore, my eyes tired from squinting at the fine work in the low light of the factory floor. Dinner was whatever I could manage to put in my mouth before I fell asleep. And I slept soundly. When I dreamed, if I dreamed at all, I dreamed of work, of rows upon rows of machines I mustn't break, of piles of pieces that unraveled, disintegrated, turned to dust, before I could turn them in and claim my pay.

Sundays I had off, and Samuel came to me, bringing food, newspapers, flowers sometimes, even though I wouldn't be there to see them bloom the next day, would instead find them drooping in the vase when I came home at night, petals blanketing the table, the piles of mail.

Letters came for Mor, and more than that, when I looked through the piles of mail he'd left behind, I found letters with postmarks from months before, letters he had evidently ignored. Bills. More bills. A postcard from Connoisseur Publications, Inc., alerting Mor that a work of his was discussed in the current issue of *PRINTS* magazine, and offering a year's subscription for $3.00. I placed correspondence like that in a separate pile, for Mor to read when he returned. An advertisement of an upcoming exhibition at the Roerich Museum. Added to the pile. A bulletin from the Artists Union. Added to the pile. A letter from the Whitney Museum. Added to the pile. A second letter from the Whitney Museum. Added to the pile. A third letter from the Whitney Museum. Added to the pile.

Normally I wouldn't even think of opening Mor's mail—normally I wouldn't even have had the chance to consider such a thing, as the mail was Mor's domain, and I only saw what he shared with me, if there was something that had come in my name, or something he deemed worth sharing.

But three letters from the Whitney Museum?

I opened the one dated earliest and had to read it twice before I fully understood: Mor had been invited to show in the exhibit. The same exhibit that Rafael, Samuel, Alfred, and Peter had celebrated being a part of that awful night. There was a form for him to fill out and return, he was to list the works he'd chosen to have in the exhibition, he was to include a brief paragraph of an artistic statement.

Oh, Mor—all of that angst and worry for nothing! I held the letter to my chest, closing my eyes for a moment before opening the other two letters, noting that the date on one of them was the night of the dinner, the night of Mor's abrupt departure. That letter said that his spot would be withdrawn if he didn't respond in a week's time. And then the last letter, confirming it: *Since we have not received your form indicating either your acceptance or refusal of this invitation within the time frame specified, we are rescinding our invitation to have your work featured in the exhibition.*

My heart sank. If only he'd opened the mail! If only he'd stopped for a moment to pay attention, to discover some good news, for once. If only he hadn't left—if only *I* hadn't left that day, if only I'd made dinner, if only we hadn't gone to the restaurant, if only he hadn't been so hurt, if only I hadn't made him so angry. He had been upset over nothing. He had left me for nothing. He had gotten what he wanted and hadn't even realized it. And now where did that leave him? Where did that leave me?

The fourth week of my employment, when I arrived at the factory, there was a line of women and girls marching, holding signs. Someone was shouting through a bullhorn. I tried to enter the building to begin my shift, but a woman stopped me, holding me by the arm.

"Are you a strikebreaker?" I recognized her as a worker from a nearby table. "I never figured you for a strikebreaker."

"Excuse me?"

"We're on strike. We won't go back unless we can get eight cents per piece. And only work til four o'clock on Saturdays."

I looked at the people around us, walking, chanting. I saw the foreman standing at the factory entrance, gesturing emphatically as he argued with another man. I had a flash of a memory, of Mor, years ago, marching as part of a demonstration in front of City Hall, proudly brandishing his hand-lettered banner: *Talk is cheap, living is not!*

"I need work," I told the woman.

"Don't we all." She laughed. "Some of us just like to get paid what we're worth."

"Either come in to work, or leave the premises immediately!" the foreman shouted.

"Well?" the woman said.

"Those who work today will be paid ten cents per piece!" the foreman yelled. "That is a guarantee!"

"Ten cents," I repeated.

"Empty promises." The woman scowled. "And even if it were true, it wouldn't last. We want changes for good. Better pay. Better hours."

The woman gestured to me, offered me a place in the line of marching women and girls, but I shook my head. "I won't break the strike, but I can't stay. I need to work."

It was immediately clear that my decision to leave was, to the women marching, essentially the same as if I had decided to break the strike. But I had to go. I had to find something else, another job, something to pay the bills, something that couldn't be stopped by a picket line; something to sustain me with Mor gone. I took the train to Queens, back to the button factory, to Mr. Kirsch, who still wasn't hiring; back to the city to Mrs. O'Brien, who still didn't need any more girls to clean houses or take in washing. Then it was lunchtime, and for once I was outside, in the sun, able to take whatever time I needed to eat the food I'd brought with me, no rats to fight with over crumbs, no looming thoughts of money wasted as I ate instead of worked. It was almost decadent to have such leisure, and I savored it, standing in the sunlight, my eyes closed for just a moment as I took a deep breath.

I ate an apple, a piece of bread, as I stood outside the subway station, watching the people go by. A violinist played on a nearby street corner, his hat on the ground, everyone rushing past him, as if he wasn't playing at all. It called to mind the violinist I'd seen on my walk to the piano store—my jailbreak, Rafael had called it—who had inspired me to find a place to practice. I packed away my lunch bag and felt around in my pocket for subway fare. I had two nickels left. The equivalent of nearly two pieces, if I had been able to work today, maybe ten, fifteen minutes' worth of work. Before I entered the station, I walked over to the violinist and put one of the nickels in his hat. His eyes remain closed, and he swayed with the music, and I paused for just a moment to listen before turning back to the station to head toward home.

Samuel refused to give hints as we walked downtown, toward the Village. He had allowed that we were walking in the direction of his studio, that we might be going to his studio, that the "something" he had for me might be waiting in his studio. But he wouldn't answer any of my questions, and he wouldn't divulge any other information, so for most of the walk we were silent.

I had been out of a job, still preparing for Mor's return, for nearly two weeks, and nothing. Just time passing, and mail addressed to him, and bills coming due for which I had no money to pay, and the empty apartment with me in it. Samuel came and got me, insisted I shower, change my clothes, leave the apartment. He had something to show me, he said. So we walked.

It was strange to walk beside him again. Everything felt different outside the world of the apartment. Outside, we were conspicuous. Outside, I was reminded of the facts. My husband was missing. Samuel was his friend. I should not be taking his hand as we walked, or putting my arm in his, so we walked like strangers, careful to avoid being too close to each other.

Soon we reached Charles Street, between Greenwich and Waverly, and he had me wait outside while he went in, evidently making sure everything was the way it should be.

Samuel covered my eyes as he guided me into the studio. He held his hands in front of my face, hovering more than touching, but I could feel my stomach leap, my face flush at his proximity after our walk apart from each other.

"I can't see," I protested.

"That's the idea. Just keep going. A few more steps . . . A little to the right . . . There. You can stop now."

I sensed that he had taken his hands away, that he was standing behind me, waiting for me to respond, but I kept my eyes closed, both to savor the moment and because I was nervous about what he had prepared for me. It reminded me of my time in the hospital, eyes closed, opening only in secret, slowly, allowing only a glimpse of the world through my blinking eyelashes before shutting tight again. I opened my eyes and saw my shoes, the floor of his studio, drop cloths spattered with colors muted by age and dust, before finally raising my eyes to take in what he had intended for me to see.

"Well?" I felt his hand hovering near the small of my back as he moved to stand beside me.

Samuel's studio was also his living space, yet it was less cramped than my apartment, more filled with sunlight, with promise. The walls were white, the ceilings tall. Though it was essentially one large room, it didn't confine or restrict. The colors of Samuel's work everywhere made it seem vibrant, welcoming. His new paintings, versions of fairy tales he had been working on in secret, he had told me, afraid of what Rafael and the others at the Collective might think, leaned against the walls. In one of the paintings, a boy with claws for hands and feet climbed along a kind of glassy surface, an animal pelt on his back. There was an eagle, a pit of twisted bodies, an apple tree. In another, a typical winter landscape hid a golden key, almost completely buried in the snow, and, in the opposite corner, beneath a snowdrift, an iron box. The third was unfinished, featuring a handless woman seated on the ground near a pear tree. The painting leaned against the wall, beside a tall window—right next to an upright piano.

It looked natural there, inevitable. As though it had always been there, waiting for me.

"Samuel," I whispered, not trusting my voice. "What have you done?"

"I've found your piano," he said.

"*My* piano?"

I walked to it, felt the silky lid, ran my hand down the left side of the case—and there it was, the gash, the legacy of the first time he helped deliver this piano to me as a surprise.

"Your piano," he said. Now it was my hands that were hovering, as if touching the instrument again would reveal it to be a mere hallucination. "I had an idea about where Mor would have had it taken—there are only a few pawn shops that even consider large musical instruments—and once I found it, I knew that the right thing to do would be to buy it back. To return it to its rightful place. Which is with you."

I turned to face him, and he took my hands.

"You should be playing," he said. "You should be performing, you should be playing on stage, for an audience. If you were my wife, I would want you to play as much as you wanted to. I wouldn't hide you away. I wouldn't keep you for myself. I would want you to share your music with everyone."

I stared at him, my face awash in tears, and felt his hands becoming tentative.

"I'm sorry," he said. "That was insensitive. Considering the circumstances."

"No." It came out as a sob, and I gripped his hands more tightly.

"You can practice here, any time you want. You can practice while I work, or even when I'm not here. I want to hear you play. I love to hear you play."

How could this be, that I should be given this piano not once, but twice? That I should have the chance to play again, to practice? How could I be deserving of such a gift? But also, how could I accept it? This had been Mor's gift, and his punishment, as much as it had been mine, and I felt suddenly wary.

"I have loved you for so long, Lise," Samuel said. "From the start, all these years."

I pulled back from him abruptly. "Don't say that."

"But it's true."

I untangled his hands from mine, and my voice was harsher than I meant it to be. "Don't talk to me about love. Love is what kept me locked in my own home. Love is what took my piano away from me in the first place."

"And it's what brought it back to you," he said. He took my hands again, caressing my fingers, my palm, the ridge of my knuckles, the fading scars on my wrists. "I want you to be able to play. I want you to be able to make music. I want you to be happy."

I allowed myself to be folded into his embrace, my cheeks wet with tears, his hands soothing my hair, my back. It felt so good to be held, to have his arms around me, to be safe.

"I don't know what that means," I whispered into his chest.

"You will," he told me. "You will."

2

And then, of course, they found the body.

The papers said it was a suicide, that he had jumped to his death.

I told everyone it was a suicide too.

But Samuel and I knew the truth.

On the floor above where Mor and I lived, there was a gap in the wire enclosing the old elevator shaft. The bottom of the shaft was littered with detritus after years of disuse. There was garbage from tenants, old rusted equipment, broken bicycles, children's toys, filth, the workings of the old elevator.

The coroner theorized that Mor had come home, drunk and despondent, and had made his way up, let himself through the opening, and fallen eight flights down. The coroner theorized that he might have lived, had he not been cut on the sharp metal awaiting him when he fell, causing him to bleed out, from a wound in his neck, primarily.

We kept quiet even as the papers characterized Mor's death as accidental. They wrote of his work, lauding him with praise, some places even calling him a genius. Finally, he had the acclaim he'd always felt he deserved.

Samuel and I waited a respectful amount of time after the funeral, and we were married. I was already nearly four months pregnant with you. We never told a soul the truth about Mor's death.

Samuel never wanted you to know. He thought it might pain you, might complicate things. He would be the only father you ever knew, he *was* the only father you ever knew, and he loved you—you know how much he loved you.

And he loved me too. Oh, how he loved me.

That is why I waited to tell you, wanting to respect his wishes that you not know while he was alive that you were anything other than his.

I understand your anger, at both of us. I understand now that you should have known, that you had a right to know. I remember what that was like, being told truths about my past that I didn't remember, that felt bewilderingly untrue, disputing the reality of my memory. I remember how unsettling that was, the groundlessness, the sense of betrayal. That is why I indulged you after you finally learned the truth, gave you so much space, allowed you the disrespect of referring to him as Samuel and not your father.

But we had our reasons. I understand if you do not understand them. But I haven't told you all of them until now.

I had to respect Samuel's wishes, after what he did for me.

Because, despite what the papers said, Mor's death was no suicide.

I killed him.

3

It had been nearly eight weeks.

I was just coming to accept that Mor might really be gone when he returned.

I had made the long walk back to the apartment that night from Samuel's, the June sun still strong as it lowered in the sky, the air still warm and humid, planning to force myself to go through the bills again, to force myself to consider what I might do if Mor never came back.

But when I tried to unlock the door to the apartment, I realized it was already open, and I found myself unprepared, filled with fear and dread.

"I see you have gotten on without me."

And there he was, at the table, his suitcase at his feet. His hair was too long, his clothes—the same clothes he had been wearing the night he left, I noted—were shabby, he was disheveled and in need of a shave. But it was Mor, home again, once again in this apartment, once again in the world.

The door to his studio was slightly ajar. Had he come back for his things? Was he planning to stay or go?

"Lise, my Lise," he said, almost a minor third.

"I am not 'your' Lise." My name came out like a hiss, my teeth clenched.

"It was a terrible thing I did, I know that now, a terrible thing." He was standing now, pleading.

"Which terrible thing?" I demanded. "Hitting me? Leaving me? Punishing me? Forbidding me to play?"

His face twisted with confusion, but also irritation, and he threw his arms open. "All of it, everything! What does it matter? I am begging your forgiveness. The specifics aren't important."

I began to understand: this wasn't a goodbye. This was an apology.

He started walking toward me, but I held up my hand.

"I was wrong, Lise, I understand now. It was wrong of me to leave."

"Eight weeks, Mor," I said, my voice breaking with angry tears. "Two months you were gone. What was I to think?"

"I'm here now," he said.

I shook my head, blinked my tears away, and walked past him to the closet. I yanked my dresses from the hangers, my things from the dresser, and put it all in a bag.

"Lise," he implored.

But I walked past him to the bathroom, grabbed my hairbrush, my toothbrush, and past him again, to the bookcase, taking my most prized music scores from the shelves. I would go to Samuel. I would tell Mor the truth. I would confess to everything, and this time I would be the one leaving, for good.

"Don't you want to know where I was, what I was doing? I made some very good connections, I have a lot of prospects now, a lot of opportunities—I did this for us, don't you see? Things will be better now, I swear it. I can take care of you. I need you."

"You need me?" A scrim of tears obscured my view, and I wiped my eyes angrily as he continued to beg me, as he walked closer to me.

"Lise, stop," he said. "What do you think you're doing? What is this madness? You're packing? You think you're going somewhere?"

I could see that he expected this to be a conversation we would continue, a chord that would resolve, that would be forgotten by the time I made him dinner.

"I'm home now," he said. "You don't need to go anywhere."

My heartbeat rushed in my ears, my hands shook from the adrenaline. "I'm leaving," I said.

He sat back down at the table heavily, sighing, his hands running through his hair, rubbing his eyes, clawing at the collar of his shirt.

"Oh, Lise, enough of this nonsense."

"It is not nonsense. I'm leaving."

"Fine. I wanted to work in my studio anyway," he said, gesturing to the door. "Just don't disturb me when you come back."

"I'm not coming back," I said. This was not the careful way I had envisioned this conversation. But I knew in my heart this was what I needed to do, what I needed to say. "I told you, I'm *leaving*. I'm leaving you."

At this he sprang up. "No."

"No?" I almost laughed. "The man who left is telling me I'm not allowed to leave?"

He came at me quickly, tearing the bag from my shoulder, spilling its contents on the floor, grabbing my arms. "You're not going anywhere."

"I am," I said. "I'm going to Samuel's."

He gripped my upper arms more tightly, shaking me, pushing me back against the wall, against the doorjamb near his studio.

"I knew it," he shouted, a crass *sforzando* on the word "knew," slamming me with the force of his certainty. "It's not enough he should steal my place in the Whitney show, he should also steal my wife?"

I tried to squirm out of his grip, but he held me pinned to the wall.

"This isn't about you," I said. "I love him. And he loves me."

This time when he hit me, it was no accident. His hand connected with the side of my face, and I staggered a bit from the shock of it, falling into the doorway, against the door to his studio. He grabbed me again, shaking me, and now his hand was around my chin, around my neck as he yelled unspeakable things at me.

The weight of him lunging at me, grabbing me, choking me, caused us to fall against the studio door, which gave way, opening, and we tumbled into the forbidden room. I fell onto a pile of papers, and he fell on top of me. I scrambled backward, trying to get out from under him, searching for purchase among the papers covering the floor, but he was able to launch himself forward and put his hands around my neck.

All around us, in massive towering piles, was his work: stacks of paintings, sketches, charcoals, oils, watercolors, notebooks, portfolio folders, every surface covered. Even his table, even the typewriter, was buried under canvases. Stacks on the floor, the bookcases filled, piled up to the ceiling, canvases leaning atop one another, sticking together, falling apart. A painting still in progress sat precariously atop another pile, the canvas stretched across an easel that was only upright due to the stack of paintings it leaned against.

There had to have been hundreds of pieces, and the ones that were visible to me appeared to be variations on the same theme. Well, you've seen them; you know. But imagine what it was like for me to realize in that moment what I was looking at. Whether they were paintings, drawings, sketches, pastels, all of it featured the same haunting subject, reiterated in various ways, and no matter the style, no matter the genre, each one had the same expression, the same gaze that met me wherever I looked, the same eyes beseeching me from every surface.

My eyes.

The endless hoard of portraits of me looked on as he gripped my neck with more and more force. I couldn't breathe, I was frantic to breathe, and I struggled, my arms and legs flailing in an attempt to break free of him. I hit the side of the table with my arm, dislodging a precarious pile, and a sheaf of papers slid over us, more sketches, along with a tumble of charcoal pencils, erasers, and a shower of something that glinted as it fell toward my face. I grabbed at the air, at the floor behind me, hoping to grip one of the pencils, hoping it would be sharp. I turned my head as much as I could with Mor's hands around my neck and saw what it was that had caught my eye. There, on the floor, were three razors. Souvenirs, I assumed, from his days of weaponizing the piano.

I grabbed the closest one before he had a chance to realize what I'd found, and I gripped it clumsily with my fingers, feeling the edge of it slicing into my skin as I plucked it from the floor and plunged it into the side of his neck, just under his jaw. His hands instinctively moved to his throat, and he looked at me with a stunned expression. The razor dug into my fingers, but I pushed it in deeper and dragged it down and across as best I could, just a little, just enough.

His blood was slippery, a deep crimson, pulsing through his fingers as he held the side of his neck, as he tried to talk. I pushed myself back, to move away from him, to get out from under him, and he fell forward, blood pooling on the pile of newspapers and sketches that lined the floor. I moved back farther, scooting myself backward into a corner, knocking into a stack of paintings and sending them scattering to the floor, surrounding me. My face stared back at me from each one, a painted hall of mirrors, judging me, and I realized as I looked into so many versions of my own face, looking back at me with a seemingly inexplicable kind of sadness, that I still held the razor in my hand, that I was bleeding, and that I had killed him.

The elevator shaft was Samuel's idea. He had seen the gnarled metal and refuse that lay at the bottom, the way the disused shaft had become a communal garbage dump for the building, the way the children liked to push things through the wire fencing to see how long it took to hit the bottom. He knew from Mor's complaining that there was a large opening in the wire on the floor above ours, how he hated the upstairs neighbor who occasionally used it to throw his trash down there, how years before a child playing there had nearly fallen through.

It would look like an accident. Or a suicide. Either way, the blood and the cut I'd made would be masked by the other injuries he would sustain in the fall.

I helped him carry Mor up the flight of stairs in the middle of the night; he pushed him through the wire and watched him fall. He cleaned my wounds. He gathered my clothes and the newspapers and sketches and everything else that was covered in blood and took them all to the incinerator. By the time the body was found, the bruises on my neck had almost healed, the cuts on my fingers no longer visible. It was easy to play the grieving widow, because I was grieving, truly, still in shock over what I had done, what we had done, and thus I was completely believable talking to the detectives, who seemed to think it was plausible that Mor had left me, come back for me, been despondent that I had taken his friend as my lover, and gotten drunk and either fallen or jumped to his death.

Samuel found a place to store all the portraits and papers from Mor's studio, someplace humidity controlled and cool, to preserve them. For all the years we were married, he paid for this. It was only after he died that I even thought to look at it all again, to organize it somehow.

And for all the years we were married, we never spoke of it. Not the art, not the obsessive number of portraits of me; not what happened that night, the second time he found me with a razor, covered in blood.

4

Which brings me to you.

I knew the moment I saw you that you were his. Red-faced and pinched, your mouth open, screaming, it was as if you were his tiny ghost, come to avenge him. Your colickyness was my punishment, I was sure of it. The shape of your nose, your chin. Your dark hair, your darkness.

Sometimes you looked at me as if you knew the truth. Your eyes with so much depth to them, with the old-soul look of someone much older, much wearier. It was hard for me not to see the accusation in your gaze, the coldness of it just before you smiled, running to me with arms open for a hug.

Sometimes I felt myself your captor more than your mother. I forbade you to create. It wasn't a conscious thought at the time, not a thoughtful, measured decision on my part; but over the years as I thought about all this, I came to understand that I did what I did because I didn't want you to be tormented by the pain of not being good enough, or by the equally exquisite pain of being too brilliant. I thought it would protect you. I thought preventing you from making art might save you from whatever madness your father had found there. I made myself distant from you. Afraid of becoming trapped under your power the way I had with Mor, afraid of losing myself to you, I held you at arm's length, never extending myself to you the way I should have.

Samuel loved you as if you had his eyes, his nose, his chin. He encouraged you, always, right from the start, never afraid of what might lie in wait for you. You remember how he was your champion, how he sheltered you from my emotions, how you and he were such a cheerful alliance. I was haunted by Mor, haunted by the Mor in you, but it was Samuel who insisted that you were not your father, would not be your father, could never be your father. So you must not blame him. Or yourself. If anyone is to blame for the distance between us, it is me.

When you found some of the paintings in the process of moving me to this place, I was shaken to be confronted, after all these years, with everything we had locked away. My face, everywhere, accusing me, holding me in judgment. Everywhere I looked, I saw my own eyes, witnesses to the truth.

This is why it is my wish that you should destroy them. When I am gone, I want you to go to the storage facility and remove everything and burn it all. All the portraits, all the correspondence, everything. I do not want his version of me to be my legacy.

So now you know everything. And I am sorry.

It has taken me a long time to understand how I wounded you, how my own wounds prevented me from understanding exactly how much I hurt you. But I do understand.

It pains me to understand it, too, to know that in trying to silence Mor the way he had silenced me—to truly silence him, and banish him from my life, to silence all traces of him—I shut down and silenced myself, which meant I silenced you. I mourned the coldness between us as I watched you grow beyond me, as I watched you live past me, away from me, apart from me, even though I pretended that was what I wanted. I mourned this as I watched you from afar, the way you loved your children, even those that weren't yours—how you always corrected me, saying of course they were yours, you loved all of them the same. I marveled at this. I marvel at you.

But I also mourn this as I finally understand that I have been complicit once again. Just as I had once allowed Mor to be my jailer, forbidding me music, I allowed him, in my treatment of you, to jail me again, forbidding me the fullness of love between mother and daughter. I wish I could say that this was his fault. In the past, I'm sure I would have. But here, at the end of my time, I see my own offenses plainly.

I couldn't see then that my worry was not protective, but destructive. I couldn't see then that my forbidding you to explore your own interests in music and art was as constricting as what he did to me. To me, they were two different things, my impulse to protect and his impulse to control. But I understand now that they are more similar than I realized.

I had hoped to inoculate you against heartache, against madness, but instead I guaranteed you would find it, as surely as if I had laid the path before you and sent you down it.

I regret our estrangement. I can only hope that you can try to understand it came from the best of impulses, all of it. As broken as I am, I tried. It came from love.

Trauma reverberates. It echoes. I know this now. It is the seed of an idea in the first three notes of a symphony, the motive that is the skeleton of not only the melodic but the harmonic structure of a piece, framing everything while the theme develops. The ominous bass figure, repeating and repeating. But I will tell you what I tell all my students, what my teacher told me: that the best performance—the best art—is, at its heart, a lie, and this lie is only allowed to grow, to thrive, to perpetuate itself and become real if both the performer and the audience enter into the illusion of it. A lie doesn't work if the person being lied to doesn't believe it.

I see that you have worked hard not to believe it. You have worked hard not to be complicit. I took this personally, yes, I admit, but even I can see what a good job you've done in your own life. I never showed you how; you figured it out by yourself. And so that gives me hope that I haven't wounded you too much. That love, wherever you find it, or even if you create it out of nothing at all, is stronger than any pain you might have.

I hope you understand now, having read all this, that this was my clumsy, self-serving attempt at an apology. But do not be alarmed, I am not asking for your forgiveness. I am only offering this to you, to read, to consider, to understand; to know the things I always wished you could have known, but which I could never say.

That is my main regret: that I could never say what you needed me to say, as your mother. I could never say the words I hear you say—sparingly, it is true, but with such sincerity—to your own children. But I say them to you now, in the hopes they are not arriving too late, and in the hopes that you are still able—still willing—to receive them. I love you. And it is the most significant achievement in my own life that I am able to see you capable of love, of loving your children so fully. In this I am learning from you still, even now, when it no longer matters anymore.

ZOEY
2020

Of all the people I had to tell, it was hardest to tell my mom. Not because I didn't think she'd accept it. But because I knew she would.

I just didn't want to have to see her face reacting, so full of worry, and then fear, and then confusion, and then relief, and then worry again, and then clarity, and then her eyes suddenly looking off into the middle distance, focused on thoughts about how she might turn this into her own story, into something that made sense for her, turn away from the chance to be fully enmeshed in the meaning of it for me in her rush to transform it into something triumphant for us both.

In English class this year, we talked a lot about etymology, which is basically like word X-rays. It's a way of thinking about words that lets you see the secret history of words that's built right into words, giving their meaning even more meaning. I'm probably not explaining it right. But like: "Trauma," the word, has a sense of turning about it. The original word means "wound," but there is a deeper root word there, buried in the *trau-* part of the word, that is *tere-*, which has as its first meaning "to rub or turn," a sense of something piercing, twisting, or threshing.

("Traum," by the way, is an entirely different word that has nothing to do with trauma. It's usually translated as "dream," but is related to the word *triegen*, which means "deceive.")

The point is, it got me thinking. Coming out as trans wasn't traumatic for me. It was more like exhaling a deep breath I hadn't realized I was holding. It was like telling the truth, finally. But I worried it might be traumatic for her? And I didn't want to have to see her face twisting, turning, didn't want to have to pierce her comforting ideas about who I am with new facts that might flood her with worry. She loves me, and she cares about me, and I knew she'd accept me no matter what. I just didn't want to have to watch the frailty of her in the act, witness her in the moment of coming to terms with it.

She was the first person I told, so I didn't even have a story yet. I just had the feeling that I couldn't have this knowledge as something that existed, without even secret words, only inside my head, and that to make it real for myself and the world, I needed to say it out loud to someone. So I tried. I stumbled. I tried to find a starting point, but everything I said felt false, and whenever I blurted something inadvertently dramatic, I could see my mom's eyes flash, simultaneously bright with worry and with strategy, framing it for herself so she could respond to me as Mom, Supportive, with Deep Wells of Empathy.

So I was clumsy at first. I talked around it. I talked about a lot of things. I used vague words like "identity" and "self." I sneaked up on it, and once I could see her coming to some sort of realization about it, I could see her sneaking up on it, too, dancing with my dance around a thing that was too big to say all at once.

But finally we reached some clarity, and I felt my body both relax and finally express the anxiety and stress of this information I'd only barely allowed myself to admit in the privacy of my own mind. I lay on the couch and she stroked my hair and told me she loved me, and maybe she was doing these things because, in her mind, she thinks that's what a Good

Mom would do, but I also allowed for the possibility that this wasn't an act, that her love was genuine, and that I really deserve it, even though I hate myself.

I don't actually hate myself. Well, I do. But, fun fact: hate has its roots in *kad-*, which means "sorrow," hatred, grief, calamity, mourning. And what I feel is both more dysphoric and less of a vibe than that. My self-hate is fundamental, just a part of who I am. An innate sense of not deserving. There's another offshoot of *kad-*, which is the Welsh word *cas*, meaning pain or anger. That's closer, I guess.

But I don't hate myself because I'm trans. Being trans is probably the only thing I feel good about myself about, if that makes any sense. My depression is a totally separate thing. I describe it like: imagine a cookie. Now add rainbow sprinkles on top. You see? Depression is the whole boring cookie; being trans is the rainbow sprinkles. If you take those sprinkles away, the cookie is still a cookie. It's still there. It's just less colorful.

The second hardest person to tell was my grandmother. Oh, and Grandpa Ted. I always forget about him. But mostly because it wasn't him I was worried about. Grandma Pauline, however, is a big mood. She's the kind of person who has ideas about you before you're even born, and then once you exist, she's got a whole life planned out for you in her imagination, which I don't know for sure if she fully realizes is not a shared reality.

So my mom and I kept it to ourselves for a while—probably too long. Once I was brave enough to ask everyone else to use the right pronouns and my new name, once I'd finally decided on a name for myself (that's a whole other story), it felt painful to have to pretend for her, to have to listen to her as she said h* and h*m and called me by my old name and act like it didn't feel like a lie. After a while it felt more hurtful to myself to keep going like that than it did to disappoint her with the truth. But I still couldn't handle an actual conversation about it. So, even though emails stress me out, I wrote her and Grandpa Ted an email. I told them that I wanted to share something with them that was important, meaningful, and exciting for me, which was that I was transgender, which meant that I'm actually a girl. I told them that this was not a crisis for me, but a relief to finally feel at peace with who I am. I told them that what I wanted them to know most was that I loved them, and that I was the same person they'd always known, the same grandchild they'd always known.

Then I broke out the list of FAQs I was sure they'd have that I in absolutely no way wanted to answer in person, for the same reasons it was difficult to tell my mom in person—I couldn't bear to watch their faces while I attempted to answer or explain. So I tried my best to cover every-thing they might possibly ask, and I mean everything, so that these kinds of uncomfortable IRL conversations might be avoided. I started off with the most basic one I thought they might have: "What is 'transgender'?" I gave them the definition (from the Human Rights Campaign website) and continued with the following:

What does being trans mean scientifically?

Are you changing your name?

What if we mess up and call you by your old name and pronouns?

Are you sure you're trans?

Is this a phase?

Aren't you too young to make a decision like this?

Aren't you too old to make a decision like this? Don't people who are *really* trans know it from the time they're very young?

Are you okay?

You don't dress like a girl. Don't you have to dress like a girl to be a girl?

Does being trans mean you like men?

Does being trans mean you like women?

What if you want to have kids?

Is being trans a mental illness?

Doesn't this mean you won't be able to have a normal life?

Are you taking medicine?

Why are you doing this to us?

Isn't life going to be so much harder for you now?

Do your friends know?

How can we learn more about this?

How can we help support you in this?

Why didn't you tell us sooner?

I wrote out answers and cited my sources, where necessary, like it was my final paper for English. Mostly I tried to reassure them. I told them they didn't have to understand it all right now, that they could simply listen to my experience and trust what I was saying. I suggested they "learn on the job" by using the language I use, calling me Zoey and referring to me as "she" and "her," and reminded them that they could also get support for themselves, whether through talking to friends who have children or grandchildren who are LGBTQ+, or finding a support group, or even speaking with a therapist. But basically, I told them, there really isn't anything you have to do other than continue to love me the way you always have.

I was nervous after I hit "send," and even more nervous to discover a response the next morning. I made my mom read it to me, and it took her a while. She just stood there silently, and I knew without even looking at her that her face was probably transforming into the world's saddest anime character, and then when she finally talked, her voice was squeaky with tears. Grandma Pauline had written back and said, "Dear Zoey, I am so pleased to make your acquaintance. Grandpa Ted and I are reading through the questions and answers you sent, and we both appreciate your thoughtfulness and thoroughness. We love you, and always will. Love, Grandma Pauline."

"Welp," I said, and my mom hugged me tight and cried all over my hoodie.

"She called you Zoey," she sobbed.

"She did," I said.

I think maybe she was more relieved than I was. But it's true, Grandma Pauline is an unpredictable person, and it really could have gone either way. I'm glad it went the way it did though.

Anyway, that's the "background, identity, interest, or talent" without which my application would be incomplete. Although honestly, applying to colleges right now seems pretty ridiculous. *List your activities.* Uhh, how about not dying during a global pandemic? *Write about a time you overcame something.* *Gestures at everything.* My guy.

Anyway, I don't know why a whole backstory is even necessary when this essay really only needs to be two words long: "I'm trans." If a college doesn't accept me, it's a hate crime.

COMMON APP ESSAY PROMPT:

The lessons we take from obstacles we encounter can be fundamental to later success. Recount a time when you faced a challenge, setback, or failure. How did it affect you, and what did you learn from the experience?

One lesson I learned recently from my mom is that it's important to "know your audience." And the reason I say that is because the whole reason I'm now doing this partial hospitalization program, supposedly curing my depression via Zoom, is because I made a joke at the doctor's.

I had to have a doctor's appointment, because my school actually believes it will be reopening again, and I needed to have my yearly physical. Joke's on them: I'm never going back to IRL classes ever again. But it turns out the joke was on me, because I had to go to the doctor's in person, because even in the middle of a pandemic, you still need to have your vaccines updated, evidently, and they haven't found a way to do that via the internet yet.

The doctor was a nurse, who had on a paper mask, a plastic face shield, and some wraparound glasses over her eyes. She kept fiddling with the glasses as they fogged up and slid down, fighting with the band of her face shield to stay on her head.

"Do you mind?" she asked me, holding up her phone. "I have a resident doing their pediatrics rotation who's shadowing me via FaceTime."

I squinted and saw a person in scrubs waving at me from the nurse's phone.

"Uh, I do kinda mind," I said, even though I felt bad for minding, and the nurse quickly turned away. It was weird enough to be interfacing with her with my mask and her mask and all this garb, like we were playacting a doctor's appointment in weird costumes; to have it all further removed into a play of a play, playing out on someone else's FaceTime for learning purposes, was too much. I heard her talking with the resident and promising to call her once the appointment was over. And then she was back, facing the computer and looking at my file.

"Okay!" she said, fake and bright. "Do you mind if Mom stays here for this part, or would you like some privacy?"

I shrugged and looked at my mom, who looked at me and shrugged back. "It's fine."

"Alrighty," the nurse said and began to look through the teen mental health questionnaire I'd filled out, the one they make us fill out at every visit. It was difficult to read any kind of facial expression, since even her eyes were somewhat obscured, but I could tell from the tone of her voice, when she started talking to me again, that she had Serious Concerns.

"Zoey, from what you've indicated here, it sounds like you have been experiencing some significant depressive episodes."

"What do you mean?"

"I mean, it says here that you have thoughts of hurting yourself or others pretty much daily."

"Just myself," I said.

"Pardon?"

"Just thoughts about hurting myself," I said, louder. "I don't care about other people."

"You don't care about other people?"

"No, I mean, I care about people. I just only want to kill *myself*. Not anyone else. So, just harming myself, not others."

She sat back in her chair. I realized I'd said the "I want to kill myself" words, the bad words, and this had likely alarmed her. But she sounded kind of calm when she spoke next. "Okay, and you have these thoughts—about killing yourself, specifically—daily, you'd say?"

I snapped my fingers into double finger guns and pointed them at her. "Passive suicidal ideation every day for six years, bro."

She couldn't see my sarcastic smile. We were literally wearing masks, obscuring ourselves, performing a charade. None of it was real. Or everything was too real. I couldn't decide which.

My mom stepped in. "Zoey uses humor as a coping mechanism," she said, talking to the nurse but really warning me to watch it. "She sees a therapist and also has a team at the gender clinic. There's no imminent danger."

"I see," the nurse said and typed for a long time in my file. Finally, she said, "So, you have suicidal thoughts, but you don't have a plan?"

"Nah," I said. "I'm bad at planning."

"Zoey, this is serious," my mom said.

"I know! I'm seriously bad at planning!"

My mom was not amused, even though this seemed like the kind of thing that would normally crack her up. "She's asking you these questions for a reason, and the way you answer them determines what kind of care she might recommend."

Then she looked at me with her eyebrows raised and her eyes urging me to get it, this message she was sending me, and I thought I did: if I kept talking like this, they'd put me in a hospital.

"Zoey," the nurse said. "I just want to be clear: You definitely don't have plans to hurt yourself? Or your mom?"

My mom and I were both caught off guard by that one.

"Hurt my *mom*?" I asked and laughed a little, because of how preposterous that sounded, but the nurse wasn't laughing, and from what I could see of her eyes, she wasn't even smiling. My mom knew how crazy this was, I could tell, she knew I would never. But I could see from both of their demeanors that I was going to need to spell it out.

"No, I don't have any plans, and I don't intend to hurt my mom."

"Or yourself?" the nurse prompted, and I could see my mom lean forward a little bit like a very restrained version of someone trying to jump in front of a moving train to stop me from saying "of course I want to hurt myself! I have suicidal ideation!" and starting this whole ridiculous line of questioning all over again.

"Not right now," I said, finally, even though that was kind of a lie, and I could see the doctor and my mom relax.

I never wanted to talk about it. With anyone. But especially not my mom. Not because I thought she wouldn't accept it or understand it, but because I *knew* she wouldn't accept it or understand it.

Actually, I didn't even tell her, she just noticed after we got back from the doctor's appointment when we were talking, when I'd forgotten to swath myself in a hoodie the way I usually do. I saw her eyes get wide first, and then I heard her voice, which sounded high-pitched and choked somehow, like she had something stuck in her throat. And then I thought, oh fuck, here we go.

"Zoey, what have you been doing to yourself?" She asked, grabbing me by the wrist, exposing my pale arm, most of the scabs still bumpy, pinkish, and red, some almost faded into nothingness. I had avoided fully taking off my hoodie at the doctor's office, citing body dysphoria, because I knew there was no way the nurse could push me on that without looking like an asshole. Instead I strategically raised my hoodie for her, lowered it when she asked me to, and pulled it to the side so my upper arm was exposed when it was time for the shots. I never took it off. So she never saw the scars.

"What does it look like," I said.

"Zoey!" She sat down in my desk chair, looking like she was going to cry, but also like she was really scared, and also like she was really mad.

"What have you been using to do this," she demanded. "How long have you been doing this? When have you been doing this? *Why* have you been doing this?"

I sat on my bed and rolled over to face the wall, pulling the blanket over my head, not wanting to answer, but she yanked the blanket off me, hard, like she was mad, not caring that it landed on the floor, that it might get dust bunnies on it from the corner of the room where they always seemed to gather.

"What," I said, and she was like, "You have to answer me, this is serious."

So I told her. I used the knives in the knife drawer upstairs, the good ones, the fancy ones, the ones with their own special sharpener. I did it at night, when no one was awake but me and the cats, who swirled around my legs, hopeful that my presence meant a midnight snack. I told her I'd done it for a while now, I didn't know how long ago it started. How long does it take cuts to heal? A few weeks, maybe? A month? My oldest ones were barely visible.

"And why," she prompted.

"Because it's the only thing that makes me feel better."

"It doesn't make you feel better. It hurts you."

"But it does make me feel better."

"But it doesn't. You only think it does," she said.

"And I'm right," I said.

"You're not. You have the proof right there on your arm: it hurts you. And it could do more than that. Those knives are sharp. You could cut too deep. You could actually kill yourself."

I didn't say anything in response because what I wanted to say was, *yes, that's the fucking idea.*

She just sat there and stared at me, and she was crying and I hated it. I had cut myself without telling her because I hadn't wanted to bother her with my bullshit, I hadn't wanted to make her feel worse than she already did, especially with her MS flaring. And yet there I was, doing both.

But then she said, "Honestly I thought you were better than this," and I didn't feel bad about it anymore because *excuse me?*

"Excuse me?" I said.

"You're better than this. Cutting is like—I don't know, it's for pretend-sad emo girls! It's cry-for-help bullshit! Don't look at me like that, you know what I mean."

"Way to shame my coping strategy," I said.

"There are a million other ways to cope," she said, crying again. "Literally, I could list a hundred things you could do instead of this. And fine, sure, I'm shaming. I'll shame you. If that's what it takes to make you stop, I'll do it, I'll do whatever. Because this scares me. This is dangerous."

I just sat on the bed, not looking at her, rubbing my fingertips over my scars. It bothered me that they were fading. This conversation honestly just made me want to do it more.

"Also. I sat there with you in the doctor's office and was like, 'Oh, don't worry, everything's fine, Zoey's just joking!' And instead you're cutting yourself?" She looked at me like she was the one who was wounded. "That makes me look like an idiot, like one of those oblivious parents."

"This isn't about you," I muttered, but she caught that I'd said something, so I had to repeat it, louder.

"It absolutely is," she said, sitting forward in my chair. "If it's about you, it's about me. You're my kid! Do you honestly think it wouldn't affect me if you hurt yourself? Why didn't you talk to me?"

I sighed and rolled my eyes because, hello, exhibit A right here. This. This conversation. This was why.

"I didn't want to worry you," I said.

"Well, too bad. Because guess what? I'm pretty fucking worried."

"Mom," I said, but she held up her hand.

"I knew you were struggling, I knew you had . . . thoughts, but I didn't think—" She drew her breath in sharply and started to sob. I sat on my bed and watched, feeling like shit, wanting to hug her but also feeling mad that I wanted to hug her, because she should be hugging me. But then she said, "Do you know how awful it is to find someone you love passed out, almost dead, barely breathing, because they tried to kill themselves?" and I felt a sickness in the pit of my stomach.

"I'm not Grandma Pauline," I said, and then I stood up and went to her, because she was really crying hard, and I could feel it, I could feel how that was for her as a little kid and how she carried it with her now. How a part of her was probably still eight years old calling 911 to say she'd found her mom in the bathtub with her wrists bleeding. Seeing my cuts probably brought it all back to her. Stupid, stupid, stupid. What a stupid fucking idiot I was.

She hugged me and we were both crying, and she said, snot from her tears getting all over my shoulder, on my hair, "You can't leave me. Promise me."

I just hugged her, because I wanted to promise, but I couldn't.

"Pinkie swear," she said into my hair. "Pinkie swear that you'll at least talk to me before you do this again."

"Okay," I said.

She pulled back to look me in the eye, to gauge if I was telling her the truth.

"Okay?"

"Okay," I said. But I didn't offer her my pinkie.

We sat on my bed, side by side, and I told her again, "I'm not like Grandma Pauline."

"I know," she said.

But, I wondered, what if I was?

As if she could hear me thinking, my mom said, "Grandma Pauline had her own issues. She had a tough start in life that made it hard for her to ever overcome it."

"I never had anything happen to me," I said. "There's no reason for me to feel this way."

My mom put an arm around my shoulders. "You don't have to have a reason to be depressed. Sometimes it's just brain chemistry."

"But there's literally no other reason for me to be like this. My life is fine. You didn't abuse me or whatever."

My mom sighed, almost like she was impatient with me, and was like, "Zoey. We're in the middle of a pandemic. Your life isn't *fine*. It's hard. It's beyond hard."

But we both knew this had been happening way before there were even warnings about a virus, before anyone knew to hoard toilet paper and antibacterial wipes and hand sanitizer, before idiots started saying masks were some kind of tool of political oppression. I have wanted to die for a long time now. The virus just gives it some added context.

"This isn't because I'm trans," I tell her, before she can suggest it. I can see as soon as I've said it that she's been wondering, that she's been waiting to connect the dots.

"But the estrogen though—it's a serious thing, it can mess with your moods. I'm not saying to stop," she said, seeing my face.

"Then don't say it."

"I'm not, it's just, maybe it's a good idea to back off. To go back to the lower dose."

My scars itch and my skin feels tight, and I only notice it because usually I never feel much of anything, and this makes me realize that I am having emotions. Probably anger. Or fear. Or both.

You can see why I didn't want to tell her. Even when I didn't want to be alone in all of this, I didn't want to tell her. Her love for me was always going to be too much. It would make me feel unworthy, and also mad. It would obscure me. It would make her launch into problem-solving mode, into being President of Operation Team Zoey, bringing all of her energy to bear on the project in front of her, which was to Make Me Better, when all I wanted was to disappear, and to not be a problem, and to not have her care so much, and to not have her feel personally attacked by my taking a knife to my skin to feel something, anything other than this persistent wish for all of this to just fucking be over.

So anyway, she made a few phone calls and got me an emergency appointment with my therapist, who I had also fooled into thinking I was just a Normal Teen Dealing with Trans Things, and then figured out how to get me into a program I could do every day and be told not to kill myself by someone who wasn't my mom.

If we weren't in the midst of this pandemic, I probably would have gone to inpatient, like most of the kids doing this partial hospitalization program, and *then* come to PHP, because PHP is where you graduate to once they let you out of the hospital. But that wasn't happening, thanks to the virus, and also to my mom insisting that inpatient would probably involve irreparable medical PTSD and she would not allow it. So that's why I'm doing this instead, Zooming into group therapy instead of school, talking about all the reasons why I'm a piece of shit and want to die.

All because I made a joke at the doctor's office.

You, a normie: Okay, Zoey, come on now. Did you mean "joke" or "cry for help"?

Me, an intellectual: Why not both?

COMMON APP ESSAY PROMPT:

Discuss an accomplishment, event, or realization that sparked a period of personal growth and a new understanding of yourself or others.

Last year I did a report on Great Gran, my Grandma Pauline's mom, for a school project about second-wave feminism. Because what's more feminist than being a single mom of half a dozen kids in the '60s, right? My mom had told me all about how basically my great grandma was killing it at a time when the tradition was that the man worked and the woman stayed home. I remember talking to GG on the phone and asking her how she felt about being a feminist, and what it was like in those days, and she laughed out loud.

"Me, a feminist? I didn't have time for all that bra-burning nonsense!"

I was surprised, because my mom had always told me these stories about GG as some kind of feminist hero, busting stereotypes and fighting for equality and making her way in a man's world. But GG dismissed it all. Arguing with her boss that she should get paid the same as the men in her office because she, too, was a "head of household"; raising all those kids on her own, back when there was no such thing as shared custody; never remarrying or relying on a man ever again: all of it was just "all in a day's work," she said.

"What do you want me to say? It was just my life. It was all I knew," she told me.

I did the report anyway, putting her picture alongside Betty Friedan, Simone de Beauvoir, and Gloria Steinem, telling her story about what it was like for her as a divorced mother of six in the 1960s. I got an A, even though my teacher said I really needed to draw a tighter line between the famous feminists and my own great-grandmother, even though I quoted the thing that all those famous feminists said, which is that the personal is political.

I sent GG the report and a photo of the trifold poster I'd made with her picture alongside all those famous people. Later, I got an email from her.

My dear Zoey,

—she always addresses her emails to me like that, "my dear," which is nice of her, but makes me sound more worthy of love than I really am—

You know, I had a lot of thinking to do after our phone call, because our conversation brought to mind a lot of things. And I think you were right, Zoey: I was a feminist. I am a feminist! I didn't know before I talked to you that a person could just be that sort of thing without marching in the streets or hating men or what have you. But now I know, from your report, that I was a feminist just by virtue of being alive and pushing back against the things life threw at me, and by teaching my kids—all of them, not just the boys—to stand on their own two feet. So thank you, Zoey. I really appreciate that you wrote your report about me, and that you gave me so much to think about. Imagine, an 87-year-old feminist! Well, that's me, I guess.

Love always,
Your Great Gran,
Anna.

I do love that about GG. How willing she is to update her story. I don't know how I'd act if I was like almost a hundred years old and some Gen Z weirdo tried to force feminism on me, but I don't think I'd be as cool as her, reevaluating my life and saying, Okay, sure, you're right, you little nihilist.

My mom and I talk a lot about stories, and the kinds of stories we tell ourselves to explain why we are the way we are. My mom seems to believe I'm stuck on telling myself bad stories only, and she's not wrong. But does a story have to *be* true to *feel* true? Telling myself a bad story about myself just feels right. And maybe feeling right is what makes the story true, and not the other way around.

I realized a long time ago that everyone has stories about themselves, and everyone has stories about other people. My mom keeps reminding me of that, when we talk about my depression, about how I want to die: that it's a story, that it's the current story I'm telling myself to explain the world; and that the story can change any time, since I'm making it up as I go along. I understand what she's getting at, but right now that's the story that feels the most true to me, and it's more powerful than her story about me, which is that I deserve to live.

People always end up telling their own stories about me, to make sense of why I'm shy, or why I'm funny, or why I'm trans. The big one that always comes up whenever I meet new friends or start some kind of new therapy is the story people imagine for themselves when they find out I don't have a dad. And see, right there, as soon as you read that, I knew exactly the kind of story that was evolving in your mind as the puzzle pieces all finally fell into place: *Aha! That's it! She has no dad! That explains everything!* But I assure you it does not.

For me, not having a dad is normal. That's just the story of my family: my mom plus me. But of course inevitably I will be asked about my dad, and inevitably when I say I don't have one, never had one, never needed one, it will become A Whole Thing and I'll have to convince whoever I'm talking to that they have not, actually, found The Source of My Sadness and cracked the code to save me.

Also, no, before you even go there, do not even begin to suggest that that's why I'm trans, because I lacked a father figure. What kind of bullshit even is that?

Not having a dad is something I feel like has just always been my life, though I guess there had to be some point when I was little, too little to remember now, where we first talked it through and it was news to me. It's just always been something I've known, nothing secret or sad about it. My therapist asked me once: Am I sad that I don't know him? That I don't have a dad? I told her no. My mom is all the parent I need, and honestly, I don't think I could take much more parenting at this point.

It's crazy all the questions people ask—do I feel like I'm missing out, don't I yearn for some kind of stable masculine influence lmao—wow, no. No thank you. Have you met men? They are not okay.

Besides, it's not such a weird thing. My mom wanted to be a mom, so she became one. Single mom by choice, sperm donor central. No actual man necessary. And that's fine. I don't need to know who my dad is to know who I am.

I do worry about other people's stories about me sometimes. I worry that their stories might somehow be more true than my stories, and that they might somehow cancel mine out. There are a lot of stories to compete with. My mom's story of me, which is that I'm funny and smart and fundamentally lovable (gross). My therapist's story of me, which is probably that I'm a mess who needs way more help than he could ever possibly be able to give me. My friends' story of me, which is that I kick ass at *Valorant* and *Overwatch*, that I send the best memes, that I make the best jokes, and that my dark humor about wanting to kill myself is just the language all of us speak to each other. My group therapy peers' collective story of me, which seems to be, from the affirmations we are all forced to say, that I always have really helpful advice for everyone else, that I'm always understanding and patient when people are working through their shit, that I'm always good for a sarcastic remark to break the tension. GG's story of me, which is that I am a "marvel" who "teaches her something new every day" and "makes her laugh" and "keeps her young." (It probably wouldn't surprise you to know she has zero issues with me being trans.) GG's story about me is the hardest of all, because she doesn't know anything about how I've been doing depression-wise, she has no idea I've been dealing with any of this. She thinks I am the best person in the world, she literally said that to me once, with the best hugs, and I think it would crush her to know how wrong her story is.

I emailed her recently, very late at night, when I was feeling discouraged and overwhelmed and stuck and desperately trying to distract myself from the impulse to quietly walk up the stairs to the kitchen and find the one steak knife I knew was still there from dinner, drying on the drying rack right out in the open, unlike everything else sharp in the house, which my mom hid somewhere, probably in her room, probably under her bed, so that I would wake her up if I tried to find it in the middle of the night, which is usually when I feel it the most, this urge to cut myself. So I wrote an email to distract myself, and it was going to just be a draft that I would never send, but for some reason I sent it. I'd forgotten that old people wake up super early, and so I was kind of shocked when I was still awake a couple of hours later and a response from her dinged at 5:30 A.M. and added itself to the thousands of unread emails I had. But I read it.

My dearest Zoey,

—she said, and I knew she was serious, because usually she just says dear, but there she was, breaking out the intensifying suffixes, and I worried she would be burdened by what I'd sent her, or worried about me or sad or concerned, but then I realized that was my own story about her because she said—

You can't imagine how pleased I was to wake up to an email from you in my inbox. Or maybe you can, and that's why you sent it. Because that is the kind of great-granddaughter you are: kind and thoughtful, the kind of great-granddaughter who would think, "What would make my great-grandmother the happiest right now? I know! An email."

I think all of us ask ourselves big questions at your age. I know I did. Of course, some of the questions I asked myself were different, because it was a different time and I had different kinds of responsibilities, and I wasn't living in the shadow of the worst virus the world has ever seen.

But I asked myself questions just the same as you, and I struggled to find answers to them. Just the same as you.

I know you didn't ask me for my advice in your email, but I wouldn't be your Great Gran if I didn't give it to you anyway. So I'm going to. I want to tell you something, Zoey—and this, my dear, is the secret to everything, so pay attention:

Keep asking the questions.

Don't worry about the answers. It's the questions that are important. Answers to the kinds of questions you're asking aren't even possible, because life isn't like a math test, where there's right answers and wrong answers, and you either get it right or you don't. You haven't been alive long enough right now to even hazard a guess at an answer, really, and I don't mean that in a condescending way, it's just the truth. Any answer you might come up with to the kinds of questions you're asking would just be stories. Or maybe theories is a better word for it—you would know, you're the one who loves words so much, and knows so much about what makes them mean what they mean.

So that's what I want to tell you. Just keep asking the questions.

And keep sending me emails. I'd really like that.

Love always,

Your Great Gran,

Anna.

COMMON APP ESSAY PROMPT:

Describe a problem you've solved or a problem you'd like to solve. It can be an intellectual challenge, a research query, an ethical dilemma—anything that is of personal importance, no matter the scale. Explain its significance to you and what steps you took or could be taken to identify a solution.

There are no rules about being trans. Just FYI. Like, for instance, you don't *have* to change your name if you don't want to. But most people kinda want to. I hadn't really thought much about it in those early days when I was waking up at 4:00 A.M., staring at my ceiling and realizing, *dude. I'm trans????* But once I told my mom, and once both of us made the shift to using "she" and "her" to refer to me—which didn't happen all at once (and there's no rule about that either, aside from basically once a person has decided on their pronouns, please use them)—I had to start thinking about it. The problem was, I had literally no idea what to call myself. This all happened the summer between sophomore and junior year, and I am what I like to call "indoorsy," so I wasn't interacting with people on a daily basis like I would be in school or whatever, which meant that I was online all the time, and the name everyone that knew me by on there was my screen name, and that wasn't going to change. Which is fine, but I'm not going to be called [redacted username] in real life.

My mom and I tried using a femme-ified version of my given name for a while, which was . . . fine? But it didn't feel like me. I looked at those online baby-name generators (gross, babies) but it was pretty much immediately overwhelming. So mostly my mom and I just avoided ever having to use a name for me, which wasn't exactly sustainable, though I did start answering pretty readily to "Hey!" My online friends and my school-friends-who-were-online either used my screen name or my Old Me name. And I just didn't make a big deal out of it. But then one day Sergio, who's been my best friend since third grade, was like *Bro. We gotta get you a name.* And thus Operation Sergio Naming Rights began.

The first thing you need to know about Sergio is that in life he basically rolled all charisma and zero intelligence. This explains how he is both perpetually on the verge of getting kicked out of school for his 2 percent—literally 2 percent—average in math class (when our friend group found that out, a bunch of us wore "Sergio: Got Milk?" T-shirts for like a week straight in solidarity) and also a folk hero among students for the diss track album he released on SoundCloud about all our teachers (yes, he is a SoundCloud rapper), using the MEAL paragraph as a kind of concept album jumping-off point, and then deleted before they found out. Our homeroom teacher told us once that probably the only reason Sergio hadn't been expelled yet was because the administration didn't think they'd be able to handle the massive student uprising that would undoubtedly occur, and I don't think he was joking.

Sergio is one of those friends who you can just talk about anything with and they don't care. I can't tell you how many intense Discord chats we've had while playing *Dark Souls III.* I say "intense," but it's not that we're constantly going deep; we just get each other—it's just that kind of mood. We've been friends for so long, ever since he walked up to me in third grade and was like, "Do you like Pokémon?" That was all it took, friends for life, no take-backs, no other questions necessary. I was low-key worried when I told him about being trans, but mostly that was just me being anxious for nothing, because of course he just immediately typed back "cool" and then killed me in-game.

I feel the need to point out here that my suddenly being trans did not transform me and Sergio into some kind of OTP. For one thing, that's not how any of this works. And for another, I like girls. Our friendship stayed exactly the same, except that now he knows the truth about me.

Anyway, as I said, at some point he finally said, *Bro, we gotta get you a name,* and I was like *Agreed,* but I had no idea how to go about it. Sergio was like, *Let the master work,* because he had just spent the past week coming up with names for his birds.

His parents had gotten him these two birds (which he named Fiona and Shrek), thinking that it would be helpful for him to have to take care of something. As though the discipline of feeding and cleaning up after birds would ignite in him a sudden determination to clean his room and shower more than once a week and do his homework and otherwise be a Productive Member of Society. Instead, he woke up one day and discovered one of the birds had laid eggs, and eventually they hatched, and now he was a Bird Dad.

OK but dude you can't just name me after the triplets in Shrek the Third, I typed, because that's exactly what he'd done with his birds. *Or after a Pokémon,* I added because, come on, this is Sergio we're talking about. He took a long time to respond and when he did, all he said was *shit*. But then eventually he had a Sergio Idea, which is ten times more potent than a regular person idea, so I had no choice but to go with it.

First he asked, *How do you feel about crowdsourcing,* and I replied, *How do you feel about having a dumb and stupid face,* but then he just jumped right into it. His idea was "Halloween in July" which meant this: basically, on July 31, which is essentially Summer Halloween anyway, everyone would come over to Sergio's parents' house in costume, and we'd have a party. For one of the party activities, Sergio would get a ton of HELLO MY NAME IS stickers from the dollar store, and everyone who came had to fill one out with at least one name suggestion for me.

And then like everyone just sticks the name stickers on you when they find you at the party, he typed.

Like pin the tail on the donkey. Except with name tag stickers. And I'm the donkey, I said.

Bro, like you can take off the ones you don't like and keep the ones you do, and then at the end of the night everyone can vote.

I mean, it was better than being named after a Pokémon.

Sergio's parents' house is a massive Victorian in Old City, and not all of it is fixed up. The basement is kind of halfway done, and one entire room was filled with old clawfoot bathtubs his parents had taken out of the millions of upstairs bathtubs and replaced with regular bathtubs or showers or whatever. He asked his mom two questions: Could he have a party in the basement, and could he fill up at least one of the bathtubs with soda or punch or something so people could drink out of it. She said yes to the first and no to the second, so it was on.

Sergio decided to go as a ceiling fan (aka wearing a T-shirt that he'd used a Sharpie to write "I heart ceilings" on, plus one of those oversized "#1" foam fingers), and I went as a VSCO Girl, both as a joke about my having transitioned into my true form as a Basic Bitch and as an opportunity to present myself for the first time in school-friend public as any kind of actual girl. My hair was longer than it had been at the end of the school year, which was the last time any of those friends had seen me, and I was able to wear it up in a scrunchie. I lived in oversized sweatshirts and leggings anyway; all I needed was a hydroflask (I took a regular water bottle and wrote "Hydroflasksksksksk" on it) and some stickers. And Sergio's naming rights idea/dollar store stickers would take care of that.

I showed up at his house early, along with two other friends, Carter (who came as a Fyre Fest sandwich) and Liv (who came as "self-care day," complete with robe and fuzzy slippers and a face mask), and of course Sergio had done nothing to prepare. So we all immediately went to the dollar store, to get the name tag stickers for me, but also to get decorations and stuff. Carter pointed out that Sergio also didn't seem to have any snacks or drinks, so we stopped at the corner store to pick up some of those too. We came back with our haul and put up janky dollar store string lights and streamers made out of tissue paper so thin it was practically invisible. We hung a giant HAPPY BIRTHDAY banner that looked like it had been designed in the '80s and had been sitting on the shelf of the dollar store ever since, and alongside that hung another giant banner that said YOU'RE 50! and another giant banner that said HAPPY RETIREMENT! Sergio didn't have any bowls or anything, so we just put all the chips and candy and stuff on a table with a sign that said to use plastic cups for both drinking and snacking.

Since Sergio's mom had said no to the bathtub-as-punch-bowl idea, we thought they could maybe be repurposed as cool places to hang out, if we moved them into the main room, but that was before we realized they each weighed a thousand pounds. Even with three of us pushing, it wouldn't budge. Finally Liv was like, "Dude, isn't this supposed to be a Halloween party anyway?" And we were all like *right*, so we took some of the dollar store string lights from the other room and put them all around the scary bathtub area, and Sergio made a sign that said HAUNTED HOUSE and taped it to the doorway, so that was perfect.

Before the rest of the kids arrived, I used one of the HELLO MY NAME IS stickers and wrote "gay disaster" on it and stuck it in the middle of my sweatshirt. Carter thought about it for a while and then wrote "Cool Person," and Liv immediately wrote "Francesca" and stuck it on my back. Sergio wrote "based" and stuck it on my arm. We were ready for the party.

It was pretty awesome that basically everyone showed up in costume. Leo came as a fidget spinner; Neil was a YouTube apology video; Rose was "sexy college admissions scandal"; Daniel was a vampire, and his girlfriend, Lucy, was Buffy; Daniel was Velma from Scooby Doo, Ben was Waldo; Luke was the FitnessGram Pacer Test; Rory was a "deviled egg" (a devil costume with a T-shirt that had an egg on it); and of course Patrick was naked (basically a long cardboard sign with skin-tone pixelated blocks). There were some other kids from Sergio's neighborhood who I didn't know but seemed cool (a ghost, Harry Potter, someone from *Game of Thrones*, Minecraft Steve, a Creeper), and I gradually collected so many stickers you could barely even see my sweatshirt.

The best part of the party was that Sergio's mom had said that since they were in the middle of redoing the basement anyway, we could destroy this one wall. So all of us were like kicking it and punching it until Rory broke through and got his foot stuck in the wall, and when he pulled it out, his shoe fell off into the wall, and then we all went crazy, pulling the wall apart until we were falling into a pile laughing.

At some point I found myself in the Haunted House, sitting in a bathtub looking up at some string lights, with Liv in the bathtub to my right, lying down with her feet up over the side, and Sergio in the bathtub to my left.

"Did you get any good names?" Liv asked.

I looked down at my sweatshirt and started reading off names, peeling off the ones I didn't like and sticking them to the bathtub.

"I mean . . ." I said. "I guess there's some okay ones? I don't know. Just none of them feel like me."

"Maybe because you don't know what 'me' feels like yet," Liv said, and Sergio leaned his head back in his tub, cupped his hands around his mouth, and bellowed, "Deep!"

"You're not wrong." I peeled off a couple more stickers. "But like, Cassandra? Natalie? Amy? Jolene? Ariana? Madonna? Penelope? I don't know."

"You know, you don't *have* to actually pick one of these names to be your name for the rest of your life," Liv said.

Sergio shot up in his bathtub. "Uh, actually, yes she does, that's the whole point of this party, to give her a name."

"So far I like this one best," I said, pointing to "gay disaster."

"What about 'Main Character'? You could be MC for short. I like that one," Sergio said, but I peeled it off and stuck it to the bathtub.

"Guys, the problem is that I have Dumb Bitch Disease. Which is not only genetic and chronic, it's also terminal."

Liv laughed, but then she asked, "For real though, are you okay? This is big. And like, I'm proud of you, but also, it's a lot."

This was before any of my other stuff had come out—before my cutting, before my blurting/making jokes at the doctor's office, before PHP or anything, before I had admitted to myself that I was depressed or struggling at all, because I was still on the high of figuring out Part One of who I was, aka a Real Girl—so I felt myself catch on what she said, like a sweater that snags on a nail, and maybe just from the exhaustion of having been so social for almost a whole day, I found myself suddenly feeling like I might cry. I was glad for the dimness, the irregular blinking of the dollar store string lights, the depth of the cool marble bathtub I was sitting in. I was glad neither of them could see my face as I said, "Yeah, I'm good."

We sat there in the kind of dark for a long while, and then Sergio was like, "Here," and he got up and came over and started peeling off all the stickers from my shirt, adding them to the collection I'd started on the side of the bathtub. Liv joined in, too, and they took off everything except the two stickers that said "based" and "gay disaster," and he said, "I'll be right back," and went to the other room, where even though half the kids were asleep, there were still people tearing apart that one wall.

When he came back, he had a sticker and a Sharpie, and he stood near one of the blinking lights to see as he wrote something carefully.

"I think this is it," he said, as he put it on my sleeve. It said, in Sergio's gnarly printing, *Zoey*.

"I like it," Liv said. "You could have gone umlauts or just z-o-e. But you went with the *Y*."

"Zoey?" I said, trying it out. It didn't feel wrong, which was honestly the closest any name had felt to being right.

"OMG, no," Liv said, smiling. "I love it. It's perfect. Right?"

Sergio looked a little embarrassed for a minute and said, "I was going to use it for one of my birds. But then I was like nah, I'll save it for you."

Honestly, I thought the tears were going to spill then and there, but I blinked for a long time until I was sure I had pushed them back in. "Dude. I'm honored. That is literally the biggest compliment. Or the biggest gift. Giving me a precious bird name," I said.

I moved the "gay disaster" and "based" stickers to my left sleeve and took the "Zoey" sticker and put it on my chest.

"Fuck yeah," Sergio said. "Now let's go introduce you to everyone!"

He and Liv started going into the other room to call everyone, telling them to come to the Haunted House because we had some news, I'd made a decision. But I just lay there in my empty bathtub, looking up at the beams in the ceiling as they shifted in the shadows of the blinking string lights, and for just a minute, I felt it in my body, this feeling of rightness, of okayness, of relief, like I'd finally fit a puzzle piece into place. And when they came back in with everyone and were like, "Hello, her name is Zoey," and everyone was like HI ZOEY, I didn't tell them all to shut up. Instead I was like, "Yo, what's up," and I really meant it.

I never thanked Sergio for coming up with my name. But I didn't have to. That's just the kind of friendship we have.

COMMON APP ESSAY PROMPT:

Reflect on a time when you questioned or challenged a belief or idea. What prompted your thinking? What was the outcome?

I remember when my mom ran out of stories.

I would ask her, when I was little, to tell me stories about what it was like when she was little, like me. I couldn't place then, but can recognize now, in hindsight, a reluctance as she considered my request. I would see her face change, but couldn't know why, and her hesitation only made me more insistent. I liked hearing about what she did and thought, the adventures she had. I imagined myself in them, listening to her tell me about the time Grandma Pauline snuck them onto a farm and let my mom pet a goat, imagining what it was like to have it nibble out of my own hand—her hand, once removed—listening to her tell me how conflicted she'd felt, even as a four-year-old, about breaking a rule, while Grandma Pauline insisted it was fine, she knew the farmer, the farmer wouldn't mind.

My mom made it funny, the way they'd tiptoed through the field and almost slipped on their way up the hill, and actually did tumble down on the way out as they scrambled to leave, how she'd rolled in the tall grass that stuck to her braids. It sounded like a magnificent adventure in her telling. I liked hearing stories about how she was the youngest one in school, and unsure of what to do, and so shy she was too scared to talk, and aware that everyone expected her to be so smart since she'd skipped a grade that they were just waiting for her to do something dumb. I liked hearing stories like that. I liked imagining my seemingly all-powerful mom as an anxious kid, a tenderhearted secret feeder of goats and respecter of rules. It made me feel like she could be me. Like I could be her, one day. A grown-up girl in the world, with stories that made sense of it.

But I remember that night, when I asked her to tell me a happy story about her life as a kid, when I asked her to tell me a *new* happy story. I remember the way she looked at me and then looked quickly away, the way when she turned back I could sense in the half-dark of my bedroom that her eyes were full, the way when she spoke her voice was tight and small.

I don't know any more happy stories, she told me.

It was only when I was older that I realized that even her happy stories had been sad ones. That she had reframed them, transformed them for herself, silently, over the years, and then transmuted them to me, perfecting them into something innocuous, harmless, benevolent, entertaining.

But when she started telling me the real stories, that's when I started feeling real. I was no longer a made-up girl listening to made-up stories about a girl who could maybe be me, if I imagined hard enough. Instead I was a real girl, listening to true stories about a girl like me who struggled to feel stable in the center of a truth that other people kept trying to lie about. Hearing the real stories about her life with Grandma Pauline opened up the world for me, and I felt initiated, accepted into the reality of complexity and nuance, and the previously satisfying happy-ending stories now seemed like pale, flabby versions of a far sturdier truth.

Once she started telling me the real stories, after she'd run out of stories, she told me the stories before the stories: The stories about Grandma Pauline and her dad, The Old Man; about Grandma Pauline's mom, my Great Gran, and how she took Pauline in as a baby even when she didn't have to. About Great Gran's mom and how she was thwarted in her career, and how that made her cold as a mom, and how that coldness just kept spreading and spreading like a frost that branched out and touched everyone. About how all of them had made their own stories pretend-happy in order to survive, and how she didn't want to do that anymore.

The thing about words and etymology, the way I like digging into the secret stories that are hidden in words, is that there's only so far back you can go. There's only so far back that languages go, that we actually know about. Some of these roots, some of these fragments? They're from hypothetical languages, protolanguage—in other words, they're from made-up languages, "best guess" languages. They're basically stories we have made up about what words mean, even though they're right there on dictionary.com and EtymologyOnline, all official and everything. And sure, you might say, well, aren't all definitions and meanings really just stories we have collectively agreed upon about words? And I would say, yeah, probably, I mean I don't know, I'm just a girl who likes words, I'm not a Professional Etymologist. But the fact that there's only so much we can know, that we can only guess at what the super ancient words really sounded like or what they felt like to the people who said them, just reminds me of how we can never know the full, true stories of other people. I can learn the stories my mom tells about my family, but I can't know the true story of what happened in my family because the story I hear from my mom is only one piece of a story that she heard from someone else and added her small part to. It's like a long-ass game of whisper-down-the-lane. Sometimes the heart of the story gets saved along the way. Sometimes it totally changes.

I didn't tell her for a long time about my being a girl. Not because I didn't want her to know, or because I didn't know myself. But because I understood the importance of living with a story for a long time, telling it to yourself with different possibilities and different intentions, before finally understanding the core of it and saying it out loud.

I also didn't tell her for a long time about being depressed. For obvious reasons.

I always tell her that it's impressive that she really did it, she really stopped the cycle of trying to live pretend-happy stories. Lots of people say they want to do things differently from their families, but she really did. It couldn't have been easy for her, figuring out how to do that, what with Grandma Pauline and all her craziness and my mom having to be the grownup all her life. But then we always laugh because I also tell her that the long chain of those girls and women in our family who grew and worked to survive all that dysfunction actually ends with me. I am the culmination of all those generations of progress. So why not go out on a high note? I'd just fuck it up anyway, if I had kids, and more than that, I don't want kids. H*ck, I don't even want to be alive. So this is where the family legacy ends. She always argues with me, tells me how insightful I am, what a good guide I would be for a kid, what an opportunity it would be to learn even more about who I am as I oversee the amazingness of a person growing into who they're meant to be.

To this, I say: I'm good. Meaning, no thanks.

Maybe, if I don't kill myself, maybe there could be some kind of future where I'm a Good Trans Gay who collects troubled teens and helps them with advice and stuff about transition or whatever their own parents don't understand. Or maybe not. The point is, I can be a person who tells stories to other people even if I don't have kids. I can be a keeper of stories, a teller of happy stories that are really sad, and sad stories that are really happy, just the way I am.

The thing is, about those true stories? The real stories? You have to tell them over and over and over to make them more powerful than the pretend stories. There's something about pretend stories that makes them root in you, the way that a scar a person might carve on the tender side of their arm might stay there, angry-red for far longer than it should be, and you have to put cream on it or something, not just one day, but every day, multiple times a day, just to get it to calm down, not even erased, just not as raised and bumpy and obvious.

It's like with my mom's piano playing. Sometimes she just plays and I hear it even though I have my headphones on, in-game, and it's a play-through of a whole song, from beginning to end. But most of the time, when I hear her, she's practicing, which means she's playing one small part over and over, breaking things down into small chunks and trying to make it perfect. And even if she does get one part pretty much perfect one day, it doesn't stay that way. The next day when she tries again, it's not perfect anymore. She has to keep practicing it, over and over, tricking herself into finding different ways to play it so that finally her muscles just remember it the right way, and she can play it right. It's something that accumulates, she told me, back when she was trying to teach me piano as a little kid. You don't just practice one day and it's over. It's every-single-day work, and sometimes you only see the results after doing it for days and days and days. (Which, hello, is why I quit playing piano.)

It's the same with those stories.

And it's the same with the stories I tell myself. I have to tell myself ten good stories to crowd out one bad one. Maybe twenty good stories, if I could even come up with that many. Or maybe it's just that I need to tell myself the same good story ten or twenty times to come close to erasing the bad one. The point is: It takes more of a good thing to even out a bad thing. It's not a one-to-one ratio. And just like with the piano practicing, it has to happen more than just once. You have to reinforce it every day. My mom says that's what love is, telling the good story, every day, to yourself and the world.

The only other story my mother ever told me was the one she had been told by her mom, who had been told it by *her* mom, who had been told it by *her* mom. And just like a game of telephone, it kind of feels like the story maybe degraded or got weirder and more fucked up as it got passed along from mother to daughter, to daughter, to daughter, to daughter. But I looked it up once, because I was curious, and it really was that weird, it really was that fucked up.

Basically, it goes like this. Once upon a time there was a girl whose father made a deal with the devil. The devil promised that if the old man gave him what was behind the man's mill, the devil would make him rich in three years' time. The old man, under the impression that nothing was behind the mill except a worthless apple tree, and thus thrilled about his luck in encountering such a stupid devil, quickly agreed to the deal. Unfortunately, standing behind the mill at that moment was, of course, his daughter. So the devil promised to return in three years to claim her.

For three years the girl lived with the knowledge of her fate, but she led a pious life and, quite literally, kept her hands clean. So when the devil returned, he couldn't take her, because she was too pure. Thwarted, he went to work on the girl's father again, and convinced the old man that the only way to rectify the situation was to chop off the girl's hands.

So he did. The old man took an axe and chopped off his daughter's hands.

But the girl was so pure, so good, her suffering so exquisite, that the tears she shed onto the ragged stumps of her wrists rendered them clean in the most spiritual sense of the word. So, once again, the devil could not claim her.

I want to point out that nowhere in this fairy tale do we ever truly know how the girl feels about any of this. About all of this. She is a cipher. Her suffering is just a fact, and we have no details about how she feels toward the father who fails her, toward her absent mother, toward the devil who engineers her fate. Whether she feels shock or betrayal upon seeing her own writhing hands on the ground, now separated from the rest of her body.

The girl, no longer useful to anyone, was cast out, sent away from her home, alone, left to fend for herself without hands. She wandered, who knows for how long, until she found herself in a royal garden, near a pear tree, starving but unable to reach the fruit. At this point, finally, there was a moment of divine intervention: an angel hovering above the garden took pity on her, plucked a pear from the tree, and fed her.

Again, I cannot emphasize this enough, we don't know what the girl thought about this, whether she wondered why an angel would help her in a royal garden but not behind the mill, the moment before the axe fell.

A royal gardener saw all of that transpire and informed the king, who promptly fell in love with the beautiful, handless girl and asked her to marry him. Once they were married, the king had his best silversmith create silver hands for her.

Was she happy about this? Did she like these immovable silver hands, clumsy, like lead weights attached to the ends of her arms; heavy as expectations, and just as rigid; fingers, but no movement; hands but no control? The story doesn't say.

After the girl was married and fitted with her silver hands, she had a son, who was born while the king was away, fighting a battle. A letter was sent to the king telling him of the blessed event, but somehow that same devil who ruined the girl's life in the first place struck again, transforming the letter so that instead of informing the king that he had a son, it said that his queen, the girl with the silver hands, had given birth to a monster.

The king responded with a letter instructing his people not to panic, but to keep the queen and their mutant offspring safe until his return. But the devil intervened yet again, changing the letter to say that the baby and the queen should be killed, and that the queen's tongue and eyes should be saved as proof. The king's mother received the letter but was unable to bring herself to follow his commands. Instead, she had a pig killed, its eyes and tongue saved as proof of the queen's death, and instructed the queen to flee with her baby.

How did she feel, fleeing in the dead of night with a baby tied to her back? Being led by an angel to a small cottage in the far woods? Did she wonder how she could possibly care for a baby with stiff silver hands, did she wonder where the angels were who could have stopped the devil at any previous point in the story?

As the girl, now a woman, made a new life for herself in the forest cottage, caring for her child, whom she named "Filled-with-Grief" (nothing personal, kid, sorry), a curious thing happened: Her silver hands fell off, and her hands began to regenerate. By the time seven years had passed, she had grown real hands as beautiful and functional as her original ones.

The king, to his credit, never fell for the devil's trickery the way the girl's father did. Upon hearing the truth from his mother, that the queen was able to escape with their child, the king set out to find them. Eventually, after seven years of searching, he stumbled upon the cottage. He met the woman and boy inside the house and told them of his quest, not recognizing them as his own wife and son. The woman informed him that she was his true wife, his queen, but he refused to believe her, for of course his wife had no hands, only silver hands, hands he had made especially for her.

Were her new hands shaking as she showed it to him, as she took a box from beneath her bed and, with her strong fingers, deftly opened it to reveal the silver hands he had made for her, that she had saved all those years after they'd fallen off? We know nothing. Events occur in the story, and the girl survives them, and the record is curiously silent about what it means, for her, personally, to endure.

The story finally ends as almost all these stories do: the king reclaimed his queen and took her and their son to return to the castle and live happily ever after.

GGG Lise told GG this story, and GG told Grandma Pauline, and Grandma Pauline told my mom, and my mom told me, with a kind of horrified fascination. I don't know what GG thought about it, or what Grandma Pauline thought about it. But I am skeptical.

I believe a different ending might be possible.

Because at the end of the story, the girl with the silver hands is a woman with real hands. Hands that regenerated only after she learned how to exist in the world with no hands, and then with silver hands, and then learned how to exist in the world alone with her child, in the woods. The real hands at the end of the story, those real hands of human flesh—they weren't bestowed upon her by some kind king or tardy angel. They're hands that she grows herself, bones and muscles and tendons and flesh pushing the heavy, inflexible silver hands away to reveal the ugly beginnings of something new: scar tissue, the pink rawness of new skin, the darkness of the veins beneath it. Hands, capable and human, born from her own body, in secret. Hands that are completely hers. Hands that make her unrecognizable to the king who searches for her for seven years.

So I believe, in the end, she doesn't return to the castle.

I believe, in the end, she hands the king the box she made with her own hands, lined with soft material she herself has spun and sewn, containing the heavy, impractical silver hands, now spotted and tarnished with age.

I believe, in the end, that she bows to him as he takes the box and uses her hands to gesture him gracefully toward the door.

Then she stays, she and her son, in the woods, no longer the girl with the silver hands, imagining she is helped by angels. No longer the recipient of things bestowed upon her—a punishment she doesn't deserve, a pear from a tree she can't reach, silver hands crafted to replace the ones cruelly taken, silver hands given out of love.

Then the king goes away, back to his castle and kingdom and intrigue and devils and angels, his heart heavy as silver, as she shuts the door behind him.

That's how it ends.

COMMON APP ESSAY PROMPT:

Share an essay on any topic of your choice. It can be one you've already written, one that responds to a different prompt, or one of your own design.

My mom has been making me learn how to drive.

"No better time to learn than during a pandemic," she said. And she's kind of right, seeing as how every day, we're practically the only ones on the road.

"You really think it's a good idea to have a person with a death wish behind the wheel?" I asked her, but all she said was *ha ha* and *get in*.

So she's been having me drive every day, as we go to IOP, which is only two hours a day, even though it literally stands for Intensive Outpatient Program, and I don't consider anything that lasts for only two hours to be legit "intensive." The drive is eerily calm. Even though things are starting to open up again, everything still looks abandoned, and all the roads are empty. I can mess up as much as I want to and probably not crash into anybody. At least, that's the idea.

The back roads are pretty, but so winding and narrow, I get scared we might tip over and roll into the trees, which line both sides and block out the sun, they're so tall.

On the freeway, it's downright creepy how alone we are, it's like a driving simulation game, some kind of GTA dystopia. There are only maybe five other cars on the road in either direction, and everything we pass is abandoned-looking, as though everyone has been raptured. Road signs flash orange messages: STAY HOME: PRACTICE SOCIAL DISTANCING and TRAVELERS FROM NEW YORK: MANDATORY QUARANTINE FOR 14 DAYS.

We're still not really supposed to be driving anywhere, unless it's for essential reasons. I guess going to Depression School counts as essential. So we're driving. I'm driving.

I don't really have a death wish. I have suicidal ideation. There's a difference.

The other thing I started after PHP ended (besides IOP) is called TMS. It's funny how all these things are acronyms. Or not funny: I guess the point is to rip out all context, take away all clues that could be buried in the actual words, leaving cold abbreviations that mean nothing, that could actually mean anything to anyone who doesn't already know. TMS is probably better-sounding than saying "shock therapy—no, not the bad kind from the olden days, the modern kind, which is fine, we swear, no worries, bro" and easier to acronymize anyway. Transcranial Magnetic Stimulation, even all spelled out, seems worlds away from "shock therapy," so even without the acronym it's designed to make it sound less awful. Also I like that there's a trans word in there. Transcranial. Through the brain, across the brain, passing through the brain. Just passing through. Just Trans Things™.

The chair looks kind of like a dentist chair, and just like at the pediatric dentist's, there's a screen where you can watch Netflix or whatever and not think about what's happening, in this particular case your brain being zapped. There's a helmet that goes on your head—kind of like a cross between a bike helmet and one of those giant hair dryer things that you see old ladies sit under in movies—and they map out which parts of your brain are supposed to get the zaps, as if they can possibly know where the "I want to kill myself" part of the brain is, and then you just sit back and let fire ants crawl on your head for like an hour.

It doesn't always feel like that. The first time, I was startled by how loud it was when it clacked on, like someone spamming a mechanical gaming keyboard on steroids, and then I felt this awful pressure, like two woodpeckers were trying to crush my skull from attacking both sides of my head. And it just didn't let up. Afterward, I told them, and they were like, why didn't you say anything, we can adjust it, and I was like, I didn't want to bother you, and they were like, dude. Please.

So they adjusted it for the next time, and gave me earplugs, and though I still notice the pressure, it's not as bad. I feel the itchy-fire-ants feeling more. My scalp is super sensitive. But I've tried all the medicines and nothing works, even the one I'm on now. So this is where we are.

What sucks is that they literally have no idea how this thing works, or if it even will work most of the time. I mean, sure, there are studies and stuff, but they don't know. And like, they tell you, okay, you might actually feel worse after the first couple of treatments, and maybe you might want to take an Advil ahead of time to prevent the headaches, but they don't tell you that for some people, it makes everything so much fucking worse that "suicidal ideation" feels like the quaintest, most bullshit way of describing how severely depressed you feel.

My mom and my doctors told me to keep going, though, and so I do, and sometimes afterward I feel okay. And when I say "okay" I mean that maybe I feel the way a normal person might feel if they were vaguely sad or disappointed, which for me translates into absolute fucking euphoria or something. I wouldn't know. I don't know what "happy" is supposed to feel like. I just know that after some sessions I feel like my body is actually connected to my brain and I notice things and there's a feeling inside me like when you're hungry and you eat a meal and it's not too little but also not too much and inside you just feel warm and full, but not so full that you want to fall asleep, you just feel . . . fine? It doesn't happen every time, and it doesn't always last for long. But the fact that it happens at all kind of gives me a little hope.

Ideation basically comes from a word that means "to see." It's this Greek verb *idein*, which we get courtesy of Plato, whose whole deal was that thinking is seeing, that if you're a true philosopher, all you have to do is look around, no training necessary, and you'll see right there in front of you the true nature of things. The sheer audacity of men, am I right?

In his philosophy, an "idea" was an archetype, a perfect thing that is the basis for everything else. "Ideal" meant "existing as an archetype," a way to describe something that's that perfect thing. And "ideate" meant to form Platonic ideas, because who wouldn't want to do that. By the time the seventeenth century rolled around, in medieval Latin, *ideat-* just meant "formed as an idea." And that's kind of the sense that still lingers today.

So when I say "suicidal ideation," it sounds scary, but all it means is that I have formed the idea that I want to commit suicide. I have seen it. And I'm okay with it, and I can't stop thinking about it.

Actually, maybe that does sound scary.

Maybe that's why at Depression School, when we talk about it, we call it SI.

We drive to Depression School, and every day I get better at figuring out turns, and when to brake, and how to change lanes. There's one road where it's straight for a long time and is also basically a hill going straight down, and I get good at coasting until the very, very end, when the car has picked up too much speed and you have to brake before you hit the turn at the bottom.

My mom asks me every day if the medication is having any effect, and if the TMS is having an effect, and every day I disappoint her by telling her the truth, which is that I don't feel different at all. I still hate myself, still can't think about a future where I exist, still want to hurt myself. She tells me that nothing is going to change things overnight, that it will be a gradual thing, that it'll seep into me little by little until one day I might notice that I don't feel so bad anymore.

Cool, I say, and she says, all exasperated, "Can you even allow for that possibility? That you might actually feel better? Or is it more important for you to stay like this?"

She gestures to my arms. The scars are almost all faded away, which makes me feel anxious, which makes me want to make new ones.

"Super fun to be blamed for my depression," I say, and she says, "Come on, you know that's not what I mean," and I say, "Sure sounds like it."

Then we just drive in silence.

I stop taking the most recent medicine, because it's not doing anything other than making me feel "activated," as my psychiatrist puts it, or "like I want to crawl out of my skin," as I put it. It takes a while, but eventually I'm able to stop jiggling my foot constantly while I sit, striding my legs through the sheets at night like I'm running underwater, waking up in a tangle, my legs vibrating.

I stop taking the medicine, but I keep going to TMS because my insurance allowed me something like thirty-six treatments, and my mom wants to get her money's worth, and also because my psych said that for some people it takes that long.

It doesn't feel like anything is happening, but I gradually notice that sometimes I actually don't think about killing myself. It'll sneak up on me, like I'll be wall-riding in *Overwatch* and I'll just be like, Whoa, I just spent five minutes forgetting to wish I was dead. And as awful as that sounds, that qualifies as progress?

My mom keeps checking in, but I am always noncommittal. I don't want to jinx it.

And at IOP, I don't talk about it at all. I like to say I have big NPC energy, which means I don't generally talk about anything directly related to me, I just give advice to other people, which is evidently "part" of the "problem," which is that I am self-abnegating and keep trying to outsmart the program directors by talking about anything other than stuff that might actually "help" me get "better." Nobody else at IOP has done TMS, so I just don't want to bring it up. I don't want the focus to be on me. Instead, I sympathize with Tony about his shitty dad, and I tell Kayla how to handle her shitty dad, and I reinforce Mia's plan to tell her shitty dad to fuck off. There are a lot of shitty dads, it turns out. I'm lucky, I guess, that I've never had a dad at all, and whenever any of the program directors bring that up, I shut it down as the potential source of all my problems, because please. If there's anything I've learned from my suicide squad peers in Depression School, it's that shitty dads are pretty much the reason for everything. Not having a dad is a huge advantage.

Anyway, the more treatments I have, the more I start to notice things that can't be jinxed away. The *kill urself* voice is still there, but it's quiet, like it is being smothered under a pillow by some other murderous part of my brain. It doesn't dominate my thoughts, and some days I almost forget about it completely. My scars are healing, and some days the skin around them is tight and feels uncomfortable, but instead of looking for something to cut with, I go to my mom's bathroom and steal her lotion, which is called Skin Food, which sounds like something a serial killer would use, and I rub it in gently until the tingling stops. I take showers.

I'm not saying I don't still hate myself. I'm just saying the hate is changing, maybe morphing back to that *kad-* root, allowing me to feel the sorrow, hatred, grief, calamity, and mourning underneath. Sometimes I cry in the shower and I don't know why, but afterward I feel like something important has happened, and I feel the exhaustion in my body, like I've been carrying an enormous barbell and finally let it drop to the floor like a "do you even lift" bro, bouncing and sending up chalk dust as it lands.

And then one day, I wake up and I feel strange. It takes me a moment to identify what it is I'm feeling. It's like a sensation of not being tired. Of not being hopeless. Of not being filled with dread. I get up and I . . . don't want to die? I have energy to go upstairs and take my meds? I feel . . . optimistic? And when it's time to go to IOP, I grab the car keys before my mom can offer, and I say, "I'll drive."

I keep it to myself in IOP, this feeling of alrightness, because it feels so fragile, but I don't fight when they ask us to journal our feelings, or when Sandy talks about using essential oils and coping techniques, or when Amy says, "Zoey, you've been quiet, what do you think about communicating with Mom when you feel unsafe?"

My mom is waiting for me in the car, doing something on her phone, probably researching other therapeutic options or trying to find some other way to save me. As I told the group at the very beginning, I lucked out with good mom RNG, she's a good one, whether or not I deserve it. She gets out and says, "It's like you're my own personal Lyft driver," and I say, "Let me get my magic wand," and we laugh about the time in the Before Times when we went somewhere in the city and the Lyft driver showed up with a sign that said "Magician on Board" and we were both like oh no but gave him five stars because when we turned him down after he asked us repeatedly if we wanted to see some magic, he seemed so sad.

On the drive home this time, the sun seems to be staring at me through the clouds, shining right at me, right on me, specifically for me. And suddenly I notice we are surrounded by trees fully leafed now, the birds soaring through the summer, the previously brown and dead banks on the sides of the road now flowering, vibrant bursts of color. All these signs of the world persisting, continuing without our say-so, even though there's a pandemic, even though I want to take myself out of it.

And just then as I drive, with the empty road in front of us making it seem as though we're the only people in the world, my mom turns up the music and it swells as it hits the chorus, and I suddenly feel it in my arms, in my chest, in the pit of my stomach, in my bones: I want to be here. I want it, this world. As fucked up as it is, as I am, as much as I hate it and fear it, as much as I hate myself and fear myself, I don't want to leave it. I don't want it to leave. The realization shimmers over me like a fever, and I feel my eyes sting with tears—imagine, having feelings in 2020—and I wipe my face, and my mom instinctively grabs for the steering wheel.

"You can't let go," she says, "even when no one's around, you can't let go."

And the sun streams into my eyes and I feel myself relax for the first time in who knows how long, and I say, "Don't worry. I don't want to."

EPILOGUE

ANNA

1983

THE WHITING GALLERY

IS PLEASED TO PRESENT FOR PUBLIC EXHIBITION

MORDECAI GOLDENBERG / LISE SANDLER:
A painter of industrial scenes and his greatest muse

Notes by Anna M. Sandler, curator

Although he was most known for his socially aware, politically minded paintings of industrial life and work in New York City of the 1920s and early '30s, Mordecai Goldenberg (1893–1934) had a subject about which he was equally passionate, but far more private.

Goldenberg was committed to a vision of himself as a "cultural worker," reflecting in his art the struggle of working-class people. Originally from Poland, he became an American citizen in 1918 and considered art not merely a vehicle for beauty and creative expression, but a means of communicating through pictorial language the strong patriotism he felt for his adopted country, and his political beliefs about the value and importance of the average worker.

In the late 1920s, Goldenberg formed, along with his closest artist friends—Peter Franklin, Alfred DeMarco, Samuel Sandler, and Rafael Sandler—a collaborative effort in the hopes of promoting themselves and their political art. Calling themselves the Collective, they shared a working space and several group exhibits, as well as a political point of view. (Most were members of the John Reed Club through 1936.) But during the early 1930s, the group began to splinter, as members' individual styles began to change and some of them moved beyond social realism and began exploring expressionism and abstraction. (Rafael Sandler, in particular, meeting with the most success.)

Abstract art was anathema to Goldenberg—it was, in his words, "irrelevant" to American life, and he had no patience for the "merely decorative." Thus, when his brand of social realism fell out of style, his career suffered. For all anyone knew, Goldenberg simply stopped working and faded into history. Though he exhibited widely at the very start of his career, it would be fair to say that since then there has been virtually no public proof of his artistic existence.

That is, until now.

I should mention here that I have a personal connection to the artist: he was my father.

I never knew him; he died before I was born. In fact, I only learned he was my father just before my mother's death, in 1971.

I was raised by my mother, Lise Goldenberg Sandler, and her second husband, the artist—and Goldenberg's friend—Samuel Sandler, who died of cancer in 1963. Though I grew up surrounded by art painted by members of the Collective, I had only ever seen a few of Goldenberg's pieces in my mother's private collection: several urban landscapes typical of his style, most of them with machines, rather than people, figuring most prominently; and, notably, a portrait of my mother.

The portrait intrigued me, as it was so different from his other works, and because in it he had managed to capture something striking and true about his subject. There was not only the refinement and sensibility of a well-trained, competent artist; there was a real sense of affection in the work that made me wonder about their relationship. But whenever I asked, my mother always characterized him as merely a family friend—my father's friend, from the Collective.

After my father, Samuel Sandler, died, my mother's health began to fail. In late 1970, in the course of moving her from her home into managed care, I discovered a cache of Goldenberg paintings and sketches in her attic—a hoard, in fact. When I came to her with my questions about what I'd found, she could deny my curiosity no longer.

She confessed to me the true nature of who Goldenberg had been to her—her first husband—and his relation to me—my father. She explained to me that what I had found was only a fraction of the work he had left behind. Around the time of his death, she told me, she had discovered over 700 oil paintings, sketches, lithographs, watercolors, and charcoals that Goldenberg had created obsessively, in secret, all of them documenting the same subject. She and Sandler had stored them for years, unsure of what to do with them. In her will, she bequeathed this work to me. She also expressed the wish that all of it be destroyed. But I could not destroy it once I had witnessed it myself.

For though I went to examine the paintings expecting a treasure trove of urban landscapes and patriotic scenes, what I found was an incredible collection of works that captured exactly what had captivated me about the portrait of his I'd seen as a child.

I discovered what you see before you: a collection of portraits, nearly 800 in number, of a single subject.

His wife.

In this exhibit, the works are displayed chronologically, to highlight the subtle changes in style over the years. The portraits of my mother from the early 1920s range from playful to somber in his treatment; his portraits from the later 1920s are often painfully hyperfocused and not all of them entirely flattering, but still with that pervading spirit of deep affection. Moving into late 1929 through early 1930, his work becomes more erratic, the color palette more garish, the lines more harsh, as though he needs boldness to clarify for himself the subject of his own work. The later stage, however, from 1931–1933, is where his work truly transforms. Some of the portraits verge on cubism, and others resemble the mathematical patterns of fractals. Color emerges from behind my mother's eyes and looms around her like bursts of psychedelia. Still others render her unrecognizable, the paintings dominated completely by obsessively detailed patterns of shape and color, a kind of ecstasy: the spirit of his wife, my mother, transformed from realistic portraiture to the essence of pure being.

It is difficult to reconcile this compulsive adoration, this beauty and love and sense of worshipfulness that he managed to capture, with the person I know as my mother, and with what I know of their history together.

My mother was a pianist, and her life was focused on her passion for music until she married Goldenberg, after which her professional training was put on hold. She struggled with what she described to me as an abusive marriage. Her music was, evidently, a source of tension between them. At first a champion of her talent, Goldenberg grew jealous of it, and it became a source of contention between them; at one point he forbade her to play the piano at all, and even had her institutionalized when she defied him. She claimed he was controlling, secretive, jealous, and rageful, and that she was afraid of him. He hid his work from her, locking himself in his studio—she had no idea that behind closed doors he was painting portrait after portrait of her—and wanted her music, her artistic nature, hidden as well.

My mother shared much of this in a letter she wrote to me shortly before she died. It was as much a gift to me as these portraits of her are—a way to see her and understand her that I had never encountered before, nor considered possible.

To me, growing up, she had always been cold, distant, inflexible, and fragile. I was constantly worried about being out of favor with her, and I never seemed to be able to predict what might cause that to happen. She was protective of me, and fearful, warning me rather than encouraging, forbidding me instead of indulging. Although my father Samuel was a loving, stable influence in my life, I chafed at the bit to leave home and establish my own life, away from her, which I did as soon as possible.

I mourned our distance and always felt somewhat responsible for it, though I couldn't understand exactly how or why. Once she told me the truth of my parentage, and recounted the many flaws of my father, I understood why: I was a painful reminder of a difficult time in her life. A literal embodiment of her abuser. Living proof that although she may have left him behind, she could never be free of him.

This was difficult to accept, because although I was told this truth as an adult—that my birth father was abusive, angry, controlling—I received the news as though I were a child. How was I to reconcile the fact that the loving father I thought I knew was no relation? That the father I'd never known had, in fact, been a bad person? That the mother I had known was not always the person I understood her to be?

But discovering these portraits of her—witnessing her as a muse, a vision—allowed me a new way of seeing her, a new way of comprehending.

She asked me to destroy these paintings. It was one of her last requests of me. But I could not. Because they offer me a version of my mother I was never able to access in life.

In these 800 paintings I see not a cold woman, but a woman who was loved, and hurt, and fundamentally misunderstood. Goldenberg's vision of her was his own limited, shortsighted version of who she was—but so was mine. I might not have known the truth about my father, but in truth my mother had been hidden from me as well. Seeing this collection of portraits, witnessing the variety of forms in which she is represented, has helped me understand there is more than one way to understand her. More importantly, it has given me a new way to understand myself and make peace with all that had been hidden from me. Exhibiting these portraits all together helps aggregate what I know about both of my parents, and becomes a way for each of them to transcend themselves.

If anyone had predicted to Mordecai Goldenberg that portraits of his wife would turn out to be his defining work, he wouldn't have deigned to entertain the notion. He believed art was political, not personal. And surely, this collection is not the political statement he intended his art to be.

If my mother knew that I had not destroyed this work but allowed her to be seen as a multifaceted, beautiful, complicated, vulnerable, full person, she would never speak to me again.

And yet I feel that these portraits of her, these tender, angry, flattering, captivating, intriguing, maddening versions of her, capture more fully than I ever could her beauty and depth and capacity for love.

I knew as soon as I found them that they did not deserve to be hidden away. When art cannot be seen, it cannot be mediated by an observer; it cannot be validated or verified, or otherwise made real by an audience. I felt strongly upon seeing these portraits of my mother, these portraits by my father, that it was no longer necessary to keep these family secrets hidden; that to fully embrace the contradictions of my past, reconcile them with my present, and find a way to move into the future, I needed witnesses to the true story of their life together, to the truth of my own life.

The only way to kill a secret is to tell it, to share it with everyone, and perhaps that is why I am so motivated to share this collection with you. The simple act of seeing this exhibition transmutes family secrets into family facts. Nothing more is hidden away, unable to be witnessed, known, felt, understood, or heard. Nothing more is set apart from us, separated or cut off from us, preventing us from understanding the fullness of our own lives.

And now that it is no longer hidden, the truth can reach us all.

MORDECAI GOLDENBERG / LISE SANDLER:
A painter of industrial scenes and his greatest muse

Opening: Saturday, September 22, 1983, noon to 6:00 P.M.
Exhibition dates: September 22–October 21

The Whiting Gallery
2 Washington Square North
New York, NY 10003
Hours: Monday through Friday, 11:00 to 6:00 P.M.
Saturday and Sunday, noon to 6:00 P.M.

PAULINE

1986

Pauline stares at the face across the room, searching for signs of recognition, signs of herself. The old woman sits in profile, looking out the window from within a cocoon of blankets. Finally, the assistant clears her throat, and Pauline collects herself and says, "Shall we?"

"Jean," the nurse says softly as they come near. "You have a visitor, Jean."

Her skin seems translucent, the thin skin of the aged, and Pauline worries she might break some of it off if she touches her. She places her hand gently on Jean's shoulder and says, "Hi, Jean? It's Paulie."

Jean doesn't register a response, so Pauline sits down across from her, on a nearby couch, and straightens the blanket slowly sliding down the side of Jean's wheelchair. The nurse takes her leave, and Jean continues to stare out the window. Pauline takes the opportunity to look at her, to really study her face. Does Pauline have her nose? Does she recognize herself in any of her features?

The room has the stale smell of old people and cleaning supplies, like a hospital, but Pauline inhales it like perfume.

"I think I remember you coming to visit me, Jean, a long time ago," she says, leaning forward and taking the old woman's hand. It feels like a tree branch, a twig she could snap if she pressed too hard. "Do you remember?"

Jean looks at her and asks, "Are you my nurse?"

"No, I'm Pauline. Paulie. Remember me?"

But this seems to agitate Jean. "I need my nurse." Her eyes now dart around the room, animating her face, and she stirs in her chair.

"What do you need, Jean? I can get it for you," Pauline says.

Jean suddenly looks at her—really looks at her, as though she sees her for the first time, and says, "What did you say your name was, dear?"

"It's Pauline," she says. She can feel her heart racing. "Sometimes you used to call me Paulie. When I was a little girl."

"If you say so, dear," Jean says. She closes her eyes. "It's hard for me to remember things, you see. What was it, what did you say—Pauline?"

"Yes, Pauline."

Jean nods. "I had a little girl once. A boy too."

"Yes, that's right," Pauline says, encouraging her with a smile that feels too wide. But Jean's face starts to crumple, as though she's wincing in pain, and a small sound escapes her, and Pauline reaches out for her hand again, trying to soothe.

"Jean? Are you okay, Jean?" she says. "Would you like to see a picture of my little girl?"

Pauline reaches into her purse and pulls out a few recent Polaroids, plus some baby photos she brought with her, in case Jean was interested. She holds out the most recent one of Hope, sitting at their upright piano, turning to smile at the camera, her long hair in high ponytails.

"This is Hope. This is my little girl. She's about to turn ten."

"What a pretty picture she is," Jean says. The photo shakes as she holds it in her hands, scrutinizing.

"And here she is in our backyard, just a little while ago. And here she is as a baby."

The photos fall to Jean's lap as she struggles to hold them, and she carefully picks them up and looks at each one.

"Don't let them take that baby," she says, pointing at the image of six-month-old Hope, pudgy and laughing in a crocheted onesie Pauline had made for her while pregnant, unable to imagine truly being a mother, having a baby who could possibly fit into something so small, who would, somehow, have to depend on her.

"No, no," Pauline tells her. "She's all mine. She's at home right now, with her father. She's fine."

"In my experience, fathers are the ones that take them away."

Pauline reaches out to take the photos back, and Jean grasps her hand.

"I didn't want to leave them, you understand. But he gave me no choice. He took them from me. I tried to come back for them a few times—"

"Yes, you came to see me once!" Pauline says. "We were all sick with the chicken pox, and my mom let you come in to visit, and you saw me on the stairs and called me Paulie."

Jean's face sharpens and she turns to Pauline with a look that seems both urgent and utterly lucid. Pauline's heart beats loudly in her ears and she nods at Jean, encouraging her to make the connection. But then her expression of understanding shifts.

"What a nice person you are, coming to visit me like this," Jean says. "Did anyone ever tell you, you have the most stunning eyes? So blue, like that. It reminds me of someone."

"Tom," Pauline says, tears on her face. "My father."

Jean pulls the blankets tighter around her and sighs. "It's been so long, my dear. Who can tell?"

HOPE

1994

On the day of the recital, Hope wakes up with a 102 fever, sweaty and confused and feeling like her body is weighted down by a million tiny barbells, making it impossible to move. Jennifer comes to her rescue, bringing her Tylenol, soup, a pair of nylons, since the only ones Hope has are ripped, ladders running up her shins. Jennifer helps her fix her hair, pops out for more supplies, stays with her until her fever is manageable, and walks with her to the back entrance of the recital hall.

"You got this," she says, squeezing Hope's hands before disappearing to join the audience. Hope hears the murmur, the sounds of people waiting for her to perform. She wipes her hands on her dress, avoiding eye contact with the voice major who serves as the stage door usher tonight, pacing the floor and willing her hands to stay warm, reviewing the opening piece in her head.

When she passes through the doorway onto the stage, she is grateful for the brightness of the main lights, which make it impossible for her to see the faces of the people she knows are there, expecting things from her.

Returning from spring break was strange. Now that she finally understood that things were over with Matthew, instead of numbness she felt loneliness and, if she was being honest with herself, grief. The sheer amount of brain space she'd let him take up, every thought centered, somehow, around what he might think or what he might say or how she might convince him to love her for real. What wasted time and energy.

She saw him around school with a new Hope, a Hope II, a freshman piano major who looked at him the way Hope must have looked at him in the beginning, dazzled by his attention. Before, this might have felt personal, a direct attack on her, designed to pull her back in or transform her into a Jennifer II, raining warnings on Hope II's deaf ears. But now, when she allowed herself to think about how it made her feel, it just made her sad.

Instead of letting the sadness spiral in on itself, she experimented with merely acknowledging that sadness and letting it go. Letting herself focus on her upcoming recital. She practiced for three-hour stretches, four hours, six hours, taking breaks to wrap her aching arms around herself and shake her hands out and rotate her wrists and crack her knuckles. The pain and fatigue she lived with didn't cease, but instead of Matthew flooding her thoughts it was Brahms, Beethoven, Chopin, Liszt, Mozart, Prokofiev—the work.

She caught him listening once, unable to play it off like he was merely walking by after she yanked open the practice room door. They looked at each other with surprise, and his face reddened as he mumbled, "Sounds good," before turning the other way and heading quickly to the stairwell.

Her ankle is almost healed now. She no longer needs to wrap it. But it aches on cold days—and now, with the fever—reminding her.

The fever makes everything shimmery, and as she walks out, into the lights, to the sound of applause, the glare dazzles her for a moment, and she feels outside of herself as she bows to the audience and settles herself onto the bench and prepares herself for the first notes.

It still feels a bit like she's watching a version of herself play as she begins. She sees the blur of her fingers in the piano's fallboard, not quite polished enough to be a mirror; she watches the strings of the grand piano stretch out before her, and the fever distorts it to make it seem as if they go on forever. A man coughs during a quiet moment. A wrapper is unwrapped. A program rustles.

Then suddenly, she can't be sure if it's from the fever as she sweats under the lights, she has a moment. Maybe not exactly like the moment Soo-Jin described to her once during a lesson, but a moment where she realizes, as she voices the Brahms, as she takes pains to bring out the middle voice, to shape the phrase, that *no one can tell what she is thinking*.

And what that means, she realizes as the sound decays around her into a breath-held silence, is that she can tell her story, in all its shameful detail, and no one will ever know exactly what it is she's said, because it's in Brahms's voice, and then Beethoven's voice, and Prokofiev's voice. Her story, coloring their music.

More than that, she realizes—as she takes up the next phrase, builds up to a crescendo, watching the bass strings stretch away from her, feeling herself vibrate as though she is a string being hit with felt hammers—that means she is safe. She can see the looming audience in her peripheral vision, but she also feels entirely alone, suspended in time, encapsulated in a bubble, in a fever of haze and sound, and she finally, *finally* understands what Soo-Jin has been trying to explain to her for the past two years, how to voice things, how to make music happen.

So her secret is free, and silent, even as she blurts it out for everyone to hear. And she tells all of it, her pain, her happiness, her doubt, her uncertainty, her foolishness, her fear; Matthew and his twisted version of love, his games; her grandfather; her mother; the icy fall, the buried eggs, the shame, the shame, the shame. *This* is the hidden music, the moment Soo-Jin was talking about, Hope is sure of it. Everything in her sight line shimmers, becomes transcendental, becomes a religious experience. For just a moment, she is transfigured, beyond pain, beyond confusion, beyond sadness, and she realizes she has the opportunity to make a new choice: to be where she is—in the middle of pain and uncertainty and everything else—and move forward anyway.

Afterward, after she has taken her bow, after she has been given flowers, after she has played the encore piece she and Soo-Jin had agreed upon in the event that things went this well; afterward, as she stands in the reception line accepting congratulations and praise, Hope can feel the gravity of Soo-Jin before she even materializes, looking at Hope from the sides of her eyes, a single eyebrow raised. Without a word, she pulls Hope into a forceful hug. Hope realizes only then how tiny Soo-Jin is, how fierce her hug is, the sheer strength of her bones, which feel like they could crush Hope, so solid and meaningful is the embrace. She stands back, her arms on Hope's shoulders, and says, "Where did this come from?"

Hope shakes her head and admits, "I don't know. I have this fever, and my hands hurt so much . . ."

Soo-Jin leans forward so Hope can hear her over the happy conversation of the reception line and squeezes her arm. "Pain is the seed of every story you will ever tell."

As Soo-Jin floats away in her floor-length gown, as dressed up as if she herself were giving the recital, Hope can see Matthew and New Hope in the line of people waiting to congratulate her. He looks at her with eyes that seem like an apology, but also like surprise, and also like regret. She smiles at him over the heads of the others and says, "I understand." It's not loud enough for him to hear, but to Hope it feels like she has shouted a benediction, and her shoulders finally fall away from her ears and she breathes in, deeply, for the first time in a long while.

As she turns her focus to accepting flowers from the old woman who comes to all the student piano recitals and brings flowers to the performers, she feels him leave, and when she looks up again, she is filled with lightness and he is gone.

ZOEY

2098

Zoey Mansfield, 96, of Philadelphia, PA, passed away on February 28, 2098. Zoey was born in May 2002 in Boston, MA. After graduating high school, she attended the University of Pennsylvania, and thereafter worked for many years as a therapist specializing in transgender care.

Everyone who knew Zoey knew of her remarkable dedication to the LGBTQ+ community, and specifically to transgender mental health. Even before she opened The Center for Life and Living in 2031, she was a fierce advocate for equitable mental health legislation, and an outspoken supporter of the rights of transgender youth. She was instrumental in the passing of Quinn's Law, which guaranteed healthcare coverage to transgender teens who emancipated themselves from their parents in order to access hormone therapy, surgery, or other treatment. She was a prolific author, known not only for her self-help books and other nonfiction, but of course for her bestselling memoir, *I Deserve Love, and Other Lies I Told Myself.* She was passionate about raising awareness around chronic suicidality and other depressive disorders, which is what inspired her to start The Center for Life and Living. The Center has, from its inception, served a population of transgender and queer youths struggling with mental health issues, and has a long-term residential program, a partial hospitalization program, and an outpatient program, all designed specifically to meet the needs of young people.

In addition to her tireless work as the director of The Center, as a political activist, and as an advocate for trans teens, Zoey was also known for her selfless generosity. Her house was always filled with what she liked to call her "found family," and anyone who spent any time there can attest to the fact that there was never a quiet moment. She pretended to only begrudgingly enjoy this, but those who knew her knew how much she loved each and every person who was a part of it. From the children she formally adopted, to her "bonus kids," to her friends and their families, she cherished them all.

Zoey is remembered by her children, Julian, Grace, and Cari; her grandchildren, Latanya, Ruby, Anna, Charlie, and Francisco; and her great-grandchildren, Eva and Lorie. She was preceded in death by her mother, Hope, and her partner of almost 60 years, Avery, who succumbed to 2097-nSARS last December.

In lieu of flowers, the family asks that you do what Zoey always encouraged everyone to do: love yourself, and others. "It's the simplest, hardest thing," she wrote in her most famous book, "and if anyone tells you it's easy, you have my permission to punch them in the face (lovingly, of course)—but you must do it. You must love. You must love yourself, and you must love others. It is a verb. It is an action. It is a calling. And it is the only thing powerful enough to counter the trauma of everyday life."

A memorial will be held at 2:00 P.M. on March 4, 2098, at The Center for Life and Living. As Zoey herself always firmly believed, everyone is welcome.

ACKNOWLEDGMENTS

This book first started out as a ghost of an idea that haunted me for years before I felt up to the challenge of writing it. I have only been able to coax it into being over the last nearly twenty years thanks to countless conversations over long walks, FaceTime, email, and texts with friends, writers, readers, and family, who have been unwavering in their support. At a certain point, when you have been working on the same book for a very long time, it starts to seem doomed, or hopeless, or even more imaginary than it already is, considering the fact that it exists only in your head. I am grateful for everyone who has humored me in this project, even (and perhaps most especially) when it seemed impossible.

Thanks to my wonderful editor, Jessica Case, who said yes to this manuscript without hesitation; to my outstanding copyeditor Stephanie Marshall Ward; and to the entire team at Pegasus, for giving it a beautiful home.

Thanks to my incredibly patient agent Laura Gross, with whom I first shared this idea in 2004, back when it was inexplicably called "Heart Like a River," and who continued to champion it for years as a manuscript I was forever working on called "The Hidden Music." Thank you for checking in on me, nudging me about this story over the years, and reading countless versions of it as it evolved into its current form.

Thanks to friends who generously shared their responses to the story over the years, including Kaitlin Costello, Judy Gitenstein, Ona Gritz,

Sue O'Doherty, Christina Li, Sandra Telep, and most especially Barbara Card Atkinson, who has read every version of the manuscript from its inception and offered invaluable feedback as a reader, writer, and a friend.

Thanks to Jeni Dahmus, archivist at the Juilliard library, for allowing me to access material from the early 1900s, including faculty handbooks, recital programs, memos, school catalogs, and photographs of the original buildings; and the folks at Manhattan School of Music, whose building was the original site of the Juilliard School from 1910 to 1969, for giving me a tour and allowing me to take notes about where Lise might have ventured in her search for a teacher.

Thanks to my piano teacher at the Boston Conservatory of Music (now Boston Conservatory at Berklee), Jung-Ja Kim, whose insight and wisdom has helped inform not only my playing but my writing as well.

Thanks to my younger daughter, Quinn, who let me mine her life experiences for Zoey, and my older daughter, Emi, for giving me young Hope's haunting line about having been a really good mommy to me when I was the baby and she was the mommy. I don't doubt it. Thanks, too, to my husband, Marc, who, it turns out, is not only fantastic in general, but is also a very good person to talk to about plot.

Thanks to my former parents-in-law, Nurit and Steve Binenbaum, who first told me the story of Moses Oley the painter and his wife Lisa, the pianist who was forbidden to play. Thank you for letting me have access to the paintings, as well as Moses and Lisa's photos and documents; for allowing me to use one of the many paintings of Lisa as part of the cover for this book; and for letting me use their lives as a jumping-off point for an entirely made-up story.

Thanks to my extended family, whose storytelling (especially about The Old Man) inspired my curiosity and imagination, and to my immediate family, including my parents, who have always encouraged me.

Finally, this book is dedicated to the memory of my grandmother, Margaret Mullinix, who was the inspiration for Anna, but also for me.